CHILDREN'S CLASSICS

The Secret Garden

FRANCES HODGSON BURNETT

The Secret Garden

PARRAGON

The Secret Garden
A Parragon Classic

This is a Siena Book
Siena is an imprint of Parragon

This edition published in 1999 by
Parragon
13 Whiteladies Road
Clifton
Bristol BS8 1PB

Printed and bound in the UK

Chapter 1

THERE IS NO ONE LEFT

When Mary Lennox was sent to Misselthwaite Manor to live with her uncle, everybody said she was the most disagreeable-looking child ever seen. It was true, too. She had a little thin face and a little thin body, thin light hair and a sour expression. Her hair was yellow, and her face was yellow because she had been born in India and had always been ill in one way or another. Her father had held a position under the English Government and had always been busy and ill himself and her mother had been a great beauty who cared only to go to parties and amuse herself with gay people. She had not wanted a little girl at all, and when Mary was born she handed her over to the care of an Ayah, who was made to understand that if she wished to please the Memsahib she must keep the child out of sight as much as possible. So when she was a sickly, fretful, ugly little baby she was kept out of the way, and when she became a sickly, fretful, toddling thing she was kept out of the way also. She never remembered seeing familiarly anything but the dark faces of her Ayah and the other native servants, and as they always obeyed her and gave her her own way in everything, because the Memsahib would be angry if she was disturbed by her crying, by the time she was six years old she was as tyrannical and selfish a little pig as ever lived. The young English governess who came to teach her to read and write disliked her so much that she gave up her place in three months, and when other governesses came to try to fill it they always went away in a shorter time than the first one. So if Mary had not chosen really to want to know how to read books, she would never have learned her letters at all.

One frightfully hot morning, when she was about nine years old, she awakened feeling very cross, and she became crosser still when she saw that the servant who stood by her bedside was not her Ayah.

"Why did you come?" she said to the strange woman. "I will not let you stay. Send my Ayah to me."

The woman looked frightened, but she only stammered that the Ayah could not come, and when Mary threw herself into a passion and beat and kicked her, she looked only more frightened and repeated that it was not possible for the Ayah to come to Missie Sahib.

There was something mysterious in the air that morning. Nothing was done in its regular order and several of the native servants seemed missing, while those whom Mary saw slunk or hurried about with ashy and scared faces. But no one would tell her anything, and her Ayah did not come. She was actually left alone as the morning went on, and at last wandered out into the garden and began to play by herself under a tree near the veranda. She pretended that she was making a flower-bed, and she stuck big scarlet hibiscus blossoms into little heaps of earth, all the time growing more and more angry and muttering to herself the things she would say and the names she would call Saidie when she returned.

"Pig! Pig! Daughter of Pigs!" she said, because to call a native a pig is the worst insult of all.

She was grinding her teeth and saying this over and over again when she heard her mother come out on the veranda with someone. She was with a fair young man, and they stood talking together in low strange voices. Mary knew the fair young man who looked like a boy. She had heard that he was a very young of officer who had just come from England. The child stared at him, but she stared most at her mother. She always did this when she had a chance to see her, because the Memsahib – Mary used to call her that oftener than anything else – was such a tall, slim, pretty person and wore such lovely clothes. Her hair was like curly silk and she had a delicate little nose which seemed to be disdaining things, and she had large laughing eyes. All her clothes were thin and floating, and Mary said they were "full of lace". They looked fuller of lace than ever this morning, but her eyes were not laughing at all. They were large and scared and lifted imploringly to the fair boy officer's face.

"Is it so very bad? Oh, is it?" Mary heard her say.

"Awfully, the young man answered in a trembling voice.

Awfully, Mrs. Lennox. You ought to have gone to the hills two weeks ago."

The Memsahib wrung her hands.

"Oh, I know I ought!" she cried. "I only stayed to go to that silly dinner-party. What a fool I was!"

At that very moment such a loud sound of wailing broke out from the servants' quarters that she clutched the young man's arm, and Mary stood shivering from head to foot. The wailing grew wilder and wilder.

"What is it? What is it?" Mrs. Lennox gasped.

"Someone has died," answered the boy of officer. "You did not say it had broken out among your servants."

"I did not know!" the Memsahib cried. "Come with me! Come with me!" and she turned and ran into the house.

After that, appalling things happened, and the mysteriousness of the morning was explained to Mary. The cholera had broken out in its most fatal form and people were dying like flies. The Ayah had been taken ill in the night, and it was because she had just died that the servants had wailed in the huts. Before the next day three other servants were dead and others had run away in terror. There was panic on every side, and dying people in all the bungalows.

During the confusion and bewilderment of the second day Mary hid herself in the nursery and was forgotten by everyone. Nobody thought of her, nobody wanted her, and strange things happened of which she knew nothing. Mary alternately cried and slept through the hours. She only knew that people were ill and that she heard mysterious and frightening sounds. Once she crept into the dining-room and found it empty, though a partly finished meal was on the table and chairs and plates looked as if they had been hastily pushed back when the diners rose suddenly for some reason. The child ate some fruit and biscuits, and being thirsty she drank a glass of wine which stood nearly filled. It was sweet, and she did not know how strong it was. Very soon it made her intensely drowsy, and she went back to her nursery and shut herself in again, frightened by cries she heard in the huts and by the hurrying sound of feet. The wine made her so sleepy that she could scarcely keep her eyes open, and she lay down on her bed and knew nothing more for a long time.

Many things happened during the hours in which she slept so heavily, but she was not disturbed by the wails and the sound of things being carried in and out of the bungalow.

When she awakened she lay and stared at the wall. The house was perfectly still. She had never known it to be so silent before. She heard neither voices nor footsteps, and wondered if everybody had got well of the cholera and all the trouble was over. She wondered also who would take care of her now her Ayah was dead. There would be a new Ayah, and perhaps she would know some new stories. Mary had been rather tired of the old ones. She did not cry because her nurse had died. She was not an affectionate child and had never cared much for anyone. The noise and hurrying about and wailing over the cholera had frightened her, and she had been angry because no one seemed to remember that he was alive. Everyone was too panic-stricken to think of a little girl no one was fond of. When people had the cholera it seemed that they remembered nothing but themselves. But if everyone had got well again, surely someone would remember and come to look for her.

But no one came, and as she lay waiting the house seemed to grow more and more silent. She heard something rustling on the matting, and when she looked down she saw a little snake gliding along and watching her with eyes like jewels. She was not frightened, because he was a harmless little thing who would not hurt her, and he seemed in a hurry to get out of the room. He slipped under the door as she watched him.

"How queer and quiet it is," she said. "It sounds as if there was no one in the bungalow but me and the snake."

Almost the next minute she heard footsteps in the compound, and then on the veranda. They were men's footsteps, and the men entered the bungalow and talked in low voices. No one went to meet or speak to them, and they seemed to open doors and look into rooms.

"What desolation!" she heard one voice say. "That pretty, pretty woman! I suppose the child, too. I heard there was a child, though no one ever saw her."

Mary was standing in the middle of the nursery when they opened the door a few minutes later. She looked an ugly, cross little thing and was frowning because she was beginning to be hungry and feel disgracefully neglected. The first man who came in was a large officer she had once seen talking to her father. He looked tired and troubled, but when he saw her he was so startled that he almost jumped back.

"Barney!" he cried out. "There is a child here A child alone! In a place like this! Mercy on us, who is she?"

"I am Mary Lennox, the little girl said, drawing herself up stiffly. She thought the man was very rude to call her father's bungalow "A place like this! I fell asleep when everyone had the cholera and I have only just wakened up. Why does nobody come?"

"It is the child no one ever saw!" exclaimed the man, turning to his companions. She has actually been forgotten!"

"Why was I forgotten?" Mary said, stamping her foot. Why does nobody come?"

The young man whose name was Barney looked at her very sadly. Mary even thought she saw him wink his eyes as if to wink tears away.

"Poor little kid!" he said. "There is nobody left to come."

It was in that strange and sudden way at Mary found out that she had neither father nor mother left; that they had died and been carried away in the night, and that the few native servants who had not died also had left the house as quickly as they could get out of it, none of them even remembering that there was a Missie Sahib. That was why the place was so quiet. It was true that there was no one in the bungalow but herself and the little rustling snake

CHAPTER 2

MISTRESS MARY QUITE CONTRARY

Mary had liked to look at her mother from a distance, and she had thought her very pretty, but as she knew very little of her, she could scarcely have been expected to love her or to miss her very much when she was gone. She did not miss her at all, in fact, and as she was a self-absorbed child she gave her entire thought to herself, as she had always done. If she had been older she would no doubt have been very anxious at being left alone in the world, but she was very young, and as she had always been taken care of, she supposed she always would be. What she thought was that she would like to know if she was going to nice people, who would be polite to her and give her her own way as her Ayah and the other native servants had done.

She knew that she was not going to stay at the English clergyman's house where she was taken at first. She did not want to stay. The English clergyman was poor and he had five children all nearly the same age and they wore shabby clothes and were always quarrelling and snatching toys from each other. Mary hated their untidy bungalow and was so disagreeable to them that after the first day or two nobody would play with her. By the second day they had given her a nickname which made her furious.

It was Basil who thought of it first. Basil was a little boy with impudent blue eyes and a turned-up nose, and Mary hated him. She was playing by herself under a tree, just as she had been playing the day the cholera broke out. She was making heaps of earth and paths for a garden and Basil came and stood near to watch her. Presently he got rather interested and suddenly made a suggestion.

"Why don't you put a heap of stones there and pretend it is a rockery?" he said. "There in the middle," and he leaned over her to point.

"Go away!" cried Mary. "I don't want boys. Go away!"

For a moment Basil looked angry, and then he began to tease. He was always teasing his sisters. He danced round and round her and made faces and sang and laughed.

Mistress Mary, quite contrary,
How does your garden grow?
With silver bells, and cockle shells,
And marigolds all in a row.

He sang it until the other children heard and laughed, too; and the crosser Mary got, the more they sang "Mistress Mary Quite Contrary"; and after that as long as she stayed with them they called her "Mistress Mary Quite Contrary" when they spoke of her to each; other, and often when they spoke to her.

"You are going to be sent home," Basil said to her, at the end of the week. "And we're glad of it."

"I am glad of it, too," answered Mary. "Where is home?"

"She doesn't know where home is!" said Basil, with seven-year-old scorn. "It's England, of course. Our grandmamma lives there, and our sister Mabel was sent to her last year. You are not going to your grandmamma. You have none. You are going to your uncle. His name is Mr. Archibald Craven."

"I don't know anything about him," snapped Mary.

"I know you don't," Basil answered. "You don't know anything. Girls never do. I heard Father and Mother talking about him. He lives in a great, big, desolate old house in the country, and no one goes near him. He's so cross he won't let them, and they wouldn't come if he would let them. He's a hunchback, and he's horrid."

"I don't believe you," said Mary; and she turned her back and stuck her fingers in her ears, because she would not listen any more.

But she thought it over a great deal afterwards; and when Mrs. Crawford told her that night that she was going to sail away to England in a few days and going to her uncle, Mr. Archibald Craven, who lived at Misselthwaite Manor, she looked so stony and stubbornly uninterested that they did not know what to think about her. They tried to be kind to her, but she only turned her face away when Mrs. Crawford attempted to kiss her, and held herself stiffly when Mr. Crawford patted her shoulder.

"She is such a plain child," Mrs. Crawford said pityingly afterward. "And her mother was such a pretty creature. She had a very pretty manner, too, and Mary has the most unattractive ways I ever saw in a child. The children call her "Mistress Mary Quite Contrary", and though it's naughty of them, one can't help understanding it."

"Perhaps if her mother had carried her pretty face and her pretty manners oftener into the nursery, Mary might have learned some pretty ways, too. It is very sad, now the poor beautiful thing is gone, to remember that many people never even knew that she had a child at all."

"I believe she scarcely ever looked at her, sighed Mrs. Crawford. "When her Ayah was dead there was no one to give a thought to the little thing. Think of the servants running away and leaving her all alone in that deserted bungalow. Colonel McGrew said he nearly jumped out of his skin when he opened the door and found her standing by herself in the middle of the room."

Mary made the long voyage to England under the care of an officer's wife, who was taking her children to leave them in a boarding-school. She was very much absorbed in her own little boy and girl, and was rather glad to hand the child over to the woman Mr. Archibald Craven sent to meet her in London. The woman was his housekeeper at Misselthwaite Manor, and her name was Mrs. Medlock. She was a stout woman, with very red cheeks and sharp black eyes. She wore a very purple dress, a black silk mantle with jet fringes on it, and a black bonnet with purple velvet flowers which stuck up and trembled when she moved her head. Mary did not like her at all, but as she very seldom liked people, there was nothing remarkable in that; besides which it was very evident Mrs. Medlock did not think much of her.

"My word! she's a plain little piece of goods!" she said. "And we'd heard that her mother was a beauty. She hasn't handed much of it down, has she, ma'am?"

"Perhaps she will improve as she grows older," the officer's wife said good-naturedly. If she were not so sallow and had a nicer expression, her features are rather good. Children alter so much.

"She'll have to alter a good deal," answered Mrs. Medlock. And there's nothing likely to improve children at Misselthwaite–if you ask me!"

They thought Mary was not listening because she was standing a little apart from them at the window of the private hotel they had gone to. She was watching the passing buses and cabs and people, but she heard quite well and was made very curious about her uncle and the place he lived in. What sort of a place was it, and what would he be like? What was a hunchback? She had never seen one. Perhaps there were none in India.

Since she had been living in other people's houses and had had no Ayah, she had begun to feel lonely and to think queer thoughts which were new to her. She had begun to wonder why she had never seemed to belong to anyone even when her father and mother had been alive. Other children seemed to belong to their fathers and mothers, but she had never seemed to really be anyone's little girl. She had had servants, and food and clothes, but no one had taken any notice of her. She did not know that this was because she was a agreeable child; but then, of course, she did not know she was disagreeable. She often thought that other people were, but she did not know that she was so herself.

She thought Mrs. Medlock the most disagreeable person she had ever seen, with her common, highly coloured face and her common fine bonnet. When the next day they set out on their journey to Yorkshire, she walked through the station to the railway carriage with her head up and trying to keep as far away from her as she could, because she did not want to seem to belong to her. It would have made her very angry to think people imagined she was her little girl.

But Mrs. Medlock was not in the least disturbed by her and her thoughts. She was the kind of woman who would "stand no nonsense from young ones". At least, that is what she would have said if she had been asked. She had not wanted to go to London just when her sister Maria's daughter was going to be married, but she had a comfortable, well-paid place as housekeeper at Misselthwaite Manor, and the only way in which she could keep it was to do at once what Mr. Archibald Crave told her to do. She never dared even to ask a question.

"Captain Lennox and his wife died of the cholera," Mr. Craven had said in his short, cold way. Captain Lennox was my wife's brother and I am their daughter's guardian. The child is to be brought here. You must go to London and bring her yourself."

So she packed her small trunk and made the journey.

Mary sat in her corner of the railway carriage and looked plain and fretful. She had nothing to read or to look at, and she had folded her thin little black-gloved hands in her lap. Her black dress made her look yellower than ever, and her limp light hair straggled from under her black crêpe hat.

"A more marred-looking young one I never saw in my life," Mrs. Medlock thought. (Marred is a Yorkshire word and means spoiled and pettish.) She had never seen a child who sat so still without doing anything; and at last she got tired of watching her and began to talk in a brisk, hard voice.

"I suppose I may as well tell you something about where you are going to," she said. "Do you know anything about your uncle."

"No," said Mary.

"Never heard your father and mother talk about him?"

"No," said Mary, frowning. She frowned because she remembered that her father and mother had never talked to her about anything in particular. Certainly they had never told her things.

"Humph," muttered Mrs. Medlock, staring at her queer, unresponsive little face. She did not say any more for a few moments, and then she began again.

"I suppose you might as well be told something-to prepare you. You are going to a queer place."

Mary said nothing at all, and Mrs. Medlock looked rather discomfited by her apparent indifference, but after taking a breath, she went on.

"Not but that it's a grand big place in a gloomy way, and Mr. Craven's proud of it in his way–and that's gloomy enough, too. The house is six hundred years old, and it's on the edge of the moor, and there's near a hundred rooms in it, though most of them's shut up and locked. And there's pictures and fine old furniture and things that's been there for ages, and there's a big park round it and gardens and trees with branches trailing to the ground–some of them." She paused and took another breath. "But there's nothing else," she ended suddenly.

Mary had begun to listen in spite of herself. It all sounded so unlike India, and anything new rather attracted her. But she did not intend to look as if she were interested. That was one of her unhappy, disagreeable ways. So she sat still.

"Well," said Mrs. Medlock. What do you think of it?

"Nothing," she answered. "I know nothing about such places."

That made Mrs. Medlock laugh a short sort of laugh.

"Eh!" she said. But you are like an old woman. Don't you care?"

"It doesn't matter," said Mary, whether I care or not."

"You are right enough there," said Mrs. Medlock. "It doesn't. What you're to be kept at Misselthwaite Manor for I don't know, unless because it's the easiest way. *He's* not going to trouble himself about you, that's sure and certain. He never troubles himself about no one."

She stopped herself as if she had just remembered something in time.

"He's got a crooked back," she said. That set him wrong. He was a sour young man and got no good of all his money and big place till he was married."

Mary's eyes turned towards her, in spite of her intention not to seem to care. She had never thought of the hunchback's being married, and she was a trifle surprised. Mrs. Medlock saw this, and as she was a talkative woman, she continued with more interest. This was one way of passing some of the time, at any rate.

"She was a sweet, pretty thing, and he'd have walked the world over to get her a blade o' grass she wanted. Nobody thought she'd marry him, but she did, and people said she married him for his money. But she didn't–she didn't," positively. "When she died–"

Mary gave a little involuntary jump.

"Oh! did she die?" she exclaimed, quite without meaning to. She had just remembered a French fairy story she had once read called *Riquet à la Houppe*. It had been about a poor hunchback and a beautiful princess, and it had made her suddenly sorry for Mr. Archibald Craven.

"Yes, she died," Mrs. Medlock answered. "And it made him queerer than ever. He cares about nobody. He won't see people. Most of the time he goes away, and when he is at Misselthwaite he shuts himself up in the West Wing and won't let anyone but Pitcher see him. Pitcher's an old fellow, but he took care of him when he was a child and he knows his ways."

It sounded like something in a book, and it did not make Mary feel cheerful. A house with a hundred rooms, nearly all shut up and with their doors locked–a house on the edge of a moor–whatsoever a moor was–sounded dreary. A man with a crooked back who shut himself up also! She stared out of the window with her lips pinched together, and it seemed quite natural that the rain should have begun to pour down in grey slanting lines and splash and stream down the window-panes. If the pretty wife had been alive, she might have made things cheerful by being something like her own mother and by running in and out and going to parties as she had done in frocks "full of lace". But she was not there any more.

"You needn't expect to see him, because ten to one you won't, said Mrs. Medlock. "And you mustn't expect that there will be people to talk to you. You'll have to play about and look after yourself. You'll be told what rooms you can go into and what rooms you're to keep out of. There's gardens enough. But when you're in the house don't go wandering and poking about. Mr. Craven won't have it."

"I shall not want to go poking about," said sour little Mary; and just as suddenly as she had begun to be rather sorry for Mr. Archibald Craven, she began to cease to be sorry and to think he was unpleasant enough to deserve all that had happened to him.

And she turned her face towards the streaming panes of the window of the railway carriage and gazed out at the grey rainstorm which looked as if it would go on for ever and ever. She watched it so long and steadily that the greyness grew heavier and heavier before her eyes and she fell asleep.

Chapter 3

ACROSS THE MOOR

She slept a long time, and when she awakened Mrs. Medlock had bought a lunch-basket at one of the stations, and they had some chicken and cold beef and bread-and-butter and some hot tea. The rain seemed to be streaming down more heavily than ever, and everybody in the station wore wet and glistening waterproofs. The guard lighted the lamps in the carriage, and Mrs. Medlock cheered up very much over her tea and chicken and beef. She ate a great deal, and afterwards fell asleep herself, and Mary sat and stared at her and watched her fine bonnet slip on one side until she herself fell asleep once more in the corner of the carriage, lulled by the splashing of the rain against the windows. It was quite dark when she awakened again. The train had stopped at a station and Mrs. Medlock was shaking her.

"You have had a sleep!" she said. "It's time to open your eyes! We're at Thwaite Station, and we've got a long drive before us."

Mary stood up and tried to keep her eyes open while Mrs. Medlock collected her parcels. The little girl did not offer to help her, because in India native servants always picked up or carried things, and it seemed quite proper that other people should wait on one.

The station was a small one, and nobody but themselves seemed to be getting out of the train. The station-master spoke to Mrs. Medlock in a rough, good-natured way, pronouncing his words in a queer broad fashion which Mary found out afterwards was Yorkshire.

"I see tha's got back," he said. An' tha's browt th' young 'un with thee."

"Aye, that's her," answered Mrs. Medlock, speaking with a Yorkshire accent herself and jerking her head over her shoulder towards Mary. How's thy missus?"

"Well enow. Th' carriage is waitin' outside for thee".

A brougham stood on the road before the little outside platform. Mary saw that it was a smart carriage and that it was a smart footman who helped her in. His long waterproof coat and the waterproof covering of his hat were shining and dripping with rain as everything was, the burly station-master included.

When he shut the door, mounted the box with the coachman, and they drove off, the little girl found herself seated in a comfortably cushioned corner, but she was not inclined to go to sleep again. She sat and looked out of the window, curious to see something of the road over which she was being driven to the queer place Mrs. Medlock had spoken of. She was not at all a timid child, and she was not exactly frightened, but she felt that there was no knowing what might happen in a house with a hundred rooms nearly all shut up–a house standing on the edge of a moor.

"What is a moor?" she said suddenly to Mrs. Medlock.

"Look out of the window in about ten minutes and you'll see," the woman answered. "We've got to drive five miles across Missel Moor before we get to the Manor. You won't see much because it's a dark night, but you can see something."

Mary asked no more questions, but waited in the darkness of her corner, keeping her eyes on the window. The carriage lamps cast rays of light a little distance ahead of them, and she caught glimpses of the things they passed. After they had left the station they had driven through a tiny village and she had seen whitewashed cottages and the lights of a public house. Then they had passed a church and a vicarage and a little shop window or so in a cottage with toys and sweets and odd things set out for sale. Then they were on the high road, and she saw hedges and trees. After that there seemed nothing different for a long time–or at least it seemed a long time to her.

At last the horses began to go more slowly, as if they were climbing up-hill, and presently there seemed to be no more hedges and no more trees. She could see nothing, in fact, but a dense darkness on either side. She leaned forward and pressed her face against the window just as the carriage gave a big jolt.

"Eh we're on the moor now sure enough," said Mrs. Medlock.

The carriage lamps shed a yellow light on a rough-looking road which seemed to be cut through bushes and low-growing things which ended in the great expanse of dark apparently spread out before and around them. A wind was rising and making a singular, wild, low, rushing sound.

"It's–it's not the sea, is it?" said Mary, looking round at her companion.

"No, not it," answered Mrs. Medlock. Nor it isn't fields nor mountains, it's just miles and miles and miles of wild land that nothing grows on but heather and gorse and broom, and nothing lives on but wild ponies and sheep."

"I feel as if it might be the sea, if there were water on it," said Mary. "It sounds like the sea just now."

"That's the wind blowing through the bushes," Mrs. Medlock said. "It's a wild, dreary enough place to my mind, though there's plenty that likes it-particularly when the heather's in bloom."

On and on they drove through the darkness, and though the rain stopped, the wind rushed by and whistled and made strange sounds. The road went up and down, and several times the carriage passed over a little bridge beneath which water rushed very fast with a great deal of noise. Mary felt as if the drive would never come to an end, and that the wide, bleak moor was a wide expanse of black ocean through which she was passing on a strip of dry land.

"I don't like it," she said to herself. "I don't like it," and she pinched her thin lips more tightly together.

The horses were climbing up a hilly piece of road when she first caught sight of a light. Mrs. Medlock saw it as soon as she did, and drew a long sigh of relief.

"Eh, I am glad to see that bit o' light twinkling," she exclaimed. It's the light in the lodge window. We shall get a good cup of tea after a bit, at all events."

It was "after a bit", as she said, for when the carriage passed through the park gates there was still two miles of avenue to drive through, and the trees (which nearly met overhead) made it seem as if they were driving through a long dark vault.

They drove out of the vault into a clear space and stopped before an immensely long but low-built house, which seemed to ramble round a stone court. At first Mary thought that there were no lights at all in the windows, but as she got out of the carriage she saw that one room in a corner upstairs showed a dull glow.

The entrance door was a huge one made of massive, curiously shaped panels of oak studded with big iron nails and bound with great iron bars. It opened into an enormous hall, which was so dimly lighted that the faces in the portraits on the walls and the figures in the suits of armour made Mary feel that she did not want to look at them. As she stood on the stone floor she looked a very small, odd little black figure, and she felt as small and lost and odd as she looked.

A neat, thin old man stood near the manservant who opened the door for them.

"You are to take her to her room," he said in a husky voice. "He doesn't want to see her. He's going to London in the morning."

"Very well, Mr. Pitcher," Mrs. Medlock answered. "So long as I know what's expected of me, I can manage."

"What's expected of you, Mrs. Medlock," Mr. Pitcher said, "is that you make sure that he's not disturbed and that he doesn't see what he doesn't want to see."

And then Mary Lennox was led up a broad staircase and down a long corridor and up a short flight of steps and through another corridor and another, until a door opened in a wall and she found herself in a room with a fire in it and a supper on a table.

Mrs. Medlock said unceremoniously:

"Well, here you are! This room and the next are where you'll live–and you must keep to them. Don't you forget that!"

It was in this way Mistress Mary arrived at Misselthwaite Manor, and she had perhaps never felt quite so contrary in all her life.

CHAPTER 4

MARTHA

When she opened her eyes in the morning it was because a young housemaid had come into her room to light the fire and was kneeling on the hearth-rug raking out the cinders noisily. Mary lay and watched her for a few moments and then began to look about the room. She had never seen a room at all like it, and thought it curious and gloomy. The walls were covered with tapestry with a forest scene embroidered on it. There were fantastically dressed people under the trees, and in the distance there was a glimpse of the turrets of a castle. There were hunters and horses and dogs and ladies. Mary felt as if she were in the forest with them. Out of a deep window she could see a great climbing stretch of land which seemed to have no trees on it, and to look rather like an endless, dull, purplish sea.

"What is that?" she said, pointing out of the window.

Martha, the young housemaid, who had just risen to her feet, looked, and pointed also.

"That there?" she said.

"Yes."

"That's th' moor," with a good-natured grin. "Does tha' like it?"

"No," answered Mary. "I hate it."

"That's because tha'rt not used to it," Martha said going back to her hearth. "Tha' thinks it's too big an' bare now. But tha' will like it."

"Do you?" inquired Mary.

"Aye, that I do," answered Martha, cheerfully polishing away at the grate. "I just love it. It's none bare. It's covered wi' growin' things as smells sweet. It's fair lovely in spring an' summer when th' gorse an' broom an' heather's in flower. It smells o' honey an' there's such a lot o' fresh air–an' th' sky looks so high an' th' bees an' skylarks makes such a nice noise hummin' an' singing'. Eh! Iwouldn't live away from th' moor for anythin'."

Mary listened to her with a grave, puzzled expression. The native servants she had been used to in India were not in the least like this. They were obsequious and servile and did not presume to talk to their masters as if they were their equals. They made salaams and called them protector of the poor and names of that sort. Indian servants were commanded to do things, not asked. It was not the custom to say "Please" and "Thank you", and Mary had always slapped her Ayah in the face when she was angry. She wondered a little what this girl would do if one slapped her in the face. She was a round, rosy, good-natured looking creature, but she had a sturdy way which made Mistress Mary wonder if she might not even slap back-if the person who slapped her was only a little girl.

"You are a strange servant," she said from her pillows, rather haughtily.

Martha sat up on her heels, with her blacking-brush in her hand, and laughed, without seeming the least out of temper.

"Eh! I know that," she said. "If there was a grand missus at Misselthwaite I should never have been even one of th' under-housemaids. I might have been let to be scullerymaid, but I'd never have been let upstairs. I'm too -common an' I talk too much Yorkshire. But this is a funny house for all it's so grand. Seems like there's neither master nor mistress except Mr. Pitcher and Mrs. Medlock. Mr. Craven, he won't be troubled about anythin' when he's here, an' he's nearly always away. Mrs. Medlock gave me th' place out o' kindness. She told me she could never have done it if Misselthwaite had been like other big houses."

"Are you going to be my servant?" Mary asked, still in her imperious little Indian way.

Martha began to rub her grate again.

"I'm Mrs. Medlock's servant," she said stoutly. "And she's Mr. Craven's-but I'm to do the housemaid's work up here an' wait on you a bit. But you won't need much waitin' on."

"Who is going to dress me?" demanded Mary.

Martha sat up on her heels again and stared. She spoke in broad Yorkshire in her amazement.

"Canna' tha' dress thysen?" she said.

"What do you mean? I don't understand your language," said Mary.

"Eh! I forgot," Martha said. Mrs. Medlock told me I'd have to be careful or you wouldn't know what I was sayin'. I mean can't you put on your own clothes?"

"No," answered Mary, quite indignantly. I never did in my life. My Ayah dressed me, of course."

"Well," said Martha, evidently not in the least aware that she was impudent, "it's time tha' should learn. Tha' cannot begin younger. It'll do thee good to wait on thysen a bit. My mother always said she couldn't see why grand people's children didn't turn out fair fools-what with nurses an' bein' washed an' dressed an' took out to walk as if they was puppies!"

"It is different in India," said Mistress Mary disdainfully. She could scarcely stand this.

But Martha was not at all crushed.

"Eh! I can see it's different," she answered almost sympathetically. "I dare say it's because there's such a lot o' blacks there instead o' respectable white people. When I heard you was comin' from India I thought you was a black too."

Mary sat up in bed, furious.

"What" she said. "What! You thought I was a native. You-you daughter of a pig! "

Martha stared and looked hot.

"Who are you callin' names?" she said. "You needn't be so vexed. That's not th' way for a young lady to talk. I've nothin' against th' blacks. When you read about 'em in tracts they're always very religious. You always read as a black's a man an' a brother. I've never seen a black an' I was fair pleased to think I was goin' to see one dose. When I come in to light your fire this mornin' I crep' up to your bed an' pulled th' cover back careful to look at you. An' there you was," disappointedly, "no more black than me–for all you're so yeller."

Mary did not even try to control her rage and humiliation.

"You thought I was a native! You dared! You don't know anything about natives! They are not people–they're servants who must salaam to you. You know nothing about India. You know nothing about anything! "

She was in such a rage and felt so hopeless before the girl's simple stare, and somehow she suddenly felt so horribly lonely and far away from everything she understood and which understood her, that she threw herself face downward on the pillows and burst into passionate sobbing. She sobbed so unrestrainedly that good-natured Yorkshire Martha was a little frightened and quite sorry for her. She went to the bed and bent over her.

"Eh! you mustn't cry like that there!" she begged. "You mustn't for sure. I didn't know you'd be vexed. I don't know anythin' about anythin' just like you said. I beg your pardon, miss. Do stop cryin'."

There was something comforting and really friendly in her queer Yorkshire speech and sturdy way which had a good effect on Mary. She gradually ceased crying and became quiet. Martha looked relieved.

"It's time for thee to get up now, she said. Mrs. Medlock said I was to carry tha' breakfast an' tea an' dinner into th' room next to this. It's been made into a nursery for thee. I'll help thee on with thy clothes if tha'll get out of bed. If th' buttons are at th' back tha' cannot button them up tha'self."

When Mary at last decided to get up, the clothes Martha took from the wardrobe were not the ones she had worn when she arrived the night before with Mrs. Medlock.

"Those are not mine," she said. "Mine are black."

She looked the thick white wool coat and dress over, and added with cool approval:

"Those are nicer than mine."

"These are th' ones tha' must put on," Martha answered. "Mr. Craven ordered Mrs. Medlock to get 'em in London. He said, 'I won't have a child dressed in black wanderin' about like a lost soul,' he said; 'It'd make the place sadder than it is. Put colour on her.' Mother she said she knew what he meant. Mother always knows what a body means. She doesn't hold with black hersel'."

"I hate black things," said Mary.

The dressing process was one which taught them both something. Martha had "buttoned up" her little sisters and brothers, but she had never seen a child who stood still and waited for another person to do things for her as if she had neither hands nor feet of her own.

"Why doesn't tha' put on tha' own shoes?" she said when Mary quietly held out her foot.

"My Ayah did it," answered Mary, staring. "It was the custom.

She said that very often–"It was the custom." The native servants were always saying it. If one told them to do a thing their ancestors had not done for a thousand years they gazed at one mildly and said, "It is not the custom" and one knew that was the end of the matter.

It had not been the custom that Mistress Mary should do anything but stand and allow herself to be dressed like a doll, but before she was ready for breakfast she began to suspect that her life at Misselthwaite Manor would end by teaching her a number of things quite new to her–things such as putting on her own shoes and stockings, and picking up things she let fall. If Martha had been a well-trained fine young lady's-maid she would have been more subservient and respectful and would have known that it was her business to brush hair, and button boots, and pick things up and lay them away. She was, however, only an untrained Yorkshire rustic who had been brought up in a moorland cottage with a swarm of little brothers and sisters who had never dreamed of doing anything but waiting on themselves and on the younger ones who were either babies in arms or just learning to totter about and tumble over things.

If Mary Lennox had been a child who was ready to be amused she would perhaps have laughed at Martha's readiness to talk, but Mary only listened to her coldly and wondered at her freedom of manner. At first she was not at all interested, but gradually, as the girl rattled on in her good-tempered, homely way, Mary began to notice what she was saying.

"Eh! you should see 'em all," she said. "There's twelve of us an' my father only gets sixteen shilling a week. I can tell you my mother's put to it to get porridge for 'em all. They tumble about on th' moor an' play there all day, an' mother says th' air of th' moor fattens 'em. She says she believes they eat th' grass same as th' wild ponies do. Our Dickon, he's twelve years old and he's got a young pony he calls his own."

"Where did he get it?" asked Mary.

"He found it on th' moor with its mother when it was a little one, an' he began to make friends with it an' give it bits o' bread an' pluck young grass for it. And it got to like him so it follows him about an' it lets him get on its back. Dickon's a kind lad an' animals like him."

Mary had never possessed an animal pet of her own and had always thought she should like one. So she began to feel a slight interest in Dickon, and as she had never been interested in anyone but herself, it was the dawning of a healthy sentiment. When she went into the room which had been made into a nursery for her, she found that it was rather like the one she had slept in. It was not a child's room, but a grown-up person's room, with gloomy old pictures on the walls and heavy old oak chairs. A table in the centre was set with a good, substantial breakfast. But she had always had a very small appetite, and she looked with something more than indifference at the first plate Martha set before her.

"I don't want it," she said.

"Tha' doesn't want thy porridge!" Martha exclaimed incredulously.

"No."

"Tha' doesn't know how good it is. Put a bit o' treacle on it or a bit o' sugar."

"I don't want it," repeated Mary.

"Eh!" said Martha. I can't abide to see good victuals go to waste. If our children was at this table they'd clean it bare in five minutes."

"Why?" asked Mary coldly.

"Why!" echoed Martha. Because they scarce ever had their stomachs full in their lives. They're as hungry as young hawks an' foxes."

"I don't know what it is to be hungry," said Mary, with the indifference of ignorance.

Martha looked indignant.

"Well, it would do thee good to try it. I can see that plain enough," she said outspokenly. "I've no patience with folks as sits an' just stares at good bread an' meat. My word! don't I wish Dickon and Phil an' Jane an' th' rest of 'em had what's here under their pinafores."

"Why don't you take it to them?" suggested Mary.

"It's not mine," answered Martha stoutly. "An' this isn't my day out. I get my day out once a month same as the rest. Then I go home an' clean up for mother an' give her a day's rest."

Mary drank some tea and ate a little toast and some marmalade.

"You wrap up warm an' run out an' play you, said Martha "It'll do you good and give you some stomach for your meat."

Mary went to the window. There were gardens and paths and big trees, but everything looked dull and wintry.

"Out? Why should I go out on a day like this?"

"Well, if tha' doesn't go out tha'lt have to stay in, an' what has tha' got to do?"

Mary glanced about her. There was nothing to do. When Mrs. Medlock had prepared the nursery she had not thought of amusement. Perhaps it would be better to go and see what the gardens were like.

"Who will go with me?" she inquired.

Martha stared.

"You'll go by yourself," she answered. You'll have to learn to play like other children does when they haven't got sisters and brothers. Our Dickon goes off on th' moor by himself an' plays for hours. That's how he made friends with th' pony. He's got sheep on th' moor that knows him, an' birds as comes an' eats out of his hand. However little there is to eat, he always saves a bit o' his bread to coax his pets."

It was really this mention of Dickon which made Mary decide to go out, though she was not aware of it. There would be birds outside, though there would not be ponies or sheep. They would be different from the birds in India and it might amuse her to look at them.

Martha found her coat and hat for her and a pair of stout little boots and she showed her her way downstairs.

"If tha' goes round that way tha'll come to th' gardens, she said, pointing to a gate in a wall of shrubbery. There's lots o' flowers in summer-time, but there's nothin' bloomin' now. She seemed to hesitate a second before she added, One of th' gardens is locked up. No one has been in it for ten years."

"Why?" asked Mary in spite of herself. Here was another locked door that added to the hundred in the strange house.

"Mr. Craven had it shut when his wife died so sudden. He

won't let no one go inside. It was her garden. He locked th' door an' dug a hole and buried th' key. There's Mrs. Medlock's bell ringing–I must run."

After she was gone Mary turned down the walk which led to the door in the shrubbery. She could not help thinking about the garden which no one had been into for ten years. She wondered what it would look like and whether there were any flowers still live in it. When she had passed through the shrubbery gate she found herself in great gardens, with wide lawns and winding walks with clipped borders. There were trees, and flower-beds, and evergreens clipped into strange shapes, and a large pool with an old grey fountain in its midst. But the flower-beds were bare and wintry and the fountain was not playing. This was not the garden which was shut up. How could a garden be shut up? You could always walk into a garden.

She was just thinking this, when she saw that, at the end of the path she was following, there seemed to be a long wall, with ivy growing over it. She was not familiar enough with England to know that she was coming upon the kitchen-gardens where the vegetables and fruit were growing. She went towards the wall and found that there was a green door in the ivy, and that it stood open. This was not the closed garden evidently, and she could go into it.

She went through the door and found that it was a garden with walls all around it and that it was only one of several walled gardens which seemed to open into one another. She saw another open green door, revealing bushes and pathways between beds containing winter vegetables. Fruit-trees were trained flat against the wall, and over some of the beds there were glass frames. The place was bare and ugly enough, Mary thought, as she stood and stared about her. It might be nicer in summer, when things were green, but there was nothing pretty about it now.

Presently an old man with a spade over his shoulder walked through the door leading from the second garden. He looked startled when he saw Mary, and then touched his cap. He had a surly old. face, and did not seem at all pleased to see her–but then she was displeased with his garden and wore her "quite contrary" expression, and certainly did not seem at all pleased to see him.

"What is this place?" she asked.

"One o' th' kitchen-gardens," he answered.

"What is that?" said Mary, pointing through the other green door.

"Another of 'em, shortly. There's another on t'other side o' th' wall an' there's th' orchard t'other side o' that.

"Can I go in them?" asked Mary.

"If tha' likes. But there's nowt to see."

Mary made no response. She went down the path and through the second green door. There she found more walls and winter vegetables and glass frames, but in the second wall there was another green door and it was not open. Perhaps it led into the garden which no one had seen for ten years. As she was not at all a timid child and always did what she wanted to do, Mary went to the green door and turned the handle. She hoped the door would not open, because she wanted to be sure she had found the mysterious garden–but it did open, quite easily and she walked through it and found herself in an orchard. There were walls all around it also and trees trained against them, and there were bare fruit-trees growing in the winter-browned grass-but there was no green door to be seen anywhere. Mary looked for it, and yet when she had entered the upper end of the garden she had noticed that the wall did not seem to end with the orchard, but to extend beyond it as if it enclosed a place at the other side. She could see the tops of trees above the wall, and when she stood still she saw a bird with a bright red breast sitting on the topmost branch of one of them, and suddenly he burst into his winter song-almost as if he had caught sight of her and was calling to her.

She stopped and listened to him, and somehow his cheerful, friendly little whistle gave her a pleased feeling–even a disagreeable little girl may be lonely, and the big closed house and big bare moor and big bare gardens had made this one feel as if there was no one left in the world but herself. If she had been an affectionate child, who had been wed to being loved, she would have broken her heart, but even though she was "Mistress Mary Quite Contrary" she was desolate, and the bright-breasted little bird brought a look into her sour little face which was almost a smile. She listened to him until he flew away. He was not like an Indian bird, and she liked him and wondered if she should ever see him again. Perhaps he lived in the mysterious garden and knew all about it.

Perhaps it was because she had nothing whatever to do that she thought so much of the deserted garden. She was curious about it, and wanted to see what it was like. Why had Mr. Archibald Craven buried the key? If he had liked his wife so much why did he hate her garden? She wondered if she should ever see him, but she knew that if she did she should not like him, and he would not like her, and that she should only stand and stare at him and say nothing, though she should be wanting dreadfully to ask him why he had done such a queer thing.

"People never like me and I never like people," she thought. And I never can talk as the Crawford children could. They were always talking and laughing and making noises.

She thought of the robin and of the way he seemed to sing his song at her, and as she remembered the tree-top he perched on she stopped rather suddenly on the path.

"I believe that tree was in the secret garden–I feel sure it was," she said. There was a wall round the place and there was no door.

She walked back into the first kitchen-garden she had entered and found the old man digging there. She went and stood beside him and watched him a few moments in her cold little way. He took no notice of her, and so at last she spoke to him.

"I have been into the other gardens," she said.

"There was nothin' to prevent thee," he answered crustily.

"I went into the orchard."

"There was no dog at th' door to bite thee," he answered.

"There was no door there into the other garden," said Mary.

"What garden?" he said in a rough voice, stopping his digging for a moment.

"The one on the other side of the wall," answered Mistress Mary. There were trees there–I saw the tops of them. A bird with a red breast was sitting on one of them, and he sang.

To her surprise the surly old weather-beaten face actually changed its expression. A slow smile spread over it and the gardener looked quite different. It made her think that it was curious how much nicer a person looked when he smiled. She had not thought of it before.

He turned about to the orchard side of his garden and began to whistle–a low, soft whistle. She could not understand how such a surly man could make such a coaxing sound.

Almost the next moment a wonderful thing happened. She heard a soft little rushing flight through the air–and it was the bird with the red breast flying to them, and he actually alighted on the big clod of earth quite near to the gardener's foot.

"Here he is," chuckled the old man, and then he poke to the bird as if he were speaking to a child.

"Where has tha' been, tha' cheeky little beggar?" he said. I've not seen thee before today. Has tha' been tha' courtin' this early in th' season? Tha'rt too for'ard."

The bird put his tiny head on one side and looked up at him with his soft bright eye, which was like a black dewdrop. He seemed quite familiar and not the least afraid. He hopped about and pecked the earth briskly, looking for seeds and insects. It actually gave Mary a queer feeling in her heart, because he was so pretty and cheerful and seemed so like a person. He had a tiny plump body and a delicate beak, and slender delicate legs.

"Will he always come when you call him?" she whispered.

"Aye, that he will. I've knowed him ever since he was a fledgling. He come out of th' nest in th' other garden, an' when first he flew over th' wall he was too weak to fly back for a few days an' we got friendly. When he went over th' wall again th' rest of th' brood was gone an' he was lonely an' he come back to me."

"What kind of a bird is he?" Mary asked.

"Doesn't tha' know? He's a robin redbreast, an' they're th' friendliest, curiousest birds alive. They're almost as friendly as dogs-if you know how to get on with 'em. Watch him peckin' about there an' lookin' round at us now an' again. He knows we're talkin' about him."

It was the queerest thing in the world to see the old fellow. He looked at the plump little scarlet-waistcoated bird as if he were both proud and fond of him.

"He's a conceited one," he chuckled. "He likes to hear folk

talk about him. An' curious–bless me, there never was his like for curiosity an' meddlin'. He's always comin' to see what I'm plantin'. He knows all th' things Mester Craven never troubles hissel' to find out. He's th' head gardener, he is."

The robin hopped about, busily pecking the soil, and now and then stopped and looked at them a little. Mary thought his black dewdrop eyes gazed at her with great curiosity. It really seemed as if he were finding out all about her. The queer feeling in her heart increased.

"Where did the rest of the brood fly to?" she asked.

"There's no knowin'. The old ones turn 'em out o' their nest an' make 'em fly, an' they're scattered before you know it. This one was a knowin' one an' he knew he was lonely."

Mistress Mary went a step nearer to the robin and looked at him very hard.

"I'm lonely," she said.

She had not known before that this was one of the things which made her feel sour and cross. She seemed to find it out when the robin looked at her and she looked at the robin.

The old gardener pushed his cap back on his bald head and stared at her a minute.

"Art tha' th' little wench from India?" he asked.

Mary nodded.

"Then no wonder tha'rt lonely. Tha'lt be lonelier before tha's done," he said.

He began to dig again, driving his spade deep into the rich black garden soil, while the robin hopped about, very busily employed.

"What is your name?" Mary inquired.

He stood up to answer her.

"Ben Weatherstaff," he answered, and then he added with a surly chuckle, "I'm lonely mysel' except when he's with me," and he jerked his thumb towards the robin. "He is th' only friend I've got."

"I have no friends at all," said Mary. "I never had. My Ayah didn't like me and I never played with anyone."

It is a Yorkshire habit to say what you think with blunt frankness, and old Ben Weatherstaff was a Yorkshire moor man.

"Tha' an' me are a good bit alike," he said. "We was wove

out of th' same cloth. We're neither of w good-lookin' an' we're both of us as sour as we look. We've got the same nasty tempers, both of us, I'll warrant!"

This was plain speaking, and Mary Lennox had never heard the truth about herself in her life. Native servants always salaamed and submitted to you, whatever you did. She had never thought much about her looks, but she wondered if she was as unattractive as Ben Weatherstaff, and she also wondered if she looked as sour as he had looked before the robin came. She actually began to wonder also if she was "nasty-tempered". She felt uncomfortable.

Suddenly a clear rippling little sound broke out near her and she turned round. She was standing a few feet from a young apple-tree, and the robin had flown on to one of its branches and had burst out into a scrap of a song. Ben Weatherstaff laughed outright.

"What did he do that for?" asked Mary.

"He's made up his mind to make friends with thee," replied Ben. "Dang me if he hasn't took a fancy to thee."

"To me?" said Mary, and she moved towards the little tree softly and looked up.

"Would you make friends with me?" she said to the robin, just as if she were speaking to a person. "Would you?" And she did not say it either in her hard little voice or in her imperious Indian voice, but in a tone so soft and eager and coaxing that Ben Weatherstaff was as surprised as she had been when she heard him whistle.

"Why," he cried out, "tha' said that as nice an' human as if tha' was a real child instead of a sharp old woman. Tha' said it almost like Dickon talks to his wild things on th' moor."

"Do you know Dickon?" Mary asked, turning round rather in a hurry.

"Everybody knows him. Dickon's wanderin' about everywhere. Th' very blackberries an' heather-bells knows him. I warrant th' foxes shows him where their cubs lies an' th' skylarks doesn't hide their nests from him.

Mary would have liked to ask some more questions. She was almost as curious about Dickon as she was about the deserted garden. But just at that moment the robin, who had ended his song, gave a little shake of his wings, spread them, and flew away. He had made his visit and had other things to do.

"He has flown over the wall!" Mary cried out, watching him. He has flown into the orchard–he has flown across the other wall–into the garden where there is no door!"

"He lives there," said old Ben. "He came out o' th' egg there. If he's courtin', he's makin' up to some young madam of a robin that lives among th' old rose-trees there."

"Rose-trees," said Mary. "Are there rose-trees?"

Ben Weatherstaff took up his spade again and began to dig. "There was ten year' ago," he mumbled.

"I should like to see them," said Mary. "Where is the green door? There must be a door somewhere."

Ben drove his spade deep and looked as uncompanionable as he had looked when she first saw him.

"There was ten year' ago, but there isn't now, he said.

"No door!" cried Mary. "There must be."

"None as anyone can find, an' none as is anyone's business. Don't be a meddlesome wench an' poke your nose where it's no cause to go. Here, I must go on with my work. Get you gone an' play you. I've no more time."

And he actually stopped digging, threw his spade over his shoulder, and walked off, without even glancing at her or saying good-bye.

Chapter 5

THE CRY IN THE CORRIDOR

At first each day which passed by for Mary Lennox was exactly like the others. Every morning she awoke in her tapestried room and found Martha kneeling upon the hearth building her fire; every morning she ate her breakfast in the nursery which had nothing amusing in it; and after each breakfast she gazed out of the window across to the huge moor, which seemed to spread out on all sides and climb up to the sky, and after she had stared for a while she realized that if she did not go out she would have to stay in and do nothing-and so she went out. She did not know that this was the best thing she could have done, and she did not know that, when she began to walk quickly or even run along the paths and down the avenue, she was stirring her slow blood and making herself stronger by fighting with the wind which swept down from the moor. She ran only to make herself warm, and she hated the wind which rushed at her face and roared and held her back as if it were some giant she could not see. But the big breaths of rough fresh air blown over the heather filled her lungs with something which was good for her whole thin body and whipped some red colour into her cheeks and brightened her dull eyes when she did not know anything about it.

But after a few days spent almost entirely out of doors, she wakened one morning knowing what it was to be hungry, and when she sat down to her breakfast she did not glance disdainfully at her porridge and push it away, but took up her spoon and began to eat it and went on eating it until her bowl was empty.

"Tha' got on well enough with that this mornin', didn't tha'?" said Martha.

"It tastes nice today," said Mary, feeling a little surprised herself.

"It's th' air of th' moor that's givin' thee stomach for tha' victuals," answered Martha. "It's lucky for thee that tha's got victuals as well as an appetite. There's been twelve in our cottage as had th' stomach an' nothing to put in it. You go on playin' you out o' doors every day an' you'll get some flesh on your bones an' you won't be so yeller."

"I don't play," said Mary. "I have nothing to play with."

"Nothin' to play with!" exclaimed Martha our children plays with sticks and stones. They just runs about an' shouts an' looks at things."

Mary did not shout, but she looked at things. There was nothing else to do. She walked round and round the gardens and wandered about the paths in the park. Sometimes she looked for Ben Weatherstaff, but though several times she saw him at work he was too busy to look at her or was too surly. Once when she was walking towards him he picked up his spade and turned away, as if he did it on purpose.

One place she went to oftener than to any other. It was the long walk outside the gardens with the walls round them. There were bare flower-beds on either side of it and against the walls ivy grew thickly. There was one part of the wall where the creeping dark green leaves were more bushy than elsewhere. It seemed as if for a long time that part had been neglected. The rest of it had been clipped and made to look neat, but at this lower end of the walk it had not been trimmed at all.

A few days after she had talked to Ben Weatherstaff, Mary stopped to notice this and wondered why it was so. She had just paused and was looking up at a long spray of ivy swinging in the wind, when she saw a gleam of scarlet and heard a brilliant chirp, and there, on the top of the wall, perched Ben Weatherstaff's robin redbreast, tilting forward to look at her with his small head on one side.

"Oh!" she cried out, "is it you–is it you? And it did not seem at all queer to her that she spoke to him as if she was sure that he would understand and answer her.

He did answer. He twittered and chirped and hopped along the wall, as if he were telling her all sorts of things. It seemed to Mistress Mary as if she understood him, too, though he was not speaking in words. It was as if he said:

"Good morning! Isn't the wind nice? Isn't the sun nice? Isn't everything nice? Let us both chirp and hop and twitter. Come on! Come on!"

Mary began to laugh, and as he hopped and took little flights along the wall she ran after him. Poor little thin, sallow, ugly Mary–she actually looked almost pretty for a moment.

"I like you! I like you!" she cried out, pattering down the walk; and she chirped and tried to whistle, which last she did not know how to do in the least. But the robin seemed to be quite satisfied and chirped and whistled back at her. At last he spread his wings and made a darting light to the top of a tree, where he perched and sang loudly.

That reminded Mary of the first time she had seen him. He

had been swinging on a tree-top then and she had been standing in the orchard. Now she was on the other side of the orchard and standing in the path outside a wall-much lower down-and there was the same tree inside.

"It's in the garden no one can go into, she said to herself. It's the garden without a door. He lives in there. How I wish I could see what it is like!"

She ran up the wall to the green door she had entered the first morning. Then she ran down the path through the other door and then into the orchard, and when she stood and looked up there was the tree on the other side of the wall, and there was the robin just finishing his song and beginning to preen his feathers with his beak.

"It is the garden," she said. "I am sure it is."

She walked round and looked closely at that side of the orchard wall, but she only found what she had found before–that there was no door in it. Then she ran through the kitchen-gardens again and out into the walk outside the long ivy-covered wall, and she walked to the end of it and looked at it, but there was no door; and then she walked to the other end, looking again, but there was no door.

"It's very queer," she said. Ben Weatherstaff said there was no door and there is no door. But there must have been one ten years ago, because Mr. Craven buried the key."

This gave her so much to think of that she began to be quite interested and feel that she was not sorry that she had come to Misselthwaite Manor. In India she had always felt hot and too languid to care much about anything. The fact was that the fresh wind from the moor had begun to blow the cobwebs out of her young brain and to waken her up a little.

She stayed out of doors nearly all day, and when she sat down to her supper at night she felt hungry and drowsy and comfortable. She did not feel cross when Martha chattered away. She felt as if she rather liked to hear her, and at last she thought she would ask her a question. She asked it after she had finished her supper and had sat down on the hearth-rug before the fire.

"Why did Mr. Craven hate the garden?" she said.

She had made Martha stay with her and Martha had not objected at all. She was very young, and used to a crowded cottage full of brothers and sisters, and she found it dull in the great servants' hall downstairs, where the footman and upper-housemaids made fun of her Yorkshire speech and looked upon her as a common little thing, and sat and whispered among themselves. Martha liked to talk, and the strange child who had lived in India, and been waited upon by "blacks", was novelty enough to attract her.

She sat down on the hearth herself without waiting to be asked.

"Art tha' thinkin' about that garden yet?" she said. I knew tha' would. That was just the way with me when I first heard about it."

"Why did he hate it?" Mary persisted.

Martha tucked her feet under her and made herself quite comfortable.

"Listen to th' wind wutherin' round the house," she said. "You could bare stand up on the moor if you was out on it tonight."

Mary did not know what wutherin' meant until she listened, and then she understood. It must mean that hollow, shuddering sort of roar which rushed round and round the house, as if the giant no one could see were buffeting it and beating at the walls and windows to try to break in. But one knew he could not get in, and somehow it made one feel very safe and warm inside a room with a real coal fire.

"But why did he hate it so?" she asked, after she had listened. She intended to know if Martha did.

Then Martha gave up her store of knowledge.

"Mind," she said, "Mrs. Medlock said it's not to be talked about. There's lots o' things in this place that's not to be talked over. That's Mr. Craven's orders. His troubles are none servants' business, he says. But for th' garden he wouldn't be like he is. It was Mrs. Craven's garden that she had made when first they were married an' she just loved it, an' they used to 'tend the flowers themselves. An' none o' th' gardeners was ever let to go in. Him an' her used to go in an' shut th' door an' stay there hours an' hours, readin' an' talkin'. An' she was just a bit of a girl an' there was an old tree with a branch bent like a seat on it. An' she made roses grow over it an' she used to sit there. But one day when she was sittin' there th' branch broke an' she fell on th' ground an' was hurt so bad that next day she died. Th' doctors thought he'd go out o' his mind an' die too. That's why he hates it. No one's never gone in since, an' he won't let anyone talk about it."

Mary did not ask any more questions. She looked at the fire and listened to the wind wutherin'. It seemed to be wutherin' louder than ever.

At that moment a very good thing was happening to her. Four good things had happened to her, in fact, since she came to Misselthwaite Manor. She had felt as if she had understood a robin and that he had understood her; she had run in the wind until her blood had grown warm; she had been healthily hungry for the first time in her life; and she had found out what it was to be sorry for someone. She was getting on.

But as she was listening to the wind she began to listen to something else. She did not know what it was, because at first she could scarcely distinguish it from the wind itself. It was a curious sound–it seemed almost as if a child were crying somewhere. Sometimes the wind sounded rather like a child crying, but presently Mistress Mary felt quite sure that this sound was inside the house, not outside it. It was far away, but it was inside. She turned round and looked at Martha.

"Do you hear anyone crying?" she said.

Martha suddenly looked confused.

"No," she answered. "It's th' wind. Sometimes it sounds as if someone was lost on th' moor an' wailin'. It's got all sorts o' sounds.

"But listen," said Mary. "It's in the house–down one of those long corridors."

And at that very moment a door must have been opened somewhere downstairs; for a great rushing draught blew along the passage and the door of the room they sat in was blown open with a crash, and as they both jumped to their feet the light was blown out and the crying sound was swept down the far corridor, so that it was to be heard more plainly than ever.

"There," said Mary. "I told you so! It is someone crying–and it isn't a grown-up person."

Martha ran and shut the door and turned the key, but before she did it they both heard the sound of a door in some far passage shutting with a bang, and then everything was quiet, for even the wind ceased "wutherin'" for a few moments.

"It was th' wind," said Martha stubbornly. "An' if it wasn't, it was little Betty Butterworth, th' scullery-maid. She's had th' toothache all day."

But something troubled and awkward in her manner made Mistress Mary stare very hard at her. She did not believe she was speaking the truth.

CHAPTER 6

"THERE WAS SOMEONE CRYING–THERE WAS!"

The next day the rain poured down in torrents again, and when Mary looked out of her window the moor was almost hidden by grey mist and cloud. There could be no going out today.

"What do you do in your cottage when it rains like this?" she asked Martha.

"Try to keep from under each other's feet mostly," Martha answered. "Eh! there does seem a lot of us then. Mother's a good-tempered woman, but she gets fair moithered. The biggest ones goes out in th' cow-shed and plays there. Dickon he doesn't mind th' wet. He goes out just th' same as if th' sun was shinin'. He says he sees things on rainy days as doesn't show when it's fair weather. He once found a little fox cub half drowned in its hole and he brought it home in th' bosom of his shirt to keep it warm. Its mother had been killed near by an' th' hole was swum out an' th' rest o' th' litter was dead. He's got it at home now. He found a half-drowned young crow another time an' he brought it home, too, an' tamed it. It's named Soot, because it's so black an' it hops an' flies about with him everywhere."

The time had come when Mary had forgotten to resent Martha's familiar talk. She had even begun to find it interesting and to be sorry when she stopped or went away. The stories she had been told by her Ayah when she lived in India had been quite unlike those Martha had to tell about the moorland cottage which held fourteen people who lived in four little rooms and never had quite enough to eat. The children seemed to tumble about and amuse themselves like a litter of rough, good-natured collie puppies. Mary was most attracted by the mother and Dickon. When Martha told stories of what "mother" said or did they always sounded comfortable.

"If I had a raven or a fox cub I could play with it," said Mary. "But I have nothing."

Martha looked perplexed.

"Can tha' knit?" she asked.

"No," answered Mary.

"Can tha' sew?"

"No."

"Can tha' read?"

"Yes."

"Then why doesn't tha' read somethin' or learn a bit o' spellin'? That's old enough to be learnin' thy books a good bit now."

"I haven't any books," said Mary. "Those I had were left in India."

"That's a pity," said Martha. "If Mrs. Medlock'd let thee go int' th' library, there's thousands o' books there."

Mary did not ask where the library was, because she was suddenly inspired by a new idea. She made up her mind to go and find it herself. She was not troubled about Mrs. Medlock. Mrs. Medlock seemed always to be in her comfortable housekeeper's sitting-room downstairs. In this queer place one scarcely ever saw anyone at all. In fact, there was no one to see but the servants, and when their master was away they lived a luxurious life below stairs, where there was a huge kitchen hung about with shining brass and pewter, and a large servants' hall where there were four or five abundant meals eaten every day, and where a great deal of lively romping went on when Mrs. Medlock was out of the way.

Mary's meals were served regularly, and Martha waited on her, but no one troubled themselves about her in the least. Mrs. Medlock came and looked at her every day or two, but no one inquired what she did or told her what to do. She supposed that perhaps this was the English way of treating children. In India she had always been attended by her Ayah, who had followed her about and waited on her, hand and foot. She had often been tired of her company. Now he was followed by nobody and was learning to dress herself, because Martha looked as though she thought she was silly and stupid when she wanted to have things handed to her and put on.

"Hasn't tha' got good sense she said once, when Mary had stood waiting for her to put on her gloves for her. "Our Susan Ann is twice as sharp as thee an' she's only four year' old. Sometimes tha' looks fair soft in th' head."

Mary had worn her contrary scowl for an hour after that, but it made her think several entirely new things.

She stood at the window for about ten minutes this morning after Martha had swept up the hearth for the last time and gone downstairs. She was thinking over the new idea which had come to her when she heard of the library. She did not care very much about the library itself, because she had read very few books; but to hear of it brought back to her mind the hundred rooms with closed doors. She wondered if they were all really locked and what she would find if she could get into any of them. Were there a hundred really? Why shouldn't she go and see how many doors she could count? It would be something to do on this morning when she could not go out. She had never been taught to ask permission to do things, and she knew nothing at all about authority, so she would not have thought it necessary to ask Mrs. Medlock if she might walk about the house, even if she had seen her.

She opened the door of the room and went into the corridor, and then she began her wanderings. It was a long corridor and it branched into other corridors and it led her up short flights of steps which mounted to others again. There were doors and doors, and there were pictures on the walls. Sometimes they were pictures of dark, curious landscapes, but oftenest they were portraits of men and women in queer, grand costumes made of satin and velvet. She found herself in one long gallery whose walls were covered with those portraits. She had never thought there could be so many in any howe. She walked slowly down this place and stared at the faces, which also seemed to stare at her. She felt as if they were wondering what a little girl from India was doing in their house. Some were pictures of children–little girls in thick satin frocks which reached to their feet and stood out about them, and boys with puffed sleeves and lace collars and long hair, or with big ruffs around their necks. She always stopped to look at the children, and wonder what their names were, and where they had gone, and why they wore such odd clothes. There was a stiff, plain little girl rather like herself. She wore a green brocade dress and held a green parrot on her finger. Her eyes had a sharp, curious look.

"Where do you live now?" said Mary aloud to her. "I wish you were here."

Surely no other little girl ever spent such a queer morning. It seemed as if there was no one in all the huge, rambling house but her own small self, wandering about upstairs and down, through narrow passages and wide ones, where it seemed to her that no one but herself had ever walked. Since so many rooms had been built, people must have lived in them, but it all seemed so empty that she could not quite believe it true.

It was not until she climbed to the second floor that she thought of turning the handle of a door. All the doors were shut, as Mrs. Medlock had said they were, but last she put her hand on the handle of one of them and turned it. She was almost frightened for a moment when she felt that it turned without difficulty and that when she pushed upon the door itself it slowly and heavily opened. It was a massive door and opened into a big bedroom. There were embroidered hangings on the wall, and inlaid furniture such as she had seen in India stood about the room. A broad window with leaded panes looked out upon the moor; and over the mantel was another portrait of the stiffly, plain little girl who seemed to stare at her more curiously than ever.

"Perhaps she slept here once said Mary. She stares at me so that she makes me feel queer."

After that she opened more doors and more. She saw so many rooms that she became quite tired and began to think that there must be a hundred, though she had not counted them. In all of them there were old pictures or old tapestries with strange scenes worked on them. There were curious pieces of furniture and curious ornaments in nearly all of them.

In one room, which looked like a lady's sitting-room, the hangings were all embroidered velvet, and in a cabinet were about a hundred little elephants made of ivory. They were of different sizes, and some had their mahouts or palanquins on their backs. Some were much bigger than the others and some were so tiny that they seemed only babies. Mary had seen caved ivory in India and she knew all about the elephants. She opened the door of the cabinet and stood on a footstool and played with these for quite a long time. When she got tired she set the elephants in order and shut the door of the cabinet.

In all her wanderings through the long corridors and the empty rooms she had seen nothing alive; but in this room she saw something. Just after she had closed the cabinet door she heard a tiny rustling sound. It made her jump and look around at the sofa by the fireplace, from which it seemed to come. In the corner of the sofa there was a cushion, and in the velvet which covered it there was a hole, and out of the hole peeped a tiny head with a pair of frightened eyes in it.

Mary crept softly across the room to look. The bright eyes belonged to a little grey mouse, and the mouse had eaten a hole into the cushion and made a comfortable nest there. Six baby mice were cuddled up asleep near her. If there was no one else alive in the hundred rooms there were seven mice who did not look lonely at all.

"If they wouldn't be so frightened I would take them back with me," said Mary.

She had wandered about long enough to feel too tired to wander any further, and she turned back. Two or three times she lost her way by turning down the wrong corridor and was obliged to ramble up and down until she found the right one; but at last she reached her own floor again, though she was some distance from her own room and did not know exactly where she was.

"I believe I have taken a wrong turning again," she said,

standing still at what seemed the end of a short passage with tapestry on the wall. "I don't know which way to go. How still everything is!"

It was while she was standing here and just after she had said this that the stillness was broken by a sound. It was another cry, but not quite like the one she had heard last night; it was only a short one, a fretful, childish whine muffled by passing through walls.

"It's nearer than it was," said Mary, her heart beating rather faster. "And it is crying."

She put her hand accidentally upon the tapestry near her, and then sprang back, feeling quite startled. The tapestry was the covering of a door which fell open and showed her that there was another part of the corridor behind it, and Mrs. Medlock was coming up it with her bunch of keys in her hand and a very cross look on her face.

"What are you doing here?" she said, and she took Mary by the arm and pulled her away. "What did I tell you?"

"I turned round the wrong corner," explained Mary. "I didn't know which way to go and I heard someone crying."

She quite hated Mrs. Medlock at the moment, but she hated her more the next.

"You didn't hear anything of the sort," said the housekeeper. "You come along back to your own nursery or I'll box your ears."

And she took her by the arm and half pushed, half pulled her up one passage and down another, until she pushed her in at the door of her own room.

"Now," she said, "you stay where you're told to stay or you'll find yourself locked up. The master had better get you a governess, same as he said he would. You're one that needs someone to look sharp after you. I've got enough to do."

She went out of the room and slammed the door after her, and Mary went and sat on the hearth-rug, pale with rage. She did not cry, but ground her teeth.

"There *was* someone crying–there *was*–there *was*!" she said to herself.

She had heard it twice now, and some time she would find out. She had found out a great deal this morning. She felt as if she had been on a long journey, and at any rate she had had something to amuse her all the time, and she had played with the ivory elephants and had seen the grey mouse and its babies in their nest in the velvet cushion.

CHAPTER 7

THE KEY OF THE GARDEN

Two days after this, when Mary opened her eyes she sat upright in bed immediately, and called to Martha.

"Look at the moor! Look at the moor!"

The rain-storm had ended and the grey mist and clouds had been swept away in the night by the wind. The wind itself had ceased and a brilliant, deep blue sky arched high over the moorland. Never, never had Mary dreamed of a sky so blue. In India skies were hot and blazing; this was of a deep, cool blue, which almost seemed to sparkle like the waters of some lovely, bottomless lake, and here and there, high, high in the arched blueness, floated small clouds of snow-white fleece. The far-reaching world of the moor itself looked softly blue instead of gloomy purple-black or awful dreary grey.

"Aye," said Martha, with a cheerful grin. "Th' storm's over for a bit. It does like this at this time o' th' year. It goes off in a night like it was pretendin' it had never been here an' never meant to come again. That's because th' springtime's on its way. It's a long way off yet, but it's comin'."

"I thought perhaps it always rained or looked dark in England," Mary said.

"Eh! no!" said Martha, sitting up on her heels among her black-lead brushes. "Nowt o'th' soart!"

"What does that mean?" asked Mary seriously. In India the

natives spoke different dialects which only a few people understood, so she was not surprised when Martha used words she did not know.

Martha laughed as she had done the first morning.

"There now," she said. "I've talked broad Yorkshire again like Mrs. Medlock said I mustn't. 'Nowt o' th' soart' means 'nothin' of the sort'," slowly and carefully, "but it takes so long to say it. Yorkshire's th' sunniest place on earth when it is sunny. I told thee tha'd like th' moor after a bit. Just you wait till you see th' gold-coloured gorse blossoms an' th' blossoms o' th' broom, an' th' heather flowerin', all purple bells, an' hundreds o' butterflies flutterin' an' bees hummin' an' skylarks soarin' up an' singin'. You'll want to get out on it at sunrise an' live out on it all day like Dickon does."

"Could I ever get there?" asked Mary wistfully, looking through her window at the far-off blue. It was so new and big and wonderful and such a heavenly colour.

"I don't know," answered Martha. "Tha's never used tha' legs since tha' was born, it seems to me. Tha' couldn't walk five mile. It's five mile to our cottage."

"I should like to see your cottage."

Martha stared at her a moment curiously before she took up her polishing brush and began to rub the grate again. She was thinking that the small plain face did not look quite as sour at this moment as it had done the first morning she saw it. It looked just a trifle like little Susan Ann's when she wanted something very much.

"I'll ask my mother about it," she said. "She's one o' them that nearly always sees a way to do things. It's my day out today an' I'm goin' home. Eh! I am glad. Mrs. Medlock thinks a lot o' mother. Perhaps she could talk to her."

"I like your mother," said Mary.

"I should think tha' did," agreed Martha, polishing away.

"I've never seen her," said Mary.

"No, tha' hasn't," replied Martha.

She sat up on her heels again and rubbed the end of her nose with the back of her hand, as if puzzled for a moment, but she ended quite positively.

"Well, she's that sensible an' hard workin' an' goodnatured an' clean that no one could help likin' her, whether they'd seen her or not. When I'm going home to her on my day out I just jump for joy when I'm crossin' th' moor."

"I like Dickon," added Mary. "And I've never seen him."

"Well," said Martha stoutly. "I've told thee that th' very birds like him an' th' rabbits an' wild sheep an' ponies, an' th' foxes themselves. I wonder," staring at her reflectively, "what Dickon would think of thee?"

"He wouldn't like me," said Mary in her stiff, cold little way. "No one does."

Martha looked reflective again.

"How does tha' like thysel'?" she inquired, really quite as if he were curious to know.

Mary hesitated a moment and thought it over.

"Not at all–really," she answered. "But I never thought of that before."

Martha grinned a little as if at some homely recollection.

"Mother said that to me once," she said. "She was at her wash-tub an' I was in a bad temper an' talkin' ill of folk an' she turns round on me an' says: 'Tha' young vixon, tha'! There tha' stands sayin' tha' doesn't like this one an' tha' doesn't like that one. How does tha' like thysel'? It made me laugh an' it brought me to my senses in a minute."

She went away in high spirits as soon as she had given Mary her breakfast. She was going to walk five miles across the moor to the cottage, and she was going to help her mother with the washing and do the week's baking and enjoy herself thoroughly.

Mary felt lonelier than ever when she knew she was no longer in the house. She went out into the garden as quickly as possible, and the first thing she did was to run round and round the fountain flower garden ten times. She counted the times carefully and when she had finished she felt in better spirits. The sunshine made the whole place look different. The high, deep, blue sky arched over Misselthwaite, as well as over the moor, and she kept lifting her face and looking up into it, trying to imagine what it would be like to lie down on one of the little snow-white clouds and float about. She went into the first kitchen-garden and found Ben Weatherstaff working there with two other gardeners. The change in the weather seemed to have done him good. He spoke to her of his own accord.

"Springtime's coming," he said. "Cannot tha' smell it?"

Mary sniffed and thought she could.

"I smell something nice and fresh and damp," she said.

"That's th' good rich earth," he answered, digging away. "It's in a good humour makin' ready to grow things. It's glad when plantin' time comes. It's dull in th' winter when it's got nowt to do. In th' flower gardens out there things will be stirrin' down below in th' dark. Th' sun's warmin' 'em. You'll see bits o' green spikes stickin' out o' th' black earth after a bit."

"What will they be?" asked Mary.

"Crocuses an' snowdrops an' daffydowndillys. Has tha' never seen them?"

"No. Everything is hot, and wet, and green after the rains in India," said Mary. "And I think things grow up in a night."

"These won't grow up in a night," said Weatherstaff. "Tha'll have to wait for 'em. They'll poke up a bit higher here, and push out a spike more there, an' uncurl a leaf this day an' another that. You watch 'em."

"I am going to," answered Mary.

Very soon she heard the soft rustling flight of wings again and she knew at once that the robin had come again. He was very pert and lively, and hopped about so close to her feet, and put his head on one side and looked at her so shyly that she asked Ben Weatherstaff a question.

"Do you think he remembers me?" she said.

"Remembers thee!" said Weatherstaff indignantly. "He knows every cabbage stump in th' gardens, let alone th' people. He's never seen a little wench here before, an' he's bent on findin' out all about thee. Tha's no need to try to hide anything from *him*."

"Are things stirring down below in the dark in that garden where he lives?" Mary inquired.

"What garden?" grunted Weatherstaff, becoming surly again.

"The one where the old rose-trees are." She could not help asking, because she wanted so much to know. "Are all the flowers dead, or do some of them come again in the summer? Are there ever any roses?"

"Ask him," said Ben Weatherstaff, hunching his shoulders towards the robin. "He's the only one as knows. No one else has seen inside it for ten year'."

Ten years was a long time, Mary thought. She had been born ten years ago.

She walked away, slowly thinking. She had begun to like the garden just as she had begun to like the robin and Dickon and Martha's mother. She was beginning to like Martha, too. That seemed a good many people to like–when you were not used to liking. She thought of the robin as one of the people. She went to her walk outside the long, ivy-covered wall over which she could see the tree-tops; and the second time she walked up and down the most interesting and exciting thing happened to her, and it was all through Ben Weatherstaff's robin.

She heard a chirp and a twitter, and when she looked at the bare flower-bed at her left side there he was hopping about and pretending to peck things out of the earth to persuade her that he had not followed her. But she knew he had followed her, and the surprise so filled her with delight that she almost trembled a little.

"You do remember me!" she cried. "You do! You are prettier than anything else in the world!"

She chirped, and talked, and coaxed and he hopped and flirted his tail and twittered. It was as if he were talking. His red waistcoat was like satin, and he puffed his tiny breast out and was so fine and so grand and so pretty that it was really as if he were showing her how important and like a human person a robin could be. Mistress Mary forgot that she had ever been contrary in her life when he allowed her to draw closer and closer to him, and bend down and talk and try to make something like robin sounds.

Oh! to think that he should actually let her come as near to him as that! He knew nothing in the world would make her put out her hand towards him or startle him in the least tiniest way. He knew it because he was a real person–only nicer than any other person in the world. She was so happy that she scarcely dared to breathe.

The flower-bed was not quite bare. It was bare of flowers because the perennial plants had been cut down for their winter rest, but there were tall shrubs and low ones which grew together at the back of the bed, and as the robin hopped about under them she saw him hop over a small pile of freshly turned-up earth. He stopped on it to look for a worm. The earth had been turned up because a dog had been trying to dig up a mole and he had scratched a deep hole.

Mary looked at it, not really knowing why the hole was there, and as she looked she saw something almost buried in the newly turned soil. It was something like a ring of rusty iron or brass, and when the robin flew up into a tree near by she put out her hand and picked the ring up. It was more than a ring, however; it was an old key which looked as if it had been buried a long time.

Mistress Mary stood up and looked at it with an almost frightened face as it hung from her finger.

"Perhaps it has been buried for ten years," she said in a whisper. "Perhaps it is the key to the garden!"

Chapter 8

THE ROBIN WHO SHOWED THE WAY

She looked at the key quite a long time. She turned it over and over, and thought about it. As I have said before, she was not a child who had been trained to ask permission or consult her elders about things. All she thought about the key was that if it was the key to the closed garden, and she could find out where the door was, she could perhaps open it and see what was inside the walls, and what had happened to the old rose-trees. It was because it had been shut up so long that she wanted to see it. It seemed as if it must be different from other places and that something strange must have happened to it during ten years. Besides that, if she liked it she could go into it every day and shut the door behind her, and she could make up some play of her own and play it quite alone, because nobody would ever know where she was, but would think the door was still locked and the key buried in the earth. The thought of that pleased her very much.

Living, as it were, all by herself in a house with a hundred mysteriously closed rooms and having nothing whatever to do to amuse herself, had set her inactive brain to work and was actually awakening her imagination. There is no doubt that the fresh, strong, pure air from the moor had a great deal to do with it. Just as it had given her an appetite, and fighting with the wind had stirred her blood, so the same things had stirred her mind. In India she had always been too hot and languid and weak to care much about anything, but in this place she was beginning to care and to want to do new things. Already she felt less "contrary", though she did not know why.

She put the key in her pocket and walked up and down her walk. No one but herself ever seemed to come there, so she could walk slowly and look at the wall, or, rather, at the ivy growing on it. The ivy was the baffling thing. Howsoever carefully she looked, she could see nothing but thickly growing, glossy, dark green leaves. She was very much disappointed. Something of her contrariness came back to her as she paced the wall and looked over it at the tree-tops inside. It seemed so silly, she said to herself, to be near it and not be able to get in. She took the key in her pocket when she went back to the house, and she made up her mind that she would always carry it with her when she went out, so that if she ever should find the hidden door she would be ready.

Mrs. Medlock had allowed Martha to sleep all night at the cottage, but she was back at her work in the morning with cheeks redder than ever and in the best of spirits.

"I got up at four o'clock," she said. Eh! it was pretty on th' moor with th' birds gettin' up an' th' rabbits scamperin' about an' th' sun risin'. I didn't walk all th' way. A man gave me a ride in his cart an' I can tell you I did enjoy myself."

She was full of stories of the delights of her day out. Her mother had been glad to see her, and they had got the baking and washing all out of the way. She had even made each of the children a dough-cake with a bit of brown sugar in it.

"I had 'em all pipin' hot when they came in from playin' on

th' moor. An' th' cottage all smelt o' nice, clean, hot bakin' an' there was a good fire, an' they just shouted for joy. Our Dickon, he said our cottage was good enough for a king to live in."

In the evening they had all sat round the fire, and Martha and her mother had sewed patches on torn clothes and mended stockings, and Martha had told them about the little girl who had come from India and who had been waited on all her life by what Martha called "blacks" until she didn't know how to put on her own stockings.

"Eh! they did like to hear about you," said Martha. "They wanted to know all about th' blacks an' about th' ship you came in. I couldn't tell 'em enough."

Mary reflected a little.

"I'll tell you a great deal more before your next day out, she said, "so that you will have more to talk about. I dare say they would like to hear about riding on elephants and camels, and about the officers going to hunt tigers."

"My word!" cried delighted Martha. It would set 'em clean off their heads. Would tha' really do that, Miss? It would be the same as a wild beast show like we heard they had in York once."

"India is quite different from Yorkshire," Mary said slowly, as she thought the matter over. "I never thought of that. Did Dickon and your mother like to hear you talk about me?"

"Why, our Dickon's eyes nearly started out o' his head, they got that round, answered Martha. "But Mother, she was put out about your seemin' to be all by yourself like. She said: 'Hasn't Mr. Craven got no governess for her, nor no nurse?' and I said: 'No, he hasn't, though Mrs. Medlock says he will when he thinks of it, but she says he mayn't think of it for two or three years."

"I don't want a governess," said Mary sharply.

"But Mother says you ought to be learnin' your book by this time an' you ought to have a woman to look after you, an' she says: 'Now Martha, you just think how you'd feel yourself, in a big place like that, wanderin' about alone, an' no mother. You do your best to cheer her up,' she says, an' I said I would."

Mary gave her a long, steady look.

"You do cheer me up," she said. "I like to hear you talk."

Presently Martha went out of the room and came back with something held in her hands under her apron.

"What does tha' think," she said, with a cheerful grin. "I've brought thee a present."

"A present!" exclaimed Mistress Mary. How could a cottage full of fourteen hungry people give anyone a present!"

"A man was drivin' across the moor peddlin'," Martha explained. "An' he stopped his cart at our door. He had pots a' pans an' odds an' ends, but Mother had no money to buy anythin'. Just as he was goin' away our 'Lizbeth Ellen called out: 'Mother, he's got skippin'- ropes with red an' blue handles.' An' Mother, she calls out quite sudden: 'Here, stop, mister! How much are they?' An' he says 'Tuppence,' an' Mother she began fumblin 'in her pocket, an' she says to me: 'Martha, tha's brought thee thy wages like a good lass, an' I've got four places to put every penny, but I'm just goin' to take tuppence out of it to buy that child a skippin'-rope,' an' she bought one, an' here it is."

She brought it out from under her apron and exhibited it quite proudly. It was a strong, slender rope with a striped red and blue handle at each end, but Mary Lennox had never seen a skipping-rope before. She gazed at it with a mystified expression.

"What is it for?" she asked curiously.

"For!" cried out Martha. "Does tha' mean that they've not got skippin'-ropes in India, for all they've got elephants and tigers and camels? No wonder most of 'em's black. This is what it's for; just watch me."

And she ran into the middle of the room and, taking a handle in each hand, began to skip, and skip, and skip, while Mary turned in her chair to stare at her, and the queer faces in the old portraits seemed to stare at her, too, and wonder what on earth this common little cottager had the impudence to be doing under their very noses. But Martha did not even see them. The interest and curiosity in Mistress Mary's face delighted her, and she went on skipping and counted as she skipped until she had reached a hundred.

"I could skip longer than that," she said when she stopped. "I've skipped as much as five hundred when I was twelve, but I wasn't as fat then as I am now, an' I was in practice."

Mary got up from her chair beginning to feel excited herself. "It looks nice," she said. "Your mother is a kind woman. Do you think I could ever skip like that?"

"You just try it," urged Martha, handing her the skipping-rope. "You can't skip a hundred at first, but if you practise you'll mount up. That's what Mother said. She says: 'Nothin' will do her more good than skippin'-rope. It's th' sensiblest toy a child can have. Let her play out in th' fresh air skippin' an' it'll stretch her legs an' arms an' give her some strength in 'em.'"

It was plain that there was not a great deal of strength in Mistress Mary's arms and legs when she first began to skip. She was not very clever at it, but she liked it so much that she did not want to stop.

"Put on tha' things and run an' skip out o' doors, said Martha. Mother said I must tell you to keep out o' doors as much as you could, even when it rains a bit, so as tha' wrap up warm."

Mary put on her coat and hat and took her skipping-rope over her arm. She opened the door to go out, and then suddenly thought of something and turned back rather slowly.

"Martha," she said, "they were your wages. It was your twopence really. Thank you." She said it stiffly because she was not used to thanking people or noticing that they did things for her. "Thank you," she said, and held out her hand because she did not know what else to do.

Martha gave her hand a clumsy little shake, as if she was not accustomed to this sort of thing either. Then she laughed.

"Eh! tha' art a queer, old-womanish thing, she said.-"If tha'd been our 'Lizabeth Ellen tha'd have given me a kiss."

Mary looked stiffer than ever.

"Do you want me to kiss you?"

Martha laughed again.

"Nay, not me," she answered. "If tha' was different, p'raps tha'd want to thysel'. But tha' isn't. Run off outside an' play with thy rope."

Mistress Mary felt a little awkward as she went out of the room. Yorkshire people seemed strange, and Martha was always rather a puzzle to her. At first she had disliked her very much, but now she did not.

The skipping-rope was a wonderful thing. She counted and skipped, and skipped and counted, until her cheeks were quite red, and she was more interested than she had ever been since she was born. The sun was shining and a little wind was blowing–not a rough wind, but one which came in delightful little gusts and brought a fresh scent of newly turned earth with it. She skipped round the fountain garden, and up one walk and down another. She skipped at last into the kitchen-garden and saw Ben Weatherstaff digging and talking to his robin, which was hopping about him. She skipped down the walk towards him and he lifted his head an,d looked at her with a curious expression. She had wondered if he would notice her. She really wanted him to see her skip.

"Well!" he exclaimed. "Upon my word! P'raps tha' art a young 'un, after all, an' p'raps tha's got child's blood in thy veins instead of sour buttermilk. Tha's skipped red into thy cheeks as sure as my name's Ben Weatherstaff. I wouldn't have believed tha' could do it."

"I never skipped before," Mary said. "I'm just beginning. I can only go up to twenty."

"Tha' keep on," said Ben. "Tha' shapes well enough at it for a young 'un that's lived with heathen. Just see how he's watchin' thee, jerking his head towards the robin. "He followed after thee yesterday. He'll be at it again today. He'll be bound to find out what th' skippin'-rope is. He's never seen one. Ehr shaking his head at the bird, "tha' curiosity will be th' death of thee some time if tha' doesn't look sharp."

Mary skipped round all the gardens and round the orchard, resting every few minutes. At length she went to her own special walk and made up her mind to try if she could skip the whole length of it. It was a good long skip, and she began slowly, but before she had gone half-way down the path she was so hot and breathless that she was obliged to stop. She did not mind much, because she had already counted up to thirty. She stopped with a little laugh of pleasure, and there, lo and behold, was the robin swaying on a long branch of ivy. He had followed her, and he greeted her with a chirp. As Mary had skipped towards him she felt something heavy in her pocket strike against her at each jump, and when she saw the robin she laughed again.

"You showed me where the key was yesterday," she said. "You ought to show me the door today; but I don't believe you know!"

The robin flew from his swinging spray of ivy on h the top of the wall and he opened his beak and sang a loud, lovely trill, merely to show off. Nothing in the world is quite as adorably lovely as a robin when he shows off–and they are nearly always doing it.

Mary Lennox had heard a great deal about Magic in her Ayah's stories, and she always said what happened almost at that moment was Magic.

One of the nice little gusts of wind rushed down the walk, and it was a stronger one than the rest. It was strong enough to wave the branches of the trees, and it was more than strong enough to sway the trailing sprays of untrimmed ivy hanging from the wall. Mary had stepped close to the robin, and suddenly the gust of wind swung aside some loose ivy trails, and more suddenly still she jumped towards it and caught it in her hand. This she did because she had seen something under it–a round knob which had been covered by the leaves hanging over it. It was the knob of a door.

She put her hands under the leaves and began to pull and push them aside. Thick as the ivy hung, it nearly all was a loose and swinging curtain, though some had crept over wood and iron Mary's heart began to thump and her hands to shake a little in her delight and excitement. The robin kept singing and twittering away and tilting his head on one side, as if he were as excited as she was. What was this under her hands which was square and made of iron and which her fingers found a hole in?

It was the lock of the door which had been closed ten years, and she put her hand in her pocket, drew out the key, and found it fitted the keyhole. She put the key in and turned it. It took two hands to do it, but it did turn.

And then she took a long breath and looked behind her up the long walk to see if anyone was coming. No one was coming. No one ever did come, it seemed, and she took another long breath, because she could not help it, and she held back the swinging curtain of ivy and pushed back the door which opened slowly–slowly.

Then she slipped through it, and shut it behind her, and stood with her back against it, looking about her and breathing quite fast with excitement, and wonder, and delight.

She was standing *inside* the secret garden.

CHAPTER 9

THE STRANGEST HOUSE ANYONE EVER LIVED IN

It was the sweetest, most mysterious-looking place anyone could imagine. The high walls which shut it in were covered with the leafless stems of climbing roses, which were so thick that they were matted together. Mary Lennox knew they were roses because she had seen a great many roses in India. All the ground was covered with grass of a wintry brown, and out of it grew clumps of bushes which were surely rose-bushes if they were alive. There were numbers of standard roses which had so spread their branches that they were like little trees. There were other trees in the garden, and one of the things which made the place look strangest and loveliest was that climbing roses had run all over them and swung down long tendrils which made light swaying curtains, and here and there they had caught at each other or at a far-reaching branch and had crept from one tree to another and made lovely bridges of themselves. There were neither leaves nor roses on them now, and Mary did not know whether they were dead or alive, but their thin grey or brown branches and sprays looked like a sort of hazy mantle spreading over everything, walls, and trees, and even brown grass, where they had fallen from their fastenings and run along the ground. It was this hazy tangle from tree to tree which made it look so mysterious. Mary had thought it must be different from other gardens which had not been left all by themselves so long; and, indeed, it was different from any other place she had ever seen in her life.

"How still it is!" she whispered. "How still!"

Then she waited a moment and listened at the stillness. The robin, who had own to his tree-top, was still as all the rest. He did not even flutter his wings; he sat without stirring, and looked at Mary.

"No wonder it is still," she whispered again. "I am the first person who has spoken in here for ten years."

She moved away from the door, stepping as softly as if she were afraid of awakening someone. She was glad that there was grass under her feet and that her steps made no sounds. She walked under one of the fairy-like arches between the trees and looked up at the sprays and tendrils which formed them.

"I wonder if they are all quite dead, she said. Is it all a quite dead garden? I wish it wasn't."

If she had been Ben Weatherstaff she could have told whether the wood was alive by looking at it, but she could only see that there were only grey or brown sprays and branches, and none showed any signs of even a tiny leaf-bud anywhere.

But she was *inside* the wonderful garden, and she could come through the door under the ivy any time, and she felt as if she had found a world all her own.

The sun was shining inside the four walls and the high arch of blue sky over this particular piece of Misselthwaite seemed even more brilliant and soft than it was over the moor. The robin flew down from his tree-top and hopped about or flew after her from one bush to another. He chirped a good deal and had a very busy air, as if he were showing her things. Everything was strange and silent, and she seemed to be hundreds of miles away from anyone, but somehow she did not feel lonely at all. All that troubled her was her wish that she knew whether all the roses were dead, or if perhaps some of them had lived and might put out leaves and buds as the weather got warmer. She did not want it to be a quite dead garden. If it were a quite alive garden, how wonderful it would be, and what thousands of roses would grow on every side!

Her skipping-rope had hung over her arm when she came

in, and after she had walked about for a while she thought she would skip round the whole garden, stopping when she wanted to look at things. There seemed to have been grass paths here and there, and in one or two corners there were alcoves of evergreen with stone seats or all moss-covered flower-urns in them.

As she came near the second of these alcoves she stopped skipping. There had once been a flower-bed in it, and she thought she saw something sticking out of the black earth–some sharp little pale green points. She remembered what Ben Weatherstaff had said, and she knelt down to look at them.

"Yes, they are tiny growing things and they *might* be crocuses or snowdrops or daffodils," she whispered.

She bent very close to them and sniffed the fresh scent of the damp earth. She liked it very much.

"Perhaps there are some other ones coming up in other places," she said. "I will go all over the garden and look."

She did not skip, but walked. She went slowly and kept her eyes on the ground. She looked in the old border-beds and among the grass, and after she had gone round, trying to miss nothing, she had found ever so many more sharp, pale green points, and she had become quite excited again.

"It isn't a quite dead garden," she cried out softly to herself. Even if the roses are dead, there are other things alive.

She did not know anything about gardening, but the grass seemed so thick in some of the places where the green points were pushing their way through that she thought they did not seem to have room enough to grow. She searched about until she found a rather sharp piece of wood and knelt down and dug and weeded out the weeds and grass until she made nice little clear places around them.

"Now they look as if they could breathe," she said, after she had finished with the first ones. "I am going to do ever so many more. I'll do all I can see. If I haven't time today I can come tomorrow.

She went from place to place, and dug and weeded, and enjoyed herself so immensely that she was led on from bed to bed and into the grass under the trees. The exercise made her so warm that she firs threw her coat off, and then her hat, and without knowing it she was smiling down on to the grass and the pale green points all the time.

The robin was tremendously busy. He was very much pleased to see gardening begun on his own estate. He had often wondered at Ben Weatherstaff. Where gardening is done all sorts of-delightful things to eat are turned up with the soil. Now here was this new kind of creature who was not half Ben's size and yet had the sense to come into his garden and begin at once.

Mistress Mary worked in her garden until it was time to go to her midday dinner. In fact she was rather late in remembering, and when she put on her coat and hat and picked up her skipping-rope, she could not believe that she had been working two or three hours. She had been actually happy all the time; and dozens and dozens of the tiny, pale green points were to be seen in cleared places, looking twice as cheerful as they had looked before when the grass and weeds had been smothering them.

I shall come back this afternoon, she said, looking all round at her new kingdom, and speaking to the trees and rose-bushes as if they heard her.

Then she ran lightly across the grass, pushed open the slow old door, and slipped through it under the ivy. She had such red cheeks and such bright eyes and ate such a dinner that Martha was delighted.

"Two pieces o' meat an' two helps o' rice-puddin'!" she said. "Eh! Mother will be pleased when I tell her what th' skippin'-rope's done for thee."

In the course of her digging with her pointed stick, Mistress Mary had found herself digging up a sort of white root rather like an onion. She had put it back in its place and patted the earth carefully down on it, and just now she wondered if Martha could tell her what it was.

"Martha," she said, "what are those white roots that look like onions?"

"They're bulbs," answered Martha. "Lots o' spring flowers grow from 'em. Th' very little ones are snowdrops an' crocuses an' th' big ones are narcissuses an' jonquils an' daffydowndillys. Th' biggest of all is lilies an' purple flags. Eh they are nice. Dickon's got a whole lot of 'em planted in our bit o' garden."

"Does Dickon know all about them?" asked Mary, a new idea taking possession of her.

"Our Dickon can make a flower grow out of a brick wall. Mother says he just whispers things out o' th' ground."

"Do bulbs live a long time, would they live years and years if no one helped them?" inquired Mary anxiously.

"They're things as helps themselves," said Martha. "That's why poor folk can afford to have 'em. If you don't trouble 'em, most of 'em'll work away underground for a lifetime an' spread out an' have little 'uns. There's a place in th' park woods here where there's snowdrops by thousands. They're the prettiest sight in Yorkshire when th' spring comes. No one knows when they was first planted."

"I wish the spring was here now," said Mary. I want to see all the things that grow in England."

She had finished her dinner and gone to her favourite seat on the hearth-rug.

"I wish–I wish I had a little spade," she said.

"Whatever does tha' want a spade for?" asked Martha laughing. "Art tha' goin' to take to diggin'? I must tell Mother that, too.

Mary looked at the fire and pondered a little. She must be careful if she meant to keep her secret kingdom. She wasn't doing any harm, but if Mr. Craven found out about the open door, he would be fearfully angry and get a new key and lock it up for ever more. She really could not bear that.

"This is such a big, lonely place," she said slowly, as if she were turning matters over in her mind. The house is lonely, and the park is lonely, and the gardens are lonely. So many places seem shut up. I never did many things in India, but there were more people to look at–natives and soldiers marching by–and sometimes bands playing, and my Ayah told me stories. There is no one to talk to here except you and Ben Weatherstaff. And you have to do your work and Ben Weatherstaff won't speak to me often. I thought if I had a little spade I could dig somewhere as he does, and I might make a little garden if he would give me some seeds.

Martha's face lighted up.

"There now!" she exclaimed, if that wasn't one of the things Mother said. She says: 'There's such a lot o' room in that big place, why don t they give her a bit for herself, even if she doesn't plant nothin' but parsley an' radishes? She'd dig an' rake away an' be right down happy over it.' Them was the very words she said."

"Were they?" said Mary. "How many things she knows, doesn't she?"

"Eh" said Martha. It's like she says: 'A woman as brings up twelve children learns something besides her A. B. C. Children's as good as 'rithmetic to set you findin' out things.'

"How much would a spade cost–a little one?" Mary asked.

"Well," was Martha's reflective answer, "at Thwaite village there's a shop or so an' I saw little garden sets with a spade an' a rake an' a fork all tied together for two shillings. An' they was stout enough to work with, too."

"I've got more than that in my purse," said Mary. "Mrs. Morrison gave me five shillings, and Mrs. Medlock gave me some money from Mr. Craven."

"Did he remember thee that much?" exclaimed Martha.

"Mrs. Medlock said I was to have a shilling a week to spend. She gives me one every Saturday. I didn't know what to spend it on."

"My word! that's riches," said Martha. "Tha' can buy anything in th' world tha' wants. The rent of our cottage is only one an' threepence, an' it's like pulling eye-teeth to get it. Now I've just thought of somethin'," putting her hands on her hips.

"What?" said Mary eagerly.

"In the shop at Thwaite they sell packages o' flower seeds for a penny each, and our Dickon, he knows which is th' prettiest ones an' how to make 'em grow. He walks over to Thwaite many a day just for th' fun of it. Does tha' know how to print letters?" suddenly.

"I know how to write," Mary answered.

Martha shook her head.

"Our Dickon can only read printin'. If tha' could print we could write a letter to him an' ask him to go an' buy th' garden tools an' th' seeds at th' same time."

"Oh! you're a good girl! Mary cried. You are, really. I didn't know you were so nice. I know I can print letters if I try. Let's ask Mrs. Medlock for a pen and ink and some paper."

"I've got some of my own," said Martha. "I bought 'em so I could print a bit a letter to Mother of a Sunday. I'll go and get it."

She ran out of the room, and Mary stood by the fire and twisted her thin little hands together with sheer pleasure.

"If I have a spade," she whispered, "I can make the earth nice and soft and dig up weeds. If I have seeds and can make flowers grow, the garden won't be dead at all–it will come alive."

She did not go out again that afternoon because when Martha returned with her pen and ink and paper she was obliged to clear the table and carry the plates and dishes downstairs, and when she got into the kitchen Mrs. Medlock was there, and told her to do something, so Mary waited for what seemed to her a long time before she came back. Then it was a serious piece of work to write to Dickon. Mary had been taught very little because her governesses had disliked her too much to stay with her. She could not spell particularly well, but she found that she could print letters when she tried. This was the letter Martha dictated to her:

My dear Dickon,

This comes hoping to find you well as it leaves me at present. Miss Mary has plenty of money and will you go to Thwaite and buy her some flower seeds and a set of garden tools to make a flower-bed. Pick the prettiest ones and easy to grow because she has never done it before and lived in India, which is different. Give my love to mother and every one of you. Miss Mary is going to tell me a lot more so that on my next day out you can hear about elephants and camels and gentlemen going hunting lions and tigers.

Your loving sister,
Martha Phoebe Sowerby

"We'll put the money in th' envelope an' I'll get th' butcher's boy to take it in his cart. He's a great friend o' Dickon's," said Martha.

"How shall I get the things when Dickon buys them?" asked Mary.

"He'll bring 'em to you himself. He'll like to walk over this way."

"Oh!" exclaimed Mary, "Then I shall see him! I never thought I should see Dickon."

"Does tha' want to see him?" asked Martha suddenly—she had looked so pleased.

"Yes, I do. I never saw a boy foxes and crows loved. I want to see him very much."

Martha gave a little start, as if she suddenly remembered something.

"Now to think," she broke out, "to think o' me forgettin' that there; an' I thought I was goin' to tell you first thing this mornin'. I asked Mother–and she said she'd ask Mrs. Medlock her own self."

"Do you mean–" Mary began.

"What I said Tuesday. Ask her if you might be driven over to our cottage some day and have a bit o' Mother's hot oat cake, an' butter, an' a glass o' milk."

It seemed as if all the interesting things were happening in one day. To think of going over the moor in the daylight and when the sky was blue! To think of going into the cottage which held twelve children!

"Does she think Mrs. Medlock would let me go?" she asked, quite anxiously.

"Aye, she thinks she would. She knows what a tidy woman Mother is and how clean she keeps the cottage."

"If I went I should see your mother as well as Dickon," said Mary, thinking it over and liking the idea very much. "She doesn't seem to be like the mothers in India."

Her work in the garden and the excitement of the afternoon ended by making her feel quiet and thoughtful. Martha stayed with her until tea-time, but they sat in comfortable quiet and talked very little. But just before Martha went downstairs for the tea-tray, Mary asked a question.

"Martha," she said, "has the scullery-maid had the toothache again today?"

Martha certainly started slightly.

"What makes thee ask that?" she said.

"Because when I waited so long for you to come back I opened the door and walked down the corridor to see if you were coming. And I heard that far-off crying again, just as we heard it the other night. There isn't a wind today, so you see it couldn't have been the wind."

"Eh!" said Martha restlessly. "Tha' mustn't go walkin' about in corridors an' listenin'. Mr. Craven would be that there angry there's no knowin' what he'd do."

"I wasn't listening," said Mary. "I was just waiting for you–and I heard it. That's three times."

"My word! There's Mrs. Medlock's bell," said Martha, and she almost ran out of the room.

"It's the strangest house anyone ever lived in," said Mary drowsily, as she dropped her head on the cushioned seat of the arm-chair near her. Fresh air, and digging, and skipping-rope had made her feel so comfortably tired that she fell asleep.

CHAPTER 10

DICKON

The sun shone down for nearly a week on the secret garden. The Secret Garden was what Mary called it when she was thinking of it. She liked the name, and she liked still more the feeling that when its beautiful old walls shut her in, no one knew where she was. It seemed almost like being shut out of the world in some fairy place. The few books she had read and liked had been fairy-story books, and she had read of secret gardens in some of the stories. Sometimes people went to sleep in them for a hundred years, which she had thought must be rather stupid. She had no intention of going to sleep, and, in fact, she was becoming wider awake every day which passed at Misselthwaite. She was beginning to like to be out of doors;

she no longer hated the wind, but enjoyed it. She could run faster, and longer, and she could skip up to a hundred. The bulbs in the secret garden must have been much astonished. Such nice clear spaces were made round them that they had all the breathing space they wanted, and really, if Mistress Mary had known it, they began to cheer up under the dark earth and work tremendously. The sun could get at them and warm them, and when the rain came down it could reach them at once, so they began to feel very much alive.

Mary was an odd, determined little person, and, now she had something interesting to be determined about, she was very much absorbed indeed. She worked and dug and pulled up weeds steadily, only becoming more pleased with her work every hour instead of tiring of it. It seemed to her like a fascinating sort of play. She found many more of the sprouting pale green points than she had ever hoped to find. They seemed to be starting up everywhere, and each day she was sure she found tiny new ones, some so tiny that they barely peeped above the earth. There were so many that she remembered what Martha had said about the "snowdrops by the thousands", and about bulbs spreading and making new ones. These had been left to themselves for ten years and perhaps they had spread, like the snowdrops, into thousands. She wondered how long it would be before they showed that they were flowers. Sometimes she stopped digging to look at the garden and try to imagine what it would be like when it was covered with thousands of lovely things in bloom.

During that week of sunshine, she became more intimate with Ben Weatherstaff. She surprised him several times by seeming to start up beside him as if she sprang out of the earth. The truth was that she was afraid that he would pick up his tools and go away if he saw her coming, so she always walked towards him as silently as possible. But, in fact, he did not object to her as strongly as he had at first. Perhaps he was secretly rather flattered by her evident desire for his elderly company. Then, also, she was more civil than she had been. He did not know that when she first saw him she spoke to him as she would have spoken to a native, and had not known that a cross, sturdy old Yorkshireman was not accustomed to salaam to his masters, and be merely commanded by them to do things.

"Tha'rt like th' robin," he said to her one morning when he lifted his head and saw her standing by him. "I never knows when I shall see thee or which side tha'll come from."

"He's friends with me now! " said Mary.

"That's like him," snapped Ben Weatherstaff. "Makin' up to th' women-folk just for vanity an' flightiness. There's nothin' he wouldn't do for th' sake o' showin' off an' flirtin' his tail-feathers. He's as full o' pride as an egg's full o' meat."

He very seldom talked much and sometimes did not even answer Mary's questions except by a grunt, but this morning he said more than usual. He stood up and rested one hobnailed boot on the top of his spade while he looked her over.

"How long has tha' been here," he jerked out.

"I think it's about a month," she answered.

"Tha's beginnin' to do Misselthwaite credit, he said. Tha' a bit fatter than tha' was an' tha's not quite so yeller. Tha' looked like a young plucked crow when tha' first came into this garden. Thinks I to myself I never set eyes on an uglier, sourer-faced young 'un."

Mary was not vain, and as she had never thought much of her looks, she was not greatly disturbed.

"I know I'm fatter," she said. "My stockings are getting tighter. They used to make wrinkles. There's the robin, Ben Weatherstaff."

There, indeed, was the robin, and she thought he looked nicer than ever. His red waistcoat was as glossy as satin and he flirted his wings and tail and tilted his head and hopped about with all sorts of lively graces. He seemed determined to make Ben Weatherstaff admire him. But Ben was sarcastic.

"Aye, there tha' art!" he said. "Tha' can put up with me for a bit sometimes when tha's got no one better. Tha's been reddenin' up thy waistcoat an' polishin' thy feathers this two weeks. I know what tha's up to. Tha's courtin' some bold young madam somewhere, tellin' thy lies to her about bein' th' finest cock robin on Missel Moor an' ready to fight all th' rest of 'em."

"Oh! look at him!" exclaimed Mary.

The robin was evidently in a fascinating, bold mood. He hopped closer and closer and looked at Ben Weatherstaff more and more engagingly. He flew on to the nearest currant-bush and tilted his head and sang a little song right at him.

"Tha' thinks tha'll get over me by doin' that," said Ben, wrinkling his face up in such a way that Mary felt sure he was trying not to look pleased. "Tha' thinks no one can stand out against thee-that's what tha' thinks."

The robin spread his wings–Mary could scarcely believe her eyes. He flew right up to the handle of Ben Weatherstaff's spade and alighted on the top of it. Then the old man's face wrinkled itself slowly into a new expression. He stood still as if he were afraid to breathe–as if he would not have stirred for the world, lest his robin should start away. He spoke quite in a whisper.

"Well, I'm danged!" he said as softly as if he were saying something quite different. "Tha' does know how to get at a chap–tha does! Tha's fair unearthly, tha's so knowin'."

And he stood without stirring–almost without drawing his breath–until the robin gave another flirt to his wings and flew away. Then he stood looking at the handle of the spade as if there might be Magic in it, and then he began to dig again and said nothing for several minutes.

But because he kept breaking into a slow grin now and then, Mary was not afraid to talk to him.

"Have you a garden of your own?" she asked.

"No. I'm a bachelor an' lodge with Martin at th' gate."

"If you had one," said Mary, "what would you plant?"

"Cabbages an' 'taters an' onions."

"But if you wanted to make a Flower-garden," persisted Mary, "what would you plant?"

"Bulbs an' sweet-smellin' things–but mostly roses."

Mary's face lighted up.

"Do you like roses?" she said.

Ben Weatherstaff rooted up a weed and threw it aside before he answered.

"Well, yes, I do. I was learned that by a young lady I was gardener to. She had a lot in a place she was fond of, an' she loved 'em like they was children–or robins. I've seen her bend over an' kiss 'em." He dragged out another weed and scowled at it. That were as much as ten year' ago."

"Where is she now?" asked Mary, much interested.

"Heaven," he answered, and drove his spade deeply into the soil, " 'cording to what parson says."

"What happened to the roses?" Mary asked again, more interested than ever.

"They was left to themselves."

Mary was becoming quite excited.

"Did they quite die? Do roses quite die when they are left to themselves?" she ventured.

"Well, I'd got to like 'em–an' I liked her–an' she liked 'em," Ben Weatherstaff admitted reluctantly. "Once or twice a year I'd go an' work at 'em a bit–prune 'em an' dig about th' roots. They run wild, but they was in rich soil, so some of 'em lived."

"When they have no leaves and look grey and brown and dry, how can you tell whether they are dead or alive?" inquired Mary.

"Wait till th' spring gets at 'em–wait till th' sun shines on th' rain an' th' rain falls on the sunshine an' then tha'll find out."

"How–how?" cried Mary, forgetting to be careful.

"Look along th' twigs an' branches an' if tha' sees a bit of a brown lump swelling here an' there, watch it after th' warm rain an' see what happens." He stopped suddenly and looked curiously at her eager face. "Why does tha' care so much about roses an' such, all of a sudden?" he demanded.

Mistress Mary felt her face grow red. She was almost afraid to answer.

"I–I want to play that–that I have a garden of my own," she stammered. "I–there is nothing for me to do. I have nothing–and no one."

"Well," said Ben Weatherstaff slowly, as he watched her, "that's true. Tha' hasn't."

He said it in such an odd way that Mary wondered if he was actually a little sorry for her. She had never felt sorry for herself; she had only felt tired and cross, because she disliked people and things so much. But now the world seemed to be changing and getting nicer. If no one found out about the secret garden, she should enjoy herself always.

She stayed with him for ten or fifteen minutes longer and asked him as many questions as she dared. He answered every one of them in his queer, grunting way, and he did not seem really cross and did not pick up his spade and leave her. He said something about roses just as she was going away, and it reminded her of the ones he had said he had been fond of.

"Do you go and see those other roses now?" she asked.

'Not been this year. My rheumatics has made me too stiff in th' joints."

He said it in his grumbling voice, and then quite suddenly he seemed to get angry with her, though she did not see why he should.

"Now look here!" he said sharply. "Don't tha' ask so many questions. Tha'rt th' worst wench for askin' questions I've ever come across. Get thee gone an' play thee. I've done talkin' for today."

And he said it so crossly that she knew there was not the least use in staying another minute. She went skipping slowly down the outside walk, thinking him over and saying to herself that, queer as it was, here was another person whom she liked, in spite of his crossness. She liked old Ben Weatherstaff. Yes, she did like him. She always wanted to try to make him talk to her. Also she began to believe that he knew everything in the world about flowers.

There was a laurel-hedged walk which curved round the secret garden and ended at a gate which opened into a wood in the park. She thought she would skip round this walk and look into the wood and see if there were any rabbits hopping about. She enjoyed the skipping very much, and when she reached the little gate she opened it and went through because she heard a low, peculiar whistling sound and wanted to find out what it was.

It was a very strange thing indeed. She quite caught her breath as she stopped to look at it. A boy was sitting under a tree, with his back against it, playing on a rough wooden pipe. He was a funny-looking boy about twelve. He looked very clean and his nose turned up and his cheeks were as red as poppies, and never had Mistress Mary seen such round and such blue eyes in any boy's face. And on the trunk of the tree he leaned against, a brown squirrel was clinging and watching him, and from behind a bush near by a cock pheasant was delicately stretching his neck to peep out, and quite near him were two rabbits sitting up and sniffing with tremulous noses–and actually it appeared as if they were all drawing near to watch him and listen to the strange, low, little call his pipe seemed to make.

When he saw Mary he held up his hand and spoke to her in a voice almost as low as and rather like his piping.

"Don't tha' move," he said. "It'd flight 'em."

Mary remained motionless. He stopped playing his pipe and began to rise from the ground. He moved so slowly that it scarcely seemed as though he were moving at all, but at last he stood on his feet and then the squirrel scampered back up into the branches of his tree, the pheasant withdrew his head, and the rabbits dropped on all fours and began to hop away, though not at all as if they were frightened.

"I'm Dickon," the boy said. "I know tha'rt Miss Mary."

Then Mary realized that somehow she had known at first that he was Dickon. Who else could have been charming rabbits and pheasants as the natives charm snakes in India? He had a wide, red, curving mouth and his smile spread all over his face.

"I got up slow," he explained, "because if tha' makes a quick move it startles 'em. A body 'as to move gentle an' speak low when wild things is about."

He did not speak to her as if they had never seen each other before, but as if he knew her quite well. Mary knew nothing about boys, and she spoke to him a little stiffly because she felt shy.

"Did you get Martha's letter?" she asked.

He nodded his curly, rust-coloured head.

"That's why I come."

He stooped to pick up something which had been lying on the ground beside him when he piped.

"I've got th' garden tools. There's a little spade an' rake an' a fork an' hoe. Eh! they are good 'uns. There's a trowel, too. An' th' woman in th' shop threw in a packet o' white poppy an' one o' blue larkspur when I bought th' other seeds."

"Will you show the seeds to me?" Mary said.

She wished she could talk as he did. His speech was so quick and easy. It sounded as if he liked her and was not the least afraid she would not like him, though he was only a common moor boy, in patched clothes and with a funny face and a rough, rusty-red head. As she came closer to him she noticed that there was a clean fresh scent of heather and grass and leaves about him, almost as if he were made of them. She liked it very much, and when she looked into his funny face with the red cheeks and round blue eyes she forgot that she had felt shy.

"Let us sit down on this log and look at them," she said.

They sat down and he took a clumsy little brown-paper package out of his coat pocket. He untied the string and inside there were ever so many neater and small packages, with a picture of a flower on each one.

"There's a lot o' mignonette an' poppies," he said. "Mignonette's th' sweetest smellin' thing as grows an' it'll grow wherever you cast it, same as poppies will. Them as'll come up an' bloom if you just whistle to 'em, them's th' nicest of all."

He stopped and turned his head quickly, his poppy-cheeked face lighting up.

"Where's that robin as is callin' us?" he said.

The chirp came from a thick holly bush, bright with scarlet berries, and Mary thought she knew whose it was.

"Is it really calling us?" she asked.

"Aye," said Dickon, as if it was the most natural thing in the world, "he's callin' someone he's friends with. That's same as sayin' 'Here I am. Look at me. I want a bit of a chat.' There he is in the bush. Whose is he?"

"He's Ben Weatherstaff's but I think he knows me a little," answered Mary.

"Aye, he knows thee," said Dickon in his low voice again. "An' he likes thee. He's took thee on. He'll tell me all about thee in a minute."

He moved quite close to the bush with the slow movement Mary had noticed before and then he made a sound almost like the robin's own twitter. The robin listened a few seconds, intently, and then answered quite as if he were replying to a question.

"Aye, he's a friend o' yours," chuckled Dickon.

"Do you think he is?" cried Mary eagerly. She did so want to know. "Do you think he really likes me?"

"He wouldn't come near thee if he didn't," answered

Dickon. "Birds is rare choosers an' a robin can flout a body worse than a man. See, he's making up to thee now. 'Cannot tha' see a chap?' he's sayin'."

And it really seemed as if it must be true. He so sidled and twittered and tilted as he hopped on his bush.

"Do you understand everything birds say?" said Mary.

Dickon's grin spread until he seemed all wide, red, curving mouth, and he rubbed his rough head.

"I think I do, and they think I do," he said. "I've lived on th' moor with 'em so long. I've watched 'em break shell and come out an' edge an' learn to fly an' begin to sing, till I think I'm one of 'em. Sometimes I think p'raps I'm a bird, or a fox, or a rabbit, or a squirrel, or even a beetle, an' I don't know it."

He laughed and came back to the log and began to talk about the flower seeds again. He told her what they looked like when they were flowers; he told her how to plant them, and watch them, and feed and water them.

"See here," he said suddenly, turning round to look at her. "I'll plant them for thee myself. Where is tha' garden?"

Mary's thin hands clutched each other as they lay on her lap. She did not know what to say, so for a whole minute she said nothing. She had never thought of this. She felt miserable. And she felt as if she went red and then pale.

"Tha's got a bit o' garden, hasn't tha?" Dickon said.

It was true that she had turned red and then pale. Dickon saw her do it, and as she still said nothing, he began to be puzzled.

"Wouldn't they give thee a bit?" he asked. "Hasn't tha' got any yet?"

She held her hands even tighter and turned her eyes towards him.

"I don't know anything about boys," she said slowly. "Could you keep a secret, if I told you one? It's a great secret, I don't know what I should do if anyone found it out. I believe I should die!" She said the last sentence quite fiercely.

Dickon looked more puzzled than ever and even rubbed his hand over his rough head again, but he answered good-humouredly.

"I'm keepin' secrets all th' time," he said. "If I couldn't keep secrets from th' other lads, secrets about foxes' cubs, an' birds' nests, n' wild things' holes, there'd be naught safe on th' moor. Aye, I can keep secrets."

Mistress Mary did not mean to put out her hand and clutch his sleeve, but she did it.

"I've stolen a garden," she said very fast. "It isn't mine. It isn't anybody's. Nobody wants it, nobody cares for it, nobody ever goes into it. Perhaps everything is dead in it already; I don't know."

She began to feel hot and as contrary as she had ever felt in her life.

"I don't care, I don't care! Nobody has any right to take it from me when I care about it and they don't. They're letting it die, all shut in by itself," she ended passionately, and she threw her arms over her face and burst out crying–poor little Mistress Mary.

Dickon's curious blue eyes grew rounder and rounder.

"Eh-h-h!" he said, drawing his exclamation out slowly, and the way he did it meant both wonder and sympathy.

"I've nothing to do," said Mary. "Nothing belongs to me. I found it myself and I got into it myself. I was only just like the robin, and they wouldn't take it from the robin."

"Where is it?" asked Dickon in a dropped voice.

Mistress Mary got up from the log at once. She knew she felt contrary again, and obstinate, and she did not care at all. She was imperious and Indian, and at the same time hot and sorrowful.

"Come with me and I'll show you," she said.

She led him round the laurel path and to the walk where the ivy grew so thickly. Dickon followed her with a queer, almost pitying, look on his face. He felt as if he were being led to look at some strange bird's nest and must move softly. When she stepped to the wall and lifted the hanging ivy he started. There was a door and Mary pushed it slowly open and they passed in together, and then Mary stood and waved her hand round defiantly.

"It's this," she said. "It's a secret garden, and I'm the only one in the world who wants it to be alive."

Dickon looked round and round about it, and round and round again.

"Eh!" he almost whispered, "it is a queer, pretty place. It's like as if a body was in a dream."

Chapter 11

THE NEST OF THE MISSEL THRUSH

For two or three minutes he stood looking round him, while Mary watched him, and then he began to walk about softly, even more lightly than Mary had walked the first time she had found herself inside the four walls. His eyes seemed to be taking in everything–the grey trees with the grey creepers climbing over them and hanging from their branches, the tangle on the wall and among the grass, the evergreen alcoves with the stone seats and tall lower urns standing in them.

"I never thought I'd see this place," he said at last in a whisper.

"Did you know about it?" asked Mary.

She had spoken aloud and he made a sign to her.

"We must talk low, he said, or someone'll hear us an' wonder what's to do in here."

"Oh! I forgot!" said Mary, feeling frightened and putting her hand quickly against her mouth. "Did you know about the garden?" she asked again when she had recovered herself.

Dickon nodded.

"Martha told me there was one as no one ever went inside, he answered. Us used to wonder what it was like."

He stopped and looked round at the lovely grey tangle about him, and his round eyes looked queerly happy.

"Eh! The nests as'll be here come springtime, he said. It'd be th' safest nestin' place in England. No one ever comin' near an' tangles o' trees an' roses to build in. I wonder all th' birds on th' moor don't build here."

Mistress Mary put her hand on his arm again without knowing it.

"Will there be roses? she whispered. "Can you tell? I thought perhaps they were all dead."

"Eh No! Not them–not all of 'em!" he answered. "Look here!"

He stepped over to the nearest tree–an old, old one with grey lichen all over its bark, but upholding a curtain of tangled sprays and branches. He took a thick knife out of his pocket and opened one of its blades.

"There's lots o' dead wood as ought to be cut out, he said. "An' there's a lot o' old wood, but it made some new last year. This here's a new bit," and he touched a shoot which looked brownish-green instead of hard, dry grey.

Mary touched it herself in an eager, reverent way.

"That one?" she said. "Is that one quite alive–quite?"

Dickon curved his wide, smiling mouth.

"It's a wick as you or me," he said; and Mary remembered that Martha had told her that "wick" meant "aliven or lively".

"I'm glad it's wick!" she cried out in her whisper. "I want them all to be wick. Let us go round the garden and count how many wick ones there are."

She quite panted with eagerness, and Dickon was as eager as she was. They went from tree to tree and from bush to bush. Dickon carried his knife in his hand and showed her things which she thought wonderful.

"They're run wild," he said, "but th' strongest ones has fair thrived on it. The delicatest ones had died out, but the others has growed an' growed, an' spread an' spread, till they's a wonder. See here!" and he pulled down a thick, grey, dry-looking branch. A body might think this was dead wood, but I don't believe it is–down to th' root. I'll cut it low down an' see."

He knelt and with his knife cut the lifeless-looking branch through, not far above the earth.

"There!" he said exultantly. "I told thee so. There's green in that wood yet. Look at it."

Mary was down on her knees before he spoke, gazing with all her might.

"When it looks a bit greenish an' juicy like that, it's wick," he explained. "When th' inside is dry an' breaks easy, like this here piece I've cut off, it's done for. There's a big root here as all this live wood sprung out of, an' if th' old wood's cut off an' it's dug round, an' took care of there'll be"–he stopped and lifted his face to look up at the climbing and hanging sprays about him–"there'll be a fountain o' roses here this summer."

They went from bush to bush and from tree to tree. He was very strong and clever with his knife and knew how to cut the dry and dead wood away, and could tell when an unpromising bough or twig still had green life in it. In the course of half an hour, Mary thought she could tell too, and when he cut through a lifeless-looking branch she would cry out joyfully under her breath when she caught sight of the least shade of moist green. The spade, and hoe, and fork were very useful. He showed her how to use the fork while he dug about the roots with the spade and stirred the earth and let the air in.

They were working industriously round one of the biggest standard roses when he caught sight of something which made him utter an exclamation of surprise.

"Why!" he cried, pointing to the grass a few feet away. "Who did that?"

It was one of Mary's own little clearings round the pale-green points.

"I did it," said Mary.

"Why, I thought tha' didn't know nothin' about gardenin'," he exclaimed.

"I don't, she answered, "but they were so little and the grass was so thick and strong, and they looked as if they had no room to breathe. So I made a place for them. I don't even know what they are."

Dickon went and knelt down by them, smiling his wide smile.

"Tha' was right," he said. "A gardener couldn't have told thee better. They'll grow now like Jack's bean-stalk. They're crocuses an' snowdrops, an' these here is narcissuses," turning to another patch, "an' here's daffydowndillys. Eh! They will be a sight."

He ran from one clearing to another.

"Tha' has done a lot o' work for such a little wench," he said, looking her over.

"I'm growing fatter," said Mary, "and I'm growing stronger. I used always to be tired. When I dig I'm not tired at all. I like to smell the earth when it's turned up."

"It's rare good for thee," he said, nodding his head wisely.

"There's naught as nice as th' smell o' good clean earth, except th' smell o' fresh growin' things when th' rain falls on 'em. I get out on th' moor many a day when it's rainin' an' I lie under a bush an' listen to th' soft swish o' drops on th' heather an' I just sniff an' sniff. My nose end fair quivers like a rabbit's, Mother says."

"Do you never catch cold?" inquired Mary, gazing at him wonderingly. She had never seen such a funny boy, or such a nice one.

"Not me," he said, grinning. "I never ketched cold since I was born. I wasn't brought up nesh enough. I've chased about th' moor in all weathers, same as th' rabbits does. Mother says I've sniffed too much fresh air for twelve year' to ever get to sniffin' with cold. I'm as tough as a whitethorn knobstick."

He was working all the time he was talking and Mary was following him and helping him with her fork or the trowel.

"There's a lot of work to do here!" he said once, looking about quite exultantly.

"Will you come again and help me to do it?" Mary begged. "I'm sure I can help, too. I can dig and pull up weeds, and do whatever you tell me. Oh! Do come, Dickon! "

"I'll come every day if tha' wants me, rain or shine," he answered stoutly. "It's th' best fun I ever had in my life–shut in here an' wakenin' up a garden."

"If you will come," said Mary, "if you will help me to make it alive I'll–I don't know what I'll do," she ended helplessly. What could you do for a boy like that?

"I'll tell thee what tha'll do," said Dickon, with his happy grin. "Tha'll get fat an' tha'll get as hungry as a young fox an' tha'll learn how to talk to th' robin same as I do. Eh! We'll have a lot o' fun."

He began to walk about, looking up in the trees and at the walls and bushes with a thoughtful expression.

"I wouldn't want to make it look like a gardener's garden, all clipped an' spick an' span, would you?" he said. "It's nicer like this with things runnin' wild, an' swingin' an' catchin' hold of each other."

"Don't let us make it tidy," said Mary anxiously. "It wouldn't seem like a secret garden if it was tidy."

Dickon stood rubbing his rusty-red head with a rather puzzled look.

"It's a secret garden sure enough," he said, "but seems like someone besides th' robin must have been in it since it was shut up ten year' ago."

"But the door was locked and the key was buried," said Mary. "No one could get in."

"That's true," he answered. "It's a queer place. Seems to me as if there'd been a bit o' prunin' done here an' there, later than ten year' ago."

"But how could it have been done?" said Mary.

He was examining a branch of a rose and he shook his head.

"Aye! How could it!" he murmured. "With th' door locked an' th' key buried."

Mistress Mary always felt that however many years she lived she should never forget that first morning when her garden began to grow. Of course, it did seem to begin to grow for her that morning. When Dickon began to clear places to plant seeds, she remembered what Basil had sung at her when he wanted to tease her.

"Are there any flowers that look like bells?" she inquired.

"Lilies o' th' valley does," he answered, digging away with the trowel, "an' there's Canterbury bells, an' campanulas."

"Let us plant some," said Mary.

"There's lilies o' th' valley here already; I saw 'em. They'll have growed too close an' we'll have to separate 'em, but there's plenty. Th' other ones take two years to bloom from seed, but I can bring you some bits o' plants from our cottage garden. Why does tha' want 'em?"

Then Mary told him about Basil and his brothers and sisters in India and of how she had hated them, and of their calling her "Mistress Mary Quite Contrary."

"They used to dance round and sing at me. They sang:

Mistress Mary, quite contrary,
How does your garden grow?
With silver bells and cockle shells,
And marigolds all in a row.

I just remembered it and it made me wonder if there were really flowers like silver bells."

She frowned a little and gave her trowel a rather spiteful dig into the earth.

"I wasn't as contrary as they were."

But Dickon laughed.

"Eh!" he said, and as he crumpled the rich black soil she saw he was sniffing up the scent of it, "there doesn't seem to be no need for no one to be contrary when there's flowers an' such like, an' such lots o' friendly wild things runnin' about makin' homes for themselves, or buildin' nests an' singin' an' whistling, does there?"

Mary, kneeling by him holding the seeds, looked at him and stopped frowning.

"Dickon," she said. "You are as nice as Martha said you were. I like you, and you make the fifth person. I never thought I should like five people."

Dickon sat up on his heels as Martha did when she was polishing the grate. He did look funny and delightful, Mary thought, with his round blue eyes and red cheeks and happy-looking turned-up nose.

"Only five folks as tha' likes?" he said. "Who is th' other four?"

"Your mother and Martha," Mary checked them of on her fingers, "and the robin and Ben Weatherstaff."

Dickon laughed so that he was obliged to stifle the sound by putting his arm over his mouth.

" I know tha' thinks I'm a queer lad," he said, "but I think tha' art th' queerest little lass I ever saw."

Then Mary did a strange thing. She leaned forward and asked him a question she had never dreamed of asking anyone before. And she tried to ask it in Yorkshire because that was his language, and in India a native was always pleased if you knew his speech.

"Does tha' like me?" she said.

"Eh!" he answered heartily, "that I does. I likes thee wonderful, an' so does th' robin, I do believe!"

"That's two, then," said Mary. "That's two for me."

And then they began to work harder than ever and more joyful. Mary was startled and sorry when she heard the big clock in the courtyard strike the hour of her midday dinner.

"I shall have to go;" she said mournfully. "And you will have to go too, won't you?"

Dickon grinned.

"My dinner's easy to carry about with me," he said. "Mother always lets me put a bit o' somethin' in my pocket."

He picked up his coat from the grass and brought out of a pocket a lumpy little bundle tied up in a quite clean, coarse, blue and white handkerchief. It held two thick pieces of bread with a slice of something laid between them.

"It's oftenest naught but bread," he said, but I've got a fine slice o' fat bacon with it today.

Mary thought it looked a queer dinner, but he seemed ready to enjoy it.

"Run on an' get thy victuals, he said. "I'll be done with mine first. I'll get some more work done before I start back home.

He sat down with his back against a tree.

"I'll call th' robin up, he said, "and give him th' rind o' th' bacon to peck at. They likes a bit o' fat wonderful."

Mary could scarcely bear to leave him. Suddenly it seemed as if he might be a sort of wood fairy who might be gone when she came into the garden again. He seemed too good to be true. She went slowly half-way to the door in the wall and then she stopped and went back.

"Whatever happens, you–you never would tell?" she said.

His poppy-coloured cheeks were distended with his first big bite of bread and bacon, but he managed to smile encouragingly.

"If tha' was a missel thrush an' showed me where thy nest was, does tha' think I'd tell anyone? Not me," he said. Tha' art as safe as a missel thrush."

And she was quite sure she was.

Chapter 12

"MIGHT I HAVE A BIT OF EARTH"

Mary ran so fast that she was rather out of breath when she reached her room. Her hair was ruffled on her forehead and her cheeks were bright pink. Her dinner was waiting on the table, and Martha was waiting near it.

"Tha's a bit late," she said. "Where has tha' been?"

"I've seen Dickon!" said Mary. "I've seen Dickon!"

"I knew he'd come," said Martha exultantly. "How does tha' like him?"

"I think–I think he's beautiful!" said Mary in a determined voice.

Martha looked rather taken aback, but she looked pleased, too.

"Well," she said, he's th' best lad as ever was born, but we never thought he was handsome. His nose turns up too much."

"I like it to turn up," said Mary.

"An' his eyes is o round," said Martha, a trifle doubtful. Though they're a nice colour."

"I like them round," said Mary. "And they are exactly the colour of the sky over the moor."

Martha beamed with satisfaction.

"Mother says he made 'em that colour with always lookin' up at th' birds an' th' clouds. But he has got a big mouth, hasn't he, now?"

"I love his big mouth," said Mary obstinately. "I wish mine were just like it."

Martha chuckled delightedly.

"It'd look rare an' funny in thy bit of a face," she said. "But I knowed it would be that way when tha' saw him. How did tha' like th' seeds an' th' garden tools?"

"How did you know he brought them?" asked Mary.

"Eh! I never thought of his not bringin' 'em. He'd be sure to bring 'em if they was in Yorkshire. He's such a trusty lad."

Mary was afraid that she might begin to ask difficult questions, but she did not. She was very much interested in the seeds and gardening tools, and there was only one moment when Mary was frightened. This was when she began to ask where the flowers were to be planted.

"Who did tha' ask about it?" she inquired.

"I haven't asked anybody yet," said Mary, hesitatingly.

"Well, I wouldn't ask th' head gardener. He's too grand, Mr. Roach is."

"I've never seen him," said Mary. "I've only seen undergardeners and Ben Weatherstaff."

"If I was you, I'd ask Ben Weatherstaff," advised Martha. "He's not half as bad as he looks, for all he's so crabbed. Mr. Craven lets him do what he likes, because he was here when Mrs. Craven was alive, an' he used to make her laugh. She liked him. Perhaps he'd find you a corner somewhere out o' the way."

"If it was out of the way and no one wanted it, no one *could* mind my having it, could they?" Mary said anxiously.

"There wouldn't be no reason," answered Martha You wouldn't do no harm."

Mary ate her dinner as quickly as she could, and when she rose from the table she was going to run to her room to put on her hat again, but Martha stopped her.

"I've got somethin' to tell you," she said. I thought I'd let you eat your dinner first. Mr. Craven came back this mornin' and I think he wants to see you."

Mary turned quite pale.

"Oh! she said. Why? Why? He didn't want to see me when I came. I heard Pitcher say he didn't."

"Well," explained Martha. Mrs. Medlock says it's because o' Mother. She was walkin' to Thwaite village an' she met him. She'd never spoke to him before, but Mrs. Craven had been to our cottage two or three times. He'd forgot, but Mother hadn't, an' she made bold to stop him. I don't know what she said to him about you, but she said somethin' as put him in th' mind to see you before he goes away again, tomorrow."

"Oh!" cried Mary, "is he going away tomorrow? I'm so glad!"

"He's goin' for a long time. He mayn't come back till

autumn or winter. He's goin' to travel in foreign places. He's always doin' it."

"Oh! I'm so glad–so glad!" said Mary thankfully.

If he did not come back until winter, or even autumn, there would be time to watch the secret garden come alive. Even if he found out then and took it away from her, she would have had that much at least.

"When do you think he will want to see–"

She did not finish the sentence, because the door opened, and Mrs. Medlock walked in. She had on her best black dress and cap, and her collar was fastened with a large brooch with a picture of a man's face on it. It was a coloured photograph of Mr. Medlock, who had died years ago, and she always wore it when she was dressed up. She looked nervous and excited.

"Your hair's rough," she said quickly. Go and brush it. Martha, help her to slip on her best dress. Mr. Craven sent me to bring her to him in his study."

All the pink left Mary's cheeks. Her heart began to thump and she felt herself changing into a stiff, plain, silent child again. She did not even answer Mrs. Medlock, but turned and walked into her bedroom, followed by Martha. She said nothing while her dress was changed, and her hair brushed, and after she was quite tidy she followed Mrs. Medlock down the corridors, in silence. What was there for her to say? She was obliged to go and see Mr. Craven, and he would not like her, and she would not like him. She knew what he would think of her.

She was taken to a part of the house she had not been into before. At last Mrs. Medlock knocked at a door, and when someone said, "Come in," they entered the room together. A man was sitting in an arm-chair before the fire, and Mrs. Medlock spoke to him.

"This is Miss Mary, sir," she said.

"You can go and leave her here. I will ring for you when I want you to take her away," said Mr. Craven.

When she went out and closed the door, Mary could only stand waiting, a plain little thing, twisting her thin hands together. She could see that the man in the chair was not so much a hunchback as a man with high, rather crooked shoulders, and he had black hair streaked with white. He turned his head over his high shoulders and spoke to her.

"Come here!" he said.

Mary went to him.

He was not ugly. His face would have been handsome if it had not been so miserable. He looked as if the sight of her worried and fretted him and as if he did not know what in the world to do with her.

"Are you well?" he asked.

"Yes," answered Mary.

"Do they take good care of you?"

"Yes."

He rubbed his forehead fretfully as he looked her over.

"You are very thin," he said.

"I am getting fatter," Mary answered, in what she knew was her stiffest way.

What an unhappy face he had! His black eyes seemed as if they scarcely saw her, as if they were seeing something else, and he could hardly keep his thoughts upon her.

"I forgot you," he said. "How could I remember you? I intended to send you a governess or nurse or someone of that sort, but I forgot."

"Please," began Mary. "Please–" and then the lump in her throat choked her.

"What do you want to say?" he inquired.

"I am–I am too big for a nurse," said Mary. "And please–please don't make me have a governess yet."

He rubbed his forehead again and stared at her.

"That was what the Sowerby woman said," he muttered absent-mindedly.

Then Mary gathered a scrap of courage.

"Is she–is she Martha's mother?" she stammered.

"Yes, I think so," he replied.

"She knows about children," said Mary. "She has twelve. She knows."

He seemed to rouse himself.

"What do you want to do?"

"I want to play out of doors," Mary answered, hoping that her voice did not tremble. "I never liked it in India. It makes me hungry here, and I am getting fatter."

He was watching her.

"Mrs. Sowerby said it would do you good. Perhaps it will," he said. "She thought you had better get stronger before you had a governess."

"It makes me feel strong when I play and the wind comes over the moor," argued Mary.

"Where do you play?" he asked next.

"Everywhere," gasped Mary. "Martha's mother sent me a skipping-rope. I skip and run–and I look about to see if things are beginning to stick up out of the earth. I don't do any harm."

"Don't look so frightened," he said in a worried voice. "You could not do any harm, a child like you! You may do what you like."

Mary put her hand up to her throat because she was afraid he might see the excited lump which she felt jump into it. She came a step nearer to him.

"May I?" she said tremulously.

Her anxious little face seemed to worry him more than ever.

"Don't look so frightened," he exclaimed. "Of course you may. I am your guardian, though I am a poor one for any child. I cannot give you time or attention. I am too ill, and wretched and distracted; but I wish you to be happy and comfortable. I don't know anything about children, but Mrs. Medlock is to see that you have all you need. I sent for you today because Mrs. Sowerby said I ought to see you. Her daughter had talked about you. She thought you needed fresh air and freedom and running about."

"She knows all about children," Mary said again in spite of herself.

"She ought to," said Mr. Craven. "I thought her rather bold to stop me on the moor, but she said Mrs. Craven had been kind to her." It seemed hard for him to speak his dead wife's name. "She is a respectable woman. Now I have seen you I think she said sensible things. Play out of doors as much as you like. It's a big place, and you may go where you like and amuse yourself as you like. Is there anything you want?" As if a sudden thought had struck him. "Do you want toys, books, dolls?"

"Might I," quavered Mary, "might I have a bit of earth?"

In her eagerness she did not realize how queer the words would sound and that they were not the ones she had meant to say. Mr. Craven looked quite startled.

"Earth!" he repeated. "What do you mean?

"To plant seeds in–to see them come alive," Mary faltered.

He gazed at her a moment and then passed his hand quickly over his eyes.

"Do you–care about gardens so much?" he said slowly.

"I didn't know about them in India," said Mary. "I was always ill and tired, and it was so hot. I sometimes made little beds in the sand and stuck flowers in them. But here it is different."

Mr. Craven got up and began to walk slowly across the room.

"A bit of earth," he said to himself, and Mary thought that somehow she must have reminded him of something. When he stopped and spoke to her his dark eyes looked almost soft and kind.

"You can have as much earth as you want," he said. "You remind me of someone close who loved the earth and things that grow. When you see a bit of earth you want," with something like a smile, "take it, child, and make it come alive."

"May I take it from anywhere–if it's not wanted?"

"Anywhere," he answered. "There! You must go now, I am tired." He touched the bell to call Mrs. Medlock. "Good-bye. I shall be away all summer."

Mrs. Medlock came so quickly that Mary thought she must have been waiting in the corridor.

"Mrs. Medlock," Mr. Craven said to her, "now I have seen the child I understand what Mrs. Sowerby meant. She must be less delicate before she begins lessons. Give her simple, healthy food. Let her run wild in the garden. Don't look after her too much. She needs liberty and fresh air and romping about. Mrs. Sowerby is to come and see her now and then, and she may sometimes go to the cottage."

Mrs. Medlock looked pleased. She was relieved to hear that she need not "look after" Mary too much. She had felt her a tiresome charge, and had, indeed, seen as little of her as she dared. In addition to this, she was fond of Martha's mother.

"Thank you, sir," she said. "Susan Sowerby and me went to

school together, and she's as sensible and good-hearted a woman as you'd find in a day's walk. I never had any children myself and she's had twelve, and there never was healthier or better ones. Miss Mary can get no harm from them. I'd always take Susan Sowerby's advice about children myself. She's what you might call healthy-minded–if you understand me."

"I understand," Mr. Craven answered. "Take Miss Mary away now and send Pitcher to me."

When Mrs. Medlock left her at the end of her own corridor Mary flew back to her room. She found Martha waiting there. Martha had, in fact, hurried back after she had removed the dinner service.

"I can have my garden!" cried Mary. "I may have it where I like! I am not going to have a governess for a long time! Your mother is coming to see me and I may go to your cottage. He says a little girl like me could not do any harm and I may do what I like–anywhere!"

"Eh!" said Martha, delighted, "that was nice of him, wasn't it?"

"Martha," said Mary solemnly, "he is really a nice man, only his face is so miserable and his forehead is all drawn together."

She ran as quickly as she could to the garden. She had been away so much longer than she had thought she should, and she knew Dickon would have to set out early on his five-mile walk. When she slipped through the door under the ivy, she saw he was not working where she had left him. The gardening tools were laid together under a tree. She ran to them, looking all round he place, but there was no Dickon to be seen. He had gone away and the secret garden was empty–except for the robin, who had just flown across the wall and sat on a standard rose-bush watching her.

"He is gone," she said woefully. "Oh! Was he–was he–was he only a wood fairy?"

Something white fastened to the standard rose-bush caught her eye. It was a piece of paper–in fact, it was a piece of the letter she had printed for Martha to send to Dickon. It was fastened on the bush with a long thorn, and in a minute she knew Dickon had left it there. There were some roughly printed letters on it and a sort of picture. At first she could not tell what it was. Then she saw it was meant for a nest with a bird sitting on it. Underneath were the printed letters, and they said:

"I will cum bak."

Chapter 13

"I AM COLIN"

Mary took the picture back to the house when she went to her supper and she showed it to Martha.

"Eh!" said Martha with great pride. I never knew our Dickon was as clever as that. That there's a picture of a missel thrush on her nest, as large as life an' twice as natural.

Then Mary knew Dickon had meant the picture to be a message. He had meant that she might be sure he would keep her secret. Her garden was her nest and she was like a missel thrush. Oh, how she did like that queer, common boy!

She hoped he would come back the very next day, and she fell asleep looking forward to the morning.

But you never know what the weather will do in Yorkshire, particularly in the springtime. She was awakened in the night by the sound of rain beating with heavy drops against her window. It was pouring down in torrents and the wind was "wuthering" round the corners and in the chimneys of the huge old house. Mary sat up in bed and felt miserable and angry.

The rain is as contrary as I ever was, she said. It came because it knew I did not want it.

She threw herself back on her pillow and buried her face. She did not cry, but she lay and hated the sound of the heavily beating rain, she hated the wind and its "wuthering". She could not go to sleep again. The mournful sound kept her awake, because she felt mournful herself. If she had felt happy it would probably have lulled her to sleep. How it wuthered" and how the big raindrops poured down and beat against the pane!

"It sounds just like a person lost on the moor and wandering on and on crying," she said.

*

She had been lying awake, turning from side to side for about an hour, when suddenly something made her sit up in bed and turn her head towards the door listening. She listened and she listened.

"It isn't the wind now," she said in a loud whisper. "That isn't the wind. It is different. It is that crying I heard before."

The door of her room was ajar and the sound came down the corridor, a far-off faint sound of fretful crying. She listened for a few minutes and each minute she became more and more sure. She felt as if she must find out what it was. It seemed even stranger than the secret garden and the buried key. Perhaps the fact that she was in a rebellious mood made her bold. She put her foot out of bed and stood on the floor.

"I am going to find out what it is," she said. "Everybody is in bed and I don't care about Mrs. Medlock–I don't care! "

There was a candle by her bedside and she took it up and went softly out of the room. The corridor looked very long and dark, but she was too excited to mind that. She thought she remembered the corners she must turn to find the short corridor with the door covered with tapestry–the one Mrs. Medlock had come through the day she lost herself. The sound had come up that passage. So she went on with her dim light, almost feeling her way, her heart beating so loud that she fancied she could hear it. The far-off, faint crying went on and led her. Sometimes it stopped for a moment or so and then began again. Was this the right corner to turn? She stopped and thought. Yes, it was. Down this passage and then to the left, and then up two broad steps, and then to the right again. Yes, there was the tapestry door.

She pushed it open very gently and closed it behind her, and she stood in the corridor and could hear the crying quite plainly, though it was not loud. It was on the other side of the wall at her left and a few yards farther on there was a door. She could see a glimmer of light coming from beneath it. The Someone was crying in that room, and it was quite a young Someone.

So she walked to the door and pushed it open, and there she was standing in the room!

It was a big room with ancient, handsome, furniture in it. There was a low fire glowing faintly on the hearth and a night-light burning by the side of a carved, four-poster bed hung with brocade, and on the bed was lying a boy, crying pitifully.

Mary wondered if she was in a real place or if she had fallen asleep again and was dreaming without knowing it.

The boy had a sharp, delicate face, the colour of ivory, and he seemed to have eyes too big for it. He had also a lot of hair which tumbled over his forehead in heavy locks and made his thin face seem smaller. He looked like a boy who had been ill, but he was crying more as if he were tired and cross than as if he were in pain.

Mary stood near the door with her candle in her hand, holding her breath. Then she crept across the room, and as she drew nearer the light attracted the boy's attention and he turned his head on his pillow and stared at her, his grey eyes opening so wide that they seemed immense.

"Who are you?" he said at last in a half-frightened whisper. "Are you a ghost?"

"No, I am not," Mary answered, her own whisper sounding half-frightened. "Are you one?"

He stared and stared and stared. Mary could not help noticing what strange eyes he had. They were agate-grey and they looked too big for his face because they had black lashes all round them.

"No," he replied, after waiting a moment or so. "I am Colin."

"Who is Colin?" she faltered.

"I am Colin Craven. Who are you?"

"I am Mary Lennox. Mr. Craven is my uncle."

"He is my father," said the boy.

"Your father!" gasped Mary. "No one ever told me he had a boy! Why didn't they?"

"Come here," he said, still keeping his strange eyes fixed on her with an anxious expression.

She came close to the bed and he put out his hand and touched her.

"You are real, aren't you?" he said. I have such real dreams very often. You might be one of them."

Mary had slipped on a woollen wrapper before she left her room and she put a piece of it between his fingers.

"Rub that and see how thick and warm it is," she said. "I will pinch you a little if you like, to show you how real I am. For a minute I thought you might be a dream, too."

"Where did you come from?" he asked.

"From my own room. The wind wuthered so I couldn't go to sleep and I heard someone crying and wanted to find out who it was. What were you crying for?"

"Because I couldn't go to sleep either, and my head ached. Tell me your name again."

"Mary Lennox. Did no one ever tell you I had come to live here?"

He was still fingering the fold of her wrapper, but he began to look a little more as if he believed in her reality.

"No," he answered. "They daren't."

"Why? asked Mary.

"Because I should have been afraid you would see me. I won't let people see me and talk me over."

"Why?" Mary asked again, feeling more mystified every moment.

Because I am like this always, ill and having to lie down. My father won't let people talk me over, either. The servants are not allowed to speak about me. If I live I may be a hunchback, but I shan't live. My father hates to think I may be like him."

"Oh, what a queer house this is!" Mary said. "What a queer house Everything is a kind of secret. Rooms are locked up and gardens are locked up–and you! Have you been locked up?"

"No. I stay in this room because I don't want to be moved out of it. It tires me too much."

"Does your father come and see you?" Mary ventured.

"Sometimes Generally when I am asleep. He doesn't want to see me."

"Why?" Mary could not help asking again.

A sort of angry shadow passed over the boy's face.

"My mother died when I was born and it makes him wretched to look at me. He thinks I don't know, but I've heard people talking. He almost hates me."

"He hates the garden, because she died," said Mary, half speaking to herself.

"What garden?" the boy asked.

"Oh! Just–just a garden she used to like," Mary stammered. "Have you been here always?"

"Nearly always. Sometimes I have been taken to places at the seaside, but I won't stay because people stare at me. I used to wear an iron thing to keep my back straight, but a grand doctor came from London to see me and said it was stupid. He told them to take it off and keep me out in the fresh air. I hate fresh air and I don't want to go out. "

"I didn't when first I came here," said Mary. "Why do you keep looking at me like that?"

"Because of the dreams that are so real," he answered rather fretfully. Sometimes when I open my eyes I don't believe I'm awake."

"We're both awake," said Mary. She glanced round the room with its high ceiling and shadowy corners and dim firelight. "It looks quite like a dream, and it's the middle of the night, and everybody in the house is asleep–everybody but us. We are wide awake."

"I don't want it to be a dream," the boy said restlessly.

Mary thought of something all at once.

"If you don't like people to see you," she began, "do you want me to go away?"

He still held the fold of her wrapper and he gave it a little pull.

"No," he said. "I should be sure you were a dream if you went. If you are real, sit down on that big footstool and talk. I want to hear about you."

Mary put down her candle on the table near the bed and sat down on the cushioned stool. She did not want to go away at all. She wanted to stay in the mysterious, hidden-away room and talk to the mysterious boy.

"What do you want me to tell you?" she said.

He wanted to know how long she had been at

Misselthwaite; he wanted to know which corridor her room was on; he wanted to know what she had been doing; if she disliked the moor as he disliked it; where she had lived before she came to Yorkshire. She answered all these questions and many more, and he lay back on his pillow and listened. He made her tell him a great deal about India and about her voyage across the ocean. She found out that because he had been an invalid he had not learned things as other children had. One of his nurses had taught him to read when he was quite little and he was always reading and looking at pictures in splendid books.

Though his father rarely saw him when he was awake, he was given all sorts of wonderful things to amuse himself with. He never seemed to have been amused, however. He could have anything he asked for and was never made to do anything he did not like to do.

"Everyone is obliged to do what pleases me," he said indifferently. "It makes me ill to be angry. No one believes I shall live to grow up."

He said it as if he was so accustomed to the idea that it had ceased to matter to him at all. He seemed to like the sound of Mary's voice. As she went on talking he listened in a drowsy, interested way. Once or twice she wondered if he were not gradually falling into a doze. But at last he asked a question which opened up a new subject.

"How old are you?" he asked.

"I am ten," answered Mary, forgetting herself for the moment, and so are you."

"How do you know that?" he demanded in a surprised voice.

"Because when you were born the garden door was locked and the key was buried. And it has been locked for ten years."

Colin half sat up, turning towards her, leaning on his elbows.

"What garden door was locked? Who did it? Where was the key buried?" he exclaimed, as if he were suddenly very much interested.

"It–it was the garden Mr. Craven hates, said Mary nervously. "He locked the door. No one–no one knew where he buried the key."

"What sort of a garden is it?" Colin persisted eagerly.

"No one has been allowed to go into it for ten years," was Mary's careful answer.

But it was too late to be careful. He was too much like herself. He, too, had had nothing to think about, and the idea of a hidden garden attracted him as it had attracted her. He asked question after question. Where was it? Had she never looked for the door? Had she never asked the gardeners?"

"They won't talk about it," said Mary. "I think they have been told not to answer questions."

"I would make them," said Colin.

"Could you?" Mary faltered, beginning to feel frightened. If he could make people answer questions, who knew what might happen?

"Everyone is obliged to please me. I told you that, he said. If I were to live, this place would some time belong to me. They all know that. I would make them tell me."

Mary had not known that she herself had been spoiled, but she could see quite plainly that this mysterious boy had been. He thought that the whole world belonged to him. How peculiar he was and how coolly he spoke of not living.

"Do you think you won't live?" she asked, partly because she was curious and partly in hope of making him forget the garden.

"I don't suppose I shall," he answered as indifferently as he had spoken before. "Ever since I remember anything I have heard people say I shan't. At first they thought I was too little to understand, and now they think I don't hear. But I do. My doctor is my father's cousin. He is quite poor and if I die he will have all Misselthwaite when my father is dead. I should think he wouldn't want me to live."

"Do you want to live?" inquired Mary.

"No," he answered, in a cross; tired fashion. But I don't want to die. When I feel ill I lie here and think about it until I cry and cry."

"I have heard you crying three times," Mary said, "but I did not know who it was. Were you crying about that?" She did so want him to forget the garden.

"I dare say," he answered. "Let us talk about something else. Talk about that garden. Don't you want to see it?"

"Yes," answered Mary in quite a low voice.

"I do," he went on persistently. "I don't think I ever really wanted to see anything before, but I want to see that garden. I want the key dug up. I want the door unlocked. I would let them take me there in my chair. That would be getting fresh air. I am going to make them open the door."

He had become quite excited and his strange eyes began to shine like stars and looked more immense than ever.

"They have to please me," he said. "I will make them take me there and I will let you go, too."

Mary's hands clutched each other. Everything would be spoiled–everything. Dickon would never come back. She would never again feel like a missel thrush with a safe-hidden nest.

"Oh, don't–don't–don't–don't do that!" she cried out.

He stared as if he thought she had gone crazy!

"Why?" he exclaimed. "You said you wanted to see it."

"I do," she answered, almost with a sob in her throat, but if you make them open the door and take you in like that it will never be a secret again."

He leaned still farther forward.

"A secret," he said. "What do you mean? Tell me."

Mary's words almost tumbled over one another.

"You see–you see," she panted, if no one knows but ourselves–if there was a door, hidden somewhere under the ivy–if there was–and we could find it; and if we could slip through it together and shut it behind us, and no one knew anyone was inside and we called it our garden and pretended that–that we were missel thrushes and it was our nest, and if we played there almost every day and dug and planted seeds and made it all come alive–"

"Is it dead?" he interrupted her.

"It soon will be if no one cares for it," she went on. The bulbs will live but the roses–"

He stopped her again as excited as she was herself.

"What are bulbs?" he put in quickly.

"They are daffodils and lilies and snowdrops. They are working in the earth now–pushing up pale-green points because the spring is coming.

"Is the spring coming?" he said. What is it like? You don't see it in rooms if you are ill."

"It is the sun shining on the rain and the rain falling on the sunshine, and things pushing up and working under the earth," said Mary. "If the garden was a secret and we could get into it we could watch the things grow bigger every day, and see how many roses are alive. Don't you see? Oh, don't you see how much nicer it would be if it was a secret?"

He dropped back on his pillow and lay there with an odd expression on his face.

"I never had a secret," he said, "except that one about not living to grow up. They don't know I know that, so it is a sort of secret. But I like this kind better."

"If you won't make them take you to the garden," pleaded Mary, "perhaps—I feel almost sure I can find out how to get in some time. And then—if the doctor wants you to go out in your chair, and if you can always do what you want to do, perhaps–perhaps we might find some boy who would push you, and we could go alone and it would always be a secret garden."

"I should–like–that," he said very slowly, his eyes looking dreamy. "I should like that. I should not mind fresh air in a secret garden."

Mary began to recover her breath and feel safer, because the idea of keeping the secret seemed to please him. She felt almost sure that if she kept on talking and could make him see the garden in his mind as she had seen it, he would like it so much that he could not bear to think that everybody might tramp into it when they chose.

"I'll tell you what I *think* it would be like, if you could go into it," she said. "It has been shut up so long things have grown into a tangle perhaps."

He lay quite still and listened while she went on talking about the roses which *might* have clambered from tree to tree and hung down–about the many birds which *might* have built their nests there because it was so safe. And then she told him about the robin and Ben Weatherstaff, and there was so much to tell about the robin and it was so easy and safe to talk about it that she ceased to feel afraid. The robin pleased him so much that he smiled until he looked almost beautiful, and at first Mary had thought that he was even plainer than herself, with his big eyes and heavy locks of hair.

"I did not know birds could be like that," he said. "But if you stay in a room you never see things. What a lot of things you know. I feel as if you had been inside that garden."

She did not know what to say, so she did not say anything. He evidently did not expect an answer and the next moment he gave her a surprise.

"I am going to let you look at something," he said. "Do you see that rose-coloured silk curtain hanging on the wall over the mantel-piece?"

Mary had not noticed it before, but she looked up and saw it. It was a curtain of soft silk hanging over what seemed to be some picture.

"Yes," she answered.

"There is a cord hanging from it," said Colin. "Go and pull it."

Mary got up, much mystified, and found the cord. When she pulled it the silk curtain ran back on rings and when it ran back it uncovered a picture. It was the picture of a girl with a laughing face. She had bright hair tied up with a blue ribbon and her gay, lovely eyes were exactly like Colin's unhappy ones, agate-grey and looking twice as big as they really were, because of the black lashes all round them.

"She is my mother," said Colin complainingly. "I don't see why she died. Sometimes I hate her for doing it."

"How queer!" said Mary.

"If she had lived I believe I should not have been ill always," he grumbled, "I dare say I should have lived, too. And my father would not have hated to look at me. I dare say I should have had a strong back. Draw the curtain again."

Mary did as she was told and returned to her footstool.

'She is much prettier than you," she said, "but her eyes are just like yours—at least they are the same shape and colour. Why is the curtain drawn over her?"

He moved uncomfortably.

"I made them do it," he said. "Sometimes I don't like to see her looking at me. She smiles too much when I am ill and miserable. Besides, she is mine, and I don't want everyone to see her."

There were a few moments of silence and then Mary spoke.

'What would Mrs. Medlock do if she found out that I had been here?" she inquired.

"She would do as I told her to do," he answered. "and I should tell her that I wanted you to come here and talk to me every day. I am glad you came."

"So am I," said Mary. "I will come as often as I can, but"-she hesitated–"I shall have to look every day for the garden door."

"Yes, you must," said Colin, and you can tell me about it afterwards."

He lay thinking a few minutes, as he had done before, and then he spoke again.

"I think you shall be a secret, too," he said. "I will not tell them until they find out. I can always send the nurse out of the room and say that I want to be by myself. Do you know Martha?"

"Yes, I know her very well," said Mary. "She waits on me."

He nodded his head towards the outer corridor.

"She is the one who is asleep in the other room. The nurse went away yesterday to stay all night with her sister and she always makes Martha attend to me when she wants to go out. Martha shall tell you when to come here."

Then Mary understood Martha's troubled look when she had asked questions about the crying.

"Martha knew about you all the time?" she said.

"Yes; she often attends to me. The nurse likes to get away from me and then Martha comes."

"I have been here a long time," said Mary. "Shall I go away now? Your eyes look sleepy."

"I wish I could go to sleep before you leave me, he said rather shyly.

"Shut your eyes," said Mary, drawing her footstool closer, and I will do what my Ayah used to do in India. I will pat your hand and stroke it and sing something quite low."

"I should like that perhaps," he said drowsily.

Somehow she was sorry for him and did not want him to lie awake, so she leaned against the bed and began to stroke and pat his hand and sing a very low little chanting song in Hindustani.

"That is nice," he said more drowsily still, and she went on chanting and stroking, but when she looked at him again his black lashes were lying close against his cheeks, for his eyes were shut and he was fast asleep. She got up softly, took her candle, and crept away without making a sound.

Chapter 14

A YOUNG RAJAH

The moor was hidden in mist when the morning came, and the rain had not stopped pouring down. There could be no going out of doors. Martha was so busy that Mary had no opportunity of talking to her, but in the afternoon she asked her to come and sit with her in the nursery. She came, bringing the stocking she was always knitting when she was doing nothing else.

"What's the matter with thee?" she asked as soon as they sat down. "Tha' looks as if tha'd somethin' to say."

"I have. I have found out what the crying was," said Mary.

Martha let her knitting drop on her knee and gazed at her with startled eyes.

"Tha' hasn't!" she exclaimed. "Never!"

"I heard it in the night," Mary went on. "And I got up and went to see where it came from. It was Colin. I found him."

Martha's face became red with fright.

"Eh! Miss Mary!" she said, half crying. "Tha' shouldn't have done it–tha' shouldn't. Tha'll get me in trouble. I never told thee nothin' about im–but tha'll get me in trouble. I shall lose my place and what'll Mother do!"

"You won't lose your place, said Mary. He was glad I came. We talked and talked and he said he was glad I came."

"Was he?" cried Martha. "Art tha' sure? Tha' doesn't know what he's like when anything vexes him. He's a big lad to cry like a baby, but when he's in a passion he'll fair scream just to frighten us. He knows us daren't call our souls our own."

"He wasn't vexed," said Mary. "I asked him if I should go away and he made me stay. He asked me questions and I sat on a big footstool and talked to him about India and about the robin and gardens. He wouldn't let me go. He let me see his mother's picture. Before I left him I sang him to sleep.

Martha fairly gasped with amazement.

"I can scarcely believe thee!" she protested. "It's as if tha'd walked straight into a lion's den. If he'd been like he is most times he'd have throwed himself into one of his tantrums and roused th' house. He won't let strangers look at him."

"He let me look at him. I looked at him all the time and he looked at me. We stared!" said Mary.

"I don't know what to do!" cried agitated Martha. If Mrs. Medlock finds out, she'll think I broke orders and told thee and I shall be packed back to Mother.

"He is not going to tell Mrs. Medlock anything about it yet. It's to be a sort of secret just at first," said Mary firmly. "And he says everybody is obliged to do as he pleases."

"Aye, that's true enough–th' bad lad!" sighed Martha, wiping her forehead with her apron.

"He says Mrs. Medlock must. And he wants me to come and talk to him every day. And you are to tell me when he wants me."

"Me!" said Martha; "I shall lose my place–I shall for sure!"

"You can't if you are doing what he wants you to do and everybody is ordered to obey him," Mary argued.

"Does tha' mean to say, cried Martha with wide-open eyes, "that he was nice to thee?"

"I think he almost liked me," Mary answered.

"Then tha' must have bewitched him!" exclaimed Martha.

"Do you mean Magic?" inquired Mary. "I've heard about Magic in India, but I can't make it. I just went into his room and I was so surprised to see him I stood and stared. And then he turned round and stared at me. And he thought I was a ghost or a dream and I thought perhaps he was. And it was so queer being there alone together in the middle of the night and not knowing about each other. And we began to ask each other questions. And when I asked him if I must go away he said I must not."

"Th' world's comin' to an end!" gasped Martha.

"What is the matter with him?" asked Mary.

"Nobody knows for sure and certain," said Martha. Mr. Craven went off his head like when he was born. Th' doctors thought he'd have to be put in a 'sylum. It was because Mrs. Craven died like I told you. He wouldn't set eyes on th' baby. He just raved and said it'd be another hunchback like him and it'd better die."

"Is Colin a hunchback?" Mary asked. "He didn't look like one."

"He isn't yet," said Martha. "But he began all wrong. Mother said that there was enough trouble raging in th' house to set any child wrong. They was afraid his back was weak an' they've always been takin' care of it–keepin' him lyin' down and not lettin' him walk. Once they made him wear a brace, but he fretted so he was downright ill. Then a big doctor came to see him an' made them take it off. He talk'd to th' other doctor quite rough–in a polite way. He said there'd been too much medicine and too much lettin' him have his own way.

"I think he's a very spoiled boy," said Mary.

"He's th' worst young nowt as ever was!" said Martha. I won't say as he hasn't been ill a good bit. He's had coughs an' colds that's nearly killed him two or three times. Once he had rheumatic fever an' once he had typhoid. Eh! Mrs. Medlock did get a fright then. He'd been out of his head an' he was talkin' to th' nurse, thinkin' he didn't know nothin', an' she said: 'He'll die this time sure enough, an' best thing for him an' for everybody.' An' she looked at him, an' there he was with his big eyes open, starin' at her as sensible as she was herself. She didn't know what'd happen, but he just stared at her an' says: 'You give me some water an' stop talkin'.' "

"Do you think he will die?" asked Mary.

"Mother says there's no reason why any child should live that gets no fresh air an' doesn't do nothin' but lie on his back an' read picture-books an' take medicine. He's weak and hates th' trouble o' bein' taken out o' doors, an' he gets cold so easy he says it makes him ill."

Mary sat and looked at the fire.

"I wonder," she said slowly, if it would not do him good to go out into a garden and watch things growing. It did me good."

"One of th' worst fits he ever had," said Martha, "was one time they took him out where the roses is by the fountain. He'd been readin' in a paper about people gettin' somethin' he called 'rose cold', an' he began to sneeze an' said he'd got it, an' then a new gardener as didn't know th' rules passed by an' looked at him curious. He threw himself into a passion an' he said he'd looked at him because he was going to be a hunchback. He cried himself into a fever an' was ill all night."

"If he ever gets angry at me, I'll never go and see him again," said Mary.

"He'll have thee if he wants thee," said Martha. "Tha' may as well know that at th' start."

Very soon afterwards a bell rang, and she rolled up her knitting.

"I dare say th' nurse wants me to stay with him a bit," she said. "I hope he's in a good temper."

She was out of the room about ten minutes and then she came back with a puzzled expression.

"Well, tha' has bewitched him," she said. "He's up on his sofa with his picture-books. He's told the nurse to stay away until six o'clock. I'm to wait in the next room. Th' minute she was gone he called me to him an' says: 'I want Mary Lennox to come and talk to me, and remember you're not to tell anyone.' You'd better go as quick as you can."

Mary was quite willing to go quickly. She did not want to see Colin as much as she wanted to see Dickon, but she wanted to see him very much.

There was a bright fire on the hearth when she entered his room, and in the daylight she saw it was a very beautiful room indeed. There were rich colours in the rugs and hangings and pictures and books on the walls, which made it look glowing and comfortable even in spite of the grey sky and falling rain. Colin looked rather like a picture himself. He was wrapped in a velvet dressing-gown and sat against a big brocaded cushion. He had a red spot on each cheek.

"Come in," he said. "I've been thinking about you all the morning."

"I've been thinking about you, too," answered Mary. "You don't know how frightened Martha is. She says Mrs. Medlock will think she told me about you and then she will be sent away."

He frowned.

"Go and tell her to come here," he said. She is in the next room."

Mary went and brought her back. Poor Martha was shaking in her shoes. Colin was still frowning.

"Have you to do what I please or have you not?" he demanded.

"I have to do what you please, sir," Martha faltered, turning quite red.

"Has Medlock to do what I please?"

"Everybody has, sir," said Martha.

"Well, then, if I order you to bring Miss Mary to me, how can Medlock send you away if she finds it out?"

"Please don't let her, sir," pleaded Martha.

I'll send *her* away if she dares to say a word about such a thing," said Master Craven. "She wouldn't like that, I can tell you."

"Thank you, sir," bobbing a curtsy. "I want to do my duty, sir."

"What I want is your duty," said Colin, more grandly still. "I'll take care of you. Now go away."

When the door closed behind Martha, Colin found Mistress Mary gazing at him as if he had set her wondering.

"Why do you look at me like that?" he asked her. "What are you thinking about?"

"I am thinking about two things."

"What are they? Sit down and tell me."

"This is the first one," said Mary, seating herself on the big stool. "Once in India I saw a boy who was a rajah. He had rubies and emeralds and diamonds stuck all over him. He spoke to his people just as you spoke to Martha. Everybody had to do everything he told them–in a minute. I think they would have been killed if they hadn't."

"I shall make you tell me about rajahs presently," he said, abut first tell me what the second thing was."

"I was thinking," said Mary, "how different you are from Dickon.

"Who is Dickon?" he said. "What a queer name!"

She might as well tell him, she thought. She could talk about Dickon without mentioning the secret garden. She had liked to hear Martha talk about him. Besides, she longed to talk about him. It would seem to bring him nearer.

"He is Martha's brother. He is twelve years old," she explained. "He is not like anyone else in the world. He can charm foxes and squirrels and birds just as the natives in India charm snakes. He plays a very soft tune on a pipe and they come and listen."

There were some big books on a table at his side, and he dragged one suddenly towards him.

"There is a picture of a snake-charmer in this," he exclaimed. "Come and look at it."

The book was a beautiful one with superb coloured illustrations and he turned to one of them.

"Can he do that?" he asked eagerly.

"He played on his pipe and they listened," Mary explained. "But he doesn't call it Magic. He says it's because he lives on the moor so much and he knows their ways. He says he feels sometimes as if he was a bird or a rabbit himself, he likes them so. I think he asked the robin questions. It seemed as if they talked to each other in soft chirps."

Colin lay back on his cushion and his eyes grew larger and larger and the spots on his cheeks burned.

"Tell me some more about him," he said.

"He knows all about eggs and nests," Mary went on. "And he knows where foxes and badgers and otters live. He keeps them secret so that other boys won't find their holes and frighten them. He knows about everything that grows or lives on the moor."

"Does he like the moor?" said Colin. "How can he when it's such a great, bare, dreary place?"

"It's the most beautiful place," protested Mary. "Thousands of lovely things grow on it, and there are thousands of little creatures all busy building nests and making holes and burrows and chippering or singing or squeaking to each other. They are so busy and having such fun under the earth or in the trees or heather. It's their world."

"How do you know all that?" said Colin, turning on his elbow to look at her.

"I have never been there once, really," said Mary, suddenly remembering. "I only drove over it in the dark. I thought it was hideous. Martha told me about it first, and then Dickon. When Dickon talks about it you feel as if you saw things and heard them, and as if you were standing in the heather with the sun shining and the gorse smelling like honey–and all full of bees and butterflies."

"You never see anything if you are ill," said Colin restlessly. He looked like a person listening to a new sound in the distance and wondering what it was.

"You can't if you stay in a room," said Mary.

"I couldn't go on the moor," he said in a resentful tone.

Mary was silent for a minute, and then she said something bold.

"You might–some time."

He moved as if he were startled.

"Go on the moor! How could I? I am going to die."

"How do you know?" said Mary unsympathetically. She didn't like the way he had of talking about dying. She did not feel very sympathetic. She felt rather as if he almost boasted about it.

"Oh, I've heard it ever since I remember," he answered crossly. They are always whispering about it and thinking I don't notice. They wish I would, too."

Mistress Mary felt quite contrary. She pinched her lips together.

"If they wished I would," she said, "I wouldn't. Who wishes you would?"

"The servants–and, of course, Dr. Craven, because he would get Misselthwaite and be rich instead of poor. He daren't say so, but he always looks cheerful when I am worse. When I had typhoid fever his face got quite fat. I think my father wishes it, too."

"I don't believe he does," said Mary quite obstinately.

That made Colin turn and look at her again.

"Don't you?" he said.

And then he lay back on his cushion and was still, as if he were thinking. And there was quite a long silence. Perhaps they were both of them thinking strange things children do not usually think of.

"I like the grand doctor from London, because he made them take the iron thing off," said Mary at last. "Did he say you were going to die?"

"No".

"What did he say?"

"He didn't whisper," Colin answered. "Perhaps he knew I hated whispering. I heard him say one thing quite aloud. He said: 'The lad might live if he would make up his mind to it. Put him in the humour.' It sounded as if he was in a temper."

"I'll tell you who would put you in the humour, perhaps," said Mary, reflecting. She felt as if she would like this thing to be settled one way or the other. "I believe Dickon would. He's always talking about live things. He never talks about dead things or things that are ill. He's always looking up in the sky to watch birds flying–or looking down at the earth to see something growing. He has such round blue eyes and they are so wide open with looking about. And he laughs such a big laugh with his wide mouth–and his cheeks are as red–as red as cherries."

She pulled her stool nearer to the sofa and her expression quite changed at the remembrance of the wide, curving mouth and wide open eyes.

"See here," she said. "Don't let us talk about dying; I don't like it. Let us talk about living. Let us talk and talk about Dickon. And then we will look at your pictures."

It was the best thing she could have said. To talk about Dickon meant to talk about the moor and about the cottage and the fourteen people who lived in it on sixteen shillings a week–and the children who got fat on the moor grass like the wild ponies. And about Dickon's mother–and the skipping-rope–and the moor with the sun on it-and about pale green points sticking up out of the black sod. And it was all so alive that Mary talked more than she had ever talked before–and Colin both talked and listened as he had ever done either before. And they both began to laugh over nothing as children will when they are happy together. And they laughed so that in the end they were making as much noise as if they had been two ordinary, healthy, natural, ten-year-old creatures–instead of a hard, little, unloving girl and a sickly boy who believed that he was going to die.

They enjoyed themselves so much that they forgot the pictures and totally forgot about the time. They had been laughing quite loudly over Ben Weatherstaff and his robin, and

Colin was actually sitting up as if he had forgotten about his weak back when he suddenly remembered something.

"Do you know there is one thing we have never once thought of?" he said. "We are cousins."

It seemed so queer that they had talked so much and never remembered this simple thing that they laughed more than ever, because they had got into the humour to laugh at anything. And in the midst of the fun the door opened and in walked Dr. Craven and Mrs. Medlock.

Dr. Craven started in actual alarm and Mrs. Medlock almost fell back because he had accidentally bumped against her.

"Good Lord!" exclaimed poor Mrs. Medlock, with her eyes almost starting out of her head. "Good Lord!"

"What is this?" said Dr. Craven, coming forward. "What does it mean?"

Then Mary was reminded of the boy rajah again. Colin answered as if neither the doctor's alarm nor Mrs. Medlock's terror were of the slightest consequence. He was as little disturbed or frightened as if an elderly cat and dog had walked into the room.

"This is my cousin, Mary Lennox," he said. "I asked her to come and talk to me. I like her. She must come and talk to me whenever I send for her."

Dr. Craven turned reproachfully to Mrs. Medlock.

"Oh, sir," she panted. "I don't know how it's happened. There's not a servant on the place that'd dare to talk–they all have their orders."

"Nobody told her anything," said Colin. She heard me crying and found me herself. I am glad she came. Don't be silly, Medlock."

Mary saw that Dr. Craven did not look pleased, but it was quite plain that he dare not oppose his patient. He sat down by Colin and felt his pulse.

"I am afraid there has been too much excitement. Excitement is not good for you, my boy," he said.

"I should be excited if she kept away," answered Colin, his eyes beginning to look dangerously sparkling. "I am better. She makes me better. The nurse must bring up her tea with mine. We will have tea together."

Mrs. Medlock and Dr. Craven looked at each other in a troubled way, but there was evidently nothing to be done.

"He does look rather better sir," ventured Mrs. Medlock. "But"–thinking the matter over–"he looked better this morning before she came into the room."

"She came into the room last night. She stayed with me a long time. She sang a Hindustani song to me and it made me go to sleep," said Colin. "I was better when I wakened up. I wanted my breakfast. I want my tea now. Tell nurse, Medlock."

Dr. Craven did not stay very long. He talked to the nurse for a few minutes when she came into the room and said a few words of warning to Colin. He must not talk too much; he must not forget that he was ill; he must not forget that he was very easily tired. Mary thought that there seemed to be a number of uncomfortable things he was not to forget.

Colin looked fretful and kept his strange, black-lashed eyes fixed on Dr. Craven's face.

"I *want* to forget it," he said at last. "She makes me forget it. That is why I want her."

Dr. Craven did not look happy when he left the room. He gave a puzzled glance at the little girl sitting on the large stool. She had become a stiff, silent child again as soon as he entered, and he could not see what the attraction was. The boy actually did look brighter, however–and he sighed rather heavily as he went down the corridor.

"They are always wanting me to eat things when I don't want to," said Colin, as the nurse brought in the tea and put it on the table by the sofa. "Now, if you'll eat I will. Those muffins look so nice and hot. Tell me about rajahs."

CHAPTER 15

NEST BUILDING

After another week of rain, the high arch of blue sky appeared again and the sun which poured down was quite hot. Though there had been no chance to see either the secret garden or Dickon, Mistress Mary had enjoyed herself very much. The week had not seemed long. She had spent hours of every day with Colin in his room, talking about rajahs or gardens or Dickon and the cottage on the moor. They had looked at the splendid books and pictures, and sometimes Mary had read things to Colin, and sometimes he had read a little to her. When he was amused and interested she thought he scarcely looked like an invalid at all, except that his face was so colourless and he was always on the sofa.

"You are a sly young one to listen and get out of your bed to go following things up like you did that night," Mrs. Medlock said once. But there's no saying it's not been a sort of blessing to the lot of us. He's not had a tantrum or a whining fit since you made friends. The nurse was just going to give up the case because she was so sick of him, but she says she doesn't mind staying now you've gone on duty with her," laughing a little.

In her talks with Colin, Mary had tried to be very cautious about the secret garden. here were certain things she wanted to find out from him, but she felt that she might find them out without asking him direct questions. In the first place, as she began to like to be with him, she wanted to discover whether he was the kind of boy you could tell a secret to. He was not in the least like Dickon, but he was evidently so pleased with the idea of a garden no one knew anything about that she thought perhaps he could be trusted. But she had not known him long enough to be sure. The second thing she wanted to find out was this: If he could be trusted–if he really could-wouldn't it be possible to take him to the garden without having anyone find it out? The grand doctor had said that he must have fresh air, and Colin had said that he would not mind fresh air in a secret garden. Perhaps if he had a great deal of fresh air and knew Dickon and the robin and saw things growing, he might not think so much about dying. Mary had seen herself in the glass sometimes lately when she had realized that she looked quite a different creature from the child she had seen when she arrived from India. This child looked nicer. Even Martha had seen a change in her.

"Th' air from th' moor has done thee good already, she had said. "Tha'rt not nigh so yeller and tha'rt not nigh so scrawny. Even tha' hair doesn't slamp down on tha' head so flat. It's got some life in it so as it sticks out a bit."

"It's like me," said Mary. "It's growing stronger and fatter. I'm sure there's more of it."

"It looks it, for sure," said Martha, ruffling it up a little round her face. "Tha'rt not half so ugly when it's that way an' there's a bit o' red in tha' cheeks."

If gardens and fresh air had been good for her, perhaps they would be good for Colin. But then, if he hated people to look at him, perhaps he would not like to see Dickon.

"Why does it make you angry when you are looked at?" she inquired one day.

"I always hated it," he answered, "even when I was very little. Then when they took me to the seaside and I used to lie in my carriage, everybody used to stare and ladies would stop and talk to my nurse and then they would begin to whisper, and I knew when they were saying I shouldn't live to grow up. Then sometimes the ladies would pat my cheeks and say 'Poor child!' Once when a lady did that I screamed out loud and bit her hand. She was so frightened she ran away."

"She thought you had gone mad like a dog," said Mary, not at all admiringly.

"I don't care what she thought," said Colin, frowning.

"I wonder why you didn't scream and bite me when I came into your room?" said Mary. Then she began to smile slowly.

"I thought you were a ghost or a dream," he said. "You can't bite a ghost or a dream, and if you scream they don't care."

"Would you hate it if–if a boy looked at you?" Mary asked uncertainly.

He lay back on his cushion and paused thoughtfully.

"There's one boy," he said quite slowly, as if he were thinking over every word, "there's one boy I believe I shouldn't mind. It's that boy who knows where the foxes live–Dickon."

"I'm sure you wouldn't mind him," said Mary.

"The birds don't and other animals, he said, still thinking it over, "perhaps that's why I shouldn't. He's a sort of animal-charmer and I am a boy animal."

Then he laughed and she laughed, too; in fact, it ended in their both laughing a great deal and finding the idea of a boy animal hiding in his hole very funny indeed.

What Mary felt afterwards was that she need not fear about Dickon.

*

On that first morning when the sky was blue again, Mary wakened very early. The sun was pouring in slanting rays through the blinds and there was something 80 joyous in the sight of it that she jumped out of bed and ran to the window. She drew up the blinds and opened the window itself, and a great waft of fresh, scented air blew in upon her. The moor was blue and the whole world looked as if something Magic had happened to it. There were tender little fluting sounds here and there and everywhere, as if scores of birds were beginning to tune up for a concert. Mary put her hand out of the window and held it in the sun.

"It's warm–warm!" she said. "It will make the green points push up and up and up, and it will make the bulbs and roots work and struggle with all their might under the earth."

She kneeled down and leaned out of the window as far as she could, breathing big breaths and sniffing the air until she laughed because she remembered what Dickon's mother had said about the end of his nose quivering like a rabbit's.

"It must be very early," she said. "The little clouds are all pink and I've never seen the sky look like this. No one is up. I don't even hear the stable-boys."

A sudden thought made her scramble to her feet.

"I can't wait! I am going to see the garden!"

She had learnt to dress herself by this time, and she put on her clothes in five minutes. She knew a small side door which she could unbolt herself, and she flew downstairs in her stocking feet and put on her shoes in the hall. She unchained and unbolted and unlocked, and when the door was open she sprang across the step with one bound, and there she was standing on the grass, which seemed to have turned green, and with the sun pouring down on her and warm, sweet wafts about her and the fluting and twittering and singing coming from every bush and tree. She clasped her hands for pure joy and looked up in the sky, and it was so blue and pink and pearly and white and flooded with springtime light that she felt as if she must flute and sing aloud herself, and knew that thrushes and robins and skylarks could not possibly help it. She ran around the shrubs and paths towards the secret garden.

"It is all different already," she said. "The grass is greener and things are sticking up everywhere and things are uncurling and green buds of leaves are showing. This afternoon I am sure Dickon will come."

The long warm rain had done strange things to the herbaceous beds which bordered the walk by the lower wall. There were things sproutin and pushing out from the roots of clumps of plants and there were actually here and there glimpses of royal purple and yellow unfurling among the stems of crocuses. Six months before Mistress Mary would not have seen how the world was waking up, but now she missed nothing.

When she had reached the place where the door hid itself under the ivy, she was startled by a curious loud sound. It was the caw-caw of a crow, and it came from the top of the wall, and when she looked up, there sat a big, glossy-plumaged, blue-black bird, looking down at her very wisely indeed. She had never seen a crow so close before, and he made her a little nervous, but the next moment he spread his wings and flapped away across the garden. She hoped he was not going to stay inside, and she pulled the door open wondering if he would. When she got fairly into the garden she saw that he probably did intend to stay, because he had alighted on a dwarf apple-tree, and under the apple-tree was lying a little reddish animal with a bushy tail, and both of them were watching the stooping body and rust-red head of Dickon, who was kneeling on the grass working hard.

Mary flew across the grass to him.

"Oh, Dickon! Dickon! " she cried out. "How could you get here so early! How could you! The sun has only just got up!"

He got up himself, laughing and glowing, and tousled; his eyes like a bit of the sky.

"Eh!" he said. "I was up long before him. How could I have stayed abed! Th' world's-all fair begun again this morning', it has. An' it's workin' an' hummin' an' scratchin' an' pipin' an' nest-buildin' an' breathin' out scents, till you've got to be out on it 'stead o' lyin' on your back. When th' sun did jump up, th' moor went mad for joy, an' I was in the midst of th' heather, an' I run like mad myself, shoutin' an' singin'. An' I come straight here. I couldn't have stayed away. Why, th' garden was lyin' here waitin'!"

Mary put her hands on her chest, panting, as if she had been running herself.

"Oh, Dickon! Dickon!" she said. "I'm so happy I can scarcely breathe."

Seeing him talking to a stranger, the little bushy-tailed animal rose from its place under the tree and came to him, and the rook, cawing one, flew down from its branch and settled quietly on his shoulder.

"This is th' little fox cub," he said, rubbing the little reddish animal's head. "It's named Captain. An' this here's Soot. Soot, he flew across th' moor with me, an' Captain he run same as if th' hounds had been after him. They both felt same as I did."

Neither of the creatures looked as if they were the least afraid of Mary. When Dickon began to walk about, Soot stayed on his shoulder and Captain trotted quietly close to his side.

"See here!" said Dickon. "See how these has pushed up, an' these an' these! An' eh! look at these here!"

He threw himself upon his knees and Mary went down beside him. They had come upon a whole clump of crocuses burst into purple and orange and gold. Mary bent her face down and kissed and kissed them.

"You never kiss a person in that way," she said when she lifted her head. "Flowers are so different."

He looked puzzled, but smiled.

"Eh!" he said, "I've kissed Mother many a time that way when I come in from th' moor after a day's roamin' an' she stood there at th' door in th' sun, lookin' so glad an' comfortable."

They ran from one part of the garden to another and found so many wonders that they were obliged to remind themselves that they must whisper or speak low. He showed her swelling leaf-buds on rose branches which had seemed dead. He showed her ten thousand new green points pushing through the mould. They put their eager young noses close to the earth and sniffed its warmed springtime breathing; they dug and pulled and laughed low with rapture until Mistress Mary' hair was as tumbled as Dickon's and her cheeks were almost as poppy red as his.

There was every joy on earth in the secret garden that morning, and in the midst of them came a delight more delightful than all, because it was more wonderful. Swiftly something flew across the wall and darted through the trees to a close-grown corner, a little flare of red-breasted bird with something hanging from its beak. Dickon stood quite still and put his hand on Mary almost as if they had suddenly found themselves laughing in a church.

"We munnot stir," he whispered in broad Yorkshire. "We munnot scarce breathe. I knowed he was mate-huntin' when I seed him last. It's Ben Weatherstaff's robin. He's buildin' his nest. He'll stay here if us don't flight him."

They settled down softly upon the grass and sat there without moving.

"Us mustn't seem as if us was watchin' him too close," said Dickon. "He'd be out with us for good if he got th' notion us was interferin' now. He'll be a good bit different till all this is over. He's settin' up housekeepin'. He'll be shyer an' readier to take things ill. He's got no time for visitin' an' gossipin'. Us must keep still a bit an' try to look as if us was grass an' trees an' bushes. Then when he's got used to seein' us I'll chirp a bit an' he'll know us'll not be in his way."

Mistress Mary was not at all sure that she knew, as Dickon seemed to, how to try to look like grass and trees and bushes. But he had said the queer thing as if it were the simplest and most natural thing in the world, and she felt it must be quite easy to him, and, indeed, she watched him for a few minutes carefully, wondering if it was possible for him to turn quietly green and put out branches and leaves. But he only sat wonderfully still, and when he spoke dropped his voice to such a softness that it was curious that she could hear him, but she could.

"It's part o' th' springtime, this nest-buildin' is," he said. "I warrant it's been goin' on in th' same way every year since th' world was begun. They've got their way o' thinkin' and doin' things, an' a body had better not meddle. You can lose a friend in spring-time easier than any other season if you're too curious."

"If we talk about him I can't help looking at him," Mary said as softly as possible. "We must talk of something else. There is something I want to tell you."

"He'll like it better if us talks o' somethin' else," said Dickon. "What is it tha's got to tell me?"

"Well–do you know about Colin?" she whispered.

He turned his head to look at her.

"What does tha' know about him?" he asked.

"I've seen him. I have been to talk to him every day this week. He wants me to come. He says I'm making him forget about being ill and dying," answered Mary.

Dickon looked actually relieved as soon as the surprise died away from his round face.

"I am glad o' that," he exclaimed. "I'm right down glad. It makes me easier. I knowed I must say nothin' about him an' I don't like havin' to hide things."

"Don't you like hiding the garden?" said Mary.

"I'll never tell about it,n he answered. "But I says to Mother: 'Mother,' I says, 'I got a secret to keep. It's not a bad 'un, tha' knows that. It's no worse than hidin' where a bird's nest is. Tha' doesn't mind it, does tha'?' "

Mary always wanted to hear about Mother.

"What did she say?" she asked, not at all afraid to hear.

Dickon grinned sweet-temperedly.

"It was just like her, what she said," he answered. "She give my head a bit of a rub an' laughed an' she says: 'Eh, lad, tha' can have all th' secrets tha' likes. I've knowed thee twelve year'."

"How did you know about Colin?" asked Mary.

"Everybody as knowed about Mester Craven knowed there was a little lad as was like to be a cripple, an' they knowed Mester Craven didn't like him to be talked about. Folks is sorry for Mester Craven because Mrs. Craven was such a pretty young lady an' they was so fond of each other. Mrs. Medlock stops in our cottage whenever she goes to Thwaite an' she doesn't mind talkin' to Mother before us children, because she knows us has been brought up to be trusty. How did tha' find out about him? Martha was in fine trouble th' last time she came home. She said tha'd heard him frettin' an' tha' was askin' questions an' she didn't know what to say."

Mary told him her story about the midnight wuthering of the wind which had wakened her and about the faint, far-off sounds of the complaining voice which had led her down the dark corridors with her candle and had ended with her opening of the door of the dimly lighted room with the carven four-poster bed in the corner. When she described the small, ivory-white face and the strange black-rimmed eyes, Dickon shook his head.

"Them's just like his mother's eyes, only hers was always laughin', they say," he said. "They say as Mr. Craven can't bear to see him when he's awake, an' it's because his eyes is so like his mother's an' yet looks so different in his miserable bit of a face."

"Do you think he wants him to die?" whispered Mary.

"No, but he wishes he'd never been born. Mother, she says that's th' worst thing on earth for a child. Them as is not wanted scarce ever thrives. Mester Craven, he'd buy anythin' as money could buy for th' poor lad, but he'd like to forget he's on earth. For one thing, he's afraid he'll look at him some day and find he's growed hunch-back."

"Colin's so afraid of it himself that he won't sit up," said Mary.

"He say he's always thinking that if he should feel a lump coming he should go crazy and scream himself to death."

"Eh! he oughtn't to lie there thinkin' things like that," said Dickon.

"No lad could get well as thought them sort o' things."

The fox was lying on the grass close by him looking up to

ask for a pat now and then, and Dickon bent down and rubbed his neck softly and thought a few minutes in silence. Presently he lifted his head and looked round the garden.

"When first we got in here," he said, "it seemed like everything was grey. Look round now and tell me if tha' doesn't see a difference."

Mary looked and caught her breath a little.

"Why!" she cried, "the grey wall is changing. It is as if a green mist were creeping over it. It's almost like a green gauze veil."

"Aye," said Dickon. An' it'll be greener and greener till th' grey's all gone. Can tha' guess what I was thinkin'?"

"I know it was something nice," said Mary eagerly. "I believe it was something about Colin."

"I was thinkin' that if he was out here he wouldn't be watchin' for lumps to grow on his back; he'd be watchin' for buds to break on th' rose-bushes, an' he'd likely be healthier," explained Dickon. I was wonderin' if us could ever get him in th' humour to come out here an' lie under th' trees in his carriage."

"I've been wondering that myself. I've thought of it almost every time I've talked to him," said Mary. "I've wondered if he could keep a secret and I've wondered if we could bring him here without anyone seeing us. I thought perhaps you could push his carriage. The doctor said he must have fresh air, and if he wants us to take him out, no one dare disobey him. He won't go out for other people, and perhaps they will be glad if he will go out with us. He could order the gardeners to keep away so they wouldn't find out."

Dickon was thinking very hard as he scratched Captain's back.

"It'd be good for him, I'll warrant," he said. "Us'd not be thinkin' he'd better never been born. We'd be just two children watchin' a garden grow, an' he'd be another. Two lads an' a little lass just lookin' on at th' springtime. I warrant it'd be better than doctor's stuff."

"He's been lying in his room so long and he's always been so afraid of his back that it has made him queer," said Mary. "He knows a good many things out of books, but he doesn't know anything else. He says he has been too ill to notice things, and he hates going out of doors and hates gardens and gardeners. But he likes to hear about this garden because it is a secret. I daren't tell him much, but he said he wanted to see it."

"Us'll have him out here some time for sure," said Dickon. "I could push his carriage well enough. Has tha' noticed how th' robin an' his mate has been workin' while we've been sittin' here? Look at him perched on that branch wonderin' where it'd be best to put that twig he's got in his beak."

He made one of his low, whistling calls, and the robin turned his head and looked at him inquiringly, still holding his twig. Dickon spoke to him as Ben Weatherstaff did, but Dickon's tone was one of friendly advice.

"Wheres' ever tha' puts it," he said, "it'll be all right. Tha' knew how to build tha' nest before tha' came out o' th' egg. Get on with thee, lad. Tha'st got no time to lose."

"Oh I do like to hear you talk to him!" Mary said, laughing delightedly. "Ben Weatherstaff scolds him and makes fun of him, but he hops about and looks as if he understood every word, and I know he likes it. Ben Weatherstaff says he is so conceited he would rather have stones thrown at him than not be noticed."

Dickon laughed too, and went on talking.

"Tha' knows us won't trouble thee," he said to the robin. "Us is near bein' wild things ourselves. Us is nest-buildin' too, bless thee. Look out tha' doesn't tell on us."

And though the robin did not answer, because his beak was occupied, Mary knew that when he flew away with his twig to his own corner of the garden, the darkness of his dew-bright eye meant that he would not tell their secret for the world.

Chapter 16

"I WON'T!" SAID MARY

They found a great deal to do that morning, and Mary was late in returning to the house and was also in such a hurry to get back to her work that she quite forgot Colin until the last moment.

"Tell Colin that I can't come and see him yet," she said to Martha. "I'm very busy in the garden."

Martha looked rather frightened.

"Eh! Miss Mary," she said, "it may put him all out of humour when I tell him that."

But Mary was not as afraid of him as other people were, and she was not a self-sacrificing person.

"I can't stay," she answered. "Dickon's waiting for me." And she ran away.

The afternoon was even lovelier and busier than the morning had been. Already nearly all the weeds were cleared out of the garden and most of the roses and trees had been pruned or dug about. Dickon had brought a spade of his own, and he had taught Mary to use all her tools, so that by this time it was plain that though the lovely wild place was not likely to become a "gardener's garden", it would be a wilderness of growing things before the springtime was over.

"There'll be apple-blossoms an' cherry-blossoms overhead," Dickon said, working away with all his might. "An' there'll be peach an' plum trees in bloom against th' walls, an' th' grass'll be a carpet o' flowers."

The little fox and the rook were as happy and busy as they were, and the robin and his mate flew backwards and forwards like tiny streaks of lightning. Sometimes the rook flapped his black wings and soared away over the tree-tops in the park. Each time he came back and perched near Dickon and cawed several times as if he were relating his adventures, and Dickon talked to him just as he had talked to the robin.

Once when Dickon was so busy that he did not answer him at first, Soot flew on to his shoulder and gently tweaked his ear with his large beak. When Mary wanted to rest a little, Dickon sat down with her under a tree, and once he took his pipe out of his pocket and played the soft, strange little notes, and two squirrels appeared on the wall and looked and listened.

"Tha's a good bit stronger than tha' was," Dickon said, looking at her as she was digging. "Tha's beginnin' to look different, for sure."

Mary was glowing with exercise and good spirits.

'I'm getting fatter and fatter every day," she said quite exultantly. "Mrs. Medlock will have to get me some bigger dresses. Martha says my hair is growing thicker. It isn't so flat and stringy."

The sun was beginning to set and sending deep gold-coloured rays slanting under the trees when they parted.

"It'll be fine tomorrow," said Dickon. "I'll be at work by sunrise."

"So will I," said Mary.

*

She ran back to the house as quickly as her feet would carry her. She wanted to tell Colin about Dickon's fox cub and the rook and about what the springtime had been doing. She felt sure he would like to hear. So it was not very pleasant when she opened the door of her room to see Martha standing waiting for her with a doleful face.

"What is the matter" she asked. "What did Colin say when you told him I couldn't come?"

"Eh!" said Martha, "I wish tha'd gone. He was nigh goin' into one o' his tantrums. There's been a nice to do all afternoon to keep him quiet. He would watch the clock all th' time."

Mary's lips pinched themselves together. She was no more used to considering other people than Colin was, and she saw no reason why an ill-tempered boy should interfere with the thing she liked best. She knew nothing about the pitifulness of people who had been ill and nervous and who did not know that they could control their tempers and need not make other people ill and nervous, too. When she had had a headache in India, she had done her best to see that everybody else also had a headache or something quite as bad. And she felt she was quite right; but, of course, now she felt that Colin was quite wrong.

He was not on his sofa when she went into his room. He was lying flat on his back in bed, and he did not turn his head towards her as she came in. This was a bad beginning, and Mary marched up to him with her stiff manner.

"Why didn't you get up?" she said.

"I did get up this morning when I thought you were coming," he answered, without looking at her. "I made them put me back in bed this afternoon. My back ached and my head ached and I was tired. Why didn't you come?"

"I was working in the garden with Dickon," said Mary.

Colin frowned and condescended to look at her.

"I won't let that boy come here if you go and stay with him instead of coming to talk to me," he said.

Mary flew into a fine passion. She could fly into a passion without making a noise. She just grew sour and obstinate and did not care what happened.

"If you send Dickon away, I'll never come into this room again," she retorted.

"You'll have to if I want you," said Colin.

"I won't!" said Mary.

"I'll make you," said Colin. "They shall drag you in."

"Shall they, Mr. Rajah!" said Mary fiercely. "They may drag me in, but they can't make me talk when they get me here. I'll sit and clench my teeth and never tell you one thing. I won't even look at you. I'll stare at the floor!"

They were a nice agreeable pair as they glared at each other. If they had been two little street boys they would have sprung at each other and had a rough-and-tumble fight. As it was, they did the next thing to it.

"You are a selfish thing!" cried Colin.

"What are you?" said Mary. "Selfish people always say that. Anyone is selfish who doesn't do what they want. You're more selfish than I am. You're the most selfish boy I ever saw."

"I'm not!" snapped Colin. "I'm not as selfish as your fine Dickon is! He keeps you playing in the dirt when he knows I am all by myself. He's selfish, if you like!"

Mary's eyes flashed fire.

"He's nicer than any other boy that ever lived!" she said. "He's–he's like an angel!" It might sound rather silly to say that, but she did not care.

"A nice angel!" Colin sneered ferociously. "He's a common cottage boy off the moor!"

"He's better than a common rajah!" retorted Mary. "He's a thousand times better!"

Because she was the stronger of the two, she was beginning to get the better of him. The truth was that he had never had a fight with anyone like himself in his life, and, upon the whole, it was rather good for him, though neither he nor Mary knew anything about that. He turned his head on his pillow and shut his eyes and a big tear was squeezed out and ran down his cheek. He was beginning to feel pathetic and sorry for himself–not for anyone else.

"I'm not as selfish as you, because I'm always ill, and I'm sure a lump is coming on my back," he said. "Besides I am dying."

"You're not!" contradicted Mary unsympathetically.

He opened his eyes quite wide with indignation. He had never heard such a thing said before. He was at once furious and slightly pleased, if a person could be both at the same time.

"I'm not?" he cried. "I am! You know I am! Everybody says so."

"I don't believe it!" said Mary sourly. "You just say that to make people sorry. I believe you're proud of it. I don't believe it! If you were a nice boy it might be true–but you're too nasty!"

In spite of his invalid back, Colin sat up in bed in quite a healthy rage.

"Get out of the room!" he shouted, and he caught hold of his pillow and threw it at her. He was not strong enough to throw it far, and it only fell at her feet, but Mary's face looked as pinched as a nut-cracker.

"I'm going," she said. "And I won't come back!"

She walked to the door, and when she reached it she turned round and spoke again.

"I was going to tell you all sorts of nice things," she said.

"Dickon brought his fox and his rook and I was going to tell you all about them. Now I won't tell you a single thing! "

She marched out of the door and closed it behind her, and there to her great astonishment she found the trained nurse standing-as if she had been listening and, more amazing still–she was laughing. She was a big, handsome young woman, who ought not to have been a trained nurse at all, as she could not bear invalids, and she was always making excuses to leave Colin to Martha or anyone else who would take her place. Mary had never liked her, and she simply stood and gazed up at her as she stood giggling into her handkerchief.

"What are you laughing at?" she asked her.

"At you two young ones," said the nurse. "It's the best thing that could happen to the sickly, pampered thing to have someone to stand up to him that's as spoiled as himself"; and she laughed into her handkerchief again. "If he'd had a young vixen of a sister to fight with, it would have been the saving of him."

"Is he going to die?"

"I don't know and I don't care," said the nurse. "Hysterics and temper are half what ails him."

"What are hysterics?" asked Mary.

"You'll find out if you work him into a tantrum after this but at any rate, you've given him something to have hysterics about, and I am glad of it."

Mary went back to her room not feeling at all as she had felt when she had come in from the garden. She was cross and disappointed, but not at all sorry for Colin. She had looked forward to telling him a great many things, and she had meant to try to make up her mind whether it would be safe to trust him with the great secret. She had been beginning to think it would be, but now she had changed her mind entirely. She would never tell him and he could stay in his room and never get any fresh air and die if he liked! It would serve him right! She felt so sour and unrelenting that for a few minutes she almost forgot about Dickon and the green veil creeping over the world and the soft wind blowing down from the moor.

Martha was waiting for her, and the trouble in her face had been temporarily replaced by interest and curiosity. There was a wooden box on the table and its cover had been removed and revealed that it was full of neat packages.

"Mr. Craven sent it to you," said Martha. "It looks as if it had picture-books in it."

Mary remembered what he had asked her the day she had gone to his room. "Do you want anything–dolls–toys–books?" She opened the package wondering if he had sent a doll, and also wondering what she should do with it if he had. But he had not sent one. There were several beautiful books such as Colin had, and two of them were about gardens and were full of pictures. There were two or three games and there was a beautiful little writing-case with a gold monogram on it and a gold pen and ink-stand.

Everything was so nice that her pleasure began to crowd her anger out of her mind. She had not expected him to remember her at all, and her hard little heart grew quite warm.

"I can write better than I can print," she said, "and the first thing I shall write-with that pen will be a letter to tell him I am much obliged."

If she had been friends with Colin she would have run to show him her presents at once, and they would have looked at the pictures and read some of the gardening books and perhaps tried playing the games, and he would have enjoyed himself so much he would never once have thought he was going to die or have put his hand on his spine to see if there was a lump coming. He had a way of doing that which she could not bear. It gave her an uncomfortable, frightened feeling because he always looked so frightened himself. He said that if he felt even quite a little lump some day he should know his hunch had begun to grow. Something he had heard Mrs. Medlock whispering to the nurse had given him the idea, and he had thought over it in secret until it was quite firmly fixed in his mind. Mrs. Medlock had said his father's back had begun to show its crookedness in that way when he was a child. He had never told anyone but Mary that most of his "tantrums", as they called them, grew out of his hysterical hidden fear. Mary had been sorry for him when he had told her.

"He always began to think about it when he was cross or tired," she said to herself. "And he has been cross today.

Perhaps–perhaps he has been thinking about it all the afternoon."

She stood still, looking down at the carpet and thinking.

"I said I would never go back again–" she hesitated, knitting her brows–"but perhaps, just perhaps, I will go and see–if he wants me–in the morning. Perhaps he'll try to throw his pillow at me again, but–I think–I'll go."

Chapter 17

A TANTRUM

She had got up very early in the morning and had worked hard in the garden, and she was tired and sleepy, so as soon as Martha had brought her supper and she had eaten it, she was glad to go to bed. As she laid her head on the pillow, she murmured to herself:

"I'll go out before breakfast and work with Dickon and then afterwards–I believe–I'll go to see him."

She thought it was the middle of the night when she was awakened by such dreadful sounds that she jumped out of bed in an instant. What was it–what was it? The next minute she felt quite sure she knew. Doors were opened and shut and there were hurrying feet in the corridors and someone was crying and screaming at the same time, screaming and crying in a horrible way.

"It's Colin," she said. "He's having one of those tantrums the nurse calls hysterics. How awful it sounds."

As she listened to the sobbing screams she did not wonder that people were so frightened that they gave him his own way in everything rather than hear them. She put her hands over her ears and felt sick and shivering.

"I don't know what to do. I don't know what to do," she kept saying. "I can't bear it."

Once she wondered if he would stop if she dared go to him, and then she remembered how he had driven her out of the room and thought that perhaps the sight of her might make him worse. Even when she pressed her hands more tightly over her ears she could not keep the awful sounds out. She hated them so and was so terrified by them that suddenly they began to make her angry, and she felt as if she should like to fly into a tantrum herself and frighten him as he was frightening her. She was not wed to anyone's temper but her own. She took her hands from her ears and sprang up and stamped her foot.

"He ought to be stopped! Somebody ought to make him stop! Somebody ought to beat him! " she cried out.

Just then she heard feet almost running down the corridor, and her door opened and the nurse came in. She was not laughing now by any means. She even looked rather pale.

"He's working himself into hysterics," she said in a great hurry. "He'll do himself harm. No one can do anything with him. You come and try, like a good child. He likes you."

"He turned me out of the room this morning," said Mary, stamping her foot in excitement.

The stamp rather pleased the nurse. The truth was that she had been afraid she might find Mary crying and hiding her head under the bed-clothes.

"That's right," she said. "You're in the right humour. You go and scold him. Give him something new to think of. Do go, child, as quick as ever you can."

It was not until afterwards that Mary realized that the thing had been funny as well as dreadful–that it was funny that all the grown-up people were so frightened that they came to a little girl just because they guessed she was almost as bad as Colin himself.

She flew along the corridor, and the nearer she got to the screams the higher her temper mounted. She felt quite wicked by the time she reached the door. She slapped it open with her hand and ran across the room to the four-poster bed.

"You stop!" she almost shouted. "You stop! I hate you. Everybody hates you! I wish everybody would run out of the house and let you scream yourself to death. You *will* scream yourself to death in a minute, and I wish you would!"

A nice, sympathetic child could neither have thought nor said such things, but it just happened that the shock of hearing them was the best possible thing for this hysterical boy whom no one had ever dared to restrain or contradict.

He had been lying on his face beating his pillow with his hands, and he actually almost jumped around, he turned so quickly at the sound of the furious little voice. His face looked dreadful, white and red, and swollen, and he was gasping and choking; but savage little Mary did not care an atom.

"If you scream another scream," she said, "I'll scream, too–and I can scream louder than you can, and I'll frighten you, I'll frighten you!"

He actually had stopped screaming because she had startled him so. The scream which had been coming almost choked him. The tears were streaming down his face and he shook all over.

"I can't stop!" he gasped, and sobbed. "I can't–I can't!"

"You can!" shouted Mary. "Half that ails you is hysterics and temper–just hysterics–hysterics–hysterics!" and she stamped each time she said it.

"I felt the lump–I felt it," choked out Colin. "I knew I should. I shall have a hunch on my back and then I shall die," and he began to writhe again and turned on his face and sobbed and wailed, but he didn't scream.

"You didn't fed a lump!" contradicted Mary fiercely. "If you did it was only a hysterical lump. Hysterics makes lumps. There's nothing the matter with your horrid back–nothing but hysterics! Turn over and let me look at it."

She liked the word "hysterics", and felt somehow as if it had an effect on him. He had probably never heard it before.

"Nurse," she commanded, "come here and show me his back this minute!"

The nurse, Mrs. Medlock, and Martha had been standing huddled together near the door staring at her, their mouths half open. All three had gasped with fright more than once. The nurse came forward as if she were half afraid. Colin was heaving with great breathless sobs.

"Perhaps he–he won't let me," she hesitated, in a low voice.

Colin heard her, however, and he gasped out between two sobs:

"Sh-show her! She-she'll see then!"

It was a poor, thin back to look at when it was bared. Every rib could be counted and every joint of the spine, though Mistress Mary did not count them as she bent over and examined them with a solemn, savage little face. She looked so sour and old-fashioned that the nurse turned her head aside to hide the twitching of her mouth. There was just a minute's silence, for even Colin tried to hold his breath while Mary looked up and down his spine, and down and up, as intently as if she had been the great doctor from London.

"There's not a single lump there!" she said at last. "There's not a lump as big as a pin-except backbone lumps, and you can only feel them because you're thin. I've got backbone lumps myself, and they used to stick out as much as yours do, until I began to get fatter, and I am not fat enough yet to hide them. There's not a lump as big as a pin. If you ever say there is again, I shall laugh!"

No one but Colin himself knew what effect those crossly spoken childish words had on him. If he had ever had anyone to talk to about his secret terrors–if he had ever dared to let himself ask questions–if he had had childish companions and had not lain on his back in the huge closed house, breathing an atmosphere heavy with the fears of people who were most of them ignorant and tired of him, he would have found out that most of his fright and illness was created by himself. But he had lain and thought of himself and his aches and weariness for hours and days and months and years. And now that an angry, unsympathetic little girl insisted obstinately that he was not at all as he thought he was, he actually felt as if she might be speaking the truth.

"I didn't know," ventured the nurse, "that he thought he had a lump on his spine. His back is weak because he won't try to sit up. I could have told him there was no lump there."

Colin gulped and turned his face a little to look at her.

"C-could you?" he said pathetically.

"Yes, sir."

"There!" said Mary, and she gulped, too.

Colin turned on his face again, and but for his long drawn broken breaths, which were the dying down of his storm of sobbing, he lay still for a minute, though great tears streamed down his face and wet the pillow. Actually the tears meant that a curious great relief had come to him. Presently he turned and looked at the nurse again, and strangely enough he was not like a rajah at all as he spoke to her.

"Do you think–I could–live to grow up?" he said.

The nurse was neither clever nor soft-hearted, but she could repeat some of the London doctor's words.

"You probably will if you will do what you are told to do, and not give way to your temper, and stay out a great deal in the fresh air."

Colin's tantrum had passed and he was weak and worn out with crying, and this perhaps made him feel gentle. He put out his hand a little towards Mary, and I am glad to say that, her own tantrum having passed, she was softened too, and met him half-way with her hand, so that it was a sort of making up.

"I'll–I'll go out with you, Mary," he said. "I shan't hate fresh air if we can find–" He remembered just in time to stop himself from saying if we can find the secret garden," and he ended shall like to go out with you you if Dickon will come and push my chair. I do so want to see Dickon and the fox and the crow."

The nurse remade the tumbled bed and shook and straightened the pillows. Then she made Colin a cup of beef-tea and gave a cup to Mary, who really was very glad to get it after her excitement. Mrs. Medlock and Martha gladly slipped away, and after everything was neat and calm and in order, the nurse looked as if she would very gladly slip away also. She was a healthy young woman -who resented being robbed of her sleep, and she yawned quite openly as she looked at Mary, who had pushed her big footstool close to the four-poster bed and was holding Colin's hand.

"You must go back and get your sleep out," she said. "He'll drop off after a while–if he's not too upset. Then I'll lie down myself in the next room."

"Would you like me to sing you that song I learned from my Ayah?" Mary whispered to Colin.

His hand pulled hers gently and he turned his tired eyes on her appealingly.

"Oh, yes!" he answered. "It's such a soft song. I shall go to sleep in a minute."

"I will put him to sleep," Mary said to the yawning nurse. "You can go if you like."

"Well," said the nurse, with an attempt at reluctance. "If he doesn't go to sleep in half an hour you must call me."

"Very well," answered Mary.

The nurse was out of the room in a minute, and as soon as she was gone Colin pulled Mary's hand again.

"I almost told," he said: "but I stopped myself in time. I won't talk and I'll go to sleep, but you said you had a whole lot of nice things to tell me. Have you–do you think you have found out anything at all about the way into the secret garden?"

Mary looked at his poor little tired face and swollen eyes and her heart relented.

"Ye-es," she answered, "I think I have. And if you will go to sleep I will tell you tomorrow."

His hand quite trembled.

"Oh, Mary!" he said. "Oh, Mary! If I could go into it I think I should live to grow up! Do you suppose that instead of singing the Ayah song–you could just tell me softly as you did that first day what you imagine it looks like inside? I am sure it will make me go to sleep."

"Yes," answered Mary. "Shut your eyes."

He closed his eyes and lay quite still and she held his hand and began to speak very slowly and in a very low voice.

"I think it has been left alone so long–that it has grown all into a lovely tangle. I think the roses have climbed and climbed and climbed until they hang from the branches and walls and creep over the ground-almost like a strange grey mist. Some of them have died, but many are alive, and when the summer comes there will be curtains and fountains of roses. I think the ground is full of daffodils and snowdrops and lilies and iris working their way out of the dark. Now the spring has begun–perhaps–perhaps–"

The soft drone of her voice was making him stiller and stiller, and she saw it and went on.

"Perhaps they are coming up through the grass–perhaps there are dusters of purple crocuses and gold ones–even now. Perhaps the leaves are beginning to break out and uncurl–and perhaps–the grey is changing and a green gauze veil is creeping–and creeping over everything. And the birds are coming to look at it–because it is–so safe and still. And perhaps–perhaps–perhaps–" very softly and slowly indeed, "the robin has found a mate–and is building a nest."

And Colin was asleep.

CHAPTER 18

"THA' MUNNOT WASTE NO TIME"

Of course, Mary did not waken early the next morning. She slept late because she was tired, and when Martha brought her breakfast she told her that though Colin was quite quiet, he was ill and feverish, as he always was after he had worn himself out with a fit of crying. Mary ate her breakfast slowly as she listened.

"He says he wishes tha' would please go and see him as soon as tha' can," Martha said. It's queer what a fancy he's took to thee. Tha' did give it him last night for sure–didn't tha'? Nobody else would have dared to do it. Eh! poor lad! He's been spoiled till salt won't save him. Mother says as th' two worst things as can happen to a child is never to have his own way–or always to have it. She doesn't know which is th' worst. Tha' was in a fine temper tha'self, too. But he says to me when I went into his room: 'Please ask Miss Mary if she'll please come an' talk to me?' Think o' him saying please! Will you go, Miss?"

"I'll run and see Dickon first," said Mary. "No, I'll go and see Colin first and tell him–I know what I'll tell him," with a sudden inspiration.

She had her hat on when she appeared in Colin's room, and for a second he looked disappointed. He was in bed, and his face was pitifully white and there were dark circles round his eyes.

"I'm glad you came," he said. "My head aches and I ache all over because I'm so tired. Are you going somewhere?"

Mary went and leaned against his bed.

"I won't be long," she said. "I'm going to Dickon, but I'll come back. Colin, it's–it's something about the secret garden."

His whole face brightened and a little colour came into it.

"Oh! is it?" he cried out. "I dreamed about it all night. I heard you say something about grey changing into green, and I dreamed I was standing in a place all filled with trembling little green leaves–and there were birds on nests everywhere and they looked so soft and still. I'll lie and think about it until you come back."

In five minutes Mary was with Dickon in their garden. The fox and the crow were with him again, and this time he had brought two tame squirrels.

"I came over on the pony this morrun'," he said. "Eh! he is a good little chap-Jump is! I brought these two in my pockets. This here one he's called Nut an' this here other one's called Shell."

When he said "Nut" one squirrel leaped on to his right shoulder, and when he said "Shell" the other one leaped on to his left shoulder.

When they sat down on the grass with-Captain curled at their feet, Soot solemnly listening on a tree and Nut and Shell nosing about close to them, it seemed to Mary that it would be scarcely bearable to leave such delightfulness, but when she began to tell her story somehow the look in Dickon's funny face gradually changed her mind. She could see he felt sorrier for Colin than she did. He looked up at the sky and all about him.

"Just listen to them birds–th' world seems full of 'em–all whistlin' an' pipin'," he said. "Look at' 'em dartin' about, an' hearken at 'em callin' to each other. Come springtime seems like as if all th' world's callin'. The leaves is uncurlin' so you can see 'em–an', my word, th' nice smells there is about!" sniffing with his happy turned-up nose. "An' that poor lad lyin' shut up an' seein' so little that he gets to thinkin' o' things as sets him screamin'. Eh! my! we mun get him out here–we mun get him watchin' an' listenin' an' sniffin' up th' air an' get him just soaked through wi' sunshine. An' we munnot lose no time about it."

When he was very much interested he often spoke quite broad Yorkshire, though at other times he tried to modify his dialect so that Mary could better understand. But she loved his broad Yorkshire, and had, in fact, been trying to learn to speak it herself. So she spoke a little now.

"Aye, that we mun," she said (which meant "Yes, indeed, we must"). I'll tell thee what w'll do first," she proceeded, and Dickon grinned, because when the little wench tried to twist her tongue into speaking Yorkshire it amused him very much. He's took a graidely fancy to thee. He wants to see thee and he wants to see Soot an' Captain. When I go back to the house to talk to him I'll ask him if tha' canna come an' see him tomorrow mornin'–an' bring tha' creatures wi' thee–an' then–in a bit, when there's more leaves out an' happen a bud or two, we'll get him to come out an' tha' shall push him in his chair an' we'll bring him here an' show him everything."

When she stopped she was quite proud of herself. She had never made a long speech in Yorkshire before, and she had remembered very well.

"Tha' mun talk a bit o' Yorkshire like that to Mester Colin," Dickon chuckled. "Tha'll make him laugh an' there's nowt as good for ill folk as laughin' is. Mother says she believes as half a hour's good laugh every mornin' 'ud cure a chap as was making ready for typhus fever."

"I'm going to talk Yorkshire to him this very day," said Mary, chuckling herself.

The garden had reached the time when every day and every night it seemed as if Magicians were passing through it drawing loveliness out of the earth and the boughs with wands. It was hard to go away and leave it all, particularly as Nut had actually crept onto her dress and Shell had scrambled down the trunk of the apple tree they sat under and stayed there looking at her with inquiring eyes. But she went back to the house and when she sat down close to Colin's bed he began to sniff as Dickon did, though not in such an experienced way.

"You smell like flowers and–and fresh things," he cried out quite joyously. "What is it you smell of? It's cool and warm and sweet all at the same time."

"It's th' wind from th' moor," said Mary. It comes o' sittin' on th' grass under a tree wi' Dickon an' wi' Captain an' Soot an' Nut an' Shell. It's th' springtime an' out o' doors an' sunshine as smells so graidely."

She said it as broadly as she could, and you do not know how broadly Yorkshire sounds until you have heard someone speak it. Colin began to laugh.

"What are you doing?" he said. "I never heard you talk like that before. How funny it sounds."

"I'm givin' thee a bit o' Yorkshire, answered Mary triumphantly. I canna talk as graidly as Dickon an' Martha can, but tha' sees I can shape a bit. Doesn't tha' understand a bit o' Yorkshire when tha' hears it? An' tha' a Yorkshire lad thysel' bred an' born! Eh! I wonder tha'rt not ashamed o' they face."

And then she began to laugh too, and they both laughed until they could not stop themselves, and they laughed until the room echoed and Mrs. Medlock opening the door to come in drew back into the corridor and stood listening, amazed.

"Well, upon my word!" she said, speaking rather broad Yorkshire herself because there was no one to hear her, and she was so astonished. "Whoever heard th' like! Whoever on earth would ha' thought it!"

There was so much to talk about. It seemed as if Colin could never hear enough of Dickon and Captain and Soot and Nut and Shell and the pony whose name was Jump. Mary had run round into the wood with Dickon to see Jump. He was a tiny little shaggy moor pony with thick locks hanging over his eyes and with a pretty face and a nuzzling velvet nose. He was rather thin with living on moor grass, but he was as tough and wiry as if the muscle in his little legs had been made of steel springs. He had lifted his head and whinnied softly the moment he saw Dickon, and he had trotted up to him and put his head across his shoulder, and then Dickon had talked into his ear and Jump had talked back in odd little whinnies and puffs and snorts. Dickon ha made him give Mary his small front hoof and kiss her on her cheek with his velvet muzzle.

"Does he really understand everything Dickon says?" Colin asked.

"It seems as if he does," answered Mary. "Dickon says anything will understand if you're friends with it for sure, but you have to be friends for sure."

Colin lay quiet a little while, and his strange grey eyes seemed to be staring at the wall, but Mary saw he was thinking.

"I wish I was friends with things," he said at last, "but I'm not. I never had anything to be friends with, and I can't bear people."

"Can't you bear me?" asked Mary.

"Yes, I can," he answered. "It's very funny, but I even like you."

"Ben Weatherstaff said I was like him," said Mary. "He said he'd warrant we'd both got the same nasty tempers. I think you are like him, too. We are all three alike–you and I and Ben Weatherstaff. He said we were neither of us much to look at, and we were as sour as we looked. But I don't feel as sour as I used to before I knew the robin and Dickon."

"Did you feel as if you hated people?"

"Yes," answered Mary, without any affectation. "I should have detested you if I had seen you before I saw the robin and Dickon."

Colin put out his thin hand and touched her.

"Mary," he said, "I wish I hadn't said what I did about sending Dickon away. I hated you when you aid he was like an angel and I laughed at you, but–but perhaps he is."

"Well, it was rather funny to say it," she admitted frankly, "because his nose does turn up and he has a big mouth and his clothes have patches all over them and he talks broad Yorkshire, but–but if an angel did come to Yorkshire and live on the moor–if there was a Yorkshire angel–I believe he'd understand the green things and know how to make them grow and he would know how to talk to the wild creatures as Dickon does, and they'd know he was friends for sure."

"I shouldn't mind Dickon looking at me," said Colin; "I want to see him."

"I'm glad you said that," answered Mary, "because–because–"

Quite suddenly it came into her mind that this was the minute to tell him. Colin knew something new was coming.

"Because what?" he cried eagerly.

Mary was so anxious that she got up from her stool and came to him and caught hold of both his hands.

"Can I trust you?" I trusted Dickon because birds trusted him. Can I trust you–for sure–*for sure*?" she implored.

Her face was so solemn that he almost whispered his answer.

"Yes–yes!"

"Well, Dickon will come to see you tomorrow morning and he'll bring his creatures with him."

"Oh! Oh!" Colin cried out in delight.

"But that's not all," Mary went on, almost pale with solemn excitement. "The rest is better. There is a door into the garden. I found it. It is under the ivy on the wall."

If he had been a strong, healthy boy, Colin would probably have shouted, "Hooray! Hooray! Hooray!" but he was weak and rather hysterical; his eyes grew bigger and bigger and he gasped for breath.

"Oh! Mary!" he cried out," with a half sob. "Shall I see it? Shall I get into it? Shall I *live* to get into it?" and he clutched her hands and dragged her towards him.

"Of course you'll see it!" snapped Mary indignantly. "Of course you'll live to get into it! Don't be silly!"

And she was so un-hysterical and natural and childish that she brought him to his senses and he began to laugh at himself, and a few minutes afterwards she was sitting on her stool again telling him not what she imagined the secret garden to be like, but what it really was, and Colin's aches and tiredness were forgotten and he was listening enraptured.

"It is just what you thought it would be," he said at last. "It sounds just as if you had really seen it. You know I said that when you told me first."

Mary hesitated about two minutes and then boldly spoke the truth.

"I had seen it–and I had been in," she said. "I found the key and got in weeks ago. But I daren't tell you–I daren't because I was so afraid I couldn't trust you–*for sure*!"

Chapter 19

"IT HAS COME!"

Of course, Dr. Craven had been sent for the morning after Colin had had his tantrum. He was always sent for at once when such a thing occurred, and he always found, when he arrived, a white, shaken boy lying on his bed, sulky and still so hysterical that he was ready to break into fresh sobbing at the least word. In fact, Dr. Craven dreaded and detested the difficulties of these visits. On this occasion he was away from Misselthwaite Manor until afternoon.

"How is he?" he asked Mrs. Medlock rather irritably when he arrived. "He will break a blood-vessel in one of those fits some day. The boy is half insane with hysteria and self-indulgence."

"Well, sir," answered Mrs. Medlock, "you'll scarcely believe your eyes when you see him. That plain, sour-faced child that's almost as bad as himself has just bewitched him. How she's done it there's no telling. The Lord knows, she's nothing to look at and you scarcely ever hear her speak, but she did what none of us dare do. She just flew at him like a little cat last night, and stamped her feet and ordered him to stop screaming, and somehow she startled him so that he actually did stop, and this afternoon—well, just come up and see, sir. It's past crediting."

The scene which Dr. Craven beheld when he entered his patient's room was indeed rather astonishing to him. As Mrs. Medlock opened the door he heard laughing and chattering. Colin was on his sofa in his dressing-gown and he was sitting up quite straight looking at a picture in one of the garden books and talking to the plain child who at that moment could scarcely be called plain at all because her face was so glowing with enjoyment.

"Those long spires of blue ones–we'll have a lot of those," Colin was announcing. "They're called Del-phiniums."

"Dickon says they're larkspurs made big and grand," cried Mistress Mary. "There are clumps there already."

Then they saw Dr. Craven and stopped. Mary became quite still and Colin looked fretful.

"I am sorry to hear you were ill last night, my boy," Dr. Craven said, a trifle nervously. He was rather a nervous man.

"I'm better now–much better," Colin answered, rather like a rajah. I'm going out in my chair in a day or two if it is fine. I want some fresh air."

Dr. Craven sat down by him and felt his pulse and looked at him curiously.

"It must be a very fine day," he said, "and you must be very careful not to tire yourself."

"Fresh air won't tire me," said the young rajah.

As there had been occasions when this same young gentleman had shrieked aloud with rage and had insisted that fresh air would give him cold and kill him, it is not to be wondered at that his doctor felt somewhat startled.

"I thought you did not like fresh air," he said.

"I don't when I am by myself," replied the rajah; "but my cousin is going out with me."

"And the nurse, of course?" suggested Dr. Craven.

"No, I will not have the nurse," so magnificently that Mary could not help remembering how the young native prince had looked with his diamonds and emeralds and pearls stuck all over him and the great rubies on the small dark hand he had waved to command his servants to approach with salaams and receive his orders.

"My cousin knows how to take care of me. I am always better when she is with me. She made me better last night. A very strong boy I know will push my carriage."

Dr. Craven felt rather alarmed. If this tiresome, hysterical boy should chance to get well, he himself would lose all chance of inheriting Misselthwaite; but he was not an unscrupulous man, though he was a weak one, and he did not intend to let him run into actual danger.

"He must be a strong boy and a steady boy," he said. "And,I must know something about him. Who is he? What is his name?"

"It's Dickon," Mary spoke up suddenly. She felt somehow that everyone who knew the moor must know Dickon. And she was right, too. She saw that in a moment Dr. Craven's serious face relaxed into a relieved smile.

"Oh, Dickon", he said. "If it is Dickon you will be safe enough. He's as strong as a moor pony, is Dickon."

"And he's trusty," said Mary. "He's th' trustiest lad i' Yorkshire." She had been talking Yorkshire to Colin and she forgot herself.

"Did Dickon teach you that?" asked Dr. Craven, laughing outright.

"I'm learning it as if it was French," said Mary, rather coldly. "It's like a native dialect in India. Very clever people try to learn them. I like it and so does Colin."

"Well, well," he said. "If it amuses you perhaps it won't do you any harm. Did you take your bromide last night, Colin?"

"No," Colin answered. "I wouldn't take it at first, and after Mary made me quiet she talked me to sleep–in a low voice–about the spring creeping into a garden."

"That sounds soothing," said Dr. Craven, more perplexed than ever and glancing sideways at Mistress Mary sitting on her stool and looking down silently at the carpet. "You are evidently better, but you must remember–"

"I don't want to remember," interrupted the rajah, appearing again. "When I lie by myself and remember I begin to have pains everywhere, and I think of things that make me begin to scream because I hate them so. If there was a doctor anywhere who could make you forget you were ill instead of remembering it, I would have him brought here." And he waved a thin hand which ought really to have been covered with royal signet rings made of rubies. "It is because my cousin makes me forget that she makes me better."

Dr. Craven had never made such a short stay after a "tantrum"; usually he was obliged to remain a very long time and do a great many things. Tis afternoon he did not give any medicine or leave any new orders, and he was spared any disagreeable scenes. When he went downstairs he looked very thoughtful, and when he talked to Mrs. Medlock in the library she felt that he was a much puzzled man.

"Well, sir," she ventured, "could you have believed it?"

"It is certainly a new state of affairs," said the doctor. "And there's no denying it is better than the old one."

"I believe Susan Sowerby's right–I do that," said Mrs. Medlock. "I stopped in her cottage on my way to Thwaite yesterday, and had a bit of talk with her. And she says to me: 'Well, Sarah Ann, she mayn't be a good child, an' she mayn't be a pretty one, but she's a child, an' children needs children.' We went to school together, Susan Sowerby and me."

"She's the best sick nurse I know," said Dr. Craven. "When I find her in a cottage I know the chances are that I shall save my patient."

Mrs. Medlock smiled. She was fond of Susan Sowerby.

"She's got a way with her, has Susan," she went on quite volubly. "I've been thinking all morning of one thing she said yesterday. She says: 'Once when I was givin' th' children a bit of a preach after they'd been fightin' I ses to 'em all, When I was at school my jography told as th' world was shaped like a orange an' I found out before I was ten that th' whole orange doesn't belong to nobody. No one owns more than his bit of a quarter an' there's times it seems like there's not enow quarters to go round. But don't you–none o' you–think as you own th' whole orange or you'll find out you're mistaken, an' you won't find it out without hard knocks." What children learns from children,' she says, 'is that there's no sense in grabbin' at th' whole orange – peel an' all. If you do, you'll likely not get even th' pips, an' them's too bitter to eat.'"

"She's a shrewd woman," said Dr. Craven, putting on his coat.

"Well, she's got a way of saying things," ended Mrs. Medlock, much pleased. "Sometimes I've said to her, 'Eh, Susan, if you was a different woman an' didn't talk such broad Yorkshire I've seen the times when I should have said you was clever.'"

*

That night Colin slept without once awakening, and when he opened his eyes in the morning he lay still and smiled without knowing it–smiled because he felt so curiously comfortable. It was actually nice to be awake, and he turned over and stretched his limbs luxuriously. He felt as if tight strings which had held him had loosened themselves and let him go. He did not know that Dr. Craven would have said that his nerves had relaxed and rested themselves. Instead of lying and staring at the wall and wishing he had not awakened, his mind was full of the plans he and Mary had made yesterday, of pictures of the garden and of Dickon and his wild creatures. It was so nice to have things to think about. And he had not been awake more than ten minutes when he heard feet running along the corridor and Mary was at the door. The next minute she was in the room and had run across to his bed, bringing with her a waft of fresh air full of the scent of the morning.

"You've been out! You've been out! There's that nice smell of leaves!" he cried.

She had been running and her hair was loose and blown, and she was bright with the air and pink-cheeked, though he could not see it.

"It's so beautiful!" she said, a little breathless with her speed. "You never saw anything so beautiful! It has *come*! I thought it had come that other morning, but it was only coming. It is here now! It has come, the Spring! Dickon says so!"

"Has it?" cried Colin, and though he really knew nothing about it, he felt his heart beat. He actually sat up in bed.

"Open the window!" he added, laughing half with joyful excitement and half at his own fancy. "Perhaps we may hear golden trumpets!"

And though he laughed, Mary was at the window in a moment and in a moment more it was opened wide and freshness and softness and scents and bird's songs were pouring through.

"That's fresh air," she said. "Lie on your back and draw in long breaths of it. That's what Dickon does when he's lying on the moor. He says he feels it in his veins and it makes him strong and he feels as if he could live for ever and ever. Breathe it and breathe it.

She was only repeating what Dickon had told her, but she caught Colin's fancy.

"'For ever and ever!' Does it make him feel like that?" he said, and he did as she told him, drawing in long deep breaths over and over again, until he felt that something quite new and delightful was happening to him.

Mary was at his bedside again.

"Things are crowding up out of the earth," she ran on in a hurry. "And there are flowers uncurling and buds on everything and the green veil has covered nearly all the grey and the birds are in such a hurry about their nests for fear they may be too late, that some of them are even fighting for places in the secret garden. And the rose-bushes look as wick as wick can be, and there are primroses in the lanes and woods, and the seeds we planted are up, and Dickon has brought the fox and the crow and the squirrels and a new-born lamb."

And then she paused for breath. The new-born lamb Dickon had found three days before lying by its dead mother among the gorse bushes on the moor. It was not the first motherless lamb he had found and he knew what to do with it. He had taken it to the cottage wrapped in his jacket and he had let it lie near the fire and had fed it with warm milk. It was a soft thing, with a darling silly baby face and legs rather long for its body. Dickon had carried it over the moor in his arms, and its feeding-bottle was in his pocket with a squirrel, and when Mary had sat under a tree with its limp warmness huddled on her lap, she had felt as if she were too full of strange joy to speak. A lamb–a lamb! a living lamb who lay on your lap like a baby!

She was describing it with great joy and Colin was listening and drawing in long breaths of air when the nurse entered. She started a little at the sight of the open window. She had sat stifling in the room many a warm day because her patient was sure that open windows gave people cold.

"Are you sure you are not chilly, Master Colin?" she inquired.

"No," was the answer. "I am breathing long breaths of fresh air. It makes you strong. I am going to get up to the sofa for breakfast and my cousin will have breakfast with me."

The nurse went away, concealing a smile, to give the order for two breakfasts. She found the servants' hall a more amusing place than the invalid's chamber, and just now everybody wanted to hear the news from upstairs. There was a great deal of joking about the unpopular young recluse who, as the cook said, "had found his master, and good for him." The servants' hall had been very tired of the tantrums, and the butler, who was a man with a family, had more than once expressed his opinion that the invalid would be all the better "for a good hiding".

When Colin was on his sofa and the breakfast for two was put upon the table, he made an announcement to the nurse in his most rajah-like manner.

"A boy, and a fox, and a crow, and two squirrels, and a new-born lamb, are coming to see me this morning. I want them brought upstairs as soon as they come," he said. "You are not to begin playing with the animals in the servants' hall and keep them there. I want them here."

The nurse gave a light gasp and tried to conceal it with a cough.

"Yes, sir," she answered.

"I'll tell you what you can do," added Colin, waving his hand. "You can tell Martha to bring them here. The boy is Martha's brother. His name is Dickon and he is an animal charmer."

"I hope the animals won't bite, Master Colin," said the nurse.

"I told you he was a charmer," said Colin austerely. "Charmers' animals never bite."

"There are snake-charmers in India," said Mary; "and they can put their snakes' heads in their mouths."

"Goodness!" shuddered the nurse.

They ate their breakfast with the morning air pouring in upon them. Colin's breakfast was a very good one, and Mary watched him with serious interest.

"You will begin to get fatter just as I did," she said. "I never wanted my breakfast when I was in India, and now I always want it."

"I wanted mine this morning," said Colin. "Perhaps it was the fresh air. When do you think Dickon will come?"

He was not long in coming. In about ten minutes Mary held up her hand.

"Listen!" she said. "Did you hear a caw?"

Colin listened and heard it, the oddest sound in the world to hear inside a house, a hoarse "caw-caw".

"Yes," he answered.

"That's Soot," said Mary. "Listen again! Do you hear a bleat–a tiny one?"

"Oh, yes!" cried Colin, quite flushing.

"That's the new-born lamb," said Mary. "He's coming."

Dickon's moorland boots were thick and clumsy, and though he tried to walk quietly they made a clumping sound as he walked through the long corridors. Mary and Colin heard him marching–marching, until he passed through the tapestry door on to the soft carpet of Colin's own passage.

"If you please, sir," announced Martha, opening the door, "if you please, sir, here's Dickon an' his creatures."

Dickon came in smiling his nicest wide smile. The new-born lamb was in his arms and the little red fox trotted by his side. Nut sat on his left shoulder and Soot on his right, and Shell's head and paws peeped out of his coat pocket.

Colin slowly sat up and stared and stared–as he had stared when he first saw Mary; but this was a stare of wonder and delight. The truth was that in spite of all he had heard he had not in the least understood what this boy would be like and that his fox and his crow and his squirrels and his lamb were so near to him and his friendliness that they seemed almost to be part of himself. Colin had never talked to a boy in his life, and he was so overwhelmed by his own pleasure and curiosity that he did not even think of speaking.

But Dickon did not feel the least shy or awkward. He had not felt embarrassed because the crow had not known his language and had only stared and had not spoken to him the first time they met. Creatures were always like that until they found out about you. He walked over to Colin's sofa and put the new-born lamb quietly on his lap, and immediately the little creature turned to the warm velvet dressing-gown and began to nuzzle and nuzzle into its folds and butt its tight-curled head with soft impatience against his side. Of course, no boy could have helped speaking then.

"What is it doing?" cried Colin. "What does it want?"

"Its wants its mother," said Dickon, smiling more and more. "I brought it to thee a bit hungry because I knowed tha'd like to see it feed."

He knelt down by the sofa and took a feeding-bottle from his pocket.

"Come on, little 'un," he said, turning the small, woolly, white head with a gentle brown hand. "This is what tha's after.

Tha'll get more out o' this than tha' will out o' silk velvet coats. There now," and he pushed the rubber tip of the bottle into the nuzzling mouth and the lamb began to suck it with ravenous ecstasy.

After that there was no wondering what to say. By the time the lamb fell asleep questions poured forth, and Dickon answered them all. He told them how he had found the lamb just as the sun was rising three mornings ago. He had been standing on the moor listening to a skylark and watching him swing higher and higher into the blue, until he was only a speck in the heights of blue.

"I'd almost lost him but for his song an' I was wonderin' how a chap could hear it when it seemed as if he'd get out o' th' world in a minute–an' just then I heard somethin' else far off among th' gorse bushes. It was a weak bleatin', an' I knowed it was a new lamb as was hungry an' I knowed it wouldn't be hungry, if it hadn't lost its mother somehow, so I set of searchin'. Eh! i did have a look for it. I went in an' out among th' gorse bushes an' round an' round an' I always seemed to take th' wrong turnin'. But at last I seed a bit o' white by a rock on top o' th' moor an' I climbed up an' found th' little 'u half dead wi' cold an' clemmin'."

While he talked, Soot flew solemnly in and out of the open window and cawed remarks about the scenery, while Nut and Shell made excursions into the big trees outside and ran up and down trunks and explored branches. Captain curled up near Dickon, who sat on the hearth-rug from preference.

They looked at the pictures in the gardening books and Dickon knew all the flowers by their country names and knew exactly which ones were already growing in the secret garden.

"I couldna' say that there name," he said, pointing to one under which was written "Aquilegia", "but us calls that a columbine, an' that there one It's a snapdragon and they both grow wild in hedges, but these is garden ones an' they're bigger and grander. There's some big clumps o' columbine in th' garden. They'll look like a bed o' blue an' white butterflies flutterin' when they're out."

"I'm going to see them," cried Colin. "I am going to see them!"

"Aye, that tha' mun," said Mary quite seriously. "An' tha' munnot lose no time about it."

CHAPTER 20

"I SHALL LIVE FOR EVER–AND EVER–AND EVER!"

But they were obliged to wait more than a week because first thee came some very windy days and then Colin was threatened with a cold, which two things happening one after the other would no doubt have thrown him into a rage, but that there was so much careful and mysterious planning to do and almost every day Dickon came in, if only for a few minutes, to talk about what was happening on the moor and in the lanes and hedges and on the borders of streams. The things he had to tell about otters' and badgers' and water-rats' houses, not to mention birds' nests and field-mice and their burrows, were enough to make you almost tremble with excitement, when you heard all the intimate details from an animal charmer and realized with what thrilling eagerness and anxiety the whole busy underworld was working.

"They're same as us," said Dickon, "only they have to build their homes every year. An' it keeps 'em so busy they fair scuffle to get 'em done."

The most absorbing thing, however, was the preparations to be made before Colin could be transported with sufficient secrecy to the garden. No one must see the chair-carriage and Dickon and Mary after they turned a certain corner of the shrubbery and entered upon the wall outside the ivied walls. As each day passed, Colin had become more and more fixed in his feeling that the mystery surrounding the garden was one of its greatest charms. Nothing must spoil that. No one must ever expect that they had a secret. People must think that he was simply going out with Mary and Dickon because he liked them and did not object to their looking at him. They had long and quite delightful talks about their work. They would go up this path and down that one and cross the other and go round among the fountain flower-beds as if they were looking at the "bedding out plants" the head gardener, Mr. Roach, had been having arranged. That would seem such a rational thing to do that no one would think it at all mysterious. They would turn into the shrubbery walks and lose themselves until they came to the long walls. It was almost as seriously and elaborately thought out as the plans of march made by great generals in time of war.

Rumours of the new and curious things which were occurring in the invalid's apartments had, of course, filtered through the servants' hall into the stableyards and out among the gardeners, but, notwithstanding this, Mr. Roach was startled one day when he received orders from Master Colin's room to the effect that he must report himself in the apartment no outsider had ever seen, as the invalid himself desired-to speak to him.

"Well, well," he said to himself, as he hurriedly changed his coat, "what's to do now? His Royal Highness that wasn't to be looked at calling up a man he's never set eyes on."

Mr. Roach was not without curiosity. He had never caught even a glimpse of the boy and had heard a dozen exaggerated stories about his uncanny looks and ways and his insane tempers. The thing he had heard oftenest was that he might die at any moment and there had been numerous fanciful descriptions of a humped back and helpless limbs, given by people who had never seen him.

"Things are changing in this house, Mr. Roach," said Mrs. Medlock, as she led him up the back staircase to the corridor on to which opened the hitherto mysterious chamber.

"Let's hope they're changing for the better," Mrs. Medlock, he answered.

"They couldn't well change for the worse," she continued; "and queer as it all is, there's them as finds their duties made a lot easier to stand up under. Don't you be surprised, Mr.

Roach, If you find yourself in the middle of a menagerie and Martha Sowerby's Dickon more at home than you or me could ever be."

There really was a sort of Magic about Dickon as Mary always privately believed. When Mr. Roach heard his name he smiled quite leniently.

"He'd be at home in Buckingham Palace or at the bottom of a coal mine," he said. "And yet it's not impudence, either. He's just fine, is that lad."

It was perhaps well he had been prepared or he might have been startled. When the bedroom door was opened a large crow, which seemed quite at home perched on the high back of a carven chair, announced the entrance of a visitor by saying "Caw-caw" quite loudly. In spite of Mrs. Medlock's warning, Mr. Roach only just escaped being sufficiently undignified to jump backwards.

The young rajah was neither in bed nor on his sofa. He was sitting in an arm-chair and a young lamb was standing by him shaking its tail in feeding-lamb fashion as Dickon knelt giving it milk from its bottle. A squirrel was perched on Dickon's bent back attentively nibbling a nut. The little girl from India was sitting on a big footstool looking on.

"Here is Mr. Roach, Master Colin," said Mrs. Medlock.

The young rajah turned and looked his servitor over–at least that was what the head gardener felt happened.

"Oh, you are Roach, are you?" he said. "I sent for you to give you some very important orders."

"Very good, sir," answered Roach, wondering if he was to receive instructions to fell all the oaks in the park or to transform the orchards into water-gardens.

"I am going out in my chair this afternoon," said Colin. "If the fresh air agrees with me I may go out every day. When I go, none of the gardeners are to be anywhere near the Long Walk by the garden walls. No one is to be there. I shall go out about two o'clock and everyone must keep away until I send word that they may go back to their work."

"Very good, sir," replied Mr. Roach, much relieved to hear that the oaks might remain and that the orchards were safe.

"Mary," said Colin, turning to her, "what is that thing you say in India when you have finished talking and want people to go?"

"You say, 'You have my permission to go,'" answered Mary.

The rajah waved his hand.

"You have my permission to go, Roach," he said. "But remember, this is very important."

"Caw-caw!" remarked the crow hoarsely, but not impolitely.

"Very good, sir. Thank you, sir," said Mr. Roach, and Mrs. Medlock took him out of the room.

Outside in the corridor, being a rather good-natured man, he smiled until he almost laughed.

"My word!" he said, "he's got a lordly way with him, hasn't he? You'd think he was a whole Royal Family rolled into one–Prince Consort and all."

"Eh!" protested Mrs. Medlock, "we've had to let him trample all over every one o£ w ever since he had feet, and he thinks that's what folks was born for."

"Perhaps he'll grow out of it, if he lives," suggested Mr. Roach.

"Well, there's one thing pretty sure," said Mrs. Medlock. "If he does live and that Indian child stays here, I'll warrant she teaches him that the whole orange does not belong to him, as Susan Sowerby says. And he'll be likely to find out the size of his own quarter."

Inside the room Colin was leaning back on his cushions.

"It's all safe now," he said." And this afternoon I shall see it–this afternoon I shall be in it!"

Dickon went back to the garden with his creatures, and Mary stayed with Colin. She did not think he looked tired, but he was very quiet before their lunch came, and he was quiet while they were eating it. She wondered why, and asked him about it.

"What big eyes you've got, Colin," she said. "When you are thinking they get as big as saucers. What are you thinking about now?"

"I can't help thinking about what it will look like," he answered.

"The garden?" asked Mary.

"The springtime," he said. "I was thinking that I've really never seen it before. I scarcely ever went out, and when I did go I ever looked at it. I didn't even think about it."

"I never saw it in India, because there wasn't any," said Mary.

Shut in and morbid as his life had been, Colin had more imagination than she had, and at least he had spent a good deal of time looking at wonderful books and pictures.

"That morning when you ran in and said 'It's come! It's come!' you made me feel quite queer. It sounded as if things were coming with a great procession and big bursts and wafts of music. I've a picture like it in one of my books–crowds of lovely people and children with garlands and branches with blossoms on them, everyone laughing and dancing and crowding and playing on pipes. That was why I said, 'Perhaps we shall hear golden trumpets,' and told you to throw open the window."

"How funny!" said Mary. "That's really just what it feels like. And if all the flowers and leaves and green things and birds, and wild creatures danced past at once, what a crowd it would be! I'm sure they'd dance and sing and flute and that would be the wafts of music."

They both laughed, but it was not because the idea was laughable, but because they both so liked it.

A little later the nurse made Colin ready. She noticed that instead of lying like a log while his clothes were put on, he sat up and made some efforts to help himself, and he talked and laughed with Mary all the time.

"This is one of his good days, sir," she said to Dr. Craven, who dropped in to inspect him. "He's in such good spirits that it makes him stronger."

"I'll call in again later in the afternoon, after he has come in," said Dr. Craven. "I must see how the going out agrees with him. I wish," in a very low voice, "that he would let you go with him."

"I'd rather give up the case this moment, sir, than even stay here while it's suggested," answered the nurse with sudden firmness.

"I hadn't really decided to suggest it," said the doctor, with his slight nervousness. "We'll try the experiment. Dickon's a lad I'd trust with a new-born child."

The strongest footman in the house carried Colin downstairs and put him in his wheeled-chair, near which Dickon waited outside. After the manservant had arranged his rugs and cushions, the rajah waved his hand to him and to the nurse.

"You have my permission to go," he said, and they both disappeared quickly, and it must be confessed, giggled, when they were safely inside the house.

Dickon began to push the wheeled-chair slowly and steadily. Mistress Mary walked beside it and Colin leaned back and lifted his face to the sky. The arch of it looked very high and the small snowy clouds seemed like white birds floating on outspread wings below its crystal blueness. The wind swept in soft big breaths down from the moor and was strange with a wild clear-scented sweetness. Colin kept lifting his thin chest to draw it in, and his big eyes looked as if it were they which were listening–listening, instead of his ears.

"There are so many sounds of singing and humming and calling out," he said. "What is that scent the puffs of wind bring?"

"It's gorse on th' moor that's openin' out," answered Dickon. "Eh! th' bees are at it wonderful today."

Not a human creature was to be caught sight of in the paths they took. In fact every gardener or gardener's lad had been witched away. But they wound in and out among the shrubbery and out and round the fountain beds, following their carefully planned route for the mere mysterious pleasure of it. But when at last they turned into the Long Walk by the ivied walls, the excited sense of an approaching thrill made them, for some curious reason they could not have explained, begin to speak in whispers.

"This is it," breathed Mary. "This is where I used to walk up and down and wonder and wonder."

"Is it?" cried Colin, and his eyes began to search the ivy with eager curiousness. "But I can see nothing," he whispered. "There is no door."

"That's what I thought," said Mary.

Then there was a lovely, breathless silence and the chair wheeled on.

"That is the garden where Ben Weatherstaff works," said Mary.

"Is it?" said Colin.

A few yards more and Mary whispered again.

"This is where the robin flew over the wall," she said.

"Is it?" cried Colin. "Oh! I wish he'd come again!"

"And that," said Mary with solemn delight, pointing under a big lilac bush, "is where he perched on the little heap of earth and showed me the key."

Then Colin sat up.

"Where? Where? There?" he cried, and his eyes were as big as the wolf's in Red Hiding Hood, when Red Riding Hood felt called upon to remark on them. Dickon stood still and the wheeled-chair stopped.

"And this," said Mary, stepping on to the bed close to the ivy, "is where I went to talk to him when he chirped at me from the top of the wall. And this is the ivy the wind blew back," and she took hold of the hanging green curtain.

"Oh! is it–" gasped Colin.

"And here is the handle, and here is the door. Dickon, push him in–push him in quickly!"

And Dickon did it with one strong, steady, splendid push.

But Colin had actually dropped back against his cushions, even though he gasped with delight, and he had covered his eyes with his hands and held them there, shutting out everything until they were inside and the chair stopped as if by magic and the door was closed. Not till then did he take them away and look round and round and round as Dickon and Mary had done. And over walls and earth and trees and swinging sprays and tendrils the fair green veil of tender little leaves had crept, and in the grass under the trees and the grey urns in the alcoves and here and there everywhere, were touches or splashes of gold and purple and white and the trees were showing pink and snow above his head, and there were fluttering of wings and faint sweet pipes and humming and scents and scents. And the sun fell warm upon his face like a hand with a lovely touch. And in wonder Mary and Dickon stood and stared at him. He looked so strange and different because a pink glow of colour had actually crept all over him–ivory face and neck and hands and all.

"I shall get well! I shall get well!" he cried out. "Mary! Dickon! I shall get well! And I shall live for ever and ever and ever!"

CHAPTER 21

BEN WEATHERSTAFF

One of the strange things about living in the world is that it is only now and then one is quite sure one is going to live for ever and ever and ever. One knows it sometimes when one gets up at the tender, solemn dawn-time and goes out and stands alone and throws one's head far back and looks up and up and watches the pale sky slowly changing and flushing and marvellous unknown things happening until the East almost makes one cry out and one's heart stands still at the strange, unchanging majesty of the rising of the sun–which has been happening every morning for thousands and thousands and thousands of years. One knows it then for a moment or so. And one knows it sometimes when one stands by oneself in a wood at sunset and the mysterious deep gold stillness slanting through and under the branches seems to be saying slowly again and again something one cannot quite hear, however much one tries. Then sometimes the immense quiet of the dark-blue at night with millions of stars waiting and watching makes one sure; and sometimes a sound of far-off music makes it true; and sometimes a look in someone's eyes.

And it was like that with Colin when he first saw and heard and felt the springtime inside the four high walls of a hidden garden. That afternoon the whole world seemed to devote itself to being perfect and radiantly beautiful and kind to one boy. Perhaps out of pure heavenly goodness the spring came and crowded everything it possibly could into that one place. More than once Dickon paused in what he was doing and stood still with a sort of growing wonder in his eyes, shaking his head softly.

"Eh! It is graidely," he said. "I'm twelve goin' on thirteen an' there's a lot o' afternoons in thirteen years, but seems to me like I never seed one as graidely as this 'ere."

"Aye, it is a graidely one," said Mary, and she sighed for

mere joy. "I'll warrant it's th' graideliest one as ever was in this world."

"Does tha' think," said Colin, with dreamy carefulness, "as happen it was made like this 'ere all o' purpose for me?"

"My word!" cried Mary admiringly, "that there is a bit o' good Yorkshire. Tha'rt shapin' first rate–that–tha' art."

And delight reigned.

They drew the chair under the plum-tree, which was snow-white with blossoms and musical with bees. It was like a king's canopy, a fairy king's. There were flowering cherry-trees near and apple-trees T whose buds were pink and white, and here and there one had burst t open wide. Between the blossoming branches of the canopy bits of blue sky looked down like wonderful eyes.

Mary and Dickon worked a little here and there and Colin watched them. They brought him things to look at–buds which were opening, buds which were tight closed, bits of twig whose leaves were just showing green, the feather of a woodpecker which had dropped on the grass, the empty shell of some bird early hatched. Dickon pushed the chair slowly round and round the garden, stopping every other moment to let him look at wonders springing out of the earth or trailing down from trees. It was like being taken in state round the country of a magic king and queen and shown all the mysterious riches it contained.

"I wonder if we shall see the robin?" said Colin.

"Tha'll see him often enow after a bit," answered Dickon. "When th' eggs hatches out th' little chap he'll be kep' so busy it'll make his head swim. Tha'll see him flyin' backward an' for'ard carryin' worms nigh as big as himsel' an' that much noise goin' on in th' nest when he gets there as fair flusters him so as he scarce knows which big mouth to drop th' &t piece in. An' gapin' beaks an' squawks on every side. Mother says as when she sees th' work a robin has to keep them gapin' beaks filled, she feels like she was a lady with nothin' to do. She says she's seen th' little chaps when it seemed like th' sweat must be droppin' off 'em, though folk can't see it."

This made them giggle so delightedly that they were obliged to cover their mouths with their hands, remembering that they must not be heard. Colin had been instructed as to the law of whispers and low voices several days before. He liked the mysteriousness of it and did his best, but in the midst of excited enjoyment it is rather difficult never to laugh above a whisper.

Every moment of the afternoon was full of new things and every hour the sunshine grew more golden. The wheeled-chair had been drawn back under the canopy and Dickon had sat down on the grass and had just drawn out his pipe when Colin saw something he had not had time to notice before.

"That's a very old tree over there, isn't it?" he said.

Dickon looked across the grass at the tree and Mary looked and there was a brief moment of stillness.

"Yes," answered Dickon, after it, and his low voice had a very gentle sound.

Mary gazed at the tree and thought.

"The branches are quite grey and there's not a single leaf anywhere," Colin went on. "It's quite dead, isn't it?"

"Aye," admitted Dickon. "But them roses as has climbed all over it will near hide every bit o' th' dead wood when they're full o' leaves an' flowers. It won't look dead then. It'll be th' prettiest of all."

Mary still gazed at the tree and thought.

"It looks as if a big branch had been broken off," said Colin. "I wonder how it was done."

"It's been done many a year," answered Dickon. "Eh!" with a sudden relieved start and laying his hand on Colin, "Look at that robin! There he is! He's been foragin' for his mate."

Colin was almost too late, but he just caught sight of him, the flash of red-breasted bird with something in his beak. He darted through the greenness and into the close-grown corner and out of sight. Colin leaned back on his cushion again, laughing a little.

"He's taking her tea to her. Perhaps it's five o'clock. I think I'd like some tea myself."

And so they were safe.

"It was Magic which sent the robin," said Mary secretly to Dickon afterwards. "I know it was Magic." For both she and Dickon had been afraid Colin might ask something about the tree whose branch had broken off ten years ago, and they had talked it over together ad Dickon had stood and rubbed his head in a troubled way.

"We mun look as if it wasn't no different from th' other trees," he had said. "We couldn't never tell him how it broke, poor lad. If he says anything about it we mun–we mun try to look cheerful."

"Aye, that we mun," had answered Mary.

But she had not felt as if she looked cheerful when she gazed at the tree. She wondered and wondered in those few moments if there was any reality in that other thing Dickon had said. He had gone on rubbing his rust-red hair in a puzzled way, but a nice comforted look had begun to grow in his blue eyes.

"Mrs Craven was a very lovely young lady," he had gone on rather hesitatingly. "An' Mother she thinks maybe she's about Misselthwaite many a time lookin' after Mester Colin, same as all mothers do when they're took out o' th' world. They have to come back, tha' sees. Happen she's been in the garden an' happen it was her set us to work, an' told us to bring him here."

Mary had thought he meant something about Magic. She was a great believer in Magic. Secretly she quite believed hat Dickon worked Magic, of course, good Magic, on everything near him and that was why people liked him so much and wild creatures knew he was their friend. She wondered, indeed, if it were not possible that his gift had brought the robin just at the right moment when Colin asked that dangerous question. She felt that his Magic was working all the afternoon and making Colin look an entirely different boy. It did not seem possible that he could be the crazy creature who had screamed and beaten and bitten his pillow. Even his ivory whiteness seemed to change. The faint glow of colour which had shown on his face and neck and hands when he first got inside the garden really never quite died away. He looked as if he were made of flesh instead of ivory or wax.

They saw the robin carry food to his mate two or three times, and it was so suggestive of afternoon tea that Colin felt they must have some.

"Go and make one of the menservants bring some in a basket to the rhododendron walk," he said. "And then you and Dickon can bring it here."

It was an agreeable idea; easily carried out, and when the white cloth was spread upon the grass, with hot tea and buttered toast and crumpets, a delightfully hungry meal was eaten, and several birds on domestic errands paused to inquire what was going on and were led into investigating crumbs with great activity. Nut and Shell whisked up trees with pieces of cake, and Soot took the entire half of a buttered crumpet into a corner and pecked at and examined and turned it over and made hoarse remarks about it until he decided to swallow it all joyfully in one gulp.

The afternoon was dragging towards its mellow hour. The sun was deepening the gold of its lances, the bees were going home and the birds were flying past less often. Dickon and Mary were sitting on the grass, the tea-basket was repacked ready to be taken back to the house, and Colin was lying against his cushions with his heavy locks pushed back from his forehead and his face looking quite a natural colour.

"I don't want this afternoon to go," he said "but I shall come back tomorrow, and the day after, and the day after, and the day after."

"You'll get plenty of fresh air, won't you?" said Mary.

"I'm going to get nothing else," he answered. "I've seen the spring now and I'm going to see the summer. I'm going to see everything grow here. I'm going to grow here myself."

"That tha' will," said Dickon. "Us'll have thee walkin' about here an' diggin' same as other folk afore long."

Colin flushed tremendously.

"Walk!" he said. "Dig! Shall I?"

Dickon's glance at him was delicately cautious. Neither he nor Mary had ever asked if anything was the matter with his legs.

"For sure tha' will," he said stoutly. Tha'–tha's got legs o' thine own, same as other folks!"

Mary was rather frightened until she heard Colin's answer.

"Nothing really ails them," he said, "but they are so thin and weak. They shake so that I'm afraid to try to stand on them."

Both Mary and Dickon drew a relieved breath.

"When tha' stops bein' afraid tha'lt stand on 'em," Dickon said with renewed cheer. "An' tha'lt stop bein' afraid in a bit."

"I shall?" said Colin, and he lay still, as if he were wondering about things.

They were really very quiet for a little while. The sun was dropping lower. It was that hour when everything stills itself, and they really had had a busy and exciting afternoon. Colin looked as if he were resting luxuriously. Even the creatures had ceased moving about and had drawn together and were resting near them. Soot had perched on a low branch and drawn up one leg and dropped the grey film drowsily over his eyes. Mary privately thought he looked as if he might snore in a minute.

In the midst of this stillness it was rather startling when Colin half lifted his head and exclaimed in a loud, suddenly alarmed whisper:

"Who is that man?"

Dickon and Mary scrambled to their feet.

"Man?" they both cried in low, quick voices.

Colin pointed to the high wall.

"Look!" he whispered excitedly. "Just look!"

Mary and Dickon wheeled about and looked. There was Ben Weatherstaff's indignant face glaring at them over the wall from the top of a ladder! He actually shook his fist at Mary.

"If I wasn't a bachelor, an' tha' was a wench o' mine, he cried, "I'd give thee a hidin'!"

He mounted another step threateningly, as if it were his energetic intention to jump down and deal with her; but as she came towards him he evidently thought better of it and stood on the top step of his ladder shaking his fist down at her.

"I never thowt much o' thee!" he harangued, "I couldna' abide thee th' first time I set eyes on thee. A scrawny, butter-milk-faced young besom, always askin' questions an' pokin' tha' nose where it wasna' wanted. I never knowed how tha' got so thick wi' me. If it hadna' been for th' robin–drat him–"

"Ben Weatherstaff," called out Mary, finding her breath. She stood below him and called up to him with a sort of gasp. "Ben Weatherstaff, it was the robin who showed me the way!"

Then it did seem as if Ben really would scramble down on her side of the wall, he was so outraged.

"Tha' young bad 'un!" he called down to her. "Layin' tha' badness on a robin–not but what he's impidint enow for anythin'. Him showin' thee th' way! Him! Eh! tha' young nowt"–she could see his next words burst out because he was overpowered by curiosity– "however i' this world did tha' get in?"

"It was the robin who showed me the way," she protested ob:stinately. "He didn't know he was doing it, but he did. And I can't tell you from here, while you're shaking your fist at me."

He stopped shaking his fist very suddenly at that very moment and his jaw actually dropped as he stared over her head at something he saw coming over the grass towards him.

At the first sound of his torrent of words Colin had been so surprised that he had only sat up and listened as if he were spellbound. But in the midst of it he had recovered himself and beckoned imperiously to Dickon.

"Wheel me over there!" he commanded. "Wheel me quite close and stop right in front of him! "

And this, if you please, this is what Ben Weatherstaff beheld and which made his jaw drop. A wheeled-chair with luxurious cushions and robes which came towards him looking rather like some sort of state coach because a young rajah leaned back in it with royal command in his great, black-rimmed eyes and a thin white hand extended haughtily towards him. And it stopped right under Ben Weatherstaff's nose. It was really no wonder his mouth dropped open.

"Do you know who I am?" demanded the rajah.

How Ben Weatherstaff stared! His red old eyes fixed themselves on what was before him as if he were seeing a ghost. He gazed and gazed and gulped a lump down his throat and did not say a word.

"Do you know who I am?" demanded Colin still more imperiously. "Answer! "

Ben Weatherstaff put his gnarled hand up and passed it over his eyes and over his forehead and then he did answer in a queer, shaky voice.

"Who tha' art?" he said. "Aye, that I do–wi' tha' mother's eyes starin' at me out o' tha' face. Lord knows how tha' come here. But tha'rt th' poor cripple."

Colin forgot that he had ever had a back. His face flushed scarlet and he sat bolt upright.

"I'm not a cripple!" he cried out furiously, "I'm not!"

"He's not!" cried Mary, almost shouting up the wall in her

fierce indignation. "He's not got a lump as big as a pin! I looked and there was none there–not one!"

Ben Weatherstaff passed his hand over his forehead again and gazed as if he could never gaze enough. His hand shook and his mouth shook and his voice shook. He was an ignorant old man and a tactless old man and he could only remember the things he had heard.

"Tha'-tha' hasn't got a crooked back?" he said hoarsely.

"No!" shouted Colin.

"Tha'–tha' hasn't got crooked legs?" quavered Ben more hoarsely yet.

It was too much. The strength which Colin usually threw into his tantrums rushed through him now in a new way. Never yet had he been accused of crooked legs–even in whispers–and the perfectly simple belief in their existence which was revealed by Ben Weatherstaff's voice was more than rajah flesh and blood could endure. His anger and insulted pride made him forget everything but this one moment, and filled him with power he had never known before, an almost unnatural strength.

"Come here!" he shouted to Dickon, and he actually began to tear the coverings off his lower limbs and disentangle himself. "Come here! Come here! This minute!"

Dickon was by his side in a second. Mary caught her breath in a short gasp and felt herself turn pale.

"He can do it! He can do it! He can do it! He can!" she gabbled over to herself under her breath as fast as she could.

There was a brief, fierce scramble, the rugs were tossed on to the ground, Dickon held Colin's arm, the thin legs were out, the thin feet were on the grass. Colin was standing upright–upright–as straight as an arrow and looking strangely tall–his head thrown back and his strange eyes flashing lightning.

"Look at me!" he flung up at Ben Weatherstaff. "Just look at me–you! Just look at me! "

He's as straight as I am," cried Dickon. He's as straight as any lad i' Yorkshire!"

What Ben Weatherstaff did Mary thought queer beyond measure. He choked and gulped and suddenly tears ran down his weather-wrinkled cheeks as he struck his old hands together.

"Eh!" he burst forth, th' lies folk tells! Tha'rt at thin as a lath an' as white as a wraith, but there's not a knob on thee. Tha'lt make a mon yet. God bless thee!"

Dickon held Colin's arms strongly, but the boy had not begun to falter. He stood straighter and straighter and looked Ben Weatherstaff in the face.

"I'm your master," he said, "when my father is away. And you are to obey me. This is my garden. Don't dare to say a word about it! You get down from that ladder and go out to the Long Walk and Miss Mary will meet you and bring you here. I want to talk to you. We did not want you, but now you will have to be in the secret. Be quick!"

Ben Weatherstaff's crabbed old face was still wet with that one queer rush of tears. It seemed as if he could not take his eyes from thin, straight Colin standing on his feet with his head thrown back.

"Eh! lad," he almost whispered. "Eh! my lad!" And then remembering himself he suddenly touched his hat gardener fashion and said, "Yes, sir! Yes, sir!" and obediently disappeared as he descended the ladder.

Chapter 22

WHEN THE SUN WENT DOWN

When his head was out of sight, Colin turned to Mary.

"Go and meet him," he said, and Mary flew across the grass to the door under the ivy.

Dickon was watching him with sharp eyes. There were scarlet spots on his cheeks and he looked amazing, but he showed no signs of falling.

"I can stand," he said, and his head was still held up and he said it quite grandly.

"I told thee tha' could as soon as tha' stopped bein' afraid," answered Dickon. "An' tha's stopped."

"Yes, I've stopped," said Colin.

Then suddenly he remembered something Mary had said.

"Are you making Magic?" he asked sharply.

Dickon's curly mouth spread in a cheerful grin.

"Tha's doin' Magic thysel'," he said. "It's same Magic as made these 'ere work out o' th' earth, and he touched with his thick boot to a clump of crocuses in the grass.

Colin looked down at them.

"Aye," he said slowly, "there couldna' be bigger Magic than that there–there couldna' be."

He drew himself up straighter than ever.

"I'm going to walk to that tree," he said, pointing to one a few feet away from him. "I'm going to be standing when Weatherstaff comes here. I can rest against the tree if I like. When I want to sit down I will sit down, but not before. Bring a rug from the chair."

He walked to the tree, and though Dickon held his arm he was wonderfully steady. When he stood against the tree trunk it was not too plain that he supported himself against it, and he still held himself so straight that he looked tall.

When Ben Weatherstaff came through the door in the wall he saw him standing there and he heard Mary muttering something under her breath.

"What art sayin'?" he asked rather testily, because he did not want his attention distracted from the long, thin, straight boy figure and proud face.

But she did not tell him. What she was saying was this:

"You can do it! You can do it! I told you you could! You can do it! You can do it! You *can*!"

She was saying it to Colin because she wanted to make Magic and keep him on his feet looking like that. She could not bear that he should give in before Ben Weatherstaff. He did not give ın. She was uplifted by a sudden feeling that he looked quite beautiful in spite of this thinness. He fixed his eyes on Ben Weatherstaff in his funny, imperious way.

"Look at me!" he commanded. "Look at me all over! Am I a hunchback? Have I got crooked legs?"

Ben Weatherstaff had not quite got over his emotion, but he had recovered a little and answered almost in his usual way.

"Not tha'," he said. "Nowt o' th' sort. What's tha' been doin' with thysel'-hidin' out o' sight an' lettin' folk think tha' was cripple an' half-witted?"

"Half-witted!" said Colin angrily. "Who thought that?"

"Lots o' fools," said Ben. "Th' world's full o' jackasses brayin' n' they bray nowt but lies. What did tha' shut thysel' up for?"

"Everyone thought I was going to die," said Colin shortly. "I'm not!"

And he said it with such decision Ben Weatherstaff looked him over, up and down, down and up.

"Tha' die!" he said with dry exultation. "Nowt o' th' sort. Tha's got too much pluck in thee. When I seed thee put tha' legs on th' ground in such a hurry I knowed tha' was all right. Sit thee down on th' rug a bit, young Mester, an' give me thy orders."

There was a queer mixture of crabbed tenderness and shrewd understanding in his manner.Mary had poured out speech as rapidly as she could as they had come down the Long Walk. The chief thing to be remembered, she had told him, was that Colin was getting well–getting well. The garden was doing it. No one must let him remember about having humps and dying.

The rajah condescended to seat himself on a rug under the tree.

"What work do you do in the gardens, Weatherstaff?" he inquired.

"Anythin' I'm told to do," answered old Ben. "I'm kep' on by favour-because she liked me."

"She?" said Colin.

"Tha' mother," answered Ben Weatherstaff.

"My mother?" said Colin, and he looked about him quietly. "This was her garden, wasn't it?"

"Aye, it was that!" and Ben Weatherstaff looked about him too. "She were main fond of it."

"It is my garden now. I am fond of it. I shall come here every day," announced Colin. "But it is to be a secret. My orders are that no one is to know that we come here. Dickon and my cousin have worked and made it come alive. I shall send for you sometimes to help–but you must come when no one can see you."

Ben Weatherstaff's face twisted itself into a dry old smile.

"I've come here before when no one saw me," he said.

"What!" exclaimed Colin. "When?"

"Th' last time I was here, rubbing his chin and looking round, "was about two year' ago."

"But no one has been in it for ten years!" cried Colin. "There was no door!"

"I'm no one," said old Ben dryly. "An' I didn't come through th' door, I come over th' wall. Th' rheumatics held me back th' last two year'."

"Tha' come an' did a bit o' prunin'!" cried Dickon. "I couldn't make out how it had been done."

"She was so fond of it–she was!" said Ben Weatherstaff slowly. "An' she was such a pretty young thing. She says to me once, 'Ben,' says she laughin', 'if ever I'm ill or if I go away you must take care of my roses.' When she did go away th' orders was no one was ever to come nigh. But I come," with grumpy obstinacy. "Over th' wall I come–until th' rheumatics stopped me–an' I did a bit of work once "year. She'd gave her order first."

"It wouldn't have been as wick as it is if tha' hadn't done it," said Dickon. "I did wonder."

"I'm glad you did it, Weatherstaff," said Colin. "You'll know how to keep the secret."

"Aye, I'll know, sir," answered Ben. "An' it'll be easier for a man wi' rheumatics to come in at th' door."

On the grass near the tree Mary had dropped her trowel. Colin stretched out his hand and took it up. An odd expression came into his face and he began to scratch at the earth. His thin hand was weak enough, but presently as they watched him–Mary with quite breathless interest–he drove the end of the trowel into the soil and turned some over.

"You can do it! You can do it!" said Mary to herself. "I tell you, you can!"

Dickon's round eyes were full of eager curiousness, but he

said not a word. Ben Weatherstaff looked on with interested face.

Colin persevered. After he had turned a few trowelfuls of soil he spoke exultantly to Dickon in his best Yorkshire.

"Tha' said as tha'd have me walkin' about here same as other folk–an' tha' said tha'd have me diggin'. I thowt tha' was just seein' to please me. This is only th' first day an' I've walked–an' here I am diggin'."

Ben Weatherstaff's mouth fell open again when he heard him, but he ended by chuckling.

"Eh!" he said, "that sounds as if tha'd got wits enow. Tha'rt a Yorkshire lad for sure. An' tha'rt diggin', too. How'd tha' like to plant a bit o' somethin? I can get thee a rose in a pot."

"Go and get it!" said Colin, digging excitedly. "Quick! Quick!"

It was done quickly enough indeed. Ben Weatherstaff went his way forgetting rheumatics. Dickon took his spade and dug the hole deeper and wider than a new digger with thin hands could make it. Mary slipped out to run and bring back a watering-can. When Dickon had deepened the hole, Colin went to turning the soft earth over and over. He looked up at the sky, flushed and glowing with the strangely new exercise, slight as it was.

"I want to do it before the sun goes quite–quite down," he said.

Mary thought that perhaps the sun held back a few minutes just on purpose. Ben Weatherstaff brought the rose in its pot from the greenhouse. He hobbled over the grass as fast as he could. He had begun to be excited, too. He knelt down by the hole and broke the pot from the mould.

"Here, lad," he said, handing the plant to Colin. "Set it in the earth thysel' same as th' king does when he goes to a new place."

The thin white hands shook a little and Colin's flush grew deeper as he set the rose in the mould and held it while old Ben made firm the earth. It was filled in and pressed down and made steady. Mary was leaning forward on her hands and knees. Soot had flown down and marched forward to see what was being done. Nut and Shell chattered about it from a cherry-tree.

"It's planted!" said Colin at last. "And the sun is only slipping over the edge. Help me up, Dickon. I want to be standing when it goes. That's part of the Magic."

And Dickon helped him, and the Magic–or whatever it was–so gave him strength that when the sun did slip over the edge and end the strange, lovely afternoon for them, there he actually stood on his two feet–laughing.

CHAPTER 23

MAGIC

Dr. Craven had been waiting some time at the house when they returned to it. He had indeed begun to wonder if it might not be wise to send someone out to explore the garden paths. When Colin was brought back to his room, the poor man looked him over seriously.

"You should not have stayed so long," he said. "You must not over-exert yourself."

"I am not tired at all," said Colin. "It has made me well. Tomorrow I am going out in the morning as well as in the afternoon."

"I am not sure that I can allow it," answered Dr. Craven. "I am afraid it would not be wise."

"It would not be wise to try to stop me," said Colin quite seriously. "I am going."

Even Mary had found out that one of Colin's chief peculiarities was that he did not know in the least what a rude little brute he was with his way of ordering people about. He had lived on a sort of desert island all his life and as he had been the king of it he had made his own manners and had had no one to compare himself with. Mary had indeed been rather like him herself, and since she had been at Misselthwaite had gradually discovered that her own manners had not been of the kind which is usual or popular. Having made this discovery, she naturally thought it of enough interest to communicate to Colin. So she sat and looked at him curiously for a few minutes after Dr. Craven had gone. She wanted to make him ask her why she was doing it, and of course she did.

"What are you looking at me for?" he said.

"I'm thinking that I am rather sorry for Dr. Craven."

"So am I," said Colin calmly, but not without an air of some satisfaction. "He won't get Misselthwaite at all now I'm not going to die."

"I'm sorry for him because of that, of course," said Mary, "but I was thinking just then that it must have been very horrid to have had to be polite for ten years to a boy who was always rude. I would never have done it."

"Am I rude?" Colin inquired undisturbedly.

"If you had been his own boy and he had been a slapping sort of man," said Mary, "he would have slapped you."

"But he daren't," said Colin.

"No, he daren't," answered Mistress Mary, thinking the thing out quite without prejudice. Nobody ever dared to do anything you didn't like–because you were going to die and things like that. You were such a poor thing."

'But," announced Colin stubbornly, "I am not going to be a poor thing. I won't let people think I'm one. I stood on my feet this afternoon."

"It is always having your own way that has made you so queer," Mary went on, thinking aloud.

Colin turned his head, frowning.

"Am I queer?" he demanded.

"Yes," answered Mary, "very. But you needn't be cross," she added impartially, "because so am I queer–and so is Ben Weatherstaff. But I am not as queer as I was before I began to like people and before I found the garden."

"I don't want to be queer," said Colin. "I am not going to be," and he frowned again with determination.

He was a very proud boy. He lay thinking for a while and then Mary saw his beautiful smile begin and gradually change his whole face.

"I shall stop being queer," he said, "if I go everyday to the garden. There is Magic in there–good Magic, you know, Mary, I am sure there is."

"So am I," said Mary.

"Even if it isn't real Magic," Colin said, "we can pretend it is. *Something* is there–*something*!"

"It's Magic," said Mary, "but not black. It's as white as snow."

They always called it Magic, and indeed it seemed like it in the months that followed–the wonderful months–the radiant months–the amazing ones. Oh! the things which happened in that garden! If you have never had a garden, you cannot understand, and if you have had a garden, you will know that it would take a whole book to describe all that came to pass there. At first it seemed that green things would never cease pushing their way through the earth, in the grass, in the beds, even in the crevices of the walls. Then the green things began to show buds, and the buds began to unfurl and show colour, every shade of blue, every shade of purple, every tint and hue of crimson. In its happy days flowers had been tucked away into every inch and hole and corner. Ben Weatherstaff had seen it done and had himself scraped out mortar from between the bricks of the wall and made pockets of earth for lovely clinging things to grow on. Iris and white lilies rose out of the grass in sheaves, and the green alcoves filled themselves with amazing armies of the blue and white flower lances of tall delphiniums or columbines or campanulas.

"She was main fond o' them–she was," Ben Weatherstaff said. "She liked them things as was allus pointin' up to th' blue sky, she used to tell. Not as she was one o' them as looked down on th' earth–not her. She loved it, but she said as th' blue sky looked so joyful."

The seeds Dickon and Mary had planted grew as if fairies had tended them. Satiny poppies of all tints danced in the breeze by the score, gaily defying flowers which had lived in the garden for years, and which it might be confessed seemed rather to wonder how such new people had got there. And the roses–the roses! Rising out of the grass, tangled round the sundial, wreathing the tree-trunks, and hanging from their branches, climbing up the walls and spreading over them with long garlands falling in cascades–they came alive day by day, hour by hour. Fair, fresh leaves, and buds–tiny at first, but swelling and working Magic until they burst and uncurled into cups of scent delicately spilling themselves over their brims and filling the garden air.

Colin saw it all, watching each change as it took place. Every morning he was brought out and every hour of each day, when it didn't rain, he spent in the garden. Even grey days pleased him. He would lie on the grass "watching things growing," he said. If you watched long enough, he declared, you could see buds unsheathe themselves. Also you could make the acquaintance of strange, busy insect things running about on various unknown but evidently serious errands, sometimes carrying tiny scraps of straw or feather or food, or climbing blades of grass as if they were trees from whose tops one could look out to explore the country. A mole throwing up its mound at the end of its burrow and making its way out at last with the long-nailed paws, which looked so like elfish hands, had absorbed him one whole morning. Ants' ways, beetles' ways, bees' ways, frogs' ways, birds' ways, plants' ways, gave him a new world to explore, and when Dickon revealed them all and added foxes' ways, otters' ways, ferrets' ways, squirrels' ways, and trouts' and water-rats' and badgers' ways, there was no end to the things to talk about and think over.

And this was not the half of the Magic. The fact that he had really once stood on his feet had set Colin thinking tremendously, and when Mary told him of the spell she had worked, he was excited and approved of it greatly. He talked of it constantly.

"Of course, there must be lots of Magic in the world," he said wisely one day, "but people don't know what it is like or how to make it. Perhaps the beginning is just to say nice things are going to happen until you make them happen. I am going to try an experiment."

The next morning when they went to the secret garden, he sent at once for Ben Weatherstaff. Ben came as quickly as he could, and found the rajah standing on his feet under a tree and looking very grand, but also very beautifully smiling.

"Good morning, Ben Weatherstaff," he said. "I want you and Dickon and Miss Mary to stand in a row and listen to me because I am going to tell you something very important."

"Aye, aye, sir!" answered Ben Weatherstaff, touching his forehead. (One of the long-concealed charms of Ben Weatherstaff was that in his boyhood he had once run away to sea and had made voyages. So he could reply like a sailor.)

"I am going to try a scientific experiment," explained the rajah. "When I grow up I am going to make great scientific discoveries and I am going to begin now with this experiment."

"Aye, aye, sir!" said Ben Weatherstaff promptly, though this was the first time he had heard of great scientific discoveries.

It was the first time Mary had heard of them, either, but even at this stage she had begun to realize that, queer as he was, Colin had read about a great many singular things and was somehow a very convincing sort of boy. When he held up his head and fixed his strange eyes on you, it seemed as if you believed him almost in spite of yourself, though he was only ten years old–going on eleven. At this moment he was especially convincing because he suddenly felt the fascination of actually making a sort of speech like a grown-up person.

"The great scientific discoveries I am going to make," he went on, "will be about Magic. Magic is a great thing, and scarcely anyone knows anything about it except a few people in old books–and Mary a little, because she was born in India, where there are fakirs. I believe Dickon knows some Magic, but perhaps he doesn't know he knows it. He charms animals and people. I would never have let him come to see me if he had not been an animal-charmer–which is a boy-charmer, too, because a boy is an animal. I am sure there is Magic in everything, only we have not sense enough to get hold of it and make it do things for us–like electricity and horses and steam."

This sounded so imposing that Ben Weatherstaff became quite excited and really could not keep still.

"Aye, aye, sir," he said, and he began to stand up quite straight.

"When Mary found this garden it looked quite dead," the orator proceeded. "Then something began pushing things up out of the soil and making things out of nothing. One day things weren't there and mother they were. I had never watched things before, and it made me feel very curious. Scientific people are always curious, and I am going to be scientific. I keep saying to myself: 'What is it? What is it?' It's something. It can't be nothing! I don't know its name, so I call it Magic. I have never seen the sun rise, but Mary and Dickon have, and from what they tell me I am sure that is Magic, too. Something pushes it up and draws it. Sometimes since I've been in the garden I've looked up through the trees at the sky and I have had a strange feeling of being happy as if something were pushing and drawing in my chest and making me breathe fast. Magic is always pushing and drawing and making things out of nothing. Everything is made out of Magic, leaves and trees, flowers and birds, badgers and foxes and squirrels and people. So it must be all around us. In this garden–in all the places. The Magic in this garden has made me stand up and know I am going to live to be a man. I am going to make the scientific experiment of trying to get some and put it in myself and make it push and draw me and make me strong. I don't know how to do it, but I think that if you keep thinking about it and calling it, perhaps it will come. Perhaps that is the first baby way to get it. When I was going to try to stand that first time, Mary kept saying to herself as fast as she could, 'You can do it! You can do it!' and I did. I had to try myself at the same time, of course, but her Magic helped me–and so did Dickon's. Every morning and evening and as often in the day-time as I can remember I am going to say, 'Magic is in me! Magic is making me well! I am going to be as strong as Dickon, as strong as Dickon!' And you must all do it, too. Tat is my experiment. Will you help, Ben Weatherstaff?"

"Aye, aye, sir!" said Ben Weatherstaff. "Aye, aye!"

"If you keep doing it every day as regularly as soldiers go through drill, we shall see what will happen and find out if the experiment succeeds. You learn things by saying them over and over and thinking about them until they stay in your mind for ever, and I think it will be the same with Magic. If you keep calling it to come to you and help you, it will get to be part of you and it will stay and do things."

"I once heard an officer in India tell my mother that there were fakirs who said words over and over thousands of times," said Mary.

"I've heard Jem Fettleworth's wife say th' same thing over

thousands o' times—callin' Jem a drunken brute," said Ben Weatherstaff dryly. "Summat allus comes o' that, sure enough. He gave her a good hidin' an' went to th' Blue Lion an' got as drunk as a lord."

Colin drew his brows together and thought a few minutes. Then he cheered up.

"Well," he said, "you see something did come of it. She used the wrong Magic until she made him beat her. If she'd used the right Magic and had said something nice, perhaps he wouldn't have got as drunk as a lord and perhaps—perhaps he might have brought her a new bonnet."

Ben Weatherstaff chuckled and there was shrewd admiration in his little old eyes.

"Tha'rt a clever lad as well as a straight-legged one, Mester Colin," he said. "Next time I see Bess Fettleworth I'll give her a bit of a hint o' what Magic will do for her. She'd be rare an' pleased if th' scientific 'experiment; worked—an' so 'ud Jem."

Dickon had stood listening to the lecture, his round.eyes shining with curious delight. Nut and $hell were on his shoulders, and he held a long-eared, white rabbit in his arm and stroked and stroked it softly while it laid its ears along its back and enjoyed itself.

"Do you think the experiment will work?" Colin asked him, wondering what he was thinking. He so often wondered what Dickon was thinking when he saw him looking at him or at one of his "creatures" with his happy, wide smile.

He smiled now, and his smile was wider than usual.

"Aye," he answered, "that I do. It'll work same as th' seeds do when th' sun shines on 'em. It'll work for sure. Shall us begin it now?"

Colin was delighted and so was Mary. Fired by recollections of fakirs and devotees in illustrations, Colin suggested that they should all sit cross-legged under the tree, which made a canopy.

"It will be like sitting in a sort of temple," said Colin. "I'm rather tired and I want to sit down."

"Eh!" said Dickon, "tha' mustn't begin by sayin' tha'rt tired. Tha' might spoil th' Magic."

Colin turned and looked at him—into his innocent, round eyes.

"That's true," he said slowly. "I must only think of the Magic."

It all seemed most majestic and mysterious when they sat down in their circle. Ben Weatherstaff felt as if he had somehow been led into appearing at a prayer-meeting. Ordinarily he was very fixed in being what he called "agen' prayer-meetin's", but this being the rajah's affair, he did not resent it, and was, indeed, inclined to be gratified at being called upon to assist. Mistress Mary felt solemnly enraptured. Dickon held his rabbit in his arm, and perhaps he made some charmer's signal no one heard, for when he sat down, cross-legged like the rest, the crow, the fox, the squirrels, and the lamb slowly drew near and made part of the circle, settling each into a place of rest as if of their own desire.

"The 'creatures' have come," said Colin gravely. "They want to help us."

Colin really looked quite beautiful, Mary thought. He held his head high as if he felt like a sort of priest, and his strange eyes had a wonderful look in them. The light shone on him through the tree canopy.

"Now we will begin," he said. "Shall we sway backwards and forwards, Mary, as if we were dervishes?"

"I canna' do no swayin' back'ard and for'ard," said Ben Weatherstaff. I've got th' rheumatics."

"The Magic will take them away," said Colin in a High Priest tone, "but we won't sway until it has done it. We will only chant."

"I canna' do no chantin," said Ben Weatherstaff, a trifle testily. "They turned me out o' th' church choir th' only time I ever tried it."

No one smiled. They were all too much in earnest. Colin's face was not even crossed by a shadow. He was thinking only of the Magic.

"Then I will chant," he said. And he began, looking like a strange boy spirit. "The sun is shining–the sun is shining. That is the Magic. The flowers are growing–the roots are stirring. That is the Magic. Being alive is the Magic–being strong is the Magic. The Magic is in me–the Magic is in me. It is in me–it is in me. It's in every one of us. It's in Ben Weatherstaff's back. Magic! Magic! Come and help!" He said it a great many times–not a thousand times, but quite a goodly number. Mary listened entranced. She felt as if it were at once queer and beautiful and she wanted him to go on and on. Ben Weatherstaff began to feel soothed into a sort of dream which was quite agreeable. The humming of the bees in the blossoms mingled with the chanting voice and drowsily melted into a doze. Dickon sat cross-legged with his rabbit asleep on his arm and a hand resting on the lamb's back. Soot had pushed away a squirrel and huddled close to him on his shoulder; the grey film dropped over his eyes. At last Colin stopped.

"Now I am going to walk round the garden," he announced.

Ben Weatherstaff's head had just drooped forward and he lifted it with a jerk.

"You have been asleep," said Colin.

"Nowt o' th' sort," mumbled Ben. "Th' sermon was good enow–but I'm bound to get out afore th' collection."

He was not quite awake yet.

"You're not in church," said Colin.

"Not me," said Ben, straightening himself. "Who said I were? I heard every bit of it. You said th' Magic was in my back. Th' doctor calls it rheumatics."

The rajah waved his hand.

"That was the wrong Magic," he said. "You will get better. You have my permission to go to your work. But come back tomorrow."

"I'd like to see thee walk round the garden," grunted Ben.

It was not an unfriendly grunt, but it was a grunt. In fact, being a stubborn old party and not having entire faith in Magic, he made up his mind that if he were sent away he would climb his ladder and look over the wall so that he might be ready to hobble back if there were any stumbling.

The rajah did not object to his staying, and so the procession was formed. It really did look like a procession. Colin was at its head with Dickon on one side and Mary on the other. Ben Weatherstaff walked behind, and the "creatures" trailed after them, the lamb and the fox cub keeping close to Dickon, the white rabbit hopping along or stopping to nibble and Soot following with the solemnity of a person who felt himself in charge.

It was a procession which moved slowly, but with dignity.

Every few yards it stopped to rest. Colin leaned on Dickon's arm and privately Ben Weatherstaff kept a sharp look-out, but now and then Colin took his hand from its support and walked a few steps alone. His head was held up all the time and he looked very grand.

"The Magic is in me!" he kept saying. "The Magic is making me strong! I can feel it! I can feel it!"

It seemed very certain that something was upholding and uplifting him. He sat on the seats in the alcoves and once or twice he sat down on the grass and several times he paused in the path and leaned on Dickon, but he would not give up until he had gone all round the garden. When he returned to the canopy tree his cheeks were flushed and he looked triumphant.

"I did it! The Magic worked!" he cried. "That is my first scientific discovery."

"What will Dr. Craven say?" broke out Mary.

"He won't say anything," Colin answered, "because he will not be told. This is to be the biggest secret of all. No one is to know anything about it until I have grown so strong that I can walk and run like any other boy. I shall come here every day in my chair and I shall be taken back in it. I won't have people whispering and asking questions and I won't let my father hear about it until the experiment has quite succeeded. Then some time when he comes back to Misselthwaite I shall just walk into his study and say: 'Here I am: I am like any other boy. I am quite well and I shall live to be a man. It has been done by a scientific experiment."

"He will think he is in a dream," cried Mary. "He won't believe his eyes."

Colin flushed triumphantly. He had made himself believe that he was going to get well, which was really more than half the battle, if he had been aware of it. And the thought which stimulated him more than any other was this imagining what his father would look like when he saw that he had a son who was as straight and strong as other fathers' sons. One of his darkest miseries in the unhealthy, morbid past days had been his hatred of being a sickly, weak-backed boy, whose father was afraid to look at him.

"He'll be obliged to believe them," he said. "One of the

things I am going to do, after the Magic works and before I begin to make scientific discoveries, is to be an athlete."

"We shall have thee takin' to boxin' in a week or so," said Ben Weatherstaff. "Tha'lt end wi' winnin' th' Belt an' bein' champion prize-fighter of all England."

Colin fixed his eyes on him sternly.

"Weatherstaff," he said, "that is disrespectful. You must not take liberties because you are in the secret. However much the Magic works, I shall not be a prize-fighter. I shall be a Scientific Discoverer."

"Ax pardon–ax pardon, sir," answered Ben, touching his forehead in salute. "I ought to have seed it wasn't a jokin' matter," but his eyes twinkled and secretly he was immensely pleased. He really did not mind being snubbed, since the snubbing meant that the lad was gaining strength and spirit.

CHAPTER 24

"LET THEM LAUGH"

The secret garden was not the only one Dickon worked in. Round the cottage on the moor there was a piece of ground enclosed by a low wall of rough stones. Early in the morning and late in the fading twilight and on all the days Colin and Mary did not see him, Dickon worked there planting or tending potatoes and cabbages, turnips and carrots and herbs for his mother. In the company of his "creatures" he did wonders there and was never tired of doing them, it seemed. While he dug or weeded he whistled or sang bits of Yorkshire moor songs or talked to Soot or Captain or the brothers and sisters he had taught to help him.

"We'd never get on as comfortable as we do," Mrs. Sowerby said, "if it wasn't for Dickon's garden. Anything'll grow for him. His 'taters and cabbages is twice th' size of anyone else's an' they've got a flavour with 'em as nobody's has."

When she found a moment to spare she liked to go out and talk to him. After supper there was still a long clear twilight to work in, and that was her quiet time. She could sit upon the low rough wall and look on and hear stories of the day. She loved this time. There were not only vegetables in this garden. Dickon had bought penny packages of flower seeds now and then and sown bright, sweet-scented things among gooseberry bushes and even cabbages and he grew borders of mignonette and pinks and pansies and things, whose seeds he could save year after year or whose roots would bloom each spring and spread in time into fine clumps. The low wall was one of the prettiest things in Yorkshire because he had tucked moorland foxglove and ferns and rock-cress and hedgerow flowers into every crevice until only here and there glimpses of the stones were to be seen.

"All a chap's got to do to make 'em thrive, Mother," he would say, "is to be friends with 'em for sure. They're just like th' 'creatures'. If they're thirsty give 'em a drink, and if they're hungry give 'em a bit o' food. They want to live same as we do. If they died I should feel as if I'd been a bad lad and somehow treated them heartless."

It was in these twilight hours that Mrs. Sowerby heard of all that happened at Misselthwaite Manor. At first she was only told that "Mester Colin" had taken a fancy to going out into the grounds with Miss Mary and that it was doing him good. But it was not long before it was agreed between the two children that Dickon's mother might "come into the secret". Somehow it was not doubted that she was "safe for sure".

So one beautiful, still evening, Dickon told the whole story, with all the thrilling details of the buried key and the robin and the grey haze which had seemed like deadness and the secret Mistress Mary had planned never to reveal. The coming of Dickon and how it had been told to him, the doubt of Mester Colin and the final drama of his introduction to the hidden domain, combined with the incident of Ben Weatherstaff's angry face peering over the wall and Mester Colin's sudden indignant strength, made Mrs. Sowerby's nice-looking face quite change colour several times.

"My word!" she said. "It was a good thing that little lass came to th' Manor. It's been th' makin' o' her an' th' savin' o' him. Standin' on his feet! An' us all thinkin' he was a poor, half-witted lad with not a straight bone in him."

She asked a great many questions and her blue eyes were full of deep thinking.

"What do they make of it at th' Manor–him being so well an' cheerful an' never complainin'?" she inquired.

"They don't know what to make of it," answered Dickon. "Every day as comes round his face looks different. It's fillin' out and doesn't look so sharp an' th' waxy colour is goin'. But he has to do his bit o' complainin'," with a highly entertained grin.

"What for, i' Mercy's name?" asked Mrs. Sowerby.

Dickon chuckled.

"He does it to keep them from guessin' what's happened. If the doctor knew he'd found out he could stand on his feet, he'd likely write and tell Mester Craven. Mester Colin's savin' th' secret to tell himself. He's goin' to practise his Magic on his legs every day till his father comes back an' then he's goin' to march into his room an' show him he's as straight as other lads. But him an' Miss Mary thinks it's best plan to do a bit o' groanin' and frettin' now an' then to throw off th' scent."

Mrs. Sowerby was laughing a low, comfortable laugh long before he had finished his last sentence.

"Eh!" she said, "that pair's enjoyin' theirselves, I'll warrant. They'll get a good bit o' play actin' out of it, an' there's nothin' children likes as much as play actin'.Let's hear what they do, Dickon, lad."

Dickon stopped weeding and sat up on his heels to tell her. His eyes were twinkling with fun.

"Mester Colin is carried down to his chair every time he goes out," he explained. "An' he flies out at John, th' footman, for not carryin' him careful enough. He makes himself as helpless-lookin' as he can an' never lifts his head until we're out o' sight o' th' house. An' he grunts an' frets a good bit when he's bein' settled into his chair. Him an' Miss Mary's both got to enjoyin' it, an' when he groans an' complains she'll say: 'Poor Colin! Does it hurt you so much? Are you so weak as that, poor Colin?'–but th' trouble is that sometimes they can scarce keep from burstin' out laughin'. When we get safe into the garden they laugh till they've no breath left to laugh with. An' they have to stuff their faces into Mester Colin's cushions to keep the gardeners from hearin', if any of 'em's about."

"Th' more they laugh th' better for 'em!" said Mrs. Sowerby, still laughing herself. "Good, healthy child laughin's better than pills any day o' th' year. That pair'll plump up for sure."

"They are plumpin' up," said Dickon. "They're that hungry they don't know how to get enough to eat without makin' talk. Mester Colin says if he keeps sendin' for more food, they won't believe he's an invalid at all. Miss Mary says she'll let him eat her share, but he says that if she goes hungry she'll get thin an' they mun both get fat at once."

Mrs. Sowerby laughed so heartily at the revelation of this difficulty that she quite rocked backwards and forwards in her blue cloak, and Dickon laughed with her.

"I'll tell thee what, lad," Mrs. Sowerby said when she could speak. "I've thought of a way to help 'em. When tha' goes to 'em in th' mornin's tha' shall take a pail o' good new milk an' I'll bake 'em a crusty cottage loaf or some buns wi' currants in 'em, same as you children like. Nothin's so good as fresh milk an' bread. Then they could take off th' edge o' their hunger while they were in their garden an' th' fine food they get indoors 'ud polish off th' corners."

"Eh! Mother!" said Dickon admiringly, "what a wonder tha' art! Tha' always sees a way out o' things. They was quite in a pother yesterday. They didn't see how they was to manage without orderin' up more food–they felt that empty inside."

"They're two young 'uns growin' fast, and health's comin' back to both of 'em. Children like that feels like young wolves an' food's flesh an' blood to 'em," said Mrs. Sowerby. Then she smiled Dickon's own curving smile. "Eh! but they're enjoyin' theirselves for sure," she said.

She was quite right. the comfortable, wonderful mother creature–and she had never been more so than when she said their "play actin'" would be their joy. Colin and Mary found it one of their most thrilling sources of entertainment. The idea of protecting themselves from suspicion had been unconsciously suggested to them first by the puzzled nurse and then by Dr. Craven himself.

"Your appetite is improving very much, Master Colin," the nurse had said one day. "You used to eat nothing, and so many things disagreed with you."

"Nothing disagrees with me now," replied Colin, and then seeing the nurse looking at him curiously, he suddenly remembered that perhaps he ought not to appear too well just yet. "At least, things don't so often disagree with me. It's the fresh air."

"Perhaps it is," said the nurse, still looking at him with a mystified expression. "But I must talk to Dr. Craven about it."

"How she stared at you!" said Mary when she went away. "As if she thought there must be something to find out."

"I won't have her finding out things," said Colin "No one must begin to find out yet."

When Dr. Craven came that morning he seemed puzzled, too. He asked a number of questions, to Colin's great annoyance.

"You stay out in the garden a great deal," he suggested. "Where do you go?"

Colin put on his favourite air of dignified indifference to opinion.

"I will not let anyone know where I go," he answered. "I go to a place I like. Everyone has orders to keep out of the way. I won't be watched and stared at. You know that!"

"You seem to be out all day, but I do not think it has done you harm–I do not think so. The nurse says that you eat much more than you have ever done before."

"Perhaps," said Colin, prompted by a sudden inspiration, "perhaps it is an unnatural appetite."

"I do not think so, as your food seems to agree with you," said Dr. Craven. "You are gaining flesh rapidly and your colour is better."

"Perhaps–perhaps I am bloated and feverish," said Colin, assuming a discouraging air of gloom. "People who are not going to live are often–different."

Dr. Craven shook his head. He was holding Colin's wrist, and he pushed up his sleeve and felt his arm.

"You are not feverish," he said thoughtfully, "and such flesh as you have gained is healthy. If we can keep this up, my boy, we need not talk of dying. Your father will be very happy to hear of this remarkable improvement."

"I won't have him told!" Colin broke forth fiercely. "It will only disappoint him if I get worse again–and I may get worse this very night. I might have a raging fever. I feel as if I might be beginning to have one now. I won't have letters written to my father–I won't–I won't! You are making me angry, and you know that is bad for me. I feel hot already. I hate being written about and being talked over as much as I hate being stared at!"

"Hush-h! my boy," Dr. Craven soothed him. "Nothing shall be written without your permission. You are too sensitive about things. You must not undo the good which has been done."

He said no more about writing to Mr. Craven, and when he saw the nurse he privately warned her that such a possibility must not be mentioned to the patient.

"The boy is extraordinarily better," he said. "His advance seems almost abnormal. But, of course, he is doing now of his own free will what we could not make him do before. Still, he excites himself very easily and nothing must be said to irritate him."

Mary and Colin were much alarmed and talked together anxiously. From this time dated their plan of "play actin".

"I may be obliged to have a tantrum," said Colin regretfully. "I don't want to have one and I'm not miserable enough now to work myself into a big one. Perhaps I couldn't have one at all. That lump doesn't come in my throat now, and I keep thinking of nice things instead of horrible ones. But if they talk about writing to my father, I shall have to do something."

He made up his mind to eat less, but unfortunately it was not possible to carry out this brilliant idea when he wakened each morning with an amazing appetite and the table near his sofa was set with a breakfast of home–made bread and fresh butter, snow-white eggs, raspberry jam, and clotted cream. Mary always breakfasted with him, and when they found themselves at the table–particularly if there were delicate slices of sizzling ham sending forth tempting odours from under a hot silver cover–they would look into each other's eyes in desperation.

"I think we shall have to eat it all this morning, Mary," Colin always ended by saying. "We can send away some of the lunch and a great deal of the dinner."

But they never found they could send away anything, and the highly polished condition of the empty plates returned to the pantry awakened much comment.

"I do wish," Colin would say also, "I do wish the slices of ham were thicker, and one muffin each is not enough for anyone."

"It's enough for a person who is going to die," answered Mary when first she heard this, "but it's not enough for a person who is going to live. I sometimes feel as if I could eat three when those nice fresh heather and gorse smells from the moor come pouring in at the open window."

The morning that Dickon–after they had been enjoying themselves in the garden for about two hours–went behind a big rose-bush and brought forth two tin pails and revealed that one was full of rich new milk with cream on the top of it, and that the other held cottage-made currant buns folded in a clean blue and white napkin, buns so carefully tucked in that they were still hot, there was a riot of surprised joyfulness. What a wonderful thing for Mrs. Sowerby to think of! What a kind, clever woman she must be! How good the buns were! And what delicious fresh milk!

"Magic is in her just as it is in Dickon," said Colin. "It makes he think of ways to do things–nice things. She is a Magic person. Tell her we are grateful, Dickon–extremely grateful."

He was given to using rather grown-up phrases at times. He enjoyed them. He liked this so much that he improved upon it.

"Tell her she has been most bounteous and our gratitude is extreme."

And then forgetting his grandeur he fell to and stuffed himself with buns and drank milk out of the pail in copious draughts in the manner of any hungry little boy who had been taking unusual exercise and breathing in moorland air and whose breakfast was more than two hours behind him.

This was the beginning of many agreeable incidents of the same kind. They actually awoke to the fact that as Mrs. Sowerby had fourteen people to provide food for she might not have enough to satisfy two extra appetites every day. So they asked her to let them send some of their shillings to buy things.

Dickon made the stimulating discovery that in the wood in the park outside the garden where Mary had first found him piping to the wild creatures, there was a deep little hollow where you could build a sort of tiny oven with stones and roast potatoes and eggs in it. Roasted eggs were a previously unknown luxury, and very hot potatoes with salt and fresh butter in them were fit for a woodland king–besides being deliciously satisfying. You could buy both potatoes and eggs and eat as many as you liked without feeling as if you were taking food out of the mouths of fourteen people.

Every beautiful morning the Magic was worked by the mystic circle under the plum-tree which-provided a canopy of thickening green leaves after its brief blossom-time was ended. After the ceremony Colin always took his walking exercise, and throughout the day he exercised his newly found power at intervals. Each day he grew stronger and could walk more steadily and cover more ground. And each day his belief in the Magic grew stronger – as well it might. He tried one experiment after another as he felt himself gaining strength, and it was Dickon who showed him the best things of all.

"Yesterday," he said one morning after an absence, "I went to Thwaite for Mother, an' near th' Blue Cow Inn I seed Bob Haworth. He's the strongest chap on th' moor. He's the champion wrestler an' he can jump higher than any other chap an' throw th' hammer farther. He's gone all th' way to Scotland for th' sports some years. He's knowed me ever since I was a little 'un an' he's a friendly sort an' I asked him some questions. Th' gentry calls him an athlete and I thought o' thee, Mester Colin, and I says: 'How did tha' make tha' muscles stick out that way, Bob? Did tha' do anythin' extra to make thysel' so strong?' An' he says: 'Well, yes, lad, I did. A strong man in a show that came to Thwaite once showed me how to exercise my arms an' legs an' every muscle in my body.' An' I says: 'Could a delicate chap make himself stronger with 'em, Bob?' an' he laughed an' says, 'Art tha' th' delicate chap?' an' I says, 'No, but I knows a young gentleman that's gettin' well of a long illness an' I wish I knowed some o' them tricks to tell him about.' I didn't say no names an' he didn't ask none. He's friendly same as I said, an' he stood up an' showed me good-natured like, an' I imitated what he did till I knowed it by heart."

Colin had been listening excitedly.

"Can you show me?" he cried. "Will you?"

"Aye, to be sure," Dickon answered, getting up. "But he says tha' mun do 'em gentle at first an' be careful not to' tire thysel'. Rest in between times an' take deep breaths an don't overdo."

"I'll be careful," said Colin. "Show me! Show me! Dickon, you are the most Magic boy in the world!"

Dickon stood up on the grass and slowly went through a carefully practical but simple series of muscle exercises. Colin watched them with widening eyes. He could do a few while he was sitting down.

Presently he did a few gently while he stood upon his already steadied feet. Mary began to do them also. Soot, who was watching the performance, became much disturbed and left his branch and hopped about restlessly because he could not do them, too.

From that time the exercises were part of the day's duties as much as the Magic was. It became possible for both Colin and Mary to do more of them each time they tried, and such appetites were the result that but for the basket Dickon put down behind the bush each morning when he arrived, they would have been lost. But the little oven in the hollow and Mrs. Sowerby's bounties were so satisfying that Mrs. Medlock and the nurse and Dr. Craven became mystified again. You can trifle with your breakfast and seem to disdain your dinner if you are full to the brim with roasted eggs and potatoes and richly frothed new milk and oat-cakes and buns and heather honey and clotted cream.

"They are eating next to nothing," said the nurse. "They'll die of starvation if they can't be persuaded to take some nourishment. And yet see how they look."

"Look!" exclaimed Mrs. Medlock indignantly. "Eh! I'm moithered to death with them. They're a pair of young Satans. Bursting their jackets one day and the next turning up their noses at the best meals Cook can tempt them with. Not a mouthful of that lovely young fowl and bread sauce did they set a fork into yesterday–and the poor woman fair *invented* a pudding for them–and back it's sent. She almost cried. She's afraid she'll be blamed if they starve themselves into their graves."

Dr. Craven came and looked at Colin long and carefully. He wore an extremely worried expression when the nurse talked with him and showed him the almost untouched tray of breakfast she had saved for him to look at–but it was even more worried when he sat down by Colin's sofa and examined him. He had been called to London on business and had not seen the boy for nearly two weeks. When young things begin to gain health they gain it rapidly. The waxen tinge had left Colin's skin and a warm rose showed through it; his beautiful eyes were clear and the hollows under them and in his cheeks and temples had filled out. His once dark, heavy locks had begun to look as if they sprang healthily from his forehead ad were soft and warm with life. His lips were fuller and of a normal colour. In fact, as an imitation of a boy who was a confirmed invalid he was a disgraceful sight. Dr. Craven held his chin in his hand and thought him over.

"I am sorry to hear that you do not eat anything," he said. "That will not do. You will lose all you have gained–and you have gained amazingly. You ate so well a short time ago."

"I told you it was an unnatural appetite," answered Colin.

Mary was sitting on her stool near by and she suddenly made a very queer sound which she tried so violently to repress that she ended by almost choking.

"What is the matter?" said Dr. Craven, turning to look at her.

Mary became quite severe in her manner.

"It was something between a sneeze and a cough," she replied, with reproachful dignity, "and it got into my throat."

"But," she said afterwards to Colin, "I couldn't stop myself. It just burst out because all at once I couldn't help remembering that last big potato you ate and the way your mouth stretched when you bit through that thick, lovely crust with jam and clotted cream on it."

"Is there any way in which those children can get food secretly?" Dr. Craven inquired of Mrs. Medlock.

"There's no way unless they dig it out of the earth or pick it off the trees," Mrs. Medlock answered. "They stay out in the grounds all day and see no one but each other. And if they want anything different to eat from what's sent up to them, they need only ask for it."

"Well," said Dr. Craven, "so long as going without food agrees with them, we need not be disturbed. The boy is a new creature."

"So is the girl," said Mrs. Medlock. "She's begun to be downright pretty since she's filled out and lost her ugly little sour look. Her hair's grown thick and healthy looking and she's got a bright colour. The glummest, ill-natured little thing she used to be, and now her and Master Colin laugh together like a pair of crazy young ones. Perhaps they're growing fat on that."

"Perhaps they are," said Dr. Craven. "Let them laugh."

Chapter 25

THE CURTAIN

And the secret garden bloomed and bloomed and every morning revealed new miracles. In the robin's nest there were eggs and the robin's mate sat upon them, keeping them warm with her feathery little breast and careful wings. At first she was very nervous, and the robin himself was indignantly watchful. Even Dickon did not go near the close-grown corner in those days, but waited until by the quiet working of some mysterious spell he seemed to have conveyed to the soul of the little pair that in the garden there was nothing which was not quite like themselves–nothing which did not understand the wonderfulness of what was happening to them–the immense, tender, terrible, heart-breaking beauty and solemnity of Eggs. If there had been one person in that garden who had not known through all his or her innermost being that if an Egg were taken away or hurt the whole world would whirl round and crash through space and come to an end–if there had been even one who did not feel it and act accordingly there could have been no happiness even in that golden springtime air. But they all knew it and felt it and the robin and his mate knew they knew it.

At first the robin watched Mary and Colin with sharp anxiety. For some mysterious reason he knew he need not watch Dickon. The first moment he set his dew-bright black eye on Dickon he knew he was not a stranger, but a sort of robin without beak or feathers. He could speak robin (which is quite a distinct language not to be mistaken for any other). To speak robin to a robin is like speaking French to a Frenchman. Dickon always spoke it to the robin himself, so the queer gibberish he used when he spoke to humans did not matter in the least. The robin thought he spoke this gibberish to them because they were not intelligent enough to understand feathered speech. His movements also were robin. They never startled one by being sudden enough to seem dangerous or threatening. Any robin could understand Dickon, so his presence was not even disturbing.

But at the outset it seemed necessary to be on guard against the other two. In the first place the boy creature did not come into the garden on his legs. He was pushed in on a thing with wheels and the skins of wild animals were thrown over him. That in itself was doubtful. Then when he began to stand up and move about he did it in a queer, unaccustomed way, and the others seemed to have to help him. The robin used to secrete himself in a bush and watch this anxiously, his head tilted first on one side and then on the other. He thought that the slow movements might mean that he was preparing to pounce, as cats do. When cats are preparing to pounce they creep over the ground very slowly. The robin talked this over with his mate a great deal for a few days, but after that he decided not to speak of the subject because her terror was so great that he was afraid it might be injurious to the Eggs.

When the boy began to walk by himself and even to move more quickly, it was an immense relief. But for a long time–or it seemed a long time to the robin–he was a source of some anxiety. He did not act as the other humans did. He seemed very fond of walking, but he had a way of sitting or lying down for a while and then getting up in a disconcerting manner to begin again.

One day the robin remembered that when he himself had been made to learn to fly by his parents he had done much the same sort of thing. He had taken short flights of a few yards and then had I been obliged to rest. So it occurred to him that this boy was learning to fly–or rather to walk. He mentioned this to his mate, and when he told her that the Eggs would probably conduct themselves in the same way after they were fledged, she was quite comforted and even became eagerly interested and derived great pleasure from watching the boy over the edge of her nest–though she always thought that the Eggs would be much cleverer and learn more quickly. But then she said indulgently that humans were always more clumsy and slow than Eggs, and most of them never seemed really to learn to fly at all. You never met them in the air or on tree-tops.

After a while the boy began to move about as the others did, but all three of the children at times did unusual things. They would stand under the trees and move their arms and legs and heads about in a way which was neither walking nor running nor sitting down. They went through these movements at intervals every day, and the robin was never able to explain to his mate what they were doing or trying to do. He could only say that he was sure that the Eggs would never flap about in such a manner, but as the boy who could speak robin fluently was doing the thing with them, birds could be quite sure that the actions were not of a dangerous nature. Of course, neither the robin nor his mate had ever heard of the champion wrestler, Bob Haworth, and his exercises for making the muscle stand out like lumps. Robins are not like human beings; their muscles are always exercised from the first, and so they develop themselves in a natural manner. If you have to fly about to find every meal you eat, your muscles do not become atrophied (atrophied means wasted away through want of use).

When the boy was walking and running about and digging and weeding like the others, the nest in the corner was brooded over by a great peace and content. Fears for the Eggs became things of the past. Knowing that your Eggs were as safe as if they were locked in a bank vault and the fact that you could watch so many curious things going on made sitting a most entertaining occupation. On wet days the "Eggs" mother sometimes felt even a little dull because the children did not come into the garden.

But even on wet days it could not be said that Mary and Colin were dull. One morning when the rain streamed down unceasingly and Colin was beginning to feel at little restive, as he was obliged to remain on his sofa because it was not safe to get up and walk about, Mary had an inspiration.

"Now that I am a real boy," Colin had said, "my legs and arms and all my body are so full of Magic that I can't keep them still. They want to be doing things all the time. Do you know that when I waken in the morning, Mary, when it's quite early and the birds are just shouting outside and everything seems just shouting for joy-even the trees and things we can't really hear-I feel as if I must jump out of bed and shout myself. And if I did it, just think what would happen!"

Mary giggled inordinately.

"The nurse would come running and Mrs. Medlock would come running and they would be sure you had gone crazy and they'd send for the doctor," she said.

Colin giggled himself. He could see how they would all look–how horrified by his outbreak and how amazed to see him standing upright.

"I wish my father would come home," he said. "I want to tell him myself. I'm always thinking about it–but we couldn't go on like this much longer. I can't stand lying still and pretending, and besides, I look too different. I wish it wasn't raining today."

It was then Mistress Mary had her inspiration.

"Colin," she began mysteriously, "do you know how many rooms there are in this house?"

"About a thousand, I suppose," he answered.

"There's about a hundred no one ever goes into," said Mary. "And one rainy day I went and looked into ever so many of them. No one ever knew, though Mrs. Medlock nearly found me out. I lost my way when I was coming back, and I stopped at the end of your corridor. That was the second time I heard you crying."

Colin started up from his sofa.

"A hundred rooms no one goes into," he said. "It sounds almost like a secret garden. Suppose we go and look at them. You could wheel me in my chair and nobody would know where we went."

"That's what I was thinking," said Mary. "No one would dare to follow us. There are galleries where you could run. We could do our exercises. There is a little Indian room where there is a cabinet full of ivory elephants. There are all sorts of rooms."

"Ring the bell," said Colin.

When the nurse came in he gave his orders.

"I want my chair," he said. "Miss Mary and I are going to look at the part of the house which is not used. John can push me as far as the picture-gallery because there are some stairs. Then he must go away and leave us alone until I send for him again."

Rainy days lost their terrors that morning. When the footman had wheeled the chair into the picture-gallery and left the two together in obedience to orders, Colin and Mary looked at each other delighted. As soon as Mary had made sure that John was really on his way back to his own quarters, Colin got out of his chair.

"I am going to run from one end of the gallery to the other," he said, "and then I am going to jump and then we will do Bob Haworth's exercises."

And they did all these things and many others. They looked at the portraits and found the plain little girl dressed in green brocade and holding the parrot on her finger.

"All these," said Colin, "must be my relations. They lived a long time ago. That parrot one, I believe, is one of my great, great, great great-aunts. She looks rather like you, Mary–not as you look now, but as you looked when you came here. You are a great deal fatter and better-looking than when I first saw you."

"So are you," said Mary, and they both laughed.

They went to the Indian room and amused themselves with the ivory elephants. They found the rose-coloured brocade boudoir and the hole in the cushion the mouse had left, but the mice had grown up and run away and the hole was empty.

They saw more rooms and made more discoveries than Mary had made on her first pilgrimage. They found new corridors and corners and flights of steps and new old pictures they liked and weird old things they did not know the use of. It was a curiously entertaining morning, and the feeling of wandering about in the same house with other people, but at the same time feeling as if one were miles away from them, was a fascinating thing.

"I'm glad we came," Colin said. "I never knew I lived in such a big, queer old place. I like it. We will ramble about every rainy day. We shall always be finding new queer corners and things."

That morning they had found among other things such good appetites that when they returned to Colin's room it was not possible to send the luncheon away untouched.

When the nurse carried the tray downstairs she slapped it down on the kitchen dresser so that Mrs. Loomis, the cook, could see the highly polished dishes and plates.

"Look at that!" she said. "This is a house of mystery, and those two children are the greatest mysteries in it."

"If they keep that up every day," said the strong young footman, John, "there'd be small wonder that he weighs twice as much today as he did a month ago. I should have to give up my place in time, for fear of doing my muscles an injury."

That afternoon Mary noticed that something new had happened in Colin's room. She had noticed it the day before, but had said nothing because she thought the change might have been made by chance. She said nothing today, but she sat and looked fixedly at the picture over the mantel. She could look at it because the curtain had been drawn aside. That was the change she noticed.

"I know what you want me to tell you," said Colin, after she had stared a few minutes. "I always know when you want me to tell you something. You are wondering why the curtain is drawn back. I am going to keep it like that."

"Why?" asked Mary.

"Because it doesn't make me angry any more to see her laughing. I wakened when it was bright moonlight two nights ago and felt as if the Magic was filling the room and making everything so splendid that I couldn't lie still. I got up and looked out of the window. The room was quite light and there was a patch of moonlight on the curtain, and somehow that made me go and pull the cord. She looked right down at me as if she were laughing because she was glad I was standing there. It made me like to look at her. I want to see her laughing like that all the time. I think she must have been a sort of Magic person perhaps."

"You are so like her now," said Mary, "that sometimes I think perhaps you are her ghost made into a boy."

That idea seemed to impress Colin. He thought it over and then answered her slowly.

"If I were her ghost–my father would be fond of me," he said.

"Do you want him to be fond of you?" inquired Mary.

"I used to hate it because he was not fond of me. If he grew fond of me I think I should tell him about the Magic. It might make him more cheerful."

CHAPTER 26

"IT'S MOTHER!"

Their belief in the Magic was an abiding thing. After the morning's incantations Colin sometimes gave them Magic lectures.

"I like to do it," he explained, "because when I grow up and make great scientific discoveries I shall be obliged to lecture about them, and so this is practice. I can only give short lectures now because I am very young, and, besides, Ben Weatherstaff would feel as if he was in church and he would go to sleep."

"T' best thing about lecturin'," said Ben, is that a chap can get up an' say aught he pleases an' no other chap can answer him back I wouldn't be again' lecturin' a bit mysel' sometimes."

But when Colin held forth under his tree old Ben fixed devouring eyes on him and kept them there. He looked him over with critical affection. It was not so much the lecture which interested him as the legs which looked straighter and stronger each day, the boyish head which held itself up so well, the once sharp chin and hollow cheeks which had filled and rounded out, and the eyes which had begun to hold the light he remembered in another pair. Sometimes when Colin felt Ben's earnest gaze meant that he was much impressed he wondered what he was reflecting on, and once, when he had seemed quite entranced, he questioned him.

"What are you thinking about, Ben Weatherstaff?" he asked.

"I was thinkin'," answered Ben, "as I'd warrant tha's gone up three or four pound this week. I was lookin' at tha' calves an' tha' shoulders. I'd like to get thee on a pair o' scales."

"It's the Magic and–and Mrs. Sowerby's buns and milk and things," said Colin. "You see, the scientific experiment has succeeded."

That morning Dickon was too late to hear the lecture. When he came he was ruddy with running and his funny face looked more twinkling than usual. As they had a good deal of weeding to do after the rains, they fell to work. They always had plenty to do after a warm, deep sinking rain. The moisture which was good for the flowers was also good for the weeds, which thrust up tiny blades of grass and points of leaves which must be pulled up before their roots took too firm hold. Colin was as good at weeding as anyone in these days, and he could lecture while he was doing it.

"The magic works best when you work yourself," he said this morning. "You can feel it in your bones and muscles. I am going to read books about bones and muscles, but I am going to write a book about Magic. I am making it up now. I keep finding out things."

It was not very long after he had said this that he laid down his trowel and stood up on his feet. He had been silent for several minutes, and they had seen that he was thinking out lectures, as he often did. When he dropped his trowel and stood upright it seemed to Mary and Dickon as if a sudden strong thought had made him do it. He stretched himself out to his tallest height and he threw out his arms exultantly. Colour glowed in his face and his strange eyes widened with joyfulness. All at once he had realized something to the full.

"Mary! Dickon!" he cried. "Just look at me!"

They stopped their weeding and looked at him.

"Do you remember that first morning you brought me in here?" he demanded.

Dickon was looking at him very hard. Being an animal-charmer, he could see more things than most people could, and many of them were things he never talked about. He saw some of them now in this boy.

"Aye, that we do," he answered.

Mary looked hard, too, but she said nothing.

"Just this minute," said Colin, "all at once I remembered it myself–when I looked at my hand digging with the trowel–and I had to stand up on my feet to see if it was real. And it s real! I'm well–I'm well!"

"Aye, that tha' art!" said Dickon.

"I'm well! I'm well!" said Colin again, and his face went quite red all over.

He had known it before in a way, he had hoped it and felt it and thought about it, but just at that minute something had rushed all through him–a sort of rapturous belief and realization, and it had been so strong that he could not help calling out.

"I shall live for ever and ever and ever he cried grandly. I shall find out thousands and thousands of things. I shall find out about people and creatures and everything that grows–like Dickon–and I shall never stop making Magic. I'm well! I'm well! I feel–I feel as if I want to shout out something–something thankful, joyful! "

Ben Weatherstaff, who had been working near a rosebush, glanced round at him.

"Tha' might sing th' Doxology," he suggested in his dryest grunt. He had no opinion of the Doxology, and he did not make the suggestion with any particular reverence.

But Colin was of an exploring mind, and he knew nothing about the Doxology.

"What is that?" he inquired.

"Dickon can sing it for thee, I'll warrant," replied Ben Weatherstaff.

Dickon answered with his all-perceiving animal-charmer's smile.

"They sing it i' church," he said. "Mother says she believes th' sky larks sings it when they gets up i' th' mornin'".

"If she says that, it must be a nice song," Colin answered. "I've never been in a church myself. I was always too ill. Sing it, Dickon. I want to hear it."

Dickon was quite simple and unaffected about it. He understood what Colin felt better than Colin did himself. He understood by a sort of instinct so natural that he did not know it was understanding. He pulled off his cap and looked round still smiling.

"Tha' must take off tha' cap", he said to Colin, "an' so mun tha', Ben–an' tha' mun stand up, tha' knows."

Colin took off his cap and the sun shone on and warmed his thick hair as he watched Dickon intently. Ben Weatherstaff scrambled up from his knees and bared his head, too, with a sort of puzzled, half-resentful look on his old face, as if he didn't know exactly why he was doing this remarkable thing.

Dickon stood out among the trees and rose-bushes and began to sing in quite a simple, matter-of-fact way, and in a nice strong boy's voice:

Praise God from whom all blessings flow,
Praise Him all creatures here below,
Praise Him above ye Heavenly Host,
Praise Father, Son, and Holy Ghost. Amen.

When he had finished, Ben Weatherstaff was standing quite still with his jaws set obstinately, but with a disturbed look in his eyes fixed on Colin. Colin's face was thoughtful and appreciative.

"It is a very nice song," he said. "I like it. Perhaps it means just what I mean when I want to shout that I am thankful to the Magic." He stopped and thought in a puzzled way. "Perhaps they are both the same thing. How can we know the exact names of everything? Sing it again, Dickon. Let us try, Mary. I want to sing it, too. How does it begin? 'Praise God from whom all blessings flow'?"

And they sang it again, and Mary and Colin lifted their voices as musically as they could, and Dickon's swelled quite loud and beautiful—and at the second line Ben Weatherstaff raspingly cleared his throat, and at the third he joined in with such vigour that it seemed almost savage, and when the "Amen" came to an end, Mary observed that the very same thing had happened to him which had happened when he found out that Colin was not a cripple—his chin was twitching and he was staring and winking, and his leathery old cheeks were wet.

"I never seed no sense in th' Doxology afore, he said hoarsely, but I may change my mind i' time. I should say tha'd gone up five pound this week, Mester Colin—five on 'em! "

Colin was looking across the garden at something attracting his attention, and his expression had become a startled one.

"Who is coming in here?" he said quickly. "Who is it?"

The door in the ivied wall had been pushed gently open and a woman had entered. She had come in with the last line of their song and she had stood still listening and looking at them. With the ivy behind her, the sunlight drifting through the trees and dappling her long blue cloak, and her nice fresh face smiling across the greenery, she was rather like a softly coloured illustration in one of Colin's books. She had wonderful affectionate eyes which seemed to take everything in—all of them, even Ben Weatherstaff and the "creatures" and every flower that was in bloom. Unexpectedly as she had appeared, not one of them felt that she was an intruder at all. Dickon's eyes lighted like lamps.

"It's Mother—that's who it is!" he cried, and he went across the grass at a run.

Colin began to move towards her, too, and Mary went with him. They both felt their pulses beat faster.

"It's Mother!" Dickon said again when they met halfway. "I knowed tha' wanted to see her an' I told her where th' door was hid."

Colin held out his hand with a sort of flushed royal shyness, but his eyes quite devoured her face.

"Even when I was ill I wanted to see you," he said, "you and Dickon and the secret garden. I'd never wanted to see anyone or anything before."

The sight of his uplifted face brought about a sudden change in her own. She flushed and the corners of her mouth shook and a mist seemed to sweep over her eyes.

"Eh! dear lad!" she broke out tremulously. "Eh! dear lad!" as if she had not know she were going to say it. She did not say, "Mester Colin," but just "dear lad" quite suddenly. She might have said it to Dickon in the same way if she had seen something in his face which touched her. Colin liked it.

"Are you surprised because I am so well?" he asked.

She put her hand on his shoulder and smiled the mist out of her eyes.

"Aye, that I am!" she said; "but tha'rt so like thy mother tha' made my heart jump."

"Do you think," said Colin a little awkwardly, "that will make my father like me?"

"Aye, for sure, dear lad," she answered, and she gave his shoulder a soft, quick pat. "He mun come home–he mun come home."

"Susan Sowerby," said Ben Weatherstaff; getting close to her. "Look at th' lad's legs, wilt tha'? They was like drumsticks i' stockin' two months ago–an' I heard folk tell as they was bandy an' knock-kneed both at th' same time. Look at 'em now! "

Susan Sowerby laughed a comfortable laugh.

"They're goin' to be fine strong lad's legs in a bit," she said. "Let him go playing', an' workin" in th' garden an' eatin' hearty an' drinkin' plenty o' good sweet milk an' there'll not be a finer pair i' Yorkshire, thank God for it."

She put both hands on Mistress Mary's shoulders and looked her little face over in a motherly fashion.

"An' thee, too!" she said. "Tha'rt grown near as hearty as our 'Lizabeth Ellen. I'l warrant tha'rt like thy mother, too. Our Martha told me as Mrs. Medlock heard she was a pretty woman. Tha'lt be like a blush-rose when tha' grows up, my little lass, bless thee."

She did not mention that when Martha came home on her "day out" and described the plain, sallow child she had said that she had no confidence whatever in what Mrs. Medlock had heard. "It doesn't stand to reason that a pretty woman could be th' mother o" such a poor" little lass," she had added obstinately.

Mary had not had time to pay much attention to her changing face. She had only known that she looked "different" and seemed to have a great deal more hair and that it was growing very fast. But remembering her pleasure in looking at the Memsahib in the past, she was glad to hear that she might some day look like her.

Susan Sowerby went round their garden with them and was told the whole story of it and shown every bush and tree which had come alive. Colin walked on one side of her and Mary on the other. Each of them kept looking up at her comfortable, rosy face, secretly curious about the delightful feeling she gave them–a sort of warm, supported feeling. It seemed as if she understood them as Dickon understood his "creatures". She stooped over the flowers and talked about them as if they were children. Soot followed her and once or twice cawed at her and flew upon her shoulder as if it were Dickon's. When they told her about the robin and the first flight of the young ones, she laughed a motherly little mellow laugh in her throat.

"I suppose learnin' 'em to fly i' like learnin' children to walk, but I'm feared I should be all in a worrit if mine had wings instead o' legs," she said.

It was because she seemed such a wonderful woman in her nice moorland cottage way that at last she was told about the Magic.

"Do you believe in Magic?" asked Colin, after he had explained about Indian fakirs. "I do hope you do."

"That I do, lad," she answered. "I never knowed it by that name, but what does th' name matter? I warrant they call it a different name i' France an' a different one i' Germany. Th' same thing as set th' seeds swellin' an' th' sun shinin' made thee a well lad an' it's th' Good Thing. It isn't like us poor fools as think it matters if us is called out of our names. Th' Big Good Thing doesn't stop to worrit, bless thee. It goes on makin' worlds by th' million–worlds like us. Never thee stop believin' in th' Big Good Thing an' knowin' th' world's full of it–an' call it what tha' likes. Tha' wert singin' to it when I come into th' garden."

"I felt so joyful," said Colin, opening his beautiful, strange eyes at her. "Suddenly, I felt how different I was–how strong my arms and legs were, you know–and how I could dig and stand–and I jumped up and wanted to shout out something to anything that would listen."

"Th' Magic listened when tha' sung th' Doxology. It would ha' listened to anything tha'd sung. It was th' joy that mattered. Eh! lad, lad–what's names to th' Joy Maker," and she gave his shoulders a quick, soft pat again.

She had packed a basket which held a regular feast this morning, and when the hungry hour came and Dickon brought it out from its hiding place, she sat down with them under their tree and watched them devour their food, laughing and quite gloating over their appetites. She was full of fun and made them laugh at all sorts of odd things. She told them stories in broad Yorkshire and taught them new words. She laughed as if she could not help it when they told her of the increasing difficulty there was in pretending that Colin was still a fretful invalid.

"You see we can't help laughing nearly all the time when we are together," explained Colin. "And it doesn't sound ill at all. We try to choke it back, but it will burst out and that sounds worse than ever."

"There's one thing that comes into my mind so often," said Mary, "and I can scarcely ever hold in when I think of it suddenly. I keep thinking suppose Colin's face should get to look like a full moon. It isn't like one yet, but he gets a tiny bit fatter every day-and suppose some morning it should look like one-what should we do!"

"Bless us all, I can see tha' has a good bit o' play actin' to do, said Susan Sowerby. But tha' won't have to keep it up much longer. Mester Craven'll come home."

"Do you think he will?" asked Colin. "Why?"

Susan Sowerby chuckled softly.

"I suppose it 'ud nigh break thy heart if he found out before tha' told him in tha' own way", she said. "Tha's laid awake nights plannin' it."

"I couldn't bear anyone else to tell him," said Colin. "I think about different ways every day. I think now I just want to run into his room."

"That'd be a fine start for him," said Susan Sowerby. "I'd like to see his face, lad. I would that! He mun come back-that he mun."

One of the things they talked of was the visit they were to make to her cottage. They planned it all. They were to drive over the moor and lunch out of doors among the heather. They would see all the twelve children and Dickon's garden and would not come back until they were tired.

Susan Sowerby got up at last to return to the house and Mrs. Medlock. It was time for Colin to be wheeled back also. But before he got into his chair he stood quite close to Susan and fixed his eyes on her with a kind of bewildered adoration and he suddenly caught hold of the fold of her blue cloak and held it fast.

"You were just what I–what I wanted," he said. "I wish you were my mother–as well as Dickon's!"

All at once Susan Sowerby bent down and drew him with her warm arms close against the bosom under the blue cloak–as if he had been Dickon's brother. The quick mist swept over her eyes.

"Eh! dear lad!" she said. Thy father mun come back to thee–he mun!"

CHAPTER 27

IN THE GARDEN

In each century since the beginning of the world wonderful things have been discovered. In the last century more amazing things were found out than in any century before. In this new century hundreds of things still more astounding will be brought to light. At first people refuse to believe that a strange new thing can be done, then they begin to hope it can't be done, then they see it can be done–then it is done and all the world wonders why it was not done centuries ago. One of the new things people began to find out in the last century was that thoughts–just mere thoughts–are as powerful as electric batteries–as good for one as sunlight is, or as bad for one as poison. To let a sad thought or a bad one get into your mind is as dangerous as letting a scarlet fever germ get into your body. If you let it stay there after it has got in you may never get over it as long as you live.

So long as Mistress Mary's mind was full of disagreeable thoughts about her dislikes and sour opinions of people and her determination not to be pleased by or interested in anything, she was a yellow-faced, sickly, bored, and wretched child. Circumstances, however, were very kind to her, though she was not at all aware of it. They began to push her about for her own good. When her mind gradually filled itself with robins, and moorland cottages crowded with children, with queer, crabbed old gardeners and common little Yorkshire housemaids, with springtime and with secret gardens coming alive day by day, and also with a moor boy and his "creatures", there was no room left for the disagreeable thoughts which affected her liver and her digestion and made her yellow and tired.

So long as Colin shut himself up in his room and thought only of his fears and weakness and his detestation of people who looked at him and reflected hourly on humps and early death, he was a hysterical, half-crazy little hypochondriac who knew nothing of the sunshine and the spring, and also did not know that he could get well and stand upon his feet if he tried to do it. When new, beautiful thoughts began to push out the old, hideous ones, life began to come back to him, his blood ran healthily through his veins, and strength poured into him like a flood. His scientific experiment was quite practical and simple and there was nothing weird about it at all. Much more surprising things can happen to anyone who, when a disagreeable or discouraged thought comes into his mind, just has the sense to remember in time and push it out by putting in an agreeable, determinedly courageous one. Two things cannot be in one place.

Where you tend a rose, my lad,
A thistle cannot grow.

While the secret garden was coming alive and two children were coming alive with it, there was a man wandering about certain far-away beautiful places in the Norwegian fjords, and the valleys and mountains of Switzerland, and he was a man who for ten years had kept his mind filled with dark and heart-broken thinking. He had not been courageous; he had never tried to put any other thoughts in the place of the dark ones. He had wandered by blue lakes and thought them; he had lain on mountain sides with sheets of deep-blue gentians blooming all about him and flower breaths filling all the air and he had thought them. A terrible sorrow had fallen upon him when he had been happy and he had let his soul fill itself with blackness and had refused obstinately to allow any rift of light to pierce through. He had forgotten and deserted his home and his duties. When he travelled about, darkness so brooded over him that the sight of him was a wrong done to other people because it was as if he poisoned the air about him with gloom. Most strangers thought he must be either half mad or a man with some hidden crime on his soul. He was a tall man with a drawn face and crooked shoulders, and the name he always entered on hotel registers was "Archibald Craven, Misselthwaite Manor, Yorkshire, England".

He had travelled far and wide since the day he saw Mistress Mary in his study and told her she might have her "bit of earth". He had been in the most beautiful places in Europe, though he had remained nowhere more than a few days. He had chosen the quietest and remotest spots. He had been on the tops of mountains whose heads were in the clouds and had looked down on other mountains when the sun rose and touched them with such light as made it seem as if the world were just being born.

But the light had never seemed to touch himself until one day when he realized that for the first time in ten years a strange thing had happened. He was in a wonderful valley in the Austrian Tyrol and he had been walking along through such beauty as might have lifted any man's soul out of shadow. He had walked a long way and it had not lifted his. But at last he had felt tired and had thrown himself down to rest on a carpet of moss by a stream. It was a clear little stream which ran quite merrily along on its narrow way through the luscious damp greenness. Sometimes it made a sound rather like very low laughter as it bubbled over and round stones. He saw birds come and dip their heads to drink it in and then flick their wings and fly away. It seemed like a thing alive and yet its tiny voice made the stillness seem deeper. The valley was very, very still.

As he sat gazing into the clear running of the water, Archibald Craven gradually felt his mind and body both grow quiet, as quiet as the valley itself. He wondered if he were going to sleep, but he was not. He sat and gazed at the sunlit water and his eyes began to see things growing at its edge. There was one lovely mass of blue forget-me-nots growing so close to the stream that its leaves were wet and at these he found himself looking as he remembered he had looked at such things years ago. He was actually thinking tenderly how lovely it was and what wonders of blue its hundreds of little blossoms were. He did not know that just that simple thought was slowly filling his mind–filling and filling it until other things were softly pushed aside. It was as if a sweet, clear spring had begun to rise in a stagnant pool and had risen and risen until at last it swept the dark water away. But of course he did not think of this himself. He only knew that the valley seemed to grow quieter and quieter as he sat and stared at the bright, delicate blueness. He did not know how long he sat there or what was happening to him, but at last he moved as if he were awakening and he got up slowly and stood on the moss carpet, drawing a long, deep, soft breath and wondering at himself. Something seemed to have been unbound and released in him, very quietly.

"What is it?" he said, almost in a whisper, and he passed his hand over his forehead. "I almost feel as if–I were alive!"

I do not know enough about the wonderfulness of undiscovered things to be able to explain how this had happened to him. Neither does anyone else yet. He did not understand at all himself–but he remembered this strange hour months afterwards when he was at Misselthwaite again and he found out quite by accident that on this very day Colin had cried out as he went into the secret garden:

"I am going to live for ever and ever and ever!"

The singular calmness remained with him the rest of the

evening, and he slept a new, reposeful sleep; but it was not with him very long. He did not know that it could be kept. By the next night he had opened the doors wide to his dark thoughts, and they had come trooping and rushing back. He left the valley and went on his wandering way again. But, strange as it seemed to him, there were minutes–sometimes half-hours–when, without his knowing why, the black burden seemed to lift itself again and he knew he was a living man and not a dead one. Slowly–slowly–for no reason that he knew of–he was coming alive with the garden.

As the golden summer changed into the deeper golden autumn he went to the Lake of Como. There he found the loveliness of a dream. He spent his days upon the crystal blueness of the lake or he walked back into the soft, thick verdure of the hills and tramped until he was tired, so that he might sleep. But by this time he had begun to sleep better, he knew, and his dreams had ceased to be a terror to him.

"Perhaps," he thought, "my body is growing stronger."

It was growing stronger but–because of the rare, peaceful hours when his thoughts were changed–his soul was slowly growing stronger, too. He began to think of Misselthwaite and wonder if he should not go home. Now and then he wondered vaguely about his boy and asked himself what he should feel when he went and stood by the carved four-poster bed again and looked down at the sharply chiselled, ivory-white face while it slept and the black lashes rimmed so startlingly the close-shut eyes. He shrank from it.

One marvel of a day he had walked so far that when he returned the moon was high and full and all the world was purple shadow and silver. The stillness of lake and shore and wood was so wonderful that he did not go into the villa he lived in. He walked down to a little flowered terrace at the water's edge and sat upon a seat and breathed in all the heavenly scents of the night. He felt the strange calmness stealing over him and it grew deeper and deeper until he fell asleep.

He did not know when he fell asleep and when he began to dream, his dream was so real that he did not feel as if he were dreaming. He remembered afterwards how intensely wide awake and alert he had thought he was. He thought that as he sat and breathed in the scent of the late roses and listened to the lapping of the water at his feet, he heard a voice calling. It was sweet and clear and happy and far away. It seemed very far, but he heard it as distinctly as if it had been at his very side.

"Archie! Archie! Archie!" it said, and then again, sweeter and clearer than before, "Archie! Archie!"

He thought he sprang to his feet, not even startled.

It was such a real voice and it seemed so natural that he should hear it.

"Lilias! Lilias!" he answered. "Lilias! Where are you?"

"In the garden," it came back like a sound from a golden flute. "In the garden!"

And then the dream ended. But he did not awaken. He slept soundly and sweetly all through the lovely night. When he did awake at last it was brilliant morning and a servant was standing staring at him. He was an Italian servant and was accustomed, as all the servants of the villa were, to accepting without question any strange thing his foreign master might do. No one ever knew when he would go out or come in or where he would choose to sleep or if he would roam about the garden or lie in the boat on the lake all night. The man held a salver with some letters on it and he waited quietly until Mr. Craven took them. When he had gone away Mr. Craven sat a few moments holding them in his hand and looking at the lake. His strange calm was still upon him and something more–a lightness, as if the cruel thing which had been done had not happened as he thought–as if something had changed. He was remembering the dream–the real, real dream.

"In the garden!" he said, wondering at himself. "In the garden! But the door is locked and the key is buried deep."

When he glanced at the letters a few minutes later, he saw that the one lying at the top of the rest was an English letter and came from Yorkshire. It was directed in a plain woman's hand, but it was not a hand he knew. He opened it, scarcely thinking of the writer, but the first words attracted his attention at once.

Dear Sir,

I am Susan Sowerby that made bold to speak to you once on the moor. It was about Miss Mary I spoke. I will make bold to speak again. Please, sir, I would come home if I was you. I think you would be glad to come and–if you will excuse me, sir–I think your lady would ask you to come if she was here,

Your obedient servant,
Susan Sowerby

Mr. Craven read the letter twice before he put it back in its envelope. He kept thinking about the dream.

"I will go back to Misselthwaite," he said. "Yes, I'll go at once."

And he went through the garden to the villa and ordered Pitcher to prepare for his return to England.

In a few days he was in Yorkshire again, and on his long railroad journey he found himself thinking of his boy as he had never thought in all the ten years past. During those years he had only wished to forget him. Now, though he did not intend to think about him, memories of him constantly drifted into his mind. He remembered the black days when he had raved like a madman because the child was alive and the mother was dead. He had refused to see it, and when he had gone to look at it at last it had been such a weak wretched thing that everyone had been sure it would die in a few days. But to the surprise of those who took care of it the days passed and it lived, and then everyone believed it would be a deformed and crippled creature.

He had not meant to be a bad father, but he had not felt like a father at all. He had supplied doctors and nurses and luxuries, but he had shrunk from the mere thought of the boy and had buried himself in his own misery. The first time after a year's absence he returned to Misselthwaite and the small miserable-looking thing languidly and indifferently lifted to his face the great grey eyes with black lashes round them, so like and yet so horribly unlike the happy eyes he had adored, he could not bear the sight of them and turned away pale as death. After that he scarcely ever saw him except when he was asleep, and all he knew of him was that he was a confirmed invalid, with a vicious, hysterical, half-insane temper. He could only be kept from furies dangerous to himself by being given his own way in every detail.

All this was not an uplifting thing to recall, but as the train whirled him through the mountain passes and golden plains, the man who was "coming alive" began to think in a new way and he thought long and steadily and deeply.

"Perhaps I have been all wrong for ten years," he said to himself. "Ten years is a long time. It may be too late to do anything–quite too late. What have I been thinking of! "

Of course this was the wrong Magic–to begin by saying "too late". Even Colin could have told him that. But he knew nothing of Magic–either black or white. This he had yet to learn. He wondered if Susan Sowerby had taken courage and written to him only because the motherly creature had realized that the boy was much worse–was fatally ill. If he had not been under the spell of the curious calmness which had taken possession of him he would have been more wretched than ever. But the calm had brought a sort of courage and hope with it. Instead of giving way to thoughts of the worst he actually found he was trying to believe in better things.

"Could it be possible that she sees that I may be able to do him good and control him?" he thought. "I will go and see her on my way to Misselthwaite."

But when on his way across the moor he stopped the carriage at the cottage, seven or eight children who were playing about gathered in a group and bobbing seven or eight friendly and polite curtsies, they told him that their mother had gone to the other side of the moor early in the morning to help a woman who had a new baby. Our Dickon, they volunteered, was over at the manor working in one of the gardens, where he spent several days each week.

Mr. Craven looked over the collection of sturdy little bodies and round, red-cheeked faces, each one grinning in its own particular way, and he awoke to the fact that they were a healthy, likeable lot. He smiled to their friendly grins, and took a golden sovereign from his pocket and gave it to our 'Lizabeth Ellen, who was the oldest.

"If you divide that into eight parts there will be half a crown for each of you", he said.

Then amid grins and chuckles and bobbing of curtsies, he

drove away, leaving ecstasy and nudging elbows and little jumps of joy behind.

The drive across the wonderfulness of the moor was a soothing thing. Why did it seem to give him a sense of home coming which he had been sure he could never feel again–that sense of the beauty of land and sky and purple bloom of distance, and a warming of the heart at drawing nearer to the great old house which had held those of his blood for six hundred years? How he had driven away from it the last time shuddering to think of its closed rooms and the boy living in the four-poster bed with the brocaded hangings. Was it possible that perhaps he might find him changed a little for the better, and that he might overcome shrinking from him? How real that dream had been–how wonderful and clear the voice which had called back to him, In the garden–In the garden!

"I will try to find the key," he said. "I will try to open the door. I must-though I don't know why."

When he arrived at the Manor the servants who received him with the usual ceremony, noticed that he looked better, and that he did not go to the remote rooms where he usually lived, attended by Pitcher. He went into the library and sent for Mrs. Medlock. She came to him somewhat excited, and curious and flustered.

"How is Master Colin, Medlock?" he inquired.

"Well, sir," Mrs. Medlock answered, "he's–he's different, in a manner of speaking."

"Worse?" he suggested.

Mrs. Medlock really was flushed.

"Well, you see, sir," she tried to explain, "neither Dr. Craven, nor the nurse, nor me can exactly make him out."

"Why is that?"

"To tell the truth, sir, Master Colin might be better and he might be changing for the worse. His appetite, sir, is past understanding–and his ways–"

"Has he become more–more peculiar?" her master asked, knitting his brows anxiously.

"That's it, sir. He's growing very peculiar–when you compare him with what he used to be. He used to eat nothing, and then suddenly he began to eat something enormous–and then he stopped again all at once and the meals were sent back just as they used to be. You never knew, sir, perhaps, that out of doors he never would let himself be taken. The things we've gone through to get him to go out in his chair would leave a body trembling like a leaf. He'd throw himself into such a state that Dr. Craven said he couldn't be responsible for forcing him. Well, sir, just without warning–not long after one of his worst tantrums, he suddenly insisted on being taken out every day by Miss Mary and Susan Sowerby's boy, Dickon, that could push his chair. He took a fancy to both Miss Mary and Dickon, and Dickon brought his tame animals, and, if you'll credit it, sir, out of doors he will stay from morning until night."

"How does he look?" was the next question.

"If he took his food natural, sir, you'd think he was putting on flesh–but we're afraid it may be a sort of bloat. He laughs sometimes in a queer way when he's alone with Miss Mary. He never used to laugh at all. Dr. Craven is coming to see you at once, if you'll allow him. He never was as puzzled in his life."

"Where is Master Colin now?" Mr. Craven asked.

"In the garden, sir. He's always in the garden–though not a human creature is allowed to go near for fear they'll look at him."

Mr. Craven scarcely heard her last words.

"In the garden!" he said, and after he had sent Mrs. Medlock away, he stood and repeated it again and again. "In the garden!"

He had to make an effort to bring himself back to the place he was standing in, and when he felt he was on earth again he turned and went out of the room. He took his way, as Mary had done, through the door in the shrubbery and among the laurels and the fountain beds. The fountain was playing now, and was encircled by beds of brilliant autumn flowers. He crossed the lawn and turned into the Long Walk by the ivied walls. He did not walk quickly, but slowly, and his eyes were on the path. He felt as if he were being drawn back to the place he had so long forsaken, and he did not know why. As he drew near to it his step became still more slow. He knew where the door was, even though the ivy hung over it–but he did not know exactly where it lay–that buried key.

So he stopped and stood still, looking about him, and almost the moment after he had paused he started and listened–asking himself if he were walking in a dream.

The ivy hung thick over the door, the key was buried under the shrubs, no human being had passed that portal for ten lonely years–and yet inside the garden there were sounds. They were the sounds of running, scuffling feet seeming to chase round and round under the kees, they were strange sounds of lowered, suppressed voices–exclamations and smothered, joyous cries. It seemed actually like the laughter of young things, the uncontrollable laughter of children who were trying not to be heard, but who in a moment or so–as their excitement mounted–would burst forth. What in heaven's name was he dreaming of–what in heaven's name did he hear? Was he losing his reason and thinking he heard things which were not for human ears? Was it that the far, dear voice had meant?

And then the moment came, the uncontrollable moment when the sounds forgot to hush themselves. The feet ran faster and faster–they were nearing the garden door–there was quick, strong, young breathing and a wild outbreak of laughing shouts which could not be contained–and the door in the wall was flung wide open, the sheet of ivy swinging back, and a boy burst through it at full speed and, without seeing the outsider, dashed almost into his arms.

Mr. Craven had extended them just in time to save him from falling as a result of his unseeing dash against him, and when he held him away to look at him in amazement at his being there he truly gasped for breath.

He was a tall boy and a handsome one. He was glowing with life, and his running had sent splendid colour leaping to his face. He threw the thick hair back from his forehead and lifted a pair of strange grey eyes–eyes full of boyish laughter and rimmed with black lashes like a fringe. It was the eyes which made Mr. Craven gasp for breath.

"Who–What? Who?" he stammered.

This was not what Colin had expected–this was not what he had planned. He had never thought of such a meeting. And yet to come dashing out–winning a race–perhaps it was even better. He drew himself up to his very tallest. Mary, who had been running with him and had dashed through the door too, believed that he managed to make himself look taller than he had ever looked before–inches taller.

"Father," he said, "I'm Colin. You can't believe it. I scarcely can myself, I'm Colin."

Like Mrs. Medlock, he did not understand what his father meant when he said hurriedly:

"In the garden! In the garden!"

"Yes," hurried on Colin. "It was the garden that did it–and Mary and Dickon and the creatures–and the Magic. No one knows. We kept it to tell you when you came. I'm well; I can beat Mary in a race. I'm going to be an athlete."

He said it all so like a healthy boy–his face flushed, his words tumbling over each other in his eagerness–that Mr. Craven's soul shook with unbelieving joy.

Colin put out his hand and laid it on his father's arm.

"Aren't you glad, father?" he ended. "Aren't you glad? I'm going to live for ever and ever and ever! "

Mr. Craven put his hands on both the boy's shoulders and held him still. He knew he dared not even try to speak for a moment.

"Take me into the garden, my boy," he said at last. "And tell me all about it."

And so they led him in.

The place was a wilderness of autumn gold and purple and violet and flaming scarlet, and on every side were sheaves of late lilies standing together–lilies which were white or white and ruby. He remembered well when the first of them had been planted that just at this season of the year their late glories should reveal themselves. Late roses climbed and hung and clustered, and the sunshine deepening the hue of the yellowing trees made one feel that one stood in an embowered temple of gold. The newcomer stood silent just as the children had done when they came into its greyness. He looked round and round.

"I thought it would be dead," he said.

"Mary thought so at first," said Colin. "But it came alive."

Then they sat down under their tree–all but Colin, who wanted to stand while he told the story.

It was the strangest thing he had ever heard, Archibald Craven thought, as it was poured forth in headlong boy fashion. Mystery and Magic and wild creatures, the weird midnight meeting–the coming of the spring–the passion of insulted pride which had dragged the young rajah to his feet to defy old Ben Weatherstaff to his face. The odd companionship, the play-acting, the great secret so carefully kept. The listener laughed until tears came into his eyes, and sometimes tears came into his eyes when he was not laughing. The Athlete, the Lecturer, the Scientific Discoverer was a laughable, lovable, healthy young human thing.

"Now," he said at the end of the story, "it need not be a secret any more. I dare say it will frighten them nearly into fits when they see me–but I am never going to get into the chair again. I shall walk back with you, Father–to the house."

*

Ben Weatherstaff's duties rarely took him away from the gardens, but on this occasion he made an excuse to carry some vegetables to the kitchen, and being invited into the servants' hall by Mrs. Medlock to drink a glass of beer, he was on the spot–as he had hoped to be–when the most dramatic event Misselthwaite Manor had seen during the present generation actually took place.

One of the windows looking upon the courtyard gave also a glimpse of the lawn. Mrs. Medlock, knowing Ben had come from the gardens, hoped that he might have caught sight of his master, and even by chance of his meeting with Master Colin.

"Did you see either of them, Weatherstaff?" she asked.

Ben took his beer-mug from his mouth and wiped his lips with the back of his hand.

"Aye, that I did," he answered with a shrewdly significant air.

"Both of them?" suggested Mrs. Medlock.

"Both of 'em," returned Ben Weatherstaff. "Thank ye kindly, ma'am, I could sup up another mug of it."

"Together?" said Mrs. Medlock, hastily overfilling his beer-mug in her excitement.

"Together, ma'am," and Ben gulped down half of his new mug at one gulp.

"Where was Master Colin? How did he look? What did they say to each other?"

"I didna hear that," said Ben, "along o' only bein' on th' step-ladder lookin' over th' wall. But I'll tell thee this. There's been things goin' on outside as you house people knows nowt about. An' what tha'll find out soon."

And it was not two minutes before he swallowed the last of his beer and waved his mug solemnly towards the window which took in, through the shrubbery, a piece of the lawn.

"Look here," he said, "if tha's curious. Look what's comin' across th' grass."

When Mrs. Medlock looked she threw up her hands and gave a little shriek, and every man and woman servant within hearing bolted across the servants' hall and stood looking through the window with their eyes almost starting out of their heads.

Across the lawn came the Master of Misselthwaite, and he looked as many of them had never seen him. And by his side, with his head up in the air and his eyes full of laughter, walked as strongly and steadily as any boy in Yorkshire–Master Colin!

Peter Pan

J. M. Barrie

Peter Pan

PARRAGON

Peter Pan
A Parragon Classic

This is a Siena Book
Siena is an imprint of Parragon

First published 1911

This edition published in 1999 by
Parragon
13 Whiteladies Road
Clifton
Bristol BS8 1PB

Printed and bound in the UK

CHAPTER 1

PETER BREAKS THROUGH

All children, except one, grow up. They soon know that they will grow up, and the way Wendy knew was this. One day when she was two years old she was playing in a garden, and she plucked another flower and ran with it to her mother. I suppose she must have looked rather delightful, for Mrs Darling put her hand to her heart and cried, "Oh, why can't you remain like this for ever!" This was all that passed between them on the subject, but henceforth Wendy knew that she must grow up. You always know after you are two. Two is the beginning of the end.

Of course they lived at 14, and until Wendy came her mother was the chief one. She was a lovely lady, with a romantic mind and such a sweet mocking mouth. Her romantic mind was like the tiny boxes, one within the other, that came from the puzzling East, however many you discover there is always one more; and her sweet mocking mouth had one kiss on it that Wendy could never get, though there it was, perfectly conspicuous in the right-hand corner.

The way Mr Darling won her was this; the many gentlemen who had been boys when she was a girl discovered simultaneously that they loved her, and they all ran to her house to propose to her except Mr Darling, who took a cab and nipped in first, and so he got her. He got all of her, except the innermost box and the kiss. He never knew about the box, and in time gave up trying for the kiss. Wendy thought Napoleon could have got it, but I can picture him trying, and then going off in a passion, slamming the door.

Mr Darling used to boast to Wendy that her mother not only loved him but respected him. He was one of those deep ones who know about stocks and shares. Of course no one really knows, but he quite seemed to know, and he often said stocks were up and shares were down in a way that would have made any woman respect him.

Mrs Darling was married in white, and at first she kept the books perfectly, almost gleefully, as if it were a game, not so much as a brussels spout was missing; but by and by whole cauliflowers dropped out, and instead of them there were pictures of babies without faces. She drew them when she should have been totting up. They were Mrs Darling's guesses.

Wendy came first, then John, then Michael.

For a week or two after Wendy came it was doubtful whether they would be able to keep her, as she was another mouth to feed. Mr Darling was frightfully proud of her, but he was very honourable, and he sat on the edge of Mrs Darling's bed, holding her and calculating expenses, while she looked at him imploringly. She wanted to risk it, come what might, but that was not his way; his way was with a pencil and a piece of paper, and if she confused him with suggestions he had to begin at the beginning again.

"Now don't interrupt," he would beg of her. "I have one pound seventeen here, and two and six at the office; I can cut off my coffee at the office, say ten shillings, making two nine and six, with your eighteen and three makes three nine seven, with five naught naught in my cheque-book makes eight nine seven – who is that moving? – eight nine seven, dot and carry seven – don't speak, my own – and the pound you lent to that man who came to the door – quiet, child – dot and carry child – there, you've done it! – did I say nine nine seven? Yes, I said nine nine seven; the question is, can we try it for a year on nine nine seven?"

"Of course we can, George," she cried. But she was prejudiced in Wendy's favour, and he was really the grander character of the two.

"Remember mumps," he warned her almost threateningly and off he went again. "Mumps one pound, that is what I have put down, but I dare say it will be more like thirty shillings – don't speak – measles one five, German measles half a guinea, makes two fifteen six – don't waggle your finger – whooping-cough, say fifteen shillings" – and so on it went, and it added up differently each time; but at last Wendy just got through, with mumps reduced to twelve six, and the two kinds of measles treated as one.

There was the same excitement over John, and Michael had even a narrower squeak; but both were kept, and soon you might have seen the three of them going in a row to Miss Fulsom's Kindergarten school, accompanied by their nurse.

Mrs Darling loved to have everything just so, and Mr Darling had a passion for being exactly like his neighbours; so, of course, they had a nurse. As they were poor owing to the amount of milk children drank, this nurse was a prim Newfoundland dog, called Nana, who had belonged to no one in particular until the Darlings engaged her. She had always thought children important, however, and the Darlings had become acquainted with her in Kensington Gardens, where she spent most of her spare time peeping into perambulators, and was much hated by careless nursemaids, whom she followed to their homes and complained of to their mistresses. She proved to be quite a treasure of a nurse. How thorough she was at bath-time; and up at any moment of the night if one of her charges made the slightest cry. Of course her kennel was in the nursery. She had a genius for knowing when a cough is a thing to have no patience with and when it needs a stocking round your throat. She believed to her last day in old-fashioned remedies like rhubarb leaf, and made sounds of contempt over all this new-fangled talk about germs, and so on. It was a lesson in propriety to see her escorting the children to school, walking sedately by their side when they were well behaved, and butting them back into line if they strayed. On John's footer days she never once forgot his sweater, and she usually carried an umbrella in her mouth in case of rain. There is a room in the basement of Miss Fulsom's school where the nurses wait. They sat on forms, while Nana lay on the floor, but that was the only difference. They affected to ignore her as of an inferior social status to themselves, and she despised their light talk. She resented visits to the nursery from Mrs Darling's friends, but if they did come she first whipped off Michael's pinafore and put him into the one with blue braiding, and smoothed out Wendy and made a dash at John's hair.

No nursery could possibly have been conducted more correctly, and Mr Darling knew it, yet he sometimes wondered uneasily whether the neighbours talked.

He had his position in the city to consider.

Nana also troubled him in another way. He had sometimes a feeling that she did not admire him. "I know she admires you tremendously, George," Mrs Darling would assure him, and then she would sign to the children to be specially nice to father. Lovely dances followed, in which the only other servant, Liza, was sometimes allowed to join. Such a midget she looked in her long skirt and maid's cap, though she had sworn, when engaged, that she would never see ten again. The gaiety of those romps! And gayest of all was Mrs Darling, who would pirouette so wildly that all you could see of her was the kiss, and then if you had dashed at her you might have got it. There never was a simpler, happier family until the coming of Peter Pan.

Mrs Darling first heard of Peter when she was tidying up her children's minds. It is the nightly custom of every good mother after her children are asleep to rummage in their minds and put things straight for next morning, repacking into their proper places the many articles that have wandered during the day. If you could keep awake (but of course you can't) you would see your own mother doing this, and you would find it very interesting to watch her. It is quite like tidying up drawers. You would see her on her knees, I expect, lingering humorously over some of your contents, wondering where on earth you had picked this thing up, making discoveries sweet and not so sweet, pressing this to her cheek as if it were as nice as a kitten, and hurriedly stowing that out of sight. When you wake in the morning, the naughtiness and evil passions with which you went to bed have been folded up small and placed at the bottom of your mind; and on the top, beautifully aired, are spread out your prettier thoughts, ready for you to put on.

I don't know whether you have ever seen a map of a person's mind. Doctors sometimes draw maps of other parts of you, and your own map can become intensely interesting, but catch them trying to draw a map of a child's mind, which is not only confused, but keeps going round all the time. There are zigzag lines on it, just like your temperature on a card, and these are probably roads in the island; for the Neverland is always more or less an island, with astonishing splashes of colour here and there, and coral reefs and rakish-looking craft in the offing, and savages and lonely lairs, and gnomes who are mostly tailors, and caves through which a river runs, and princes with six elder brothers, and a hut fast going to decay, and one very small old lady with a hooked nose. It would be an easy map if that were all; but there is also first day at school, religion, fathers, the round pond, needlework, murders, hangings, verbs that take the dative, chocolate-pudding day, getting into braces, say ninety-nine, threepence for pulling out your tooth yourself, and so on; and either these are part of the island or they are another map showing through, and it is all rather confusing, especially as nothing will stand still.

Of course the Neverlands vary a good deal. John's, for instance, had a lagoon with flamingoes flying over it at which John was shooting, while Michael, who was very small, had a flamingo with lagoons flying over it. John lived in a boat turned upside down on the sands, Michael in a wigwam, Wendy in a house of leaves deftly sewn together. John had no friends, Michael had friends at night, Wendy had a pet wolf forsaken by its parents; but on the whole the Neverlands have a family resemblance, and if they stood still in a row you could say of them that they have each other's nose, and so forth. On these magic shores children at play are for ever beaching their coracles. We too have been there; we can still hear the sound of the surf, though we shall land no more.

Of all delectable islands the Neverland is the snuggest and most compact; not large and sprawly, you know, with tedious distances between one adventure and another, but nicely crammed. When you play at it by day with the chairs and table-cloth, it is not in the least alarming but in the two minutes before you go to sleep it becomes very nearly real. That is why there are night-lights.

Occasionally in her travels through her children's minds Mrs Darling found things she could not understand, and of these quite the most perplexing was the word Peter. She knew of no Peter, and yet he was here and there in John and Michael's minds, while Wendy's began to be scrawled all over with him. The name stood out in bolder letters than any of the other words, and as Mrs Darling gazed she felt that it had an oddly cocky appearance.

"Yes, he is rather cocky," Wendy admitted with regret. Her mother had been questioning her.

"But who is he, my pet?"

"He is Peter Pan, you know, mother."

At first Mrs Darling did not know, but after thinking back into her childhood she just remembered a Peter Pan who was said to live with the fairies. There were odd stories about him; as that when children died he went part of the way with them, so that they should not be frightened. She had believed in him at the time, but now that she was married and full of sense she quite doubted whether there was any such person.

"Besides," she said to Wendy, "he would be grown up by this time."

"Oh no, he isn't grown up," Wendy assured her confidently, "and he is just my size." She meant that he was her size in both mind and body; she didn't know how she knew it, she just knew it.

Mrs Darling consulted Mr Darling, but he smiled pooh-pooh. "Mark my words," he said, "it is some nonsense Nana has been putting into their heads; just the sort of idea a dog would leave. Leave it alone, and it will blow over."

But it would not blow over; and soon the troublesome boy gave Mrs Darling quite a shock.

Children have the strangest adventures without being troubled by them. For instance, they may remember to mention, a week after the event happened, that when they were in the wood they met their dead father and had a game with him. It was in this casual way that Wendy one morning made a disquieting revelation. Some leaves of a tree had been found on the nursery floor, which certainly were not there when the children went to bed, and Mrs Darling was puzzling over them when Wendy said with a tolerant smile:

"I do believe it is that Peter again!"

"Whatever do you mean, Wendy?"

"It is so naughty of him not to wipe," Wendy said, sighing. She was a tidy child.

She explained in quite a matter-of-fact way that she thought Peter sometimes came to the nursery in the night and sat on the foot of her bed and played on his pipes to her. Unfortunately she never woke, so she didn't know how she knew, she just knew.

"What nonsense you talk, precious. No one can get into the house without knocking."

"I think he comes in by the window," she said.

"My love, it is three floors up."

"Were not the leaves at the foot of the window, mother?"

It was quite true; the leaves had been found very near the window.

Mrs Darling did not know what to think, for it all seemed so natural to Wendy that you could not dismiss it by saying she had been dreaming.

"My child," the mother cried, "why did you not tell me of this before?"

"I forgot," said Wendy lightly. She was in a hurry to get her breakfast.

Oh, surely she must have been dreaming.

But, on the other hand, there were the leaves. Mrs Darling examined them carefully; they were skeleton leaves, but she was sure they did not come from any tree that grew in England. She crawled about the floor, peering at it with a candle for marks of a strange foot. She rattled the poker up the chimney and tapped the walls. She let down a tape from the window to the pavement, and it was a sheer drop of thirty feet, without so much as a spout to climb up by.

Certainly Wendy had been dreaming.

But Wendy had not been dreaming, as the very next night showed, the night on which the extraordinary adventures of these children may be said to have begun.

On the night we speak of all the children were once more in bed. It happened to be Nana's evening off, and Mrs Darling had bathed and sung to them till one by one they had let go her hand and slid away into the land of sleep.

All were looking so safe and cosy that she smiled at her fears now and sat down tranquilly by the fire to sew.

It was something for Michael, who on his birthday was getting into shirts. The fire was warm, however, and the nursery dimly lit by three night-lights, and presently the sewing lay on Mrs Darling's lap. Then her head nodded, oh, so gracefully. She was asleep. Look at the four of them, Wendy and Michael over there, John here, and Mrs Darling by the fire. There should have been a fourth night-light.

While she slept she had a dream. She dreamt that the Neverland had come too near and that a strange boy had broken through from it. He did not alarm her, for she thought she had seen him before in the faces of many women who have no children. Perhaps he is to be found in the faces of some mothers also. But in her dream he had rent the film that obscures the Neverland, and she saw Wendy and John and Michael peeping through the gap.

The dream by itself would have been a trifle, but while she was dreaming the window of the nursery blew open, and a boy did drop on the floor. He was accompanied by a strange light, no bigger than your fist, which darted about the room like a living thing; and I think it must have been this light that wakened Mrs Darling.

She started up with a cry, and saw the boy, and somehow she knew at once that he was Peter Pan. If you or I or Wendy had been there we should have seen that he was very like Mrs Darling's kiss. He was a lovely boy, clad in skeleton leaves and the juices that ooze out of trees; but the most entrancing thing about him was that he had all his first teeth. When he saw she was a grown-up, he gnashed the little pearls at her.

CHAPTER 2

THE SHADOW

Mrs Darling screamed, and, as if in answer to a bell, the door opened, and Nana entered, returned from her evening out. She growled and sprang at the boy, who leapt lightly through the window. Again Mrs Darling screamed, this time in distress for him, for she thought he was killed, and she ran down into the street to look for his little body, but it was not there; and she looked up, and in the black night she could see nothing but what she thought was a shooting star.

She returned to the nursery, and found Nana with something in her mouth, which proved to be the boy's shadow. As he leapt at the window Nana had closed it quickly, too late to catch him, but his shadow had not had time to get out; slam went the window and snapped it off.

You may be sure Mrs Darling examined the shadow carefully, but it was quite the ordinary kind.

Nana had no doubt of what was the best thing to do with this shadow. She hung it out at the window, meaning "He is sure to come back for it; let us put it where he can get it easily without disturbing the children."

But unfortunately Mrs Darling could not leave it hanging out at the window; it looked so like the washing and lowered the whole tone of the house. She thought of showing it to Mr Darling, but he was totting up winter great-coats for John and Michael, with a wet towel round his head to keep his brain clear, and it seemed a shame to trouble him; besides, she knew exactly what he would say: "It all comes of having a dog for a nurse."

She decided to roll the shadow up and put it away carefully in a drawer, until a fitting opportunity came for telling her husband. Ah me!

The opportunity came a week later, on that never-to-be-forgotten Friday. Of course it was a Friday.

"I ought to have been specially careful on a Friday," she used to say afterwards to her husband, while perhaps Nana was on the other side of her, holding her hand.

"No, no," Mr Darling always said, "I am responsible for it all. I, George Darling, did it. *Mea culpa, mea culpa.*" He had had a classical education.

They sat thus night after night recalling that fatal Friday, till every detail of it was stamped on their brains and came through on the other side like the faces on a bad coinage.

"If only I had not accepted that invitation to dine at 27," Mrs Darling said.

"If only I had not poured my medicine into Nana's bowl," said Mr Darling.

"If only I had pretended to like the medicine," was what Nana's wet eyes said.

"My liking for parties, George."

"My fatal gift of humour, dearest."

"My touchiness about trifles, dear master and mistress."

Then one or more of them would break down altogether; Nana at the thought, "It's true, it's true, they ought not to have had a dog for a nurse." Many a time it was Mr Darling who put the handkerchief to Nana's eyes.

"That fiend!" Mr Darling would cry, and Nana's bark was the echo of it, but Mrs Darling never upbraided Peter; there was something in the right-hand corner of her mouth that wanted her not to call Peter names.

They would sit there in the empty nursery, recalling fondly every smallest detail of that dreadful evening. It had begun so uneventfully, so precisely like a hundred other evenings, with Nana putting on the water for Michael's bath and carrying him to it on her back.

"I won't go to bed," he had shouted, like one who still believed that he had the last word on the subject. "I won't, I won't. Nana, it isn't six o'clock yet. Oh dear, oh dear, I shan't love you any more, Nana, I tell you I won't be bathed, I won't, I won't!"

Then Mrs Darling had come in, wearing her white evening-gown. She had dressed early because Wendy so loved to see her in her evening-gown, with the necklace George had given her. She was wearing Wendy's bracelet on her arm; she had asked for the loan of it. Wendy so loved to lend her bracelet to her mother.

She had found her two older children playing at being herself and father on the occasion of Wendy's birth, and John was saying:

"I am happy to inform you, Mrs Darling, that you are now a mother," in just a tone as Mr Darling himself may have used on the real occasion.

Wendy had danced with joy, just as the real Mrs Darling must have done.

Then John was born, with the extra pomp that he received due to the birth of a male, and Michael came from his bath to ask to be born also, but John said brutally that they did not want any more.

Michael had nearly cried. "Nobody wants me," he said, and of course the lady in evening-dress could not stand that.

"I do," she said. "I so want a third child."

"Boy or girl?" asked Michael, not too hopefully.

"Boy."

Then he had leapt into her arms. Such a little thing for Mr and Mrs Darling and Nana to recall now, but not so little if that was to be Michael's last night in that nursery.

They go on with their recollections.

"It was then that I rushed in like a tornado, wasn't it?" Mr Darling would say, scorning himself, and indeed he had been like a tornado.

Perhaps there was some excuse for him. He, too, had been dressing for the party, and all had gone well with him until he came to his tie. It is an astounding thing to have to tell, but this man, though he knew about stocks and shares, had no real mastery of his tie. Sometimes the thing yielded to him without a contest, but there were occasions when it would have been better for the house if he had swallowed his pride and used a made-up tie!

This was such an occasion. He came rushing into the nursery with the crumpled little brute of a tie in his hand.

"Why, what is the matter, father, dear?"

"Matter!" he yelled; he really yelled. "This tie, it will not tie." He became dangerously sarcastic. "Not round my neck! Round the bedpost! Oh yes, twenty times have I made it up round the bedpost, but round my neck, no! Oh dear no! begs to be excused!"

He thought Mrs Darling was not sufficiently impressed, and he went on sternly. "I warn you of this, mother, that unless this tie is round my neck we don't go out to dinner tonight, and if I don't go out to dinner tonight, I never go to the office again, and if I don't go to the office again, you and I starve, and our children will be flung into the streets."

Even then Mrs Darling was placid. "Let me try, dear," she said, and indeed that was what he had come to ask her to do; and with her nice cool hands she tied his tie for him, while the children stood around to see their fate decided. Some men would have resented her being able to do it so easily, but Mr Darling was far too fine a nature for that; he thanked her carelessly, at once forgot his rage, and in another moment was dancing round the room with Michael on his back.

"How wildly we romped!" said Mrs Darling now, recalling it.

"Our last romp!" Mr Darling groaned.

"Oh George, do you remember Michael suddenly said to me, "How did you get to know me, mother?"

"I remember!"

"They were rather sweet, don't you think, George?"

"And they were ours, ours, and now they are gone."

The romp had ended with the appearance of Nana, and most unluckily Mr Darling collided against her, covering his trousers with hairs. They were not only new trousers but they were the first he ever had with braid on them, and he had to bite his lip to prevent the tears coming. Of course Mrs Darling brushed him, but he began to talk again about its being a mistake to have a dog for a nurse.

"George, Nana is a treasure."

"No doubt, but I have an uneasy feeling at times that she looks upon the children as puppies."

"Oh no, dear one, I feel sure she knows they have souls."

"I wonder," Mr Darling said thoughtfully, "I wonder." It was an opportunity, his wife felt, for telling him about the boy. At first he pooh-poohed the story, but he became thoughtful when she showed him the shadow.

"It is nobody," he said, examining it carefully, "but he does look a scoundrel."

"We were still discussing it, you remember," says Mr Darling, "when Nana came in with Michael's medicine. You will never carry the bottle in your mouth again, Nana, and it is all my fault."

Strong man though he was, there is no doubt that he had behaved rather foolishly over the medicine. If he had a weakness, it was for thinking that all his life he had taken medicine boldly; and so now, when Michael dodged the spoon in Nana's mouth, he had said reprovingly, "Be a man, Michael."

"Won't; won't," Michael cried naughtily. Mrs Darling left the room to get a chocolate for him, and Mr Darling thought this showed want of firmness.

"Mother, don't pamper him," he called after her. "Michael, when I was your age I took medicine without a murmur. I said 'Thank you, kind parents, for giving me bottles to make me well.'"

He really thought this was true, and Wendy, who was now in her night-gown, believed it also, and she said, to encourage Michael, "That medicine you sometimes take, father, is much nastier, isn't it?"

"Ever so much nastier," Mr Darling said bravely, "and I would take it now as an example to you, Michael, if I hadn't lost the bottle."

He had not exactly lost it; he had climbed in the dead of night to the top of the wardrobe and hidden it there. What he did not know was that the faithful Liza had found it, and put it back on his wash-stand.

"I know where it is, father," Wendy cried, always glad to be of service. "I'll bring it," and she was off before he could stop her. Immediately his spirits sank in the strangest way.

"John," he said, shuddering, "it's most beastly stuff. It's that nasty, sticky, sweet kind."

"It will soon be over, father," John said cheerily, and then in rushed Wendy with the medicine in a glass.

"I have been as quick as I could," she panted.

"You have been wonderfully quick," her father retorted, with a vindictive politeness that was quite thrown away upon her. "Michael first," he said doggedly.

"Father first," said Michael, who was of a suspicious nature.

"I shall be sick, you know," Mr Darling said threateningly.

"Come on, father," said John.

"Hold your tongue, John," his father rapped out.

Wendy was quite puzzled. "I thought you took it quite easily, father."

"That is not the point," he retorted. "The point is, that there is more in my glass than in Michael's spoon." His proud heart was nearly bursting. "And it isn't fair; I would say it though it were with my last breath – it isn't fair."

"Father, I am waiting," said Michael coldly.

"It's all very well to say you are waiting; so am I waiting."

"Father's a cowardy custard."

"So are you a cowardy custard."

"I'm not frightened."

"Neither am I frightened."

"Well, then, take it."

"Well, then you take it."

Wendy had a splendid idea. "Why not both take it at the same time?"

"Certainly," said Mr Darling. "Are you ready, Michael?"

Wendy gave the words, one, two, three, and Michael took his medicine, but Mr Darling slipped his behind his back.

There was a yell of rage from Michael, and "O father!" Wendy exclaimed.

"What do you mean by 'O father'?' Mr Darling demanded. "Stop that row, Michael. I meant to take mine, but I – I missed it."

It was dreadful the way all the three were looking at him, just as if they did not admire him. "Look here, all of you," he said entreatingly, as soon as Nana had gone into the bathroom. "I have just thought of a splendid joke. I shall pour my medicine into Nana's bowl, and she will drink it, thinking it is milk!"

It was the colour of milk; but the children did not have their father's sense of humour, and they looked at him reproachfully as he poured the medicine into Nana's bowl. "What fun," he said doubtfully, and they did not dare expose him when Mrs Darling and Nana returned.

"Nana, good dog," he said, patting her. "I have put a little milk into your bowl, Nana."

Nana wagged her tail, ran to the medicine, and began lapping it. Then she gave Mr Darling such a look, not an angry look, she showed him the great red tear that makes us so sorry for noble dogs, and crept into her kennel.

Mr Darling was frightfully ashamed of himself, but he would not give in. In a horrid silence Mrs Darling smelt the bowl. "O George," she said, "it's your medicine!"

"It was only a joke," he roared, while she comforted her boys, and Wendy hugged Nana. "Much good," he said bitterly, "my wearing myself to the bone trying to be funny in this house."

And still Wendy hugged Nana. "That's right," he shouted. "Coddle her! Nobody coddles me. Oh dear no! I am only the breadwinner, why should I be coddled, why, why, why!"

"George," Mrs Darling entreated him, "not so loud; the servants will hear you." Somehow they had got into the way of calling Liza the servants.

"Let them," he answered recklessly. "Bring in the whole world. But I refuse to allow that dog to lord it in my nursery for an hour longer."

The children wept, and Nana ran to him beseechingly, but he waved her back. He felt he was a strong man again. "In vain, in vain," he cried; "the proper place for you is the yard, and there you go to be tied up this instant."

"George, George," Mrs Darling whispered, "remember what I told you about that boy."

Alas, he would not listen. He was determined to show who was master in that house, and when commands would not draw Nana from the kennel, he lured her out of it with honeyed words, and seizing her roughly, dragged her from the nursery. He was ashamed of himself, and yet he did it.

It was all owing to his too affectionate nature, which craved for admiration. When he had tied her up in the backyard, the wretched father went and sat in the passage, with his knuckles to his eyes.

In the meantime Mrs Darling had put the children to bed in unwonted silence and lit their night-lights. They could hear Nana barking, and John whimpered, "It is because he is chaining her up in the yard," but Wendy was wiser.

"That is not Nana's unhappy bark," she said, little guessing what was about to happen; "that is her bark when she smells danger."

Danger!

"Are you sure, Wendy?"

"Oh yes."

Mrs Darling quivered and went to the window. It was securely fastened. She looked out, and the night was peppered with stars. They were crowding round the house, as if curious to see what was to take place there, but she did not notice this, nor that one or two of the smaller ones winked at her. Yet a nameless fear clutched at her heart and made her cry, "Oh, how I wish that I wasn't going to a party tonight!"

Even Michael, already half asleep, knew that she was perturbed, and he asked, "Can anything harm us, mother, after the night-lights are lit?"

"Nothing, precious," she said; "they are the eyes a mother leaves behind her to guard her children."

She went from bed to bed singing enchantments over them, and little Michael flung his arms round her. "Mother," he cried, "I'm glad of you." They were the last words she was to hear from him for a long time.

No. 27 was only a few yards distant, but there had been a slight fall of snow, and Father and Mother Darling picked their way over it deftly not to soil their shoes. They were already the only persons in the street, and all the stars were watching them. Stars are beautiful, but they may not take an active part in anything, they must just look on for ever. It is a punishment put on them for something they did so long ago that no star now knows what it was. So the older ones have become glassy-eyed and seldom speak (winking is the star language), but the little ones still wonder. They are not really friendly to Peter, who has a mischievous way of stealing up behind them and trying to blow them out; but they are so fond of fun that they were on his side tonight, and anxious to get the grown-ups out of the way. So as soon as the door of 27 closed on Mr and Mrs Darling there was a commotion in the firmament, and the smallest of all the stars in the Milky Way screamed out:

"Now, Peter!"

CHAPTER 3

COME AWAY, COME AWAY!

For a moment after Mr and Mrs Darling left the house the night-lights by the beds of the three children continued to burn clearly. They were awfully nice little night-lights, and one cannot help wishing that they could have kept awake to see Peter, but Wendy's light blinked and gave such a yawn that the other two yawned also, and before they could close their mouths all the three went out.

There was another light in the room now, a thousand times brighter than the night-lights, and in the time we have taken to say this, it has been in all the drawers in the nursery, looking for Peter's shadow, rummaged the wardrobe and turned every pocket inside out. It was not really a light; it made this light by flashing about so quickly, but when it came to rest for a second you saw it was a fairy, no longer than your hand, but still growing. It was a girl called Tinker Bell, exquisitely gowned in a skeleton leaf, cut low and square, through which her figure could be seen to the best advantage. She was slightly inclined to *embonpoint.*

A moment after the fairy's entrance the window was blown open by the breathing of the little stars, and Peter dropped in. He had carried Tinker Bell part of the way, and his hand was still messy with the fairy dust.

"Tinker Bell," he called softly, after making sure that the children were asleep. "Tink, where are you?" She was in a jug for a moment, and liking it extremely; she had never been in a jug before.

"Oh, do come out of that jug, and tell me, do you know where they put my shadow?"

The loveliest tinkle as of golden bells answered him. It is the fairy language. You ordinary children can never hear it, but if you were to hear it you would know that you had heard it once before.

Tink said that the shadow was in the big box. She meant the chest of drawers, and Peter jumped at the drawers, scattering their contents to the floor with both hands, as kings toss ha'pence to the crowd. In a moment he had recovered his shadow, and in his delight he forgot that he had shut Tinker Bell up in the drawer.

If he thought at all, but I don't believe he ever thought, it was that he and his shadow, when brought near each other, would join like drops of water; and when they did not he was appalled. He tried to stick it on with soap from the bathroom, but that also failed. A shudder passed through Peter, and he sat on the floor and cried.

His sobs woke Wendy, and she sat up in bed. She was not alarmed to see a stranger crying on the nursery floor; she was only pleasantly interested.

"Boy," she said courteously, "why are you crying?"

Peter could be exceedingly polite also, having learned the grand manner at fairy ceremonies, and he rose and bowed to her beautifully. She was much pleased, and bowed beautifully to him from the bed.

"What's your name?" he asked.

"Wendy Moira Angela Darling," she replied with some satisfaction. "What is your name?"

"Peter Pan."

She was already sure that he must be Peter, but it did seem a comparatively short name.

"Is that all?"

"Yes," he said rather sharply. He felt for the first time that it was a shortish name.

"I'm so sorry," said Wendy Moira Angela.

"It doesn't matter," Peter gulped.

She asked where he lived.

"Second to the right," said Peter, "and then straight on till morning."

"What a funny address!"

Peter had a sinking feeling. For the first time he felt that perhaps it was a funny address.

"No, it isn't," he said.

"I mean," Wendy said nicely, remembering that she was hostess, "is that what they put on the letters?"

He wished she had not mentioned letters.

"Don't get any letters," he said contemptuously.

"But your mother gets letters?"

"Don't have a mother," he said. Not only had he no mother, but he had not the slightest desire to have one. He thought them very over-rated persons. Wendy, however, felt at once that she was in the presence of a tragedy.

"O Peter, no wonder you were crying," she said, and got out of bed and ran to him.

"I wasn't crying about mothers," he said rather indignantly. "I was crying because I can't get my shadow to stick on. Besides, I wasn't crying."

"It has come off?"

"Yes."

Then Wendy saw the shadow on the floor, looking so draggled, and she was frightfully sorry for Peter. "How awful!" she said, but she could not help smiling when she saw that he had been trying to stick it on with soap. How exactly like a boy!

Fortunately she knew at once what to do. "It must be sewn on," she said, just a little patronizingly.

"What's sewn?" he asked.

"You're dreadfully ignorant."

"No, I'm not."

But she was exulting in his ignorance. "I shall sew it on for you, my little man," she said, though he was as tall as herself, and she got out her housewife, and sewed the shadow on to Peter's foot.

"I dare say it will hurt a little," she warned him.

"Oh, I shan't cry," said Peter, who was already of the opinion that he had never cried in his life. And he clenched his teeth and did not cry; and soon his shadow was behaving properly, though still a little creased.

"Perhaps I should have ironed it," Wendy said thoughtfully; but Peter, boylike, was indifferent to appearances, and he was now jumping about in the wildest glee. Alas, he had already forgotten that he owed his bliss to Wendy. He thought he had attached the shadow himself. "How clever I am," he crowed rapturously, "oh, the cleverness of me!"

It is humiliating to have to confess that this conceit of Peter was one of his most fascinating qualities. To put it with brutal frankness, there never was a cockier boy.

But for the moment Wendy was shocked. "You conceited boy," she exclaimed with frightful sarcasm; "of course I did nothing!"

"You did a little," Peter said carelessly, and continued to dance.

"A little!" she replied with hauteur; "if I am no use I can at least withdraw"; and she sprang in the most dignified way into bed and covered her face with the blankets.

To induce her to look up he pretended to be going away, and when this failed he sat on the end of the bed and tapped her gently with his foot. "Wendy," he said, "don't withdraw. I can't help crowing, Wendy, when I'm pleased with myself." Still she would not look up, though she was listening eagerly. "Wendy," he continued in a voice that no woman had ever yet been able to resist, "Wendy, one girl is more use than twenty boys."

Now Wendy was every inch a woman, though there were not very many inches, and she peeped out of the bedclothes.

"Do you really think so, Peter?"

"Yes, I do."

"I think it's perfectly sweet of you," she declared, "and I'll get up again"; and she sat with him on the side of the bed. She also said she would give him a kiss if he liked, but Peter did not know what she meant, and he held out his hand expectantly.

"Surely you know what a kiss is?" she asked, aghast.

"I shall know when you give it to me," he replied stiffly; and not to hurt his feelings she gave him a thimble.

"Now," said he, "shall I give you a kiss?" and she replied with a slight primness, "If you please." She made herself rather cheap by inclining her face towards him, but he merely dropped an acorn button into her hand; so she slowly returned her face to where it had been before, and said nicely that she would wear his kiss on the chain round her neck. It was lucky that she did put it on that chain, for it was afterwards to save her life.

When people in our set are introduced, it is customary for them to ask each other's age, and so Wendy, who always liked to do the correct thing, asked Peter how old he was. It was not really a happy question to ask him; it was like an examination paper that asks grammar, when what you want to be asked is Kings of England.

"I don't know," he replied uneasily, "but I am quite young." He really knew nothing about it; he had merely suspicions, but he said at a venture, "Wendy, I ran away the day I was born."

Wendy was quite surprised, but interested; and she indicated in the charming drawing-room manner, by a touch on her night-gown, that he could sit nearer her.

"It was because I heard father and mother," he explained in a low voice, "talking about what I was to be when I became a man." He was extraordinarily agitated now. "I don't want ever to be a man," he said with passion. "I want always to be a little boy and to have fun. So I ran away to Kensington Gardens and lived a long long time among the fairies."

She gave him a look of the most intense admiration, and he thought it was because he had run away, but it was really because he knew fairies. Wendy had lived such a home life that to know fairies struck her as quite delightful. She poured out questions about them, to his surprise, for they were rather a nuisance to him, getting in his way and so on, and indeed he sometimes had to give them a hiding. Still, he liked them on the whole, and he told her about the beginning of fairies.

"You see, Wendy, when the first baby laughed for the first time, its laugh broke into a thousand pieces, and they all went skipping about, and that was the beginning of fairies."

Tedious talk this, but being a stay-at-home she liked it.

"And so," he went on good-naturedly, "there ought to be one fairy for every boy and girl."

"Ought to be? Isn't there?"

"No. You see, children know such a lot now, they soon don't believe in fairies, and every time a child says, 'I don't believe in fairies,' there is a fairy somewhere that falls down dead."

Really, he thought they had now talked enough about fairies, and it struck him that Tinker Bell was keeping very quiet. "I can't think where she has gone to,"he said, rising, and he called Tink by name. Wendy's heart went flutter with a sudden thrill.

"Peter," she cried, clutching him, "you don't mean to tell me that there is a fairy in this room!"

"She was here just now," he said a little impatiently. "You don't hear her, do you?" and they both listened.

"The only sound I hear," said Wendy, "is like a tinkle of bells."

"Well, that's Tink, that's the fairy language. I think I hear her too."

The sound came from the chest of drawers, and Peter made a merry face. No one could ever look quite so merry as Peter, and the loveliest of gurgles was his laugh. He had his first laugh still.

"Wendy," he whispered gleefully, "I do believe I shut her up in the drawer!"

He let poor Tink out of the drawer, and she flew about the nursery, screaming with fury. "You shouldn't say such things," Peter retorted. "Of course I'm very sorry, but how could I know you were in the drawer?"

Wendy was not listening to him. "O Peter," she cried, "if she would only stand still and let me see her!"

"They hardly ever stand still," he said, but for one moment Wendy saw the romantic figure come to rest on the cuckoo clock. "O the lovely!" she cried, though Tink's face was still distorted with passion.

"Tink," said Peter amiably, "this lady says she wishes you were her fairy."

Tinker Bell answered insolently.

"What does she say, Peter?"

He had to translate. "She is not very polite. She says you are a great ugly girl, and that she is my fairy."

He tried to argue with Tink. "You know you can't be my fairy, Tink, because I am a gentleman and you are a lady."

To this Tink replied in these words, "You silly ass," and

disappeared into the bathroom. "She is quite a common fairy," Peter explained apologetically; "she is called Tinker Bell because she mends the pots and kettles."

They were together in the arm-chair by this time, and Wendy plied him with more questions.

"If you don't live in Kensington Gardens now—"

"Sometimes I do still."

"But where do you live mostly now?"

"With the lost boys."

"Who are they?"

"They are the children who fall out of their perambulators when the nurse is looking the other way. If they are not claimed in seven days they are sent far away to the Neverland to defray expenses. I'm captain."

"What fun it must be!"

"Yes," said cunning Peter, "but we are rather lonely. You see we have no female companionship."

"Are none of the others girls?"

"Oh no, girls, you know, are much too clever to fall out of their prams."

This flattered Wendy immensely. "I think," she said, "it is perfectly lovely the way you talk about girls; John there just despises us."

For reply Peter rose and kicked John out of bed, blankets and all; one kick. This seemed to Wendy rather forward for a first meeting, and she told him with spirit that he was not captain in her house. However, John continued to sleep so placidly on the floor that she allowed him to remain there. "And I know you meant to be kind," she said, relenting, "so you may give me a kiss."

For a moment she had forgotten his ignorance about kisses. "I thought you would want it back," he said a little bitterly, and offered to return her the thimble.

"Oh dear," said the nice Wendy, "I don't mean a kiss, I mean a thimble."

"What's that?"

"It's like this." She kissed him.

"Funny!" said Peter gravely. "Now shall I give you a thimble?"

"If you wish to," said Wendy, keeping her head erect this time.

Peter thimbled her, and almost immediately she screeched. "What is it, Wendy?"

"It was exactly as if someone was pulling my hair."

"That must have been Tink. I never knew her so naughty before."

And indeed Tink was darting about again, using offensive language.

"She says she will do that to you, Wendy, every time I give you a thimble."

"But why?"

"Why, Tink?"

Again Tink replied, "You silly ass." Peter could not understand why, but Wendy understood; and she was just slightly disappointed when he admitted that he came to the nursery window not to see her but to listen to stories.

"You see I don't know any stories. None of the lost boys know any stories."

"How perfectly awful," Wendy said.

"Do you know," Peter asked, "why swallows build in the eaves of houses? It is to listen to the stories. O Wendy, your mother was telling you such a lovely story."

"Which story was it?"

"About the prince who couldn't find the lady who wore the glass slipper."

"Peter," said Wendy excitedly, "that was Cinderella, and he found her, and they lived happy ever after."

Peter was so glad that he rose from the floor, where they had been sitting, and hurried to the window. "Where are you going?" she cried with misgiving.

"To tell the other boys."

"Don't go, Peter," she entreated, "I know such lots of stories."

Those were her precise words, so there can be no denying that it was she who first tempted him.

He came back, and there was a greedy look in his eye now which ought to have alarmed her, but did not.

"Oh, the stories I could tell to the boys!" she cried, and then Peter gripped her and began to draw her towards the window.

"Let me go!" she ordered him.

"Wendy, do come with me and tell the other boys."

Of course she was very pleased to be asked, but she said, "Oh dear, I can't. Think of mummy! Besides, I can't fly."

"I'll teach you."

"Oh, how lovely to fly."

"I'll teach you how to jump on the wind's back, and then away we go."

"Oo!" she exclaimed rapturously.

"Wendy, Wendy, when you are sleeping in your silly bed you might be flying about with me saying funny things to the stars."

"Oo!"

"And, Wendy, there are mermaids."

"Mermaids! With tails?"

"Such long tails."

"Oh," cried Wendy, "to see a mermaid!"

He had become frightfully cunning. "Wendy," he said, "how we should all respect you."

She was wriggling her body in distress. It was quite as if she were trying to remain on the nursery floor.

But he had no pity for her.

"Wendy," he said, the sly one, "you could tuck us in at night."

"Oo!"

"None of us has ever been tucked in at night."

"Oo," and her arms went out to him.

"And you could darn our clothes, and make pockets for us. None of us has any pockets."

How could she resist? "Of course it's awfully fascinating!" she cried. "Peter, would you teach John and Michael to fly too?"

"If you like," he said indifferently; and she ran to John and Michael and shook them. "Wake up," she cried, "Peter Pan has come and he is to teach us to fly."

John rubbed his eyes. "Then I shall get up," he said. Of course he was on the floor already. "Hallo," he said, "I am up!"

Michael was up by this time also, looking as sharp as a knife with six blades and a saw, but Peter suddenly signed silence. Their faces assumed the awful craftiness of children listening for sounds from the grown-up world. All was still as salt. Then everything was right. No, stop! Everything was wrong. Nana, who had been barking distressfully all the evening, was quiet now. It was her silence they had heard.

"Out with the light! Hide! Quick!" cried John, taking command for the only time throughout the whole adventure. And thus when Liza entered, holding Nana, the nursery seemed quite its old self, very dark; and you could have sworn you heard its three wicked inmates breathing angelically as they slept. They were really doing it artfully from behind the window curtains.

Liza was in a bad temper, for she was mixing the Christmas puddings in the kitchen, and had been drawn away from them, with a raisin still on her cheek, by Nana's absurd suspicions. She thought the best way of getting a little quiet was to take Nana to the nursery for a moment, but in custody of course.

"There, you suspicious brute," she said, not sorry that Nana was in disgrace, "they are perfectly safe, aren't they? Every one of the little angels sound asleep in bed. Listen to their gentle breathing."

Here, Michael, encouraged by his success, breathed so loudly that they were nearly detected. Nana knew that kind of breathing, and she tried to drag herself out of Liza's clutches.

But Liza was dense. "No more of it, Nana," she said sternly, pulling her out of the room. "I warn you if you bark again I shall go straight for master and missus and bring them home from the party, and then, oh, won't master whip you, just."

She tied the unhappy dog up again, but do you think Nana ceased to bark? Bring master and missus home from the party! Why, that was just what she wanted. Do you think she cared whether she was whipped so long as her charges were safe? Unfortunately Liza returned to her puddings, and Nana, seeing that no help would come from her, strained and strained at the chain until at last she broke it. In another moment she had burst into the dining room of 27 and flung up her paws to heaven, her most expressive way of making a communication. Mr and Mrs Darling knew at once that something terrible was happening in their nursery, and without a good-bye to their hostess they rushed into the street.

But it was now ten minutes since three scoundrels had been breathing behind the curtains; and Peter Pan can do a great deal in ten minutes.

We now return to the nursery.

"It's all right," John announced, emerging from his hiding-place. "I say, Peter, can you really fly?"

Instead of troubling to answer him Peter flew round the room, taking in the mantlepiece on the way.

"How topping!" said John and Michael.

"How sweet!" cried Wendy.

"Yes, I'm sweet, oh, I am sweet!" said Peter, forgetting his manners again.

It looked delightfully easy, and they tried it first from the floor and then from the beds, but they always went down instead of up.

"I say, how do you do it?" asked John, rubbing his knee. He was quite a practical boy.

"You just think lovely wonderful thoughts," Peter explained, "and they lift you up in the air."

He showed them again.

"You're so nippy at it," John said; "couldn't you do it very slowly once?"

Peter did it both slowly and quickly. "I've got it now, Wendy!" cried John, but soon he found he had not. Not one of them could fly an inch, though even Michael was in words of two syllables, and Peter did not know A from Z.

Of course Peter had been trifling with them, for no one can fly unless the fairy dust has been blown on him. Fortunately, as we have mentioned, one of his hands was messy with it, and he blew some on each of them, with the most superb results.

"Now just wriggle your shoulders this way," he said "and let go."

They were all on their beds, and gallant Michael let go first. He did not quite mean to let go, but he did it, and immediately he was borne across the room.

"I flewed!" he screamed while still in mid-air.

John let go and met Wendy near the bathroom.

"Oh, lovely!"

"Oh, ripping!"

"Look at me!"

"Look at me!"

"Look at me!"

They were not nearly so elegant as Peter, they could not help kicking a little, but their heads were bobbing against the ceiling, and there is almost nothing so delicious as that. Peter gave Wendy a hand at first, but had to desist, Tink was so indignant.

Up and down they went, and round and round. Heavenly was Wendy's word.

"I say," cried John, "why shouldn't we all go out!"

Of course it was to this that Peter had been luring them.

Michael was ready; he wanted to see how long it took him to do a billion miles. But Wendy hesitated.

"Mermaids!" said Peter again.

"Oh!"

"And there are pirates."

"Pirates," cried John, seizing his Sunday hat, "let us go at once."

It was just at this moment that Mr and Mrs Darling hurried with Nana out of 27. They ran into the middle of the street to look up at the nursery window; and, yes, it was still shut, but the room was ablaze with light, and most heart-gripping sight of all, they could see in shadow on the curtain three little figures in night attire circling round and round, not on the floor but in the air.

Not three figures, four!

In a tremble they opened the street door. Mr Darling would have rushed upstairs, but Mrs Darling signed to him to go softly. She even tried to make her heart go softly.

Will they reach the nursery in time? If so, how delightful for them, and we shall all breathe a sigh of relief, but there will be no story. On the other hand, if they are not in time, I solemnly promise that it will all come right in the end.

They would have reached the nursery in time had it not been that the little stars were watching them. Once again the stars blew the window open, and that smallest star of all called out:

"Look out, Peter!"

Then Peter knew that there was not a moment to lose. "Come," he cried imperiously, and soared out at once into the night followed by John and Michael and Wendy.

Mr and Mrs Darling and Nana rushed into the nursery too late. The birds were flown.

CHAPTER 4

THE FLIGHT

"Second on the right, and straight on till morning."

That, Peter had told Wendy, was the way to Neverland; but even birds, carrying maps and consulting them at windy corners, could not have sighted it with these instructions. Peter, you see, just said anything that came into his head.

At first his companions trusted him implicitly, and so great were the delights of flying that they wasted time circling round church spires or any other tall objects on the way that took their fancy.

John and Michael raced, Michael getting a start.

They recalled with contempt that not so long ago they had thought themselves fine fellows for being able to fly round a room.

Not so long ago. But how long ago? They were flying over the sea before this thought began to disturb Wendy seriously. John thought it was their second sea and their third night.

Sometimes it was dark and sometimes light, and now they were very cold and again too warm. Did they really feel hungry at times, or were they merely pretending because Peter had such a jolly new way of feeding them? His way was to pursue birds who had food in their mouths suitable for humans and snatch it from them; then the birds would follow and snatch it back; and they would all go chasing each other gaily for miles, parting at last with mutual expressions of good-will. But Wendy noticed with gentle concern that Peter did not seem to know that this was rather an odd way of getting your bread and butter, nor even that there are other ways.

Certainly they did not pretend to be sleepy, they were sleepy; and that was a danger, for the moment they popped off, down they fell. The awful thing was that Peter thought this funny.

"There he goes again!" he would cry gleefully, as Michael suddenly dropped like a stone.

"Save him, save him!" cried Wendy, looking with horror at the cruel sea far below. Eventually Peter would dive through the air, and catch Michael just before he could strike the sea, and it was lovely the way he did it; but he always waited till the last moment, and you felt it was his cleverness that interested him and not the saving of human life. Also he was fond of variety, and the sport that engrossed him one moment would suddenly cease to engage him, so there was always the possibility that the next time you fell he would let you go.

He could sleep in the air without falling, by merely lying on his back and floating, but this was, partly at least, because he was so light that if you got behind him and blew he went faster.

"Do be more polite to him," Wendy whispered to John, when they were playing "Follow my Leader".

"Then tell him to stop showing off," said John.

When playing Follow my Leader, Peter would fly close to the water and touch each shark's tail in passing, just as in the street you may run your finger along an iron railing. They could not follow him in this with much success, so perhaps it was rather like showing off, especially as he kept looking behind to see how many tails they missed.

"You must be nice to him," Wendy impressed on her brothers. "What would we do if he were to leave us?"

"We could go back," Michael said.

"How could we ever find our way back without him?"

"Well, then, we could go on," said John.

"That is the awful thing, John. We should have to go on, for we don't know how to stop."

This was true; Peter had forgotten to show them how to stop.

John said that if the worst came to the worst, all they had to do was to go straight on, for the world was round, and so in time they must come back to their own window.

"And who is to get food for us, John?"

"I nipped a bit out of that eagle's mouth pretty neatly, Wendy."

"After the twentieth try," Wendy reminded him. "And even though we became good at picking up food, see how we bump against clouds and things if he is not near to give us a hand."

Indeed they were constantly bumping. They could now fly strongly, though they still kicked far too much; but if they saw a cloud in front of them, the more they tried to avoid it, the more certainly did they bump into it. If Nana had been with them she would have had a bandage round Michael's forehead by this time.

Peter was not with them for the moment, and they felt rather lonely up there by themselves. He could go so much faster than they that he would suddenly shoot out of sight, to have some adventure in which they had no share. He would come down laughing over something fearfully funny he had been saying to a star, but he had already forgotten what it was, or he would come up with mermaid scales still sticking to him, and yet not be able to say for certain what had been happening. It was really rather irritating to children who had never seen a mermaid.

"And if he forgets them so quickly," Wendy argued, "how can we expect that he will go on remembering us?"

Indeed, sometimes when he returned he did not remember them, at least not well. Wendy was sure of it. She saw recognition come into his eyes as he was about to pass them the time of day and go on; once even she had to tell him her name.

"I'm Wendy," she said agitatedly.

He was very sorry. "I say, Wendy," he whispered to her, "always if you see me forgetting you, just keep on saying

'I'm Wendy', and then I'll remember."

Of course this was rather unsatisfactory. However, to make amends he showed them how to lie out flat on a strong wind that was going their way, and this was such a pleasant change that they tried it several times and found they could sleep thus with security. Indeed they would have slept longer, but Peter tired quickly of sleeping, and soon he would cry in his captain voice, "We get off here." So with occasional tiffs, but on the whole rollicking, they drew near the Neverland; for after many moons they did reach it, and, what is more, they had been going pretty straight all the time, not perhaps so much owing to the guidance of Peter or Tink as because the island was out looking for them. It is only thus that anyone may sight those magic shores.

"There it is," said Peter calmly.

"Where, where?"

"Where all the arrows are pointing."

Indeed a million golden arrows were pointing out the island to the children, all directed by their friend the sun, who wanted them to be sure of their way before leaving them for the night.

Wendy and John and Michael stood on tiptoe in the air to get their first sight of the island. Strange to say, they all recognized it at once, and until fear fell upon them they hailed it, not as something long dreamt of and seen at last, but as a familiar friend to whom they were returning home for the holidays.

"John, there's the lagoon."

"Wendy, look at the turtles burying their eggs in the sand."

"I say, John, I see your flamingo with the broken leg."

"Look, Michael, there's your cave."

"John, what's that in the brushwood?"

"It's a wolf with her whelps. Wendy, I do believe that's your little whelp."

"There's my boat, John, with her sides stove in."

"No, it isn't. Why, we burned your boat."

"That's her, at any rate, I say, John, I see the smoke of the redskin camp."

"Where? Show me, and I'll tell you by the way the smoke curls whether they are on the war-path."

"There, just across the Mysterious River."

"I see now. Yes, they are on the war-path right enough."

Peter was a little annoyed with them for knowing so much; but if he wanted to lord it over them his triumph was at hand, for have I not told you that anon fear fell upon them?

It came as the arrows went, leaving the island in gloom.

In the old days at home the Neverland had always begun to look a little dark and threatening by bedtime. Then unexplored patches arose in it and spread; black shadows moved about in them; the roar of the beasts of prey was quite different now, and above all, you lost the certainty that you would win. You were quite glad that the night-lights were on. You even liked Nana to say that this was just the mantelpiece over here, and that the Neverland was all make-believe.

Of course the Neverland had been make-believe in those days; but it was real now, and there were no night-lights, and it was getting darker every moment, and where was Nana?

They had been flying apart, but they huddled close to Peter now. His careless manner had gone at last, his eyes were sparkling, a tingle went through them every time they touched his body. They were now over the fearsome island, flying so low that sometimes a tree grazed their feet. Nothing horrid was visible in the air, yet their progress had become slow and laboured, exactly as if they were pushing their way through hostile forces. Sometimes they hung in the air until Peter had beaten on it with his fists.

"They don't want us to land," he explained.

"Who are they?" Wendy whispered, shuddering.

But he could not or would not say. Tinker Bell had been asleep on his shoulder, but now he wakened her and sent her on in front.

Sometimes he poised himself in the air, listening intently with his hand to his ear, and again he would stare down with eyes so bright that they seemed to bore two holes to earth. Having done these things, he went on again.

His courage was almost appalling. "Do you want an adventure now," he said casually to John, "or would you like to have your tea first?"

Wendy said "tea first" quickly, and Michael pressed her hand in gratitude, but the braver John hesitated.

"What kind of adventure?" he asked cautiously.

"There's a pirate asleep in the pampas just beneath us," Peter told him. "If you like, we'll go down and kill him."

"I don't see him," John said after a long pause.

"I do."

"Suppose," John said a little huskily, "he were to wake up."

Peter spoke indignantly. "You don't think I would kill him while he was sleeping! I would wake him first, and then kill him. That's the way I always do."

"I say! Do you kill many?"

"Tons."

John said "how ripping", but decided to have tea first. He asked if there were many pirates on the island just now, and Peter said he had never known so many.

"Who is captain now?"

"Hook," answered Peter; and his face became very stern as he said that hated word.

"Jas. Hook?"

"Aye."

Then indeed Michael began to cry, and even John could speak in gulps only, for they knew Hook's reputation.

"He was Blackbeard's bo'sun," John whispered huskily. "He is the worst of them all. He is the only man of whom Barbecue was afraid."

"That's him," said Peter.

"What is he like? Is he big?"

"He is not so big as he was."
"How do you mean?"
"I cut off a bit of him."
"You!"
"Yes, me," said Peter sharply.
"I wasn't meaning to be disrespectful."
"Oh, all right."
"But, I say, what bit?"
"His right hand."
"Then he can't fight now?"
"Oh, can't he just!"
"Left-hander?"
"He had an iron hook instead of a right hand, and he claws with it."
"Claws!"
"I say, John," said Peter.
"Yes."
"Say, 'Aye, aye, sir.'"
"Aye, aye, sir."
"There is one thing, Peter continued, "that every boy who serves under me had to promise, and so must you."
John paled.
"It is this, if we meet Hook in open fight, you must leave him to me."
"I promise," John said loyally.
For the moment they were feeling less eerie, because Tink was flying with them, and in her light they could distinguish each other. Unfortunately she could not fly so slowly as they, and so she had to go round and round them in a circle in which they moved as in a halo. Wendy quite liked it, until Peter pointed out the drawback.
"She tells me," he said, "that the pirates sighted us before the darkness came, and got Long Tom out."
"The big gun?"
"Yes. And of course they must see her light, and if they guess we are near it they are sure to let fly."

"Wendy!"

"John!"

"Michael!"

"Tell her to go away at once, Peter," the three cried simultaneously, but he refused.

"She thinks we have lost the way," he replied stiffly, "and she is rather frightened. You don't think I would send her away all by herself when she is frightened!"

For a moment the circle of light was broken, and something gave Peter a loving little pinch.

"Then tell her," Wendy begged, "to put out her light."

"She can't put it out. That is about the only thing fairies can't do. It just goes out of itself when she falls asleep, same as the stars."

"Then tell her to sleep at once," John almost ordered.

"She can't sleep except when she's sleepy. It is the only other thing fairies can't do."

"Seems to me," growled John, "these are the only two things worth doing."

Here he got a pinch, but not a loving one.

"If only one of us had a pocket," Peter said, "we could carry her in it." However, they had set off in such a hurry that there was not a pocket between the four of them.

He had a happy idea. John's hat!

Tink agreed to travel by hat if it was carried in the hand. John carried it, though she had hoped to be carried by Peter. Presently Wendy took the hat, because John said it struck against his knee as he flew; and this, as we shall see, led to mischief, for Tinker Bell hated to be under an obligation to Wendy.

In the black topper the light was completely hidden, and they flew on in silence. It was the stillest silence they had ever known, broken once by a distant lapping, which Peter explained was the wild beasts drinking at the ford, and again by a rasping sound that might have been the branches of trees rubbing together, but he said it was the redskins sharpening their knives.

Even these noises ceased. To Michael the loneliness was dreadful. "If only something would make a sound!" he cried.

As if in answer to his request, the air was rent by the most tremendous crash he had ever heard. The pirates had fired Long Tom at them.

The roar of it echoed through the mountains, and the echoes seemed to cry savagely, "Where are they, where are they, where are they?"

Thus sharply did the terrified three learn the difference between an island of make-believe and the same island come true.

When at last the heavens were steady again, John and Michael found themselves alone in the darkness. John was treading the air mechanically, and Michael without knowing how to float was floating.

"Are you shot?" John whispered tremulously.

"I haven't tried yet," Michael whispered back.

We know now that no one had been hit. Peter, however, had been carried by the wind of the shot far out to sea, while Wendy was blown upwards with no companion but Tinker Bell.

It would have been well for Wendy if at that moment she had dropped the hat.

I don't know whether the idea came suddenly to Tink, or whether she had planned it on the way, but she at once popped out of the hat and began to lure Wendy to her destruction.

Tink was not all bad; or, rather, she was all bad just now, but, on the other hand, sometimes she was all good. Fairies have to be one thing or the other, because being so small they unfortunately have room for one feeling only at a time. They are, however, allowed to change, only it must be a complete change. At present she was full of jealousy of Wendy. What she said in her lovely tinkle Wendy could not of course understand, and I believe some of it was bad words, but it sounded kind, and she flew back and forward, plainly meaning "Follow me, and all will be well."

What else could poor Wendy do? She called to Peter and John and Michael, and got only mocking echoes in reply. She did not yet know that Tink hated her with the fierce hatred of a very woman. And so, bewildered, and now staggering in her flight, she followed Tink to her doom.

CHAPTER 5

THE ISLAND COME TRUE

Feeling that Peter was on his way back, the Neverland had again woke into life. We ought to use the pluperfect and say wakened, but woke is better and was always used by Peter.

In his absence things are usually quiet on the island. The fairies take an hour longer in the morning, the beasts attend to their young, the redskins feed heavily for six days and nights, and when pirates and lost boys meet they merely bite their thumbs at each other. But with the coming of Peter, who hates lethargy, they are all under way again: if you put your ear to the ground now, you would hear the whole island seething with life.

On this evening the chief forces of the island were disposed as follows. The lost boys were out looking for Peter, the pirates were out looking for the lost boys, the redskins were out looking for the pirates, and the beasts were out looking for the redskins. They were going round and round the island, but they did not meet because all were going at the same rate.

All wanted blood except the boys, who liked it as a rule, but tonight were out to greet their captain. The boys on the island vary, of course, in numbers, according as they get killed and so on; and when they seem to be growing up, which is against the rules, Peter thins them out; but at this time there were six of them, counting the Twins as two. Let us pretend to lie here among the sugar-cane and watch them as they steal by in single file, each with his hand on his dagger.

They are forbidden by Peter to look in the least like him, and they wear the skins of bears slain by themselves, in which they are so round and furry that when they fall they roll. They have therefore become very sure-footed.

The first to pass is Tootles, not the least brave but the most unfortunate of all that gallant band. He had been in fewer adventures than any of them, because the big things constantly happened just when he had stepped round the corner; all would be quiet; he would take the opportunity of going off to gather a few sticks for firewood, and then when he returned the others would be sweeping up the blood. The ill luck had given a gentle melancholy to his countenance, but instead of souring his nature had sweetened it, so that he was quite the humblest of the boys. Poor kind Tootles, there is danger in the air for you tonight. Take care lest an adventure is now offered you, which, if accepted, will plunge you in deepest woe. Tootles, the fairy Tink, who is bent on mischief this night, is looking for a tool, and she thinks you the most easily tricked of the boys. 'Ware Tinker Bell.

Would that he could hear us, but we are not really on the island, and he passes by, biting his knuckles.

Next comes Nibs, the gay and debonair, followed by Slightly, who cuts whistles out of the trees and dances ecstatically to his own tunes. Slightly is the most conceited of the boys. He thinks he remembers the days before he was lost, with their manners and customs, and this has given his nose an offensive tilt. Curly is fourth; he is a pickle, and so often has he had to deliver up his person when Peter said sternly, "Stand forth the one who did this thing," that now at the command he stands forth automatically whether he has done it or not. Last come the

Twins, who cannot be described because we should be sure to be describing the wrong one. Peter never quite knew what twins were, and his band were not allowed to know anything he did not know, so these two were always vague about themselves, and did their best to give satisfaction by keeping close together in an apologetic sort of way.

The boys vanish in the gloom, and after a pause, but not a long pause, for things go briskly on the island, come the pirates on their track. We hear them before they are seen, and it is always the same dreadful song:

"Avast belay, yo ho, heave to,
A-pirating we go,
And if we're parted by a shot
We're sure to meet below!"

A more villainous-looking lot never hung in a row on Execution dock. Here, a little in advance, ever and again with his head to the ground listening, his great arms bare, pieces of eight in his ears as ornaments, is the handsome Italian Cecco, who cut his name in letters of blood on the back of the governor of the prison at Goa. That gigantic black behind him has had many names since he dropped the one with which dusky mothers still terrify their children on the banks of the Guidjo-mo. Here is Bill Jukes, every inch of him tattooed, the same Bill Jukes who got six dozen on the *Walrus* from Flint before he would drop the bag of moidores; and Cookson, said to be Black Murphy's brother (but this was never proved); and Gentlemen Starkey, once an usher in a public school and still dainty in his ways of killing; and Skylights (Morgan's Skylights); and the Irish bo'sun Smee, an oddly genial man who stabbed, so to speak, without offence, and was the only Nonconformist in Hook's crew; and Noodler, whose hands were fixed on backwards; and Robt. Mullins and Alf Mason and many another ruffian long known and feared on the Spanish Main.

In the midst of them, the blackest and largest jewel in the dark setting, reclined James Hook, or, as he wrote himself, Jas. Hook, of whom it is said he was the only man that the Sea-Cook feared. He lay at ease in a rough chariot drawn and propelled by his men, and instead of a right hand he had the iron hook with which ever and anon he encouraged them to increase their pace. As dogs this terrible man treated and addressed them, and as dogs they obeyed him. In person he was cadaverous and blackavized, and his hair was dressed in long curls, which at a little distance looked like black candles, and gave a singularly threatening expression to his handsome countenance. His eyes were of the blue of the forget-me-not, and of a profound melancholy, save when he was plunging his hook into you, at which time two red spots appeared in them and lit them up horribly. In manner, something of the grand seigneur still clung to him, so that he even ripped you up with an air, and I have been told that he was a *raconteur* of repute. He was never more sinister than when he was most polite, which is probably the truest test of breeding; and the elegance of his diction, even when he was swearing, no less than the distinction of his demeanour, showed him one of a different caste from his crew. A man of indomitable courage, it was said of him that the only thing he shied at was the sight of his own blood, which was thick and of an unusual colour. In dress he somewhat aped the attire associated with the name of Charles II, having heard it said in some earlier period of his career that he bore a strange resemblance to the ill-fated Stuarts; and in his mouth he had a holder of his own contrivance which enabled him to smoke two cigars at once. But undoubtedly the grimmest part of him was his iron claw.

Let us now kill a pirate, to show Hook's method. Skylights will do. As they pass, Skylights lurches clumsily against him, ruffling his lace collar; the hook shoots forth, there is a tearing sound and one screech, then the body is kicked aside, and the pirates pass on. He has not even taken the cigars from his mouth.

Such is the terrible man against whom Peter Pan is pitted. Which will win?

On the trail of the pirates, stealing noiselessly down the war-path, which is not visible to inexperienced eyes, come the redskins, every one of them with his eyes peeled. They carry tomahawks and knives, and their naked bodies gleam with paint and oil. Strung around them are scalps, of boys as well as of pirates, for these are the Piccaninny tribe, and not to be confused with the softer-hearted Delawares or the Hurons. In the van, on all fours, is Great Big Little Panther, a brave of so many scalps that in his present position they somewhat impede his progress. Bringing up the rear, the place of greatest danger, comes Tiger Lily, proudly erect, a princess in her own right. She is the most beautiful of dusky Dianas and the belle of the Piccaninnies, coquettish, cold and amorous by turns; there is not a brave who would not have the wayward thing to wife, but she staves off the altar with a hatchet. Observe how they pass over fallen twigs without making the slightest noise. The only sound to be heard is their somewhat heavy breathing. The fact is that they are all a little fat just now after the heavy gorging, but in time they will work this off. For the moment, however, it constitutes their chief danger.

The redskins disappear as they have come, like shadows, and soon their place is taken by the beasts, a great and motley procession: lions, tigers, bears, and the innumerable smaller savage things that flee from them, for every kind of beast, and, more particularly, all the maneaters, live cheek by jowl on the favoured island. Their tongues are hanging out, they are hungry tonight.

When they have passed, comes the last figure of all, a gigantic crocodile. We shall see for whom she is looking presently.

The crocodile passes, but soon the boys appear again, for the procession must continue indefinitely until one of the parties stops or changes its pace. Then quickly they will be on top of each other.

All are keeping a sharp look out in front, but none suspects that the danger may be creeping up from behind. This shows how real the island was.

The first to fall out of the moving circle was the boys. They flung themselves down on the sward, close to their underground home.

"I do wish Peter would come back," every one of them said nervously, though in height and still more in breadth they were all larger than their captain.

"I am the only one who is not afraid of the pirates," Slightly said, in the tone that prevented his being a general favourite; but perhaps some distant sound disturbed him, for he added hastily, "but I wish he would come back, and tell us whether he has heard anything more about Cinderella."

They talked of Cinderella, and Tootles was confident that his mother must have been very like her.

It was only in Peter's absence that they could speak of mothers, the subject being forbidden by him as silly.

"All I remember about my mother," Nibs told them, "is that she often said to father, 'Oh, how I wish I had a cheque-book of my own.' I don't know what a cheque-book is, but I should just love to give my mother one."

While they talked they heard a distant sound. You or I, not being wild things of the woods, would have heard nothing, but they heard it, and it was the grim song:

"Yo ho, yo ho, the pirate life,
The flag o' skull and bones,
A merry hour, a hempen rope,
And hey for Davy Jones."

At once the lost boys – but where are they? They are no longer there. Rabbits could not have disappeared more quickly.

I will tell you where they are. With the exception of Nibs, who has darted away to reconnoitre, they are already in their home under the ground, a very delightful residence of which we shall see a good deal presently. But how have they reached it? for there is no entrance to be seen, not so much as a pile of brushwood which, if removed, would disclose the mouth of a cave. Look closely, however, and you may note that there are here seven large trees, each having in its hollow trunk a hole as large as a boy. These are the seven entrances to the home under the ground, for which Hook has been searching in vain these many moons. Will he find it tonight?

As the pirates advanced, the quick eye of Starkey sighted Nibs disappearing through the wood, and at once his pistol flashed out. But an iron claw gripped his shoulder.

"Captain, let go," he cried, writhing.

Now for the first time we hear the voice of Hook. It was a black voice. "Put back that pistol first," it said threateningly.

"It was one of those boys you hate. I could have shot him dead."

"Aye, and the sound would have brought Tiger Lily's redskins upon us. Do you want to lose your scalp?"

"Shall I after him, Captain," asked pathetic Smee, "and tickle him with Johnny Corkscrew?" Smee had pleasant names for everything, and his cutlass was Johnny Corkscrew, because he wriggled it in the wound. One could mention many lovable traits in Smee. For instance, after killing, it was his spectacles he wiped instead of his weapon.

"Johnny's a silent fellow," he reminded Hook.

"Not now, Smee," Hook said darkly. "He is only one, and I want to mischief all the seven. Scatter and look for them."

The pirates disappeared among the trees, and in a moment their captain and Smee were alone. Hook heaved a heavy sigh; and I know not why it was, perhaps it was because of the soft beauty of the evening, but there came over him a desire to confide to his faithful bo'sun the story of his life. He spoke long and earnestly, but what it was all about Smee, who was rather stupid, did not know in the least.

Anon he caught the word Peter.

"Most of all," Hook was saying passionately, "I want their captain, Peter Pan. 'Twas he cut off my arm." He brandished the hook threateningly. "I've waited long to shake his hand with this. Oh, I'll tear him."

"And yet," said Smee, "I have often heard you say that hook was worth a score of hands, for combing the hair and other homely uses."

"Aye," the captain answered, "if I was a mother I would pray to have my children born with this instead of that," and he cast a look of pride upon his iron hand and one of scorn upon the other. Then again he frowned.

"Peter flung my arm," he said, wincing, "to a crocodile that happened to be passing by."

"I have often," said Smee, "noticed your strange dread of crocodiles."

"Not of crocodiles," Hook corrected him, "but of that one crocodile." He lowered his voice. "It liked my arm so much, Smee, that it has followed me ever since, from sea to sea and from land to land, licking its lips for the rest of me."

"In a way," said Smee, "it's a sort of compliment."

"I want no such compliments," Hook barked petulantly. "I want Peter Pan, who first gave the brute its taste for me."

He sat down on a large mushroom, and now there was a quiver in his voice. "Smee," he said huskily, "that crocodile would have had me before this, but by a lucky chance it swallowed a clock which goes tick tick inside it, and so before it can reach me I hear the tick and bolt." He laughed, but in a hollow way.

"Some day," said Smee, "the clock will run down, and then he'll get you."

Hook wetted his dry lips. "Aye," he said, "that's the fear that haunts me."

Since sitting down he had felt curiously warm. "Smee," he said, "this seat is hot." He jumped up. "Odds bobs, hammer and tongs, I'm burning."

They examined the mushroom, which was of a size and solidity unknown on the mainland; they tried to pull it up, and it came away at once in their hands, for it had no root. Stranger still, smoke began at once to ascend. The pirates looked at each other. "A chimney!" they both exclaimed.

They had indeed discovered the chimney of the home under the ground. It was the custom of the boys to stop it with a mushroom when enemies were in the neighbourhood.

Not only smoke came out of it. There came also children's voices, for so safe did the boys feel in their hiding-place that they were gaily chattering. The pirates listened grimly, and then replaced the mushroom. They looked around them and noted the holes in the seven trees.

"Did you hear them say Peter Pan's from home?" Smee whispered, fidgeting with Johnny Corkscrew.

Hook nodded. He stood for a long time lost in thought, and at last a curdling smile lit up his swarthy face. Smee had been waiting for it. "Unrip your plan, captain," he cried eagerly.

"To return to the ship," Hook replied slowly through his teeth, "and cook a large rich cake of a jolly thickness with green sugar on it. There can be but one room below, for there is but one chimney. The silly moles had not the sense to see that they did not need a door apiece. That shows they have no mother. We will leave the cake on the shore of the mermaids' lagoon. These boys are always swimming about there, playing with the mermaids. They will find the cake and they will gobble it up, because, having no mother, they don't know how dangerous 'tis to eat rich damp cake." He burst into laughter, not hollow laughter now, but honest laughter. "Aha, they will die."

Smee had listened with growing admiration.

"It's the wickedest, prettiest policy ever I heard of," he cried, and in their exultation they danced and sang:

"Avast, belay, when I appear,
By fear they're overtook;
Naught's left upon your bones when you
Have shaken claws with Hook."

They began the verse, but they never finished it, for another sound broke in and stilled them. It was at first such a tiny sound that a leaf might have fallen on it and smothered it, but as it came nearer it was more distinct.

Tick tick tick tick.

Hook stood shuddering, one foot in the air.

"The crocodile," he gasped, and bounded away, followed by his bo'sun.

It was indeed the crocodile. It has passed the redskins, who were now on the trail of the other pirates. It oozed on after Hook.

Once more the boys emerged into the open; but the dangers of the night were not yet over, for presently Nibs rushed breathless into their midst, pursued by a pack of wolves. The tongues of the pursuers were hanging out; the baying of them was horrible.

"Save me, save me!" cried Nibs, falling on the ground.

"But what can we do, what can we do?"

It was a high compliment to Peter that at that dire moment their thoughts turned to him.

"What would Peter do?" they cried simultaneously.

Almost in the same breath they added, "Peter would look at them through his legs."

And then, "Let us do what Peter would do."

It is quite the most successful way of defying wolves, and as one boy they bent and looked through their legs. The next moment is the long one; but victory came quickly, for as the boys advanced upon them in this terrible attitude, the wolves dropped their tails and fled.

Now Nibs rose from the ground, and the others thought that his staring eyes saw the wolves. But it was not wolves he saw.

"I have seen a wonderful thing," he cried as they gathered round him eagerly. "A great white bird. It is flying this way."

"What kind of a bird, do you think?"

"I don't know," Nibs said, awestruck, "but it looks so weary, and as it flies it moans, 'Poor Wendy'."

"Poor Wendy?"

"I remember," said Slightly instantly, "there are birds called Wendies."

"See, it comes," cried Curly, pointing to Wendy in the heavens.

Wendy was now almost overhead, and they could hear her plaintive cry. But more distant came the shrill voice of Tinker Bell. The jealous fairy had now cast off all disguise of friendship, and was darting at her victim from every direction, pinching savagely each time she touched.

"Hallo, Tink," cried the wondering boys.

Tink's reply rang out: "Peter wants you to shoot the Wendy."

It was not in their nature to question when Peter ordered. "Let us do what Peter wishes," cried the simple boys. "Quick, bows and arrows."

All but Tootles popped down their trees. He had a bow and arrow with him, and Tink noted it, and rubbed her little hands.

"Quick, Tootles, quick," she screamed. "Peter will be so pleased."

Tootles excitedly fitted the arrow to his bow. "Out of the way, Tink," he shouted; and then he fired, and Wendy fluttered to the ground with an arrow in her breast.

Chapter 6

THE LITTLE HOUSE

Foolish Tootles was standing like a conqueror over Wendy's body when the other boys sprang, armed, from their trees.

"You are too late," he cried proudly, "I have shot the Wendy, Peter will be so pleased with me."

Overhead Tinker Bell shouted "Silly ass!" and darted into hiding. The others did not hear her. They had crowded round Wendy, and as they looked a terrible silence fell upon the wood. If Wendy's heart had been beating they would all have heard it.

Slightly was the first to speak. "This is no bird," he said in a scared voice. "I think it must be a lady."

"A lady?" said Tootles, and fell a-trembling.

"And we have killed her," Nibs said hoarsely.

They all whipped off their caps.

"Now I see," Curly said; "Peter was bringing her to us." He threw himself sorrowfully on the ground.

"A lady to take care of us at last," said one of the twins, "and you have killed her."

They were sorry for him, but sorrier for themselves, and when he took a step nearer them they turned from him.

Tootles' face was very white, but there was a dignity about him now that had never been there before.

"I did it," he said, reflecting. "When ladies used to come to me in dreams, I said, 'Pretty mother, pretty mother.' But when at last she really came, I shot her."

He moved slowly away.

"Don't go," they called in pity.

"I must," he answered, shaking; "I am so afraid of Peter."

It was at this tragic moment that they heard a sound which made the heart of every one of them rise to his mouth. They heard Peter crow.

"Peter!" they cried, for it was always thus that he signalled his return.

"Hide her," they whispered, and gathered hastily around Wendy. But Tootles stood aloof.

Again came that ringing crow, and Peter dropped in front of them. "Greeting, boys," he cried, and mechanically they saluted, and then again was silence.

He frowned.

"I am back," he said hotly, "why do you not cheer?"

They opened their mouths, but the cheers would not come. He overlooked it in his haste to tell the glorious tidings.

"Great news, boys," he cried. "I have brought at last a mother for you all."

Still no sound, except a little thud from Tootles as he dropped on his knees.

"Have you not seen her?" said Peter, becoming troubled. "She flew this way."

"Ah me," one voice said, and another said, "Oh, mournful day."

Tootles rose. "Peter," he said quietly, "I will show her to you"; and when the others would still have hidden her he said, "Back, twins, let Peter see."

So they all stood back, and let him see, and after he had looked for a little time he did not know what to do next.

"She is dead," he said uncomfortably. "Perhaps she is frightened at being dead."

He thought of hopping off in a comic sort of way till he was out of sight of her, and then never going near the spot any more. They would all have been glad to follow if he had done this.

But there was the arrow. He took it from her heart and faced his band.

"Whose arrow?" he demanded sternly.

"Mine, Peter," said Tootles on his knees.

"Oh, dastard hand," Peter said, and he raised the arrow to use it as a dagger.

Tootles did not flinch. He bared his breast. "Strike, Peter," he said firmly, "strike me."

Twice did Peter raise the arrow, and twice did his hand fall. "I cannot strike," he said with awe, "there is something stays my hand."

All looked at him in wonder, save Nibs, who fortunately looked at Wendy.

"It is she," he cried, "the Wendy lady; see, her arm."

Wonderful to relate, Wendy had raised her arm. Nibs bent over her and listened reverently. "I think she said 'Poor Tootles'," he whispered.

"She lives," Peter said briefly.

Slightly cried instantly, "The Wendy lady lives."

Then Peter knelt beside her and found his button. You remember she had put it on a chain that she wore round her neck.

"See," he said, "the arrow struck against this. It is the kiss I gave her. It has saved her life."

"I remember kisses," Slightly interposed quickly, "let me see it. Aye, that's a kiss."

Peter did not hear him. He was begging Wendy to get better quickly, so that he could show her the mermaids. Of course she could not answer yet, being still in a frightful faint; but from overhead came a wailing note.

"Listen to Tink," said Curly, "she is crying because the Wendy lives."

Then they had to tell Peter of Tink's crime, and almost never had they seen him look so stern.

"Listen, Tinker Bell," he cried; "I am your friend no more. Begone from me for ever."

She flew on to his shoulder and pleaded, but he brushed her off. Not until Wendy again raised her arm did he relent sufficiently to say, "Well, not for ever, but for a whole week."

Do you think Tinker Bell was grateful to Wendy for raising her arm? Oh dear no, never wanted to pinch her so much. Fairies indeed are strange, and Peter, who understood them best, often cuffed them.

But what to do with Wendy in her present delicate state of health?

"Let us carry her down into the house," Curly suggested.

"Aye," said Slightly, "that is what one does with ladies."

"No, no," Peter said, "you must not touch her. It would not be sufficiently respectful."

"That," said Slightly, "is what I was thinking."

"But if she lies there," Tootles said, "she will die."

"Aye, she will die," Slightly admitted, "but there is no way out."

"Yes, there is," cried Peter. "Let us build a little house round her."

They were all delighted. "Quick," he ordered them, "bring me each of you the best of what we have. Gut our house. Be sharp."

In a moment they were as busy as tailors the night before a wedding. They skurried this way and that, down for bedding, up for firewood, and while they were at it, who should appear but John and Michael. As they dragged along the ground they fell asleep standing, stopped, woke up, moved another step and slept again.

"John, John," Michael would cry, "wake up. Where is Nana, John, and mother?"

And then John would rub his eyes and mutter, "It is true, we did fly."

You may be sure they were very relieved to find Peter.

"Hallo, Peter," they said.

"Hallo," replied Peter amicably, though he had quite forgotten them. He was very busy at the moment measuring Wendy with his feet to see how large a house she would need. Of course he meant to leave room for chairs and a table. John and Michael watched him.

"Is Wendy asleep?" they asked.

"Yes."

"John," Michael proposed, "let us wake her and get her to make supper for us"; but as he said it some of the other boys rushed on carrying branches for the building of the house. "Look at them!" he cried.

"Curly," said Peter in his most captainy voice, "see that these boys help in the building of the house."

"Aye, aye, sir."

"Build a house?" exclaimed John.

"For the Wendy," said Curly.

"For Wendy?" John said aghast. "Why, she is only a girl."

"That," explained Curly, "is why we are her servants."

"You? Wendy's servants!"

"Yes," said Peter, "and you also. Away with them."

The astounded brothers were dragged away to hack and hew and carry. "Chairs and a fender first," Peter ordered. "Then we shall build the house round them."

"Aye," said Slightly, "that is how a house is built; it all comes back to me."

Peter thought of everything. "Slightly," he ordered, "fetch a doctor."

"Aye, aye," said Slightly at once, and disappeared, scratching his head. But he knew Peter must be obeyed, and he returned in a moment, wearing John's hat and looking solemn.

"Please, sir," said Peter, going to him, "are you a doctor?"

The difference between him and the other boys at such a time was that they knew it was make-believe, while to him make-believe and true were exactly the same thing. This sometimes troubled them, as when they had to make-believe that they had had their dinners.

If they broke down in their make-believe he rapped them on the knuckles.

"Yes, my little man," anxiously replied Slightly, who had chapped knuckles.

"Please, sir," Peter explained, "a lady lies very ill."

She was lying at their feet, but Slightly had the sense not to see her.

"Tut, tut, tut," he said, "where does she lie?"

"In yonder glade."

"I will put a glass thing in her mouth," said Slightly; and he made-believe to do it, while Peter waited. It was an anxious moment when the glass thing was withdrawn.

"How is she?" inquired Peter.

"Tut, tut, tut," said Slightly, "this has cured her."

"I am glad," Peter cried.

"I will call again in the evening," Slightly said; "give her beef tea out of a cup with a spout to it"; but after he had returned the hat to John he blew big breaths, which was his habit on escaping from a difficulty.

In the meantime the wood had been alive with the sound of axes; almost everything needed for a cosy dwelling already lay at Wendy's feet.

"If only we knew," said one, "the kind of house she likes best."

"Peter," shouted another, "she is moving in her sleep."

"Her mouth opens," cried a third, looking respectfully into it. "Oh, lovely!"

"Perhaps she is going to sing in her sleep," said Peter. "Wendy, sing the kind of house you would like to have."

Immediately, without opening her eyes, Wendy began to sing:

"I wish I had a pretty house,
The littlest ever seen,
With funny little red walls
And roof of mossy green."

They gurgled with joy at this, for by the greatest good luck the branches they had brought were sticky with red sap, and all the ground was carpeted with moss. As they rattled up the little house they broke into song themselves:

"We've built the little walls and roof
And made a lovely door,
So tell us, mother Wendy,
What are you wanting more?"

To this she answered rather greedily:

"Oh, really, next I think I'll have
Gay windows all about,

With roses peeping in, you know,
And babies peeping out."

With a blow of their fists they made windows, and large yellow leaves were the blinds. But roses—?

"Roses," cried Peter sternly.

Quickly they made-believe to grow the loveliest roses up the walls.

Babies?

To prevent Peter ordering babies they hurried into song again:

"We've made the roses peeping out,
The babies are at the door,
We cannot make ourselves, you know,
'Cos we've been made before."

Peter, seeing this to be a good idea, at once pretended that it was his own. The house was quite beautiful, and no doubt Wendy was very cosy within, though, of course, they could no longer see her. Peter strode up and down, ordering finishing touches. Nothing escaped his eagle eye. Just when it seemed absolutely finished:

"There's no knocker at the door," he said.

They were very ashamed, but Tootles gave the sole of his shoe, and it made an excellent knocker.

Absolutely finished now, they thought.

Not a bit of it. "There's no chimney," Peter said; "we must have a chimney."

"It certainly does need a chimney," said John importantly. This gave Peter an idea. He snatched the hat off John's head, knocked out the bottom, and put the hat on the roof. The little house was so pleased to have such a capital chimney that, as if to say thank you, smoke immediately began to come out of the hat.

Now really and truly it was finished. Nothing remained to do but to knock.

"All look your best," Peter warned them; "first impressions are awfully important."

He was glad no one asked him what first impressions are; they were all too busy looking their best.

He knocked politely; and now the wood was as still as the children, not a sound to be heard except from Tinker Bell, who was watching from a branch and openly sneering.

What the boys were wondering was, would anyone answer the knock? If a lady, what would she be like?

The door opened and a lady came out. It was Wendy. They all whipped off their hats.

She looked properly surprised, and this was just how they had hoped she would look.

"Where am I?" she said.

Of course Slightly was the first to get his word in. "Wendy lady," he said rapidly, "for you we built this house."

"Oh, say you're pleased," cried Nibs.

"Lovely, darling house," Wendy said, and they were the very words they had hoped she would say.

"And we are your children," cried the twins.

They all went on their knees, and holding out their arms cried, "O Wendy lady, be our mother."

"Ought I?" Wendy said, all shining. "Of course it's frightfully fascinating, but you see I am only a little girl, I have no real experience."

"That doesn't matter," said Peter, as if he were the only person present who knew all about it, though he was really the one who knew least. "What we need is just a nice motherly person."

"Oh dear!" Wendy said, "you see I feel that is exactly what I am."

"It is, it is," they all cried; "we saw it at once."

"Very well," she said, "I will do my best. Come inside at once, you naughty children; I am sure your feet are damp. And before I put you to bed I have just time to finish the story of Cinderella."

In they went; I don't know how there was room for them, but you can squeeze very tight in the Neverland. And that was the first of the many joyous evenings they had with Wendy. By and by she tucked them up in the great bed in the home under the trees, but she herself slept that night in the little house, and Peter kept watch outside with drawn sword, for the pirates could be heard carousing far away and the wolves were on the prowl. The little house looked so cosy and safe in the darkness with a bright light showing through its blinds, and the chimney smoking beautifully, and Peter standing on guard.

After a time he fell asleep, and some unsteady fairies had to climb over him on their way home from an orgy. Any of the other boys obstructing the fairy path at night they would have mischiefed, but they just tweaked Peter's nose and passed on.

Chapter 7

THE HOME UNDER THE GROUND

One of the first things Peter did next day was to measure Wendy and John and Michael for hollow trees. Hook, you remember, had sneered at the boys for thinking they needed a tree apiece, but this was ignorance, for unless your tree fitted you it was difficult to go up and down, and no two of the boys were quite the same size. Once you fitted, you drew in your breath at the top, and down you went at exactly the right speed, while to ascend you drew in and let out alternately, and so wriggled up. Of course, when you have mastered the action you are able to do these things without thinking of them, and then nothing can be more graceful.

But you simply must fit, and Peter measures you for your tree as carefully as for a suit of clothes: the only difference being that the clothes are made to fit you, while you have to be made to fit the tree. Usually it is done quite easily, as by your wearing too many garments or too few; but if you are bumpy in awkward places or the only available tree is an odd shape, Peter does some things to you, and after that you fit. Once you fit, great care must be taken to go on fitting, and this, as Wendy was to discover to her delight, keeps a whole family in perfect condition.

Wendy and Michael fitted their trees at the first try, but John had to be altered a little.

After a few days' practice they could go up and down as gaily as buckets in a well. And how ardently they grew to love their home under the ground; especially Wendy. It consisted of one large room, as all houses should do, with a floor in which you could dig if you wanted to go fishing, and in this flow grew stout mushrooms of a charming colour, which were used as stools. A Never tree tried hard to grow in the centre of the room, but every morning they sawed the trunk through, level with the floor. By tea-time it was always about two feet high, and then they put a door on top of it, the whole thus becoming a table; as soon as they cleared away, they sawed off the trunk again, and thus there was more room to play. There was an enormous fire-place which was in almost any part of the room where you cared to light it, and across this Wendy stretched strings, made of fibre, from which she suspended her washing. The bed was tilted against the wall by day, and let down at 6.30, when it filled nearly half the room; and all the boys except Michael slept in it, lying like sardines in a tin. There was a strict rule against turning round until one gave the signal, when all turned at once. Michael should have used it also, but Wendy would have a baby, and he was the littlest, and you know what women are, and the short and the long of it is that he was hung up in a basket.

It was rough and simple, and not unlike what baby bears would have made of an underground house in the same circumstances. But there was one recess in the wall, no larger than a bird-cage, which was the private apartment of Tinker Bell. It could be shut off from the rest of the home by a tiny curtain, which Tink, who was most fastidious, always kept drawn when dressing or undressing. No woman, however large, could have had a more exquisite boudoir and bedchamber combined. The couch, as she always called it, was a genuine Queen Mab, with club legs; and she varied the bedspreads according to what fruit-blossom was in season. Her mirror was a Puss-in-boots, of which there are now only three, unchipped, known to the fairy dealers; the wash-stand was Pie-crust and reversible, the chest of drawers an authentic Charming the Sixth, and the carpet and rugs of the best (the early) period of Margery and Robin. There was a chandelier from Tiddlywinks for the look of the thing, but of course she lit the residence herself. Tink was very contemptuous of the rest of the house, as indeed was perhaps inevitable; and her chamber, though beautiful, looked rather conceited, having the appearance of a nose permanently turned up.

I suppose it was all especially entrancing to Wendy, because those rampagious boys of hers gave her so much to do. Really there were whole weeks when, except perhaps with a stocking in the evening, she was never above ground. The cooking, I can tell you, kept her nose to the pot. Their chief food was roasted bread-fruit, yams, coconuts, baked pig, mammee-apples, tappa rolls and bananas, washed down with calabashes of poe-poe; but you never exactly knew whether there would be a real meal or just a make-believe, it all depended upon Peter's whim. He could eat, really eat, if it was part of a game, but he could not stodge just to feel stodgy, which is what most children like better than anything else; the next best thing being to talk about it. Make-believe was so real to him that during a meal of it you could see him getting rounder. Of course it was trying, but you simply had to follow his lead, and if you could prove to him that you were getting loose for your tree he let you stodge.

Wendy's favourite time for sewing and darning was after they had all gone to bed. Then, as she expressed it, she had a breathing time for herself; and she occupied it in making new things for them, and putting double pieces on the knees, for they were all most frightfully hard on their knees.

When she sat down to a basketful of their stockings, every heel with a hole in it, she would fling up her arms and exclaim, "Oh dear, I am sure I sometimes think spinsters are to be envied."

Her face beamed when she exclaimed this.

You remember about her pet wolf. Well, it very soon discovered that she had come to the island and it found her out, and they just ran into each other's arms. After that it followed her about everywhere.

As time wore on did she think much about the beloved parents she had left behind? This is a difficult question, because it is quite impossible to say how time does wear on in the Neverland, where it is calculated by moons and suns, and there are ever so many more of them than on the mainland. But I am afraid that Wendy did not really worry about her father and mother; she was absolutely confident that they would always keep the window open for her to fly back by, and this gave her complete ease of mind. What did disturb her at times was that John remembered his parents vaguely only, as people he had once known, while Michael was quite willing to believe that she was really his mother. These things scared her a little, and nobly anxious to do her duty, she tried to fix the old life in their minds by setting them examination papers on it, as like as possible to the ones she used to do at school. The other boys thought this awfully interesting and insisted on joining, and they made slates for themselves, and sat round the table, writing and thinking hard about the questions she had written on another slate and passed round. They were the most ordinary questions – "What colour was the colour of Mother's eyes? Which was taller, Father or Mother? Was Mother blonde or brunette? Answer all three questions if possible." "(A) Write an essay of not less than 40 words on How I spent my last Holidays, or The Characters of Father and Mother compared. Only one of these to be attempted." Or "(1) Describe Mother's laugh; (2) Describe Father's laugh; (3) Describe Mother's Party Dress; (4) Describe the Kennel and its Inmate."

They were just everyday questions like these, and when you could not answer them you were told to make a cross and it was really dreadful what a number of crosses even John made. Of course the only boy who replied to every question was Slightly, and no one could have been more hopeful of coming out first, but his answers were perfectly ridiculous, and he really came out last: a melancholy thing.

Peter did not compete. For one thing he despised all mothers except Wendy, and for another he was the only boy on the island who could neither write nor spell; not the smallest word. He was above all that sort of thing.

By the way, the questions were all written in the past tense. What was the colour of Mother's eyes, and so on. Wendy, you see, had been forgetting too.

Adventures, of course, as we shall see, were of daily occurrence; but about this time Peter invented, with Wendy's help, a new game that fascinated him enormously, until he suddenly had no more interest in it, which, as you have been told, was what always happened with his games. It consisted in pretending not to have adventures, in doing the sort of thing John and Michael had been doing all their lives: sitting on stools flinging balls in the air, pushing each other, going out for walks and coming back without having killed so much as a grizzly. To see Peter doing nothing on a stool was a great sight; he could not help looking solemn at such times, to sit still seemed to him such a comic thing to do. He boasted that he had gone a walk for the good of his health.

For several suns these were the most novel of all adventures to him; and John and Michael had to pretend to be delighted also; otherwise he would have treated them severely.

He often went out alone, and when he came back you were never absolutely certain whether he had had an adventure or not. He might have forgotten it so completely that he said nothing about it; and then when you went out you found the body; and, on the other hand, he might say a great deal about it, and yet you could not find the body. Sometimes he came home with his head bandaged, and then Wendy cooed over him and bathed it in lukewarm water, while he told a dazzling tale. But she was never quite sure, you know. There were, however, many adventures which she knew to be true because she was in them herself, and there were still more that were at least partly true, for the other boys were in them and said they were wholly true. To describe them all would require a book as large as an English-Latin, Latin-English Dictionary, and the most we can do is to give one as a specimen of an average hour on the island. The difficulty is which one to choose. Should we take the brush with the redskins at Slightly's Gulch? It was a sanguinary affair, and especially interesting as showing one of Peter's peculiarities, which was that in the middle of a fight he would suddenly change sides. At the Gulch, when victory was still in the balance, sometimes leaning this way and sometimes that, he called out, "I'm a redskin today; what are you, Tootles?" And Tootles answered "Redskin; what are you, Nibs?" and Nibs said, "Redskin; what are you, Twin?" and so on; and they were all redskins; and of course this would have ended the fight had not the real redskins, fascinated by Peter's methods, agreed to be lost boys for that once, and so at it they all went again, more fiercely than ever.

The extraordinary upshot of this adventure was – but we have not decided yet that this is the adventure we are to narrate. Perhaps a better one would be the night attack by the redskins on the house under the ground, when several of them stuck in the hollow trees and had to be pulled out like corks. Or we might tell how Peter saved Tiger Lily's life in the Mermaids' Lagoon, and so made her his ally.

Or we could tell of that cake the pirates cooked so that the boys might eat it and perish; and how they placed it in one cunning spot after another; but always Wendy snatched it from the hands of her children, so that in time it lost its succulence, and became as hard as a stone, and was used as a missile, and Hook fell over it in the dark.

Or suppose we tell of the birds that were Peter's friends, particularly of the Never bird that built in a tree overhanging the lagoon, and how the nest fell into the water, and still the bird sat on her eggs, and Peter gave orders that she was not to be disturbed. That is a pretty story, and the end shows how grateful a bird can be; but if we tell it we must also tell the whole adventure of the lagoon, which would of course be telling two adventures rather than just one. A shorter adventure, and quite as exciting, was Tinker Bell's attempt, with the help of some street fairies, to have the sleeping Wendy conveyed on a great floating leaf to the mainland. Fortunately the leaf gave way and Wendy woke, thinking it was bath-time, and swam back. Or again, we might choose Peter's defiance of the lions, when he drew a circle round him on the ground with an arrow and defied them to cross it; and though he waited for hours, with the other boys and Wendy looking on breathlessly from trees, not one of them dared to accept his challenge.

Which of these adventures shall we choose? The best way will be to toss for it.

I have tossed, and the lagoon has won. This almost makes one wish that the Gulch or the cake or Tink's leaf had won. Of course I could do it again, and make it best out of three; however, perhaps fairest to stick to the lagoon.

CHAPTER 8

THE MERMAIDS' LAGOON

If you shut your eyes and are a lucky one, you may see at times a shapeless pool of lovely pale colours suspended in the darkness; then if you squeeze your eyes tighter, the pool begins to take shape, and the colours become so vivid that with another squeeze they must go on fire. But just before they go on fire you see the lagoon. This is the nearest you ever get to it on the mainland, just one heavenly moment; if there could be two moments you might see the surf and hear the mermaids singing.

The children often spent long summer days on this lagoon, swimming or floating most of the time, playing the mermaid games in the water and so forth. You must not think from this that the mermaids were on friendly terms with them; on the contrary, it was among Wendy's lasting regrets that all the time she was on the island she never had a civil word from one of them. When she stole softly to the edge of the lagoon she might see them by the score, especially on the Marooners' Rock, where they loved to bask, combing out their hair in a lazy way that quite irritated her; or she might even swim, on tiptoe as it were, to within a yard of them, but then they saw her and dived, probably splashing her with their tails, not by accident, but intentionally.

They treated all the boys in the same way, except of course Peter, who chatted with them on Marooners' Rock by the hour, and sat on their tails when they got cheeky. He gave Wendy one of their combs.

The most haunting time at which to see them is at the turn of the moon, when they utter strange wailing cries; but the lagoon is dangerous for mortals then, and until the evening of which we have now to tell, Wendy had never seen the lagoon by moonlight, less from fear, for of course Peter would have accompanied her, than because she had strict rules about every one being in bed by seven. She was often at the lagoon, however, on sunny days after rain, when the mermaids come up in extraordinary numbers to play with their bubbles. The bubbles of many colours made in rainbow water they treat as balls, hitting them gaily from one to another with their tails, and trying to keep them in the rainbow till they burst. The goals are at each end of the rainbow, and the keepers only are allowed to use their hands. Sometimes hundreds of mermaids will be playing in the lagoon at a time, and it is quite a pretty sight.

But the moment the children tried to join in they had to play by themselves, for the mermaids immediately disappeared. Nevertheless we have proof that they secretly watched the interlopers, and were not above taking an idea from them; for John introduced a new way of hitting the bubble, with the head instead of the hand, and the mermaid goal-keepers adopted it. This is the one mark that John has left on the Neverland.

It must also have been rather pretty to see the children resting on a rock for half an hour after their midday meal. Wendy insisted on their doing this, and it had to be a real rest even though the meal was make-believe. So they lay there in the sun, and their bodies glistened in it, while she sat beside them and looked important.

It was one such day, and they were all on Marooners' Rock. The rock was not much larger than their great bed, but of course they all knew how not to take up much room, and they were dozing, or at least lying with their eyes shut, and pinching occasionally when they thought Wendy was not looking. She was very busy, stitching.

While she stitched a change came to the lagoon. Little shivers ran over it, and the sun went away and shadows stole across the water, turning it cold. Wendy could no longer see to thread her needle, and when she looked up, the lagoon that had always hitherto been such a laughing place seemed formidable and unfriendly.

It was not, she knew, that night had come, but something as dark as night had come. No, worse than that. It had not come, but it had sent that shiver through the sea to say that it was coming. What was it?

There crowded upon her all the stories she had been told of Marooners' Rock, so called because evil captains put sailors on it and leave them there to drown. They drown when the tide rises, for then it is submerged.

Of course she should have roused the children at once; not merely because of the unknown that was stalking towards them, but because it was no longer good for them to sleep on a rock grown chilly. But she was a young mother and she did not know this; she thought you simply must stick to your rule about half an hour after the midday meal. So, though fear was upon her, and she longed to hear male voices, she would not waken them. Even when she heard the sound of muffled oars, though her heart was in her mouth, she did not waken them. She stood over them to let them have their sleep out. Was it not brave of Wendy?

It was well for those boys then that there was one among them who could sniff danger even in his sleep. Peter sprang erect, as wide awake at once as a dog, and with one warning cry he roused the others.

He stood motionless, one hand to his ear.

"Pirates!" he cried. The others came closer to him. A strange smile was playing about his face, and Wendy saw it and shuddered. While that smile was on his face no one dared address him; all they could do was to stand ready to obey. The order came sharp and incisive.

"Dive!"

There was a gleam of legs, and instantly the lagoon seemed deserted. Marooners' Rock stood alone in the forbidding waters, as if it were itself marooned.

The boat drew nearer. It was the pirate dinghy, with three figures in her, Smee and Starkey, and the third a captive, no other than Tiger Lily. Her hands and ankles were tied, and she knew what was to be her fate. She was to be left on the rock to perish, an end to one of her race more terrible than death by fire or torture, for is it not written in the book of the tribe that there is no path through water to the happy hunting-ground? Yet her face was impassive; she was the daughter of a chief, she must die as a chief's daughter, it is enough.

They had caught her boarding the pirate ship with a knife in her mouth. No watch was kept on the ship, it being Hook's boast that the wind of his name guarded the ship for a mile around. Now her fate would help to guard it also. One more wail would go the round in that wind by night.

In the gloom that they brought with them the two pirates did not see the rock till they crashed into it.

"Luff, you lubber," cried an Irish voice that was Smee's; "Here's the rock. Now, then, what we have to do is to hoist the redskin on to it, and leave her there to drown."

It was the work of one brutal moment to land the beautiful girl on the rock; she was too proud to offer a vain resistance.

Quite near the rock, but out of sight, two heads were bobbing up and down, Peter's and Wendy's. Wendy was crying, for it was the first tragedy she had seen. Peter had seen many tragedies, but he had forgotten them all. He was less sorry than Wendy for Tiger Lily; it was two against one that angered him, and he meant to save her. An easy way would have been to wait until the pirates had gone, but he was never one to choose the easy way.

There was almost nothing he could not do, and he now imitated the voice of Hook.

"Ahoy there, you lubbers," he called. It was a marvellous imitation.

"The captain," said the pirates, staring at each other in surprise.

"He must be swimming out to us," Starkey said, when they had looked for him in vain.

"We are putting the redskin on the rock," Smee called out.

"Set her free," came the astonishing answer.

"Free!"

"Yes, cut her bonds and let her go."

"But, captain—"

"At once, d'ye hear," cried Peter, "or I'll plunge my hook in you."

"This is queer," Smee gasped.

"Better do what the captain orders," said Starkey nervously.

"Aye, aye," Smee said, and he cut Tiger Lily's cords. At once like an eel she slid between Starkey's legs into the water.

Of course Wendy was very elated over Peter's cleverness; but she knew that he would be elated also and very likely crow and thus betray himself, so at once her hand went out to cover his mouth. But it was stayed even in the act, for "Boat ahoy!" rang over the lagoon in Hook's voice, and this time it was not Peter who had spoken.

Peter may have been about to crow, but his face puckered in a whistle of surprise instead.

"Boat ahoy!" again came the cry.

Now Wendy understood. The real Hook was also in the water.

He was swimming to the boat, and as his men showed a light to guide him he had soon reached them. In the light of the lantern Wendy saw his hook grip the boat's side; she saw his evil swarthy face as he rose dripping from the water, and, quaking, she would have liked to swim away, but Peter would not budge. He was tingling with life and also top-heavy with conceit. "Am I not a wonder, oh, I am a wonder!" he whispered to her; and though she thought so also, she was really glad for the sake of his reputation that no one heard him except herself.

He signed to her to listen.

The two pirates were very curious to know what had brought their captain to them, but he sat with his head on his hook in a position of profound melancholy.

"Captain, is all well?" they asked timidly, but he answered with a hollow moan.

"He sighs," said Smee.

"He sighs again," said Starkey.

"And yet a third time he sighs," said Smee.

"What's up, captain?"

Then at last he spoke passionately.

"The game's up," he cried, "those boys have found a mother."

Affrighted though she was, Wendy swelled with pride.

"O evil day," cried Starkey.

"What's a mother?" asked the ignorant Smee.

Wendy was so shocked that she exclaimed, "He doesn't know!" and always after this she felt that if she could have a pet pirate Smee would be her one.

Peter pulled her beneath the water, for Hook had started up, crying, "What was that?"

"I heard nothing," said Starkey, raising the lantern over the waters, and as the pirates looked they saw a strange sight. It was the nest I have told you of, floating on the lagoon, and the Never bird was sitting on it.

"See," said Hook in answer to Smee's question, "that is a mother. What a lesson! The nest must have fallen into the water, but would the mother desert her eggs? No!"

There was a break in his voice, as if for a moment he recalled innocent days when – but he brushed away his weakness with his hook.

Smee, much impressed, gazed at the bird as the nest was borne past, but the more suspicious Starkey said, "If she is a mother, perhaps she is hanging about here to help Peter."

Hook winced. "Aye," he said, "that is the fear that haunts me."

He was roused from this dejection by Smee's eager voice.

"Captain," said Smee, "could we not kidnap these boys' mother and make her our mother?"

"It is a princely scheme," cried Hook, and at once it took practical shape in his great brain. "We will seize the children and carry them to the boat: the boys we will make walk the plank, and Wendy shall be our mother."

Again Wendy forgot herself.

"Never!" she cried, and bobbed.

"What was that?"

But they could see nothing. They thought it must have been but a leaf in the wind. "Do you agree, my bullies?" asked Hook.

"There is my hand on it," they both said.

"And there is my hook. Swear."

They all swore. By this time they were on the rock and suddenly Hook remembered Tiger Lily.

"Where is the redskin?" he demanded abruptly.

He had a playful humour at moments, and they thought this was one of the moments.

"That is all right, captain," Smee answered complacently, "we let her go."

"Let her go!" cried Hook.

"'Twas your own orders," the bos'un faltered.

"You called over the water to us to let her go," said Starkey.

"Brimstone and gall," thundered Hook, "what cozening is here?" His face had gone black with rage, but he saw that they believed their words, and he was startled. "Lads," he said, shaking a little, "I gave no such order."

"It is passing queer," Smee said, and they all fidgeted uncomfortably. Hook raised his voice, but there was a quiver in it.

"Spirit that haunts this dark lagoon tonight," he cried, "dost hear me?"

Of course Peter should have kept quiet, but of course he did not. He immediately answered in Hook's voice:

"Odds, bobs, hammer and tongs, I hear you."

In that supreme moment Hook did not blanch, even at the gills, but Smee and Starkey clung to each other in terror.

"Who are you, stranger, speak?" Hook demanded.

"I am James Hook," replied the voice, "captain of the *Jolly Roger*."

"You are not; you are not," Hook cried hoarsely.

"Brimstone and gall," the voice retorted, "say that again, and I'll cast anchor in you."

Hook tried a more ingratiating manner. "If you are Hook," he said almost humbly, "come, tell me, who am I?"

"A codfish," replied the voice, "only a codfish."

"A codfish!" Hook echoed blankly; and it was then, but not till then, that his proud spirit broke. He saw his men draw back from him.

"Have we been captained all this time by a codfish?" they muttered. "It is lowering to our pride."

They were his dogs snapping at him, but, tragic figure though he had become, he scarcely heeded them. Against such fearful evidence it was not their belief in him that he needed, it was his own. He felt his ego slipping from him. "Don't desert me, bully," he whispered hoarsely to it.

In his dark nature there was a touch of the feminine, as in all the great pirates, and it sometimes gave him intuitions. Suddenly he tried the guessing game.

"Hook," he cried, "have you another voice?"

Now Peter could never resist a game, and he answered blithely in his own voice, "I have."

"And another name?"

"Aye, aye."

"Vegetable?" asked Hook.

"No."

"Mineral?"

"No."

"Animal?"

"Yes."

"Man?"

"No!" This answer rang out scornfully.

"Boy?"

"Yes."

"Ordinary boy?"

"No!"

"Wonderful boy?"

To Wendy's pain the answer that rang out this time was "Yes."

"Are you in England?"

"No."

"Are you here?"

"Yes."

Hook was completely puzzled. "You ask him some questions," he said to the others, wiping his damp brow.

Smee reflected. "I can't think of a thing," he said regretfully.

"Can't guess, can't guess," crowed Peter. "Do you give it up?"

Of course in his pride he was carrying the game too far, and the miscreants saw their chance.

"Yes, yes," they answered eagerly.

"Well, then," he cried, "I am Peter Pan."

Pan!

In a moment Hook was himself again, and Smee and Starkey were his faithful henchmen.

"Now we have him," Hook shouted. "Into the water, Smee. Starkey, mind the boat. Take him dead or alive."

He leaped as he spoke, and simultaneously came the gay voice of Peter.

"Are you ready, boys?"

"Aye, aye," from various parts of the lagoon.

"Then lam into the pirates."

The fight was short and sharp. First to draw blood was John, who gallantly climbed into the boat and held Starkey.

There was a fierce struggle, in which the cutlass was torn from the pirate's grasp. He wriggled overboard and John leapt after him. The dinghy drifted away.

Here and there a head bobbed up in the water, and there was a flash of steel, followed by a cry or a whoop. In the confusion some struck at their own side. The corkscrew of Smee got Tootles in the fourth rib, but he was himself pinked in turn by Curly. Farther from the rock Starkey was pressing Slightly and the twins hard.

Where all this time was Peter? He was seeking bigger game.

The others were all brave boys, and they must not be blamed for backing from the pirate captain. His iron claw made a circle of dead water round him, from which they fled like affrighted fishes.

But there was one who did not fear him: there was one prepared to enter that circle.

Strangely, it was not in the water that they met. Hook rose to the rock to breathe, and at the same moment Peter scaled it on the opposite side. The rock was slippery as a ball, and they had to crawl rather than climb. Neither knew the other was coming. Each feeling for a grip met the other's arm: in surprise they raised their heads; their faces were almost touching; so they met.

Some of the greatest heroes have confessed that just before they fell to they had a sinking. Had it been so with Peter at that moment I would admit it. After all, this was the only man that the Sea-Cook had feared. But Peter had no sinking, he had one feeling only, gladness; and he gnashed his pretty teeth with joy. Quick as thought he snatched a knife from Hook's belt and was about to drive it home, when he saw that he was higher up the rock than his foe. It would not have been fighting fair. He gave the pirate a hand to help him up.

It was then that Hook bit him.

Not the pain of this but its unfairness was what dazed Peter. It made him quite helpless. He could only stare, horrified.

Every child is affected thus the first time he is treated unfairly. All he thinks he has a right to when he comes to you to be yours is fairness. After you have been unfair to him he will love you again, but he will never afterwards be quite the same boy. No one ever gets over the first unfairness; no one except Peter. He often met it, but he always forgot it. I suppose that was the real difference between him and all the rest.

So when he met it now it was like the first time; and he could just stare, helpless. Twice the iron hand clawed him.

A few minutes afterwards the other boys saw Hook in the water striking wildly for the ship; no elation on his pestilent face now, only white fear, for the crocodile was in dogged pursuit of him. On ordinary occasions the boys would have swum alongside cheering; but now they were uneasy, for they had lost both Peter and Wendy, and were scouring the lagoon for them, calling them by name. They found the dinghy and went home in it, shouting, "Peter, Wendy," as they went, but no answer came save the mocking laughter of the mermaids. "They must be swimming back or flying," the boys concluded. They were not very anxious, they had such faith in Peter. They chuckled, boylike, because they would be late for bed; and it was all Mother Wendy's fault!

When their voices died away there came cold silence over the lagoon, and then a feeble cry.

"Help, help!"

Two small figures were beating against the rock; the girl had fainted and lay on the boy's arm. With a last effort Peter pulled her up the rock and then lay down beside her. Even as he also fainted he saw that the water was rising. He knew that they would soon be drowned, but he could do not more.

As they lay side by side a mermaid caught Wendy by the feet, and began pulling her softly into the water. Peter, feeling her slip from him, woke with a start, and was just in time to draw her back. But he had to tell her the truth.

"We are on the rock, Wendy," he said, "but it is growing smaller. Soon the water will be over it."

She did not understand even now.

"We must go," she said almost brightly.

"Yes," he answered faintly.

"Shall we swim or fly, Peter?"

He had to tell her.

"Do you think you could swim or fly as far as the island, Wendy, without my help?"

She had to admit that she was too tired.

He moaned.

"What is it?" she said, anxious about him at once.

"I can't help you, Wendy. Hook wounded me. I can neither fly nor swim."

"Do you mean we shall both be drowned?"

"Look how the water is rising."

They put their hands over their eyes to shut out the sight. They thought they would soon be no more. As they sat thus something brushed against Peter as light as a kiss, and stayed there, as if saying timidly, "Can I be of any use?"

It was the tail of a kite, which Michael had made some days before. It had torn itself out of his hand and floated away.

"Michael's kite," Peter said without interest, but next moment he had seized the tail, and was pulling the kite towards him.

"It lifted Michael off the ground," he cried; "why should it not carry you?"

"Both of us!"

"It can't lift two; Michael and Curly tried."

"Let us draw lots," Wendy said bravely.

"And you a lady; never." Already he had tied the tail round her. She clung to him; she refused to go without him; but with a "Good-bye, Wendy," he pushed her from the rock; and in a few minutes she was borne out of his sight. Peter was alone on the lagoon.

The rock was very small now; soon it would be submerged. Pale rays of light tiptoed across the waters; and by and by there was to be heard a sound at once the most musical and the most melancholy in the world: the mermaids calling to the moon.

Peter was not quite like the other boys; but he was afraid at last. A tremor ran through him, like a shudder passing over the sea; but on the sea one shudder follows another till there are hundreds of them, and Peter felt just the one. Next moment he was standing erect on the rock again, with that smile on his face and a drum beating within him. It was saying, "To die will be an awfully big adventure."

CHAPTER 9

THE NEVER BIRD

The last sounds Peter heard before he was quite alone were the mermaids retiring one by one to their bedchambers under the sea. He was too far away to hear their doors shut; but every door in the coral caves where they live rings a tiny bell when it opens or closes (as in all the nicest houses on the mainland), and he heard the bells.

Steadily the waters rose till they were nibbling at his feet; and to pass the time until they made their final gulp, he watched the only thing moving on the lagoon. He thought it was a piece of floating paper, perhaps part of the kite, and wondered idly how long it would take to drift ashore.

Presently he noticed as an odd thing that it was undoubtedly out upon the lagoon with some definite purpose, for it was fighting the tide, and sometimes winning; and when it won, Peter, always sympathetic to the weaker side, could not help clapping; it was such a gallant piece of paper.

It was not really a piece of paper; it was the Never bird, making desperate efforts to reach Peter on her nest. By working her wings, in a way she had learned since the nest fell into the water, she was able to some extent to guide her strange craft, but by the time Peter recognized her she was very exhausted. She had come to save him, to give him her nest, though there were eggs in it. I rather wonder at the bird, for though he had been nice to her, he had also sometimes tormented her. I can suppose only that, like Mrs Darling and the rest of them, she was melted because he had all his first teeth.

She called out to him what she had come for, and he called out to her what was she doing there; but of course neither of them understood the other's language. In fanciful stories people can talk to the birds freely, and I wish for the moment I could pretend that this was such a story, and say that Peter replied immediately to the Never bird; but truth is best, and I want to tell only what really happened. Well, not only could they not understand each other, but they forgot their manners.

"I – want – you – to – get – into – the – nest," the bird called, speaking as slowly and distinctly as possible, "and – then – you – can – drift – ashore, but – I – am – too – tired – to – bring – it – any – nearer – so – you – must – try – to – swim – to – it."

"What are you quacking about?" Peter answered. "Why don't you let the nest drift as usual?"

"I – want – you –" the bird said, and repeated it all over.

Then Peter tried slow and distinct.

"What – are – you – quacking – about?" and so on.

The Never bird became irritated; they have very short tempers.

"You dunderheaded little jay," she screamed, "why don't you do as I tell you?"

Peter felt that she was calling him names, and at a venture he retorted hotly:

"So are you!"

Then rather curiously they both snapped out the same remark:

"Shut up!"

"Shut up!"

Nevertheless the bird was determined to save him if she could, and by one last mighty effort she propelled the nest against the rock. Then up she flew; deserting her eggs, so as to make her meaning clear.

Then at last he understood, and clutched the nest and waved his thanks to the bird as she fluttered overhead. It was not to receive his thanks, however, that she hung there in the sky; it was not even to watch him get into the nest; it was to see what he did with her eggs.

There were two large white eggs, and Peter lifted them up and reflected. The bird covered her face with her wings, so as not to see the last of her eggs; but she could not help peeping between the feathers.

I forget whether I have told you that there was a stave on the rock, driven into it by some buccaneers of long ago to mark the site of buried treasure. The children had discovered the glittering hoard, and when in mischievous mood used to fling showers of moidores, diamonds, pearls and pieces of eight to the gulls, who pounced upon them for food, and then flew away, raging at the scurvy trick that had been played upon them. The stave was still there, and on it Starkey had hung his hat, a deep tarpaulin, watertight, with a broad brim. Peter put the eggs into this hat and set it on the lagoon. It floated beautifully.

The Never bird saw at once what he was up to, and screamed her admiration of him; and, alas, Peter crowed his agreement with her. Then he got into the nest, reared the stave in it as a mast, and hung up his shirt for a sail. At the same moment the bird fluttered down upon the hat and once more sat snugly on her eggs. She drifted in one direction, and he was borne off in another, both cheering.

Of course when Peter landed he beached his barque in a place where the bird would easily find it; but the hat was such a great success that she abandoned her nest. It drifted about till it went to pieces, and often Starkey came to the shore of the lagoon, and with many bitter feelings, watched the bird sitting on his hat. As we shall not see her again, it may be worth mentioning here that all Never birds now build in that shape of nest, with a broad brim on which the youngsters take an airing.

Great were the rejoicings when Peter reached the home under the ground almost as soon as Wendy, who had been carried hither and thither by the kite. Every boy had adventures to tell; but perhaps the biggest adventure of all was that they were several hours late for bed. This so inflated them that they did various dodgy things to get staying up still longer, such as demanding bandages; but Wendy, though glorying in having them all home again safe and sound, was scandalized by the lateness of the hour, and cried, "To bed, to bed", in a voice that had to be obeyed. Next day, however, she was awfully tender, and gave out bandages to every one; and they played till bedtime at limping about and carrying their arms in slings.

Chapter 10

THE HAPPY HOME

One important result of the brush on the lagoon was that it made the redskins their friends. Peter had saved Tiger Lily from a dreadful fate, and now there was nothing she and her braves would not do for him. All night they sat above, keeping watch over the home under the ground and awaiting the big attack by the pirates which obviously could not be much longer delayed. Even by day they hung about, smoking the pipe of peace, and looking almost as if they wanted tit-bits to eat.

They called Peter the Great White Father, prostrating themselves before him; and he liked this tremendously, so that it was not really good for him.

"The Great White Father," he would say to them in a very lordly manner, as they grovelled at his feet, "is glad to see the Piccaninny warriors protecting his wigwam from the pirates."

"Me Tiger Lily," that lovely creature would reply. "Peter Pan save me, me his velly nice friend. Me no let pirates hurt him."

She was far too pretty to cringe in this way, but Peter thought it his due, and he would answer condescendingly. "It is good. Peter Pan has spoken."

Always when he said "Peter Pan has spoken", it meant that they must now shut up, and they accepted it humbly in that spirit; but they were by no means so respectful to the other boys, whom they looked upon as just ordinary braves. They said "How-do?" to them, and things like that; and what annoyed the boys was that Peter seemed to think this all right.

Secretly Wendy sympathized with them a little, but she was far too loyal a housewife to listen to any complaints against father. "Father knows best," she always said, whatever her private opinion might be. Her private opinion was that the redskins should not call her squaw.

We have now reached the evening that was to be known among them as the Night of Nights, because of its adventures and their upshot. The day, as if quietly gathering its forces, had been almost uneventful, and now the redskins in their blankets were at their posts above, while, below, the children were having their evening meal; all except Peter, who had gone out to get the time. The way you got the time on the island was to find the crocodile, and then stay near him till the clock struck.

This meal happened to be a make-believe tea, and they sat round the board, guzzling in their greed; and really, what with their chatter and recriminations, the noise, as Wendy said, was positively deafening. To be sure, she did not mind noise, but she simply would not have them grabbing things, and then excusing themselves by saying that Tootles had pushed their elbow. There was a fixed rule that they must never hit back at meals, but should refer the matter of dispute to Wendy by raising the right arm politely and saying, "I complain of So-and-So"; but what usually happened was that they forgot to do this or did it too much.

"Silence," cried Wendy when for the twentieth time she had told them that they were not all to speak at once. "Is your calabash empty, Slightly, darling?"

"Not quite empty, Mummy," Slightly said, after looking into an imaginary mug.

"He hasn't even begun to drink his milk," Nibbs interposed.

This was telling, and Slightly seized his chance.

"I complain of Nibs," he cried promptly.

John, however, had held up his hand first.

"Well, John?"

"May I sit in Peter's chair, as he is not here?"

"Sit in father's chair, John!" Wendy was scandalized. "Certainly not."

"He is not really our father," John answered. "He didn't even know how a father does till I showed him."

This was grumbling. "We complain of John," cried the twins.

Tootles held up his hand. He was so much the humblest of them, indeed he was the only humble one, that Wendy was specially gentle with him.

"I don't suppose," Tootles said diffidently, "that I could be father."

"No, Tootles."

Once Tootles began, which was not very often, he had a silly way of going on.

"As I can't be father," he said heavily, "I don't suppose, Michael, you would let me be baby?"

"No, I won't," Michael rapped out. He was already in his basket.

"As I can't be baby," Tootles said, getting heavier and heavier, "do you think I could be a twin?"

"No, indeed," replied the twins; "it's awfully difficult to be a twin."

"As I can't be anything important," said Tootles, "would any of you like to see me do a trick?"

"No," they all replied.

Then at last he stopped. "I hadn't really any hope," he said.

The hateful telling broke out again.

"Slightly is coughing on the table."

"The twins began with mammee-apples."

"Curly is taking both tappa rolls and yams."

"Nibs is speaking with his mouth full."

"I complain of the twins."

"I complain of Curly."

"I complain of Nibs."

"Oh dear, oh dear," cried Wendy, "I'm sure I sometimes think that children are more trouble than they are worth."

She told them to clear away, and sat down to her work-basket: a heavy load of stockings and every knee with a hole in it as usual.

"Wendy," remonstrated Michael, "I'm too big for a cradle."

"I must have somebody in a cradle," she said almost tartly, "and you are the littlest. A cradle is such a nice homely thing to have about a house."

While she sewed they played round her; such a group of happy faces and dancing limbs lit up by that romantic fire. It had become a very familiar scene this in the home under the ground, but we are looking on it for the last time.

There was a step above, and Wendy, you may be sure, was the first to recognize it.

"Children, I hear your father's step. He likes you to meet him at the door."

Above, the redskins crouched before Peter.

"Watch well, braves, I have spoken."

And then, as so often before, the gay children dragged him from his tree. As so often before, but never again.

He had brought nuts for the boys as well as the correct time for Wendy.

"Peter, you just spoil them, you know," Wendy simpered.

"Aye, old lady," said Peter, hanging up his gun.

"It was me told him mothers are called old lady," Michael whispered to Curly.

"I complain of Michael," said Curly instantly.

The first twin came to Peter. "Father, we want to dance."

"Dance away, my little man," cried Peter, who was in high good humour.

"But we want you to dance."

Peter was really the best dancer among them, but he pretended to be scandalized.

"Me! My old bones would rattle."

"And Mummy too."

"What," cried Wendy, "the mother of such an armful, dance!"

"But on a Saturday night," Slightly insinuated.

It was not really Saturday night, at least it may have been, for they had long lost count of the days; but always if they wanted to do anything special they said this was Saturday night, and then they did it.

"Of course it is Saturday night, Peter," Wendy said, relenting.

"People of our figure, Wendy."

"But it is only among our own progeny."

"True, true."

So they were told they could dance, but they must put on their nighties first.

"Ah, old lady," Peter said aside to Wendy, warming himself by the fire and looking down at her as she sat turning a heel, "there is nothing more pleasant of an evening for you and me when the day's toil is over than to rest by the fire with the little ones near by."

"It is sweet, Peter, isn't it?" Wendy said, frightfully gratified. "Peter, I think Curly has your nose."

"Michael takes after you."

She went to him and put her hand on his shoulder.

"Dear Peter," she said, "with such a large family, of course, I have now passed my best, but you don't want to change me, do you?"

"No, Wendy."

Certainly he did not want a change, but he looked at her uncomfortably; blinking, you know, like one not sure whether he was awake or asleep.

"Peter, what is it?"

"I was just thinking," he said, a little scared. "It is only make-believe, isn't it, that I am their father?"

"Oh yes," Wendy said primly.

"You see," he continued apologetically, "it would make me seem so old to be their real father."

"But they are ours, Peter, yours and mine."

"But not really, Wendy?" he asked anxiously.

"Not if you don't wish it," she replied; and she distinctly heard his sigh of relief. "Peter," she asked, trying to speak firmly, "what are your exact feelings for me?"

"Those of a devoted son, Wendy."

"I thought so," she said, and went and sat by herself at the extreme end of the room.

"You are so queer," he said, frankly puzzled, "and Tiger Lily is just the same. There is something she wants to be to me, but she says it is not my mother."

"No, indeed, it is not," Wendy replied with frightful emphasis. Now we know why she was prejudiced against the redskins.

"Then what is it?"

"That isn't for a lady to tell."

"Oh, very well," Peter said, a little nettled. "Perhaps Tinker Bell will tell me."

"Oh yes, Tinker Bell will tell you," Wendy retorted scornfully. "She is an abandoned little creature."

Here Tink, who was in her boudoir, eavesdropping, squeaked out something impudent.

"She says she glories in being abandoned," Peter interpreted.

He had a sudden idea. "Perhaps Tink wants to be my mother?"

"You silly ass!" cried Tinker Bell in a passion.

She had said it so often that Wendy needed no translation.

"I almost agree with her," Wendy snapped. Fancy Wendy snapping. But she had been much tried, and she little knew what was to happen before the night was out. If she had known she would not have snapped.

None of them knew. Perhaps it was best not to know. Their ignorance gave them one more glad hour; and as it was to be their last hour on the island, let us rejoice that there were sixty minutes in it. They sang and danced in their nightgowns. Such a deliciously creepy song it was, in which they pretended to be frightened at their own shadows; little witting that so soon shadows would close in upon them, from whom they would shrink in real fear. So uproariously gay was the dance, and how they buffeted each other on the bed and out of it! It was a pillow fight rather than a dance, and when it was finished, the pillows insisted on one bout more, like partners who know that they may never meet again. The stories they told, before it was time for Wendy's good-night story! Even Slightly tried to tell a story that night, but the beginning was so fearfully dull that it appalled even himself, and he said gloomily:

"Yes, it is a dull beginning. I say, let us pretend that it is the end."

And then at last they all got into bed for Wendy's story, the story they loved best, the story Peter hated. Usually when she began to tell this story he left the room or put his hands over his ears; and possibly if he had done either of those things this time they might all still be on the island. But tonight he remained on his stool; and we shall see what happened.

CHAPTER 11

WENDY'S STORY

"Listen, then," said Wendy, settling down to her story, with Michael at her feet and seven boys in the bed. "There was once a gentleman—"

"I had rather he had been a lady," Curly said.

"I wish he had been a white rat," said Nibs.

"Quiet," their mother admonished them. "There was a lady also, and—"

"O Mummy," cried the first twin, "you mean that there is a lady also, don't you? She is not dead, is she?"

"Oh, no."

"I am awfully glad she isn't dead," said Tootles. "Are you glad, John?"

"Of course I am."

"Are you glad, Nibs?"

"Rather."

"Are you glad, Twins?"

"We are just glad."

"Oh dear," sighed Wendy.

"Little less noise there," Peter called out, determined that she should have fair play, however beastly a story it might be in his opinion.

"The gentleman's name," Wendy continued, "was Mr Darling, and her name was Mrs Darling."

"I knew them," John said, to annoy the others.

"I think I knew them," said Michael rather doubtfully.

"They were married, you know," explained Wendy, "and what do you think they had?"

"White rats," cried Nibs, inspired.

"No."

"It's awfully puzzling," cried Tootles, who knew the story by heart.

"Quiet, Tootles. They had three descendants."

"What is descendants?"

"Well, you are one, Twin."

"Do you hear that, John? I am a descendant."

"Descendants are only children," said John.

"Oh dear, oh dear," sighed Wendy. "Now, these three children had a faithful nurse called Nana; but Mr Darling was angry with her and chained her up in the yard; and so all the children flew away."

"It's an awfully good story," said Nibs.

"They flew away," Wendy continued, "to the Neverland, where the lost children are."

"I just thought they did," Curly broke in excitedly. "I don't know how it is, but I just thought they did."

"O Wendy," cried Tootles, "was one of the lost children called Tootles?"

"Yes, he was."

"I am in a story. Hurrah, I am in a story, Nibs."

"Hush. Now, I want you to consider the feelings of the unhappy parents with all their children flown away."

"Oo!" they all moaned, though they were not really considering the feelings of the unhappy parents one jot.

"Think of the empty beds!"

"Oh!"

"It's awfully sad," the first twin said cheerfully.

"I don't see how it can have a happy ending," said the second twin. "Do you Nibs?"

"I'm frightfully anxious."

"If you knew how great is a mother's love," Wendy told them triumphantly, "you would have no fear." She had now come to the part that Peter hated.

"I do like a mother's love," said Tootles, hitting Nibs with a pillow. "Do you like a mother's love, Nibs?"

"I do just," said Nibs, hitting back.

"You see," Wendy said complacently, "our heroine knew that the mother would always leave the window open for her children to fly back by; so they stayed away for years and had a lovely time."

"Did they ever go back?"

"Let us now," said Wendy, bracing herself for her finest effort, "take a peep into the future"; and they all gave themselves the twist that makes peeps into the future easier. "Years have rolled by; and who is this elegant lady of uncertain age alighting at London Station?"

"O Wendy, who is she?" cried Nibs, every bit as excited as if he didn't know.

"Can it be – yes – no – it is – the fair Wendy!"

"Oh!"

"And who are the two noble portly figures accompanying her, now grown to man's estate? Can they be John and Michael? They are!"

"Oh!"

"'See, dear brothers,' says Wendy, pointing upwards, 'There is the window still standing open. Ah, now we are rewarded for our sublime faith in mother's love.' So up they flew to their mummy and daddy; and pen cannot describe the happy scene, over which we draw a veil."

That was a story, and they were as pleased with it as the fair narrator herself. Everything just as it should be, you see.

Off we skip like the most heartless things in the world, which is what children are, but so attractive; and we have an entirely selfish time; and then when we have need of special attention we nobly return for it, confident that we shall be embraced instead of smacked.

So great indeed was their faith in a mother's love that they felt they could afford to be callous for a bit longer.

But there was one there who knew better; and when Wendy finished he uttered a hollow groan.

"What is it, Peter?" she cried, running to him, thinking he was ill. She felt him solicitously, lower down than his chest. "Where is it, Peter?"

"It isn't that kind of pain," Peter replied darkly.

"Then what kind is it?"

"Wendy, you are wrong about mothers."

They all gathered round him in affright, so alarming was his agitation; and with a fine candour he told them what he had hitherto concealed.

"Long ago," he said, "I thought like you that my mother would always keep the window open for me; so I stayed away for moons and moons and moons, and then flew back; but the window was barred, for mother had forgotten all about me, and there was another little boy sleeping in my bed."

I am not sure that this was true, but Peter thought it was true; and it scared them.

"Are you sure mothers are like that?"

"Yes."

So this was the truth about mothers. The toads!

Still it is best to be careful; and no one knows so quickly as a child when he should give in. "Wendy, let us go home," cried John and Michael together.

"Yes," she said, clutching them.

"Not tonight?" asked the lost boys bewildered. They knew in what they called their hearts that one can get on quite well without a mother, and that it is only the mothers who think you can't.

"At once," Wendy replied resolutely, for the horrible thought had come to her: "Perhaps mother is in half-mourning by this time."

This dread made her forgetful of what must be Peter's feelings, and she said to him rather sharply, "Peter, will you make the necessary arrangements?"

"If you wish it," he replied as coolly as if she had asked him to pass the nuts.

Not so much as a sorry-to-lose-you between them! If she did not mind the parting, he was going to show her, was Peter, that neither did he.

But of course he cared very much; and he was so full of wrath against grown-ups, who, as usual, were spoiling everything, that as soon as he got inside his tree he breathed intentionally quick short breaths at the rate of about five to a second. He did this because there is a saying in the Neverland that every time you breathe, a grown-up dies; and Peter was killing them off vindictively as fast as possible.

Then having given the necessary instructions to the redskins he returned to the home, where an unworthy scene had been enacted in his absence. Panic-stricken at the thought of losing Wendy, the lost boys had advanced upon her threateningly.

"It will be worse than before she came," they cried.

"We shan't let her go."

"Let's keep her prisoner."

"Aye, chain her up."

In her extremity an instinct told her to which of them to turn.

"Tootles," she cried, "I appeal to you."

Was it not strange? She appealed to Tootles, quite the silliest one.

Grandly, however, did Tootles respond. For that one moment he dropped his silliness and spoke with dignity.

"I am just Tootles," he said, "and nobody minds me. But the first who does not behave to Wendy like an English gentleman I will blood him severely."

He drew his hanger; and for that instant his sun was at noon. The others held back uneasily. Then Peter returned, and they saw at once that they would get no support from him. He would keep no girl in Neverland against her will.

"Wendy," he said, striding up and down, "I have asked the redskins to guide you through the wood, as flying tires you so."

"Thank you, Peter."

"Then," he continued in the short sharp voice of one accustomed to be obeyed, "Tinker Bell will take you across the sea. Wake her, Nibs."

Nibs had to knock twice before he got an answer, though Tink had really been sitting up in bed listening for some time.

"Who are you? How dare you? Go away!" she cried.

"You are to get up, Tink," Nibs called, "and take Wendy on a journey."

Of course Tink had been delighted to hear that Wendy was going; but she was jolly well determined not to be her courier, and she said so in still more offensive language. Then she pretended to be asleep again.

"She says she won't," Nibs exclaimed, aghast at such insubordination, whereupon Peter went sternly towards the young lady's chamber.

"Tink," he rapped out, "if you don't get up and dress at once I will open the curtains, and then we shall all see you in your *négligée*."

This made her leap to the floor. "Who said I wasn't getting up?" she cried.

In the meantime the boys were gazing very forlornly at Wendy, now equipped with John and Michael for the journey. By this time they were dejected, not merely because they were about to lose her, but also because they felt that she was going off to something nice to which they had not been invited. Novelty was beckoning to them as usual.

Crediting them with a nobler feeling, Wendy melted.

"Dear ones," she said, "if you will all come with me I feel almost sure I can get my father and mother to adopt you."

The invitation was meant specially for Peter; but each of the boys was thinking exclusively of himself, and at once they jumped with joy.

"But won't they think us rather a handful?" Nibs asked in the middle of his jump.

"Oh, no," cried Wendy, rapidly thinking it out, "it will only mean having a few beds in the drawing-room; they can be hidden behind screens on first Thursdays."

"Peter, can we go?" they all cried imploringly. They took it for granted that if they went he would go also, but really they scarcely cared. Thus children are ever ready, when novelty knocks, to desert their dearest ones.

"All right," Peter replied with a bitter smile; and immediately they rushed to get their things.

"And now, Peter," Wendy said, thinking she had put everything right, "I am going to give you your medicine before you go." She loved to give them medicine, and undoubtedly gave them too much. Of course it was only water; but it was out of a calabash, and she always shook the calabash and counted the drops, which gave it a certain medicinal quality. On this occasion, however, she did not give Peter his draught for just as she had prepared it, she saw a look on his face that made her heart sink.

"Get your things, Peter," she cried, shaking.

"No," he answered, pretending indifference, "I am not going with you, Wendy."

"Yes, Peter."

"No."

To show that her departure would leave him unmoved, he skipped up and down the room, playing gaily on his heartless pipes. She had to run about after him, though it was rather undignified.

"To find your mother," she coaxed.

Now, if Peter had ever quite had a mother, he no longer missed her. He could do very well without one. He had thought them out, and remembered only their bad points.

"No, no," he told Wendy decisively; "perhaps she would say I was old, and I just want always to be a little boy and to have fun."

"But, Peter—"

"No."

And so the others had to be told.

"Peter isn't coming."

Peter not coming! They gazed blankly at him, their sticks over their backs, and on each stick a bundle. Their first thought was that if Peter was not going he had probably changed his mind about letting them go.

But he was far too proud for that. "If you find your mothers," he said darkly, "I hope you will like them."

The awful cynicism of this made an uncomfortable impression, and most of them began to look rather doubtful. After all, their faces said, were they not noodles to want to go?

"Now then," cried Peter, "no fuss, no blubbering; good-bye, Wendy"; and he held out his hand cheerily, quite as if they must really go now, for he had something important to do.

She had to take his hand, as there was no indication that he would prefer a thimble.

"You will remember about changing your flannels, Peter?" she said, lingering over him. She was always so particular about their flannels.

"Yes."

"And you will take your medicine?"

"Yes."

That seemed to be everything; and an awkward pause followed. Peter, however, was not the kind that breaks down before people. "Are you ready, Tinker Bell?" he called out.

"Aye, aye."

"Then lead the way."

Tink darted up the nearest tree; but no one followed her, for it was at this moment that the pirates made their dreadful attack upon the redskins. Above, where all had been so still, the air was rent with shrieks and the clash of steel. Below, there was dead silence. Mouths opened and remained open. Wendy fell on her knees, but her arms were extended towards Peter. All arms were extended to him, as if suddenly blown in his direction; they were beseeching him mutely not to desert them. As for Peter, he seized his sword, the same he thought he had slain Barbecue with; and the lust of battle was in his eye.

CHAPTER 12

THE CHILDREN ARE CARRIED OFF

The pirate attack had been a complete surprise; a sure proof that the unscrupulous Hook had conducted it improperly, for to surprise redskins fairly is beyond the wit of the white man.

By all the unwritten laws of savage warfare it is always the redskin who attacks, and with the wiliness of his race he does it just before the dawn, at which time he knows the courage of the whites is at its lowest ebb. The white men have in the meantime made a rude stockade on the summit of yonder undulating ground, at the foot of which a stream runs; for it is destruction to be too far from water. There they await the onslaught, the inexperienced ones clutching their revolvers and treading on twigs, but the old hands sleeping tranquilly until just before the dawn. Through the long black night the savage scouts wriggle, snake-like, among the grass without stirring a blade. The brushwood closes behind them as silently as sand into which a mole has dived. Not a sound is to be heard, save when they give vent to a wonderful imitation of the lonely call of the coyote. The cry is answered by other braves; and some of them do it even better than the coyotes, who are not very good at it. So the chill hours wear on, and the long suspense is horribly trying to the paleface who has to live through it for the first time; but to the trained hand those ghastly calls and still ghastlier silences are but an imitation of how the night is marching.

That this was the usual procedure was so well known to Hook that in disregarding it he cannot be excused on the pleas of ignorance.

The Piccaninnies, on their part, trusted implicitly to his honour, and their whole action of the night stands out in marked contrast to his. They left nothing undone that was consistent with the reputation of their tribe. With that alertness of the senses which is at once the marvel and despair of civilized peoples, they knew that the pirates were on the island from the moment one of them trod on a dry stick; and in an incredibly short space of time the coyote cries began. Every foot of ground between the spot where Hook had landed his forces and the home under the trees was stealthily examined by braves, wearing their moccasins with the heels in front. They found only one hillock with a stream at its base, so that Hook had no choice; here he must establish himself and wait for just before the dawn. Everything being thus mapped out with almost diabolical cunning, the main body of the redskins folded their blankets around them, and in the phlegmatic manner that is to them the pearl of manhood squatted above the children's home, awaiting the cold moment when they should deal pale death.

Here dreaming, though wide awake, of the exquisite tortures to which they were to put him at break of day, those confiding savages were found by the treacherous Hook. From the accounts afterwards supplied by such of the scouts as escaped the carnage, he does not seem even to have paused at the rising ground, though it is certain that in that grey light he must have seen it: no thought of waiting to be attacked appears from first to last to have visited his subtle mind; he would not even hold off till the night was nearly spent; on he pounded with no policy but to fall to. What could the bewildered scouts do, masters as they were of every warlike artifice save this one, but trot helplessly after him, exposing themselves fatally to view, the while they gave pathetic utterance to the coyote cry.

Around the brave Tiger Lily were a dozen of her stoutest warriors, and they suddenly saw the perfidious pirates bearing down upon them. Fell from their eyes then the film through which they had looked at victory. No more would they torture at the stake. For them the happy hunting-grounds now. They knew it; but as their fathers' sons they acquitted themselves. Even then they had time to gather in a phalanx that would have been hard to break had they risen quickly, but this they were forbidden to do by the traditions of their race. It is written that the noble savage must never express surprise in the presence of the white. Thus terrible as the sudden appearance of the pirates must have been to them, they remained stationary for a moment, not a muscle moving; as if the foe had come by invitation. Then, indeed, the tradition gallantly upheld, they seized their weapons, and the air was torn with the war-cry, but it was now too late.

It is no part of ours to describe what was a massacre rather than a fight. Thus perished many of the flowers of the Piccaninny tribe. Not all unavenged did they die, for with Lean Wolf fell Alf Mason, to disturb the Spanish Main no more; and among others who bit the dust were Geo. Scourie, Chas. Turley, and the Alsatian Foggerty. Turley fell to the tomahawk of the terrible Panther, who ultimately cut a way through the pirates with Tiger Lily and a small remnant of the tribe.

To what extent Hook is to blame for his tactics on this occasion is for the historian to decide. Had he waited on the rising ground till the proper hour he and his men would probably have been butchered; and in judging him it is only fair to take this into account. What he should perhaps have done was to acquaint his opponents that he proposed to follow a new method. On the other hand this, as destroying the element of surprise, would have made his strategy of no avail, so that the whole question is beset with difficulties. One cannot at least withhold a reluctant admiration for the wit that had conceived so bold a scheme, and the fell genius with which it was carried out.

What were his own feelings about himself at that triumphant moment? Fain would his dogs have known, as breathing heavily and wiping their cutlasses, they gathered at a discreet distance from his hook, and squinted through their ferret eyes at this extraordinary man. Elation must have been in his heart, but his face did not reflect it: ever a dark and solitary enigma, he stood aloof from his followers in spirit as in substance.

The night's work was not yet over, for it was not the redskins he had come out to destroy; they were but the bees to be smoked, so that he should get at the honey. It was Pan he wanted, Pan and Wendy and their band, but chiefly Pan.

Peter was such a small boy that one tends to wonder at the man's hatred of him. True, he had flung Hook's arm to the crocodile; but even this and the increased insecurity of life to which it led, owing to the crocodile's pertinacity, hardly account for a vindictiveness so relentless and malignant. The truth is that there was a something about Peter which goaded the pirate captain to frenzy. It was not his courage, it was not his engaging appearance, it was not—. There is no beating about the bush, for we know quite well what it was, and have got to tell. It was Peter's cockiness.

This had got on Hook's nerves; it made his iron claw twitch, and at night it disturbed him like an insect. While Peter lived, the tortured man felt that he was a lion in a cage into which a sparrow had come.

The question now was how to get down the trees, or how to get his dogs down. He ran his greedy eyes over them, searching for the thinnest ones. They wriggled uncomfortably, for they knew that he would not scruple to ram them down with poles.

In the meantime, what of the boys? We have seen them at the first clang of weapons, turned as it were into stone figures, open-mouthed, all appealing with outstretched arms to Peter; and we return to them as their mouths close, and their arms fall to their sides. The pandemonium above has ceased almost as suddenly as it arose, passed like a fierce gust of wind; but they know that in the passing it has determined their fate.

Which side has won?

The pirates, listening avidly at the mouths of the trees, heard the question put by every boy, and alas, they also heard Peter's answer.

"If the redskins have won," he said, "they will beat the tom-tom; it is always their sign of victory."

Now Smee had found the tom-tom, and was at that moment sitting on it. "You will never hear the tom-tom again," he muttered, but inaudibly of course, for strict silence had been enjoined. To his amazement Hook signed him to beat the tom-tom; and slowly there came to Smee an understanding of the dreadful wickedness of the order. Never, probably, had this simple man admired Hook so much.

Twice Smee beat upon the instrument, and then stopped to listen gleefully.

"The tom-tom," the miscreants heard Peter cry; "an Indian victory!"

The doomed children answered with a cheer that was music to the black hearts above, and almost immediately they repeated their good-byes to Peter. This puzzled the pirates, but all their other feelings were swallowed by a base delight that the enemy were about to come up the trees. They smirked at each other and rubbed their hands. Rapidly and silently Hook gave his orders: one man to each tree, and the others to arrange themselves in a line two yards apart.

CHAPTER 13

DO YOU BELIEVE IN FAIRIES?

The more quickly this horror is disposed of the better. The first to emerge from his tree was Curly. He rose out of it into the arms of Cecco, who flung him to Smee, who flung him to Starkey, who flung him to Bill Jukes, who flung him to Noodler, and so he was tossed from one to another till he fell at the feet of the black pirate. All the boys were plucked from their trees in this ruthless manner; and several of them were in the air at a time, like bales of goods flung from hand to hand.

A different treatment was accorded to Wendy, who came last. With ironical politeness Hook raised his hat to her, and offering her his arm, escorted her to the spot where the others were being gagged. He did it with such an air, he was so frightfully *distingué*, that she was too fascinated to cry out. She was only a little girl.

Perhaps it is tell-tale to divulge that for a moment Hook entranced her, and we tell on her only because her slip led to strange results. Had she haughtily unhanded him (and we would have loved to write it of her), she would have been hurled through the air like the others, and then Hook would probably not have been present at the tying of the children; and had he not been at the tying he would not have discovered Slightly's secret, and without the secret he could not presently have made his foul attempt on Peter's life.

They were tied to prevent their flying away, doubled up with their knees close to their ears; and for the trussing of them the black pirate had cut a rope into nine equal pieces. All went well until Slightly's turn came, when he was found to be like those irritating parcels that use up all the string in going round and leave no tags with which to tie a knot. The pirates kicked him in their rage, just as you kick the parcel (though in fairness you should kick the string); and strange to say it was Hook who told them to belay their violence. His lip was curled with malicious triumph. While his dogs were merely sweating because every time they tried to pack the unhappy lad tight in one part he bulged out in another, Hook's master mind had gone far beneath Slightly's surface, probing not for effects but for causes; and his exultation showed that he had found them. Slightly, white to the gills, knew that Hook had surprised his secret, which was this, that no boy so blown out would use a tree wherein an average man need stick. Poor Slightly, most wretched of all the children now, for he was in a panic about Peter, bitterly regretted what he had done. Madly addicted to the drinking water when he was hot, he had swelled in consequence to his present girth, and instead of reducing himself to fit his tree he had, unknown to the others, whittled his tree to make it fit him.

Sufficient of this Hook guessed to persuade him that Peter at last lay at his mercy; but no word of the dark design that now formed in the subterranean caverns of his mind crossed his lips; he merely signed that the captives were to be conveyed to the ship, and that he would be alone.

How to convey them? Hunched up in their ropes they might indeed be rolled downhill like barrels, but most of the way lay through a morass. Again Hook's genius surmounted difficulties. He indicated that the little house must be used as a conveyance. The children were flung into it, four stout pirates raised it on their shoulders, the others fell in behind, and singing the hateful pirate chorus the strange procession set off through the wood. I don't know whether any of the children were crying; if so, the singing drowned the sound; but as the little house disappeared in the forest, a brave though tiny jet of smoke issued from its chimney as if defying Hook.

Hook saw it, and it did Peter a bad service. It dried up any trickle of pity for him that may have remained in the pirate's infuriated breast.

The first thing he did on finding himself alone in the fast-falling night was to tiptoe to Slightly's tree, and make sure that it provided him with a passage. Then for long he remained brooding; his hat of ill omen on the sward, so that a gentle breeze which had arisen might play refreshingly through his hair. Dark as were his thoughts his blue eyes were as soft as the periwinkle. Intently he listened for any sound from the nether world, but all was as silent below as above; the house under the ground seemed to be but one more empty tenement in the void. Was that boy asleep, or did he stand waiting at the foot of Slightly's tree, with his dagger in his hand?

There was no way of knowing, save by going down. Hook let his cloak slip softly to the ground, and then biting his lip till a lewd blood stood on them, he stepped into the tree. He was a brave man; but for a moment he had to stop there and wipe his brow, which was dripping like a candle. Then silently he let himself go into the unknown.

He arrived unmolested at the foot of the shaft, and stood still again, biting his breath, which had almost left him. As his eyes became accustomed to the dim light various objects in the home under the trees took shape; but the only one on which his greedy gaze rested, long sought for and found at last, was the great bed. On the bed lay Peter fast asleep.

Unaware of the tragedy being enacted above, Peter had continued, for a little time after the children left, to play gaily on his pipes: no doubt rather a forlorn attempt to prove to himself that he did not care. Then he decided not to take his medicine, so as to grieve Wendy. Then he lay down on the bed outside the coverlet, to vex her still more; for she had always tucked them inside it, because you never know that you may not grow chilly at the turn of the night. Then he nearly cried; but it struck him how indignant she would be if he laughed instead; so he laughed a haughty laugh and fell asleep in the middle of it.

Sometimes, though not often, he had dreams, and they were more painful than the dreams of other boys. For hours he could not be separated from these dreams, though he wailed piteously in them. They had to do, I think, with the riddle of his existence. At such times it had been Wendy's custom to take him out of bed and sit with him on her lap, soothing him in dear ways of her own invention, and when he grew calmer to put him back to bed before he quite woke up, so that he should not know of the indignity to which she had subjected him. But on this occasion he had fallen at once into a dreamless sleep. One arm dropped over the edge of the bed, one leg was arched, and the unfinished part of his laugh was stranded on his mouth, which was open, showing the little pearls.

Thus defenceless, Hook found him. He stood silent at the foot of the tree looking across the chamber at his enemy. Did no feeling of compassion disturb his sombre breast? The man was not wholly evil; he loved flowers (I have been told) and sweet music (he was himself no mean performer on the harpsichord); and let it be frankly admitted, the idyllic nature of the scene stirred him profoundly. Mastered by his better self, he would have returned reluctantly up the tree but for one thing.

What stayed him was Peter's impertinent appearance as he slept. The open mouth, the drooping arm, the arched knee: they were such a personification of cockiness as, taken together, will never again, one may hope, be presented to eyes so sensitive to their offensiveness. They steeled Hook's heart. If his rage had broken him into a hundred pieces every one them would have disregarded the incident, and leapt at the sleeper.

Though a light from the one lamp shone dimly on the bed Hook stood in darkness himself, and at the first stealthy step forward he discovered an obstacle, the door of Slightly's tree. It did not entirely fill the aperture, and he had been looking over it. Feeling for the catch, he found to his fury that it was low down, beyond his reach. To his disordered brain it seemed then that the irritating quality in Peter's face and figure visibly increased, and he rattled the door and flung himself against it. Was his enemy to escape him after all?

But what was that? The red in his eye had caught sight of Peter's medicine standing on a ledge within easy reach. He fathomed what it was straightaway, and immediately he knew that the sleeper was in his power.

Lest he should be taken alive, Hook always carried about his person a dreadful drug, blended by himself of all the death-dealing rings that had come into his possession. These he had boiled down into a yellow liquid quite unknown to science, which was probably the most virulent poison in existence.

Five drops of this he now added to Peter's cup. His hand shook, but it was in exultation rather than in shame. As he did it he avoided glancing at the sleeper, but not lest pity should unnerve him; merely to avoid spilling. Then one long gloating look he cast upon his victim, and turning, wormed his way with difficulty up the tree. As he emerged at the top he looked the very spirit of evil breaking from its hole. Donning his hat at its most rakish angle, he wound his cloak around him, holding one end in front as if to conceal his person from the night, of which it was the blackest part, and muttering strangely to himself stole away through the trees.

Peter slept on. The light fluttered and went out, leaving the tenement in darkness; but still he slept. It must have been not less than ten o'clock by the crocodile, when he suddenly sat up in his bed, wakened by he knew not what. It was a soft cautious tapping on the door of his tree.

Soft and cautious, but in that stillness it was sinister. Peter felt for his dagger till his hand gripped it. Then he spoke.

"Who is that?"

For long there was no answer: then again the knock.

"Who are you?"

No answer.

He was thrilled, and he loved being thrilled. In two strides he reached his door. Unlike Slightly's door it filled the aperture, so that he could not see beyond it, nor could the one knocking see him.

"I won't open unless you speak," Peter cried.

Then at last the visitor spoke, in a lovely bell-like voice.

"Let me in, Peter."

It was Tink, and quickly he unbarred to her. She flew in excitedly, her face flushed and her dress stained with mud.

"What is it?"

"Oh, you could never guess," she cried, and offered him three guesses. "Out with it!" he shouted; and in one ungrammatical sentence, as long as the ribbons conjurers pull from their mouths, she told of the capture of Wendy and the boys.

Peter's heart bobbed up and down as he listened. Wendy bound, and on the pirate ship; she who loved everything to be just so!

"I'll rescue her," he cried, leaping at his weapons. As he leapt he thought of something he could do to please her. He could take his medicine.

His hand closed on the fatal draught.

"No!" shrieked Tinker Bell, who had heard Hook muttering about his deed as he sped through the forest.

"Why not?"

"It is poisoned."

"Poisoned? Who could have poisoned it?"

"Hook."

"Don't be silly. How could Hook have got down here?"

Alas, Tinker Bell could not explain this, for even she did not know the dark secret of Slightly's tree. Nevertheless

Hook's words had left no room for doubt. The cup was poisoned.

"Besides," said Peter, quite believing himself, "I never fell asleep."

He raised the cup. No time for words now; time for deeds: and with one of her lightning movements Tink got between his lips and the draught, and drained it to the dregs.

"Why, Tink, how dare you drink my medicine?"

But she did not answer. Already she was reeling in the air.

"What is the matter with you?" cried Peter, suddenly afraid.

"It was poisoned, Peter," she told him softly; "and now I am going to be dead."

"O Tink, did you drink it to save me?"

"Yes."

"But why Tink?"

Her wings would scarcely carry her now, but in reply she alighted on his shoulder and gave his chin a loving bite. She whispered in his ear, "You silly ass"; and then, tottering to her chamber, lay down on the bed.

His head almost filled the fourth wall of her little room as he knelt near her in distress. Every moment her light was growing fainter; and he knew that if it went out she would be no more. She liked his tears so much that she put out her beautiful finger and let them run over it.

Her voice was so low that at first he could not make out what she said. Then he made it out. She was saying that she thought she could get well again if children believed in fairies.

Peter flung out his arms. There were no children there, and it was night-time; but he addressed all who might be dreaming of the Neverland, and who were therefore nearer to him than you think; boys and girls in their nighties, and naked papooses in their baskets hung from trees.

"Do you believe?" he cried.

Tink sat up in bed almost briskly to listen to her fate.

She fancied she heard answers in the affirmative, and then again she wasn't sure.

"What do you think?" she asked Peter.

"If you believe," he shouted to them, "clap your hands; don't let Tink die."

Many clapped.

Some didn't.

A few little beasts hissed.

The clapping stopped suddenly, as if countless mothers had rushed to their nurseries to see what on earth was happening; but already Tink was saved. First her voice grew strong; then she popped out of bed; then she was flashing through the room more merry and impudent than ever. She never thought of thanking those who believed, but she would have liked to get at the ones who had hissed.

"And now to rescue Wendy."

The moon was riding in a cloudy heaven when Peter rose from his tree, begirt with weapons and wearing little else, to set out upon his perilous quest. It was not such a night as he would have chosen. He had hoped to fly, keeping not far from the ground so that nothing unwonted should escape his eyes; but in that fitful light to have flown low would have meant trailing his shadow through the trees, thus disturbing the birds and acquainting a watchful foe that he was astir.

He regretted now that he had given the birds of the island such strange names that they are very wild and difficult of approach.

There was no other course but to press forward in redskin fashion, at which happily he was an adept. But in what direction, for he could not be sure that the children had been taken to the ship? A slight fall of snow had obliterated all footmarks; and a deathly silence pervaded the island, as if for a space Nature stood still in horror of the recent carnage. He had taught the children something of the forest lore that he had himself learned from Tiger Lily and Tinker Bell, and knew that in their dire hour they were not likely to forget it.

Slightly, if he had an opportunity, would blaze the trees, for instance, Curly would drop seeds, and Wendy would leave her handkerchief at some important place. But morning was needed to search for such guidance, and he could not wait. The upper world had called him, but would give no help.

The crocodile passed him, but not another living thing, not a sound, not a movement; and yet he knew well that sudden death might be at the next tree, or stalking him from behind.

He swore this terrible oath: "Hook or me this time."

Now he crawled forward like a snake; and again, erect, he darted across a space on which the moonlight played: one finger on his lip and his dagger at the ready. He was frightfully happy.

CHAPTER 14

THE PIRATE SHIP

One green light squinting over Kidd's Creek, which is near the mouth of the pirate river, marked where the brig, the *Jolly Roger*, lay, low in the water; a rakish-looking craft foul to the hull, every beam in her detestable, like ground strewn with mangled feathers. She was the cannibal of the seas, and scarce needed that watchful eye, for she floated immune in the horror of her name.

She was wrapped in the blanket of night, through which no sound from her could have reached the shore. There was little sound, and none agreeable save the whir of the ship's sewing machine at which Smee sat, ever industrious and obliging, the essence of the commonplace, pathetic Smee. I know not why he was so infinitely pathetic, unless it were because he was so pathetically unaware of it; but even strong men had to turn hastily from looking at him, and more than once on summer evenings he had touched the fount of Hook's tears and made it flow. Of this, as of almost everything else, Smee was quite unconscious.

A few of the pirates leant over the bulwarks drinking in the miasma of the night; others sprawled by barrels over games of dice and cards; and the exhausted four who had carried the little house lay prone on the deck, where even in their sleep they rolled skilfully to this side and that out of Hook's reach, lest he should claw them mechanically in passing.

Hook trod the deck in thought. O man unfathomable. It was his hour of triumph. Peter had been removed for ever from his path, and all the other boys were on the brig, about to walk the plank. It was his grimmest deed since the days when he had brought Barbecue to heel; and knowing as we do how vain a tabernacle is man, could we be surprised had he now paced the dock unsteadily, bellied out by the winds of his success?

But there was no elation in his gait, which kept pace with the action of his sombre mind. Hook was profoundly dejected.

He was often thus when communing with himself on board ship in the quietude of the night. It was because he was so terribly alone. This inscrutable man never felt more alone than when surrounded by his dogs. They were socially so inferior to him.

Hook was not his true name. To reveal who he really was would even at this date set the country in a blaze; but as those who read between the lines must already have guessed, he had been at a famous public school; and its traditions still clung to him like garments, with which indeed they are largely concerned. Thus it was offensive to him even now to board a ship in the same dress in which he grappled her; and he still adhered in his walk to the school's distinguished slouch. But above all he retained the passion for good form.

Good form! However much he may have degenerated, he still knew that this is all that really matters.

From far within him he heard a creaking as of rusty portals, and through them came a stern tap-tap-tap, like hammering in the night when one cannot sleep. "Have you been good form today?" was their eternal question.

"Fame, fame, that glittering bauble, it is mine," he cried.

"Is it quite good form to be distinguished at anything?" the tap-tap from his school replied.

"I am the only man whom Barbecue feared," he urged; "and Flint himself feared Barbecue."

"Barbecue, Flint – what house?" came the cutting retort.

Most disquieting reflection of all, was it not bad form to think about good form?

His vitals were tortured by this problem. It was a claw within him sharper than the iron one; and as it tore him, the perspiration dripped down his sallow countenance and streaked his doublet. Oft-times he drew his sleeve across his face, but there was no damming that trickle.

Ah, envy not Hook.

There came to him a presentiment of his early dissolution. It was as if Peter's terrible oath had boarded the ship. Hook felt a gloomy desire to make his dying speech, lest presently there should be no time for it.

"Better for Hook," he cried, "if he had had less ambition." It was in his darkest hours only that he referred to himself in the third person.

"No little children love me."

Strange that he should think of this, which had never troubled him before; perhaps the sewing machine brought it to his mind. For long he muttered to himself, staring at Smee, who was hemming placidly, under the conviction that all children feared him.

Feared him! Feared Smee! There was not a child on board the brig that night who did not already love him. He had said horrid things to them and hit them with the palm of his hand, because he could not hit with his fist; but they had only clung to him more. Michael had tried on his spectacles.

To tell poor Smee that they thought him lovable! Hook itched to do it, but it seemed too brutal. Instead, he revolved this mystery in his mind: why do they find Smee lovable? He pursued the problem like the sleuth-hound that he was. If Smee was lovable, what was it that made him so? A terrible answer suddenly presented itself: "Good form?"

Had the bo'sun good form without knowing it, which is the best form of all?

He remembered that you have to prove you don't know you have it before you are eligible for Pop.

With a cry of rage he raised his iron hand over Smee's head; but he did not tear. What arrested him was this reflection:

"To claw a man because he is good form, what would that be?"

"Bad form!"

The unhappy Hook was as impotent as he was damp, and he fell forward like a cut flower.

His dogs thinking him out of the way for a time, discipline instantly relaxed; and they broke into a bacchanalian dance, which brought him to his feet at once; all traces of human weakness gone, as if a bucket of water had passed over him.

"Quiet, you scugs," he cried, "or I'll cast anchor in you": and at once the din was hushed. "Are all the children chained, so they cannot fly away?"

"Aye, aye."

"Then hoist them up."

The wretched prisoners were dragged from the hold, all except Wendy, and ranged in line in front of him. For a time he seemed unconscious of their presence. He lolled at his ease, humming, not unmelodiously, snatches of a rude song, and fingered a pack of cards. Ever and anon the light from his cigar gave a touch of colour to his face.

"Now then, bullies," he said briskly, "six of you walk the plank tonight, but I have room for two cabin boys. Which of you is it to be?"

"Don't irritate him unnecessarily," had been Wendy's instructions in the hold; so Tootles stepped forward politely. Tootles hated the idea of signing under such a man, but an instinct told him that it would be prudent to lay responsibility on an absent person; and though a somewhat silly boy, he knew that mothers alone are always willing to be the buffer. All children know this about mothers, and despise them for it, but make constant use of it.

So Tootles explained prudently, "You see, sir, I don't think my mother would like me to be a pirate. Would your mother like you to be a pirate, Slightly?"

He winked at Slightly, who said mournfully, "I don't think so," as if he wished things had been otherwise. "Would your mother like you to be a pirate, Twin?"

"I don't think so," said the first twin, as clever as the others. "Nibs, would—"

"Stow this gab," roared Hook, and the spokesmen were dragged back. "You boy," he said, addressing John, "you look as if you had a little pluck in you. Didst never want to be a pirate, my hearty?"

Now John had sometimes experienced this hankering at maths prep.; and he was struck by Hook's picking him out.

"I once thought of calling myself Red-handed Jack," he said diffidently.

"And a good name too. We'll call you that here, bully, if you join."

"What do you think, Michael?" asked John.

"What would you call me if I join?" Michael demanded.

"Blackbeard Joe."

Michael was naturally impressed. "What do you think, John?" He wanted John to decide, and John wanted him to decide.

"Shall we still be respectful subjects of the King?" John inquired.

Through Hook's teeth came the answer: "You would have to swear, 'Down with the King.'"

Perhaps John had not behaved very well so far, but he shone out now.

"Then I refuse," he cried, banging the barrel in front of Hook.

"And I refuse," cried Michael.

"Rule Britannia!" squeaked Curly.

The infuriated pirates buffeted them in the mouth; and Hook roared out, "That seals your doom. Bring up their mother. Get the plank ready."

They were only boys, and they went white as they saw Jukes and Cecco preparing the fatal plank. But they tried to look brave when Wendy was brought up.

No words of mine can tell you how Wendy despised those pirates. To the boys there was at least some glamour in the pirate calling, but all that she saw was that the ship had not been scrubbed for years. There was not a port-hole, on the grimy glass of which you might not have written with your finger, "Dirty pig"; and she had already written it on several. But as the boys gathered round her she had no thought, of course, save for them.

"So, my beauty," said Hook, as if he spoke in syrup, "you are to see your children walk the plank."

Fine gentleman though he was, the intensity of his communings had soiled his ruff, and suddenly he knew that she was gazing at it. With a hasty gesture he tried to hide it, but he was too late.

"Are they to die?" asked Wendy, with a look of such frightful contempt that he nearly fainted.

"They are," he snarled. "Silence all," he called gloatingly, "For a mother's last words to her children."

At this moment Wendy was grand. "These are my last words, dear boys," she said firmly. "I feel that I have a message to you from your real mothers, and it is this: 'We hope our sons will die like English gentlemen.'"

Even the pirates were awed; and Tootles cried out hysterically. "I am going to do what my mother hopes. What are you to do, Nibs?"

"What my mother hopes. What are you to do, Twin?"

"What my mother hopes. John, what are—?"

But Hook had found his voice again.

"Tie her up," he shouted.

It was Smee who tied her to the mast. "See here, honey," he whispered, "I'll save you if you promise to be my mother."

But not even for Smee would she make such a promise. "I would almost rather have no children at all," she said disdainfully.

It is sad to know that not a boy was looking at her as Smee tied her to the mast; the eyes of all were on the plank; that last little walk they were about to take. They were no longer able to hope that they would walk it manfully, for the capacity to think had gone from them; they could stare and shiver only.

Hook smiled on them with his teeth closed, and took a step towards Wendy. His intention was to turn her face so that she should see the boys walking the plank one by one. But he never reached her, he never heard the cry of anguish he hoped to wring from her. He heard something else instead.

It was the terrible tick-tick of the crocodile.

They all heard it – pirates, boys, Wendy; and immediately every head was blown in one direction; not to the water whence the sound proceeded, but towards Hook. All knew that what was about to happen concerned him alone, and that from being actors they were suddenly become spectators.

Very frightful was it to see the change that came over him. It was as if he had been clipped at every joint. He fell in a little heap.

The sound came steadily nearer; and in advance of it came this ghastly thought. "The crocodile is about to board the ship."

Even the iron claw hung inactive; as if knowing that it was no intrinsic part of what the attacking force wanted. Left so fearfully alone, any other man would have lain with his eyes shut where he fell: but the gigantic brain of Hook was still working, and under its guidance he crawled on his knees along the deck as far from the sound as he could go. The pirates respectfully cleared a passage for him, and it was only when he brought up against the bulwarks that he spoke.

"Hide me," he cried hoarsely.

They gathered round him; all eyes averted from the thing that was coming aboard. They had no thought of fighting it. It was Fate.

Only when Hook was hidden from them did curiosity loosen the limbs of the boys so that they could rush to the ship's side to see the crocodile climbing it. Then they got the strangest surprise of this Night of Nights; for it was no crocodile that was coming to their aid. It was Peter.

He signed to them not to give vent to any cry of admiration that might rouse suspicion. Then he went on ticking.

CHAPTER 15

"HOOK OR ME THIS TIME"

Odd things happen to all of us on our way through life without our noticing for a time that they have happened. Thus, to take an instance, we suddenly discover that we have been deaf in one ear for we don't know how long, but, say, half an hour. Now such an experience had come that night to Peter. When last we saw him he was stealing across the island with one finger to his lips and his dagger at the ready.

He had seen the crocodile pass by without noticing anything peculiar about it, but by and by he remembered that it had not been ticking. At first he thought this eerie, but soon he concluded rightly that the clock had run down.

Without giving a thought to what might be the feelings of a fellow-creature thus abruptly deprived of its closest companion, Peter at once considered how he could turn the catastrophe to his own use; and he decided to tick, so that wild beasts should believe he was the crocodile and let him pass unmolested. He ticked superbly, but with one unforeseen result. The crocodile was among those who heard the sound, and it followed him, though whether with the purpose of regaining what it had lost or merely as a friend under the belief that it was again ticking itself, will never be certainly known, for, like all slaves to a fixed idea, it was a stupid beast.

Peter reached the shore without mishap, and went straight on; his legs encountering the water as if quite unaware that they had entered a new element. Thus many animals pass from land to water, but no other human of whom I know. As he swam he had but one thought: "Hook or me this time." He had ticked so long that he now went on ticking without knowing that he was doing it. Had he known he would have stopped, for to board the brig by the help of the tide, though an ingenious idea, had not occurred to him.

On the contrary, he thought he had scaled her side as noiseless as a mouse; and he was amazed to see the pirates cowering from him, with Hook in their midst as abject as if he had heard the crocodile.

The crocodile! No sooner did Peter remember it than he heard the ticking. At first he thought the sound did come from the crocodile, and he looked behind him swiftly. Then he realized that he was doing it himself, and in a flash he understood the situation. "How clever of me," he thought at once, and signed to the boys not to burst into applause.

It was at this moment that Ed Teynte the quartermaster emerged from the forecastle and came along the deck. Now, reader, time what happened by your watch. Peter struck true and deep. John clapped his hands on the ill-fated pirate's mouth to stifle the dying groan. He fell forward. Four boys caught him to prevent the thud. Peter gave the signal, and the carrion was cast overboard. There was a splash, and then silence. How long has it taken?

"One!" (Slightly had begun to count.)

None too soon, Peter, every inch of him on tiptoe, vanished into the cabin; for more than one pirate was screwing up his courage to look round. They could hear each other's distressed breathing now, which showed them that the more terrible sound had passed.

"It's gone, captain," Smee said, wiping his spectacles. "All's still again."

Slowly Hook let his head emerge from his ruff, and listened so intently that he could have caught the echo of the tick. There was not a sound, and he drew himself up firmly to his full height.

"Then here's to Johnny Plank," he cried brazenly, hating the boys more than ever because they had seen him unbend. He broke into the villainous ditty:

"Yo ho, yo ho, the frisky plank,
You walks along it so,
Till it goes down and you goes down
To Davy Jones below!"

To terrorize the prisoners the more, though with a certain loss of dignity, he danced along an imaginary plank, grimacing at them as he sang; and then when he finished he cried, "Do you want a touch of the cat before you walk the plank?"

At that they fell on their knees. "No, no," they cried so piteously that every pirate smiled.

"Fetch the cat, Jukes," said Hook; "it's in the cabin."

The cabin! Peter was in the cabin! The children gazed at each other.

"Aye, aye," said Jukes blithely, and he strode into the cabin. They followed him with their eyes; they scarce knew that Hook had resumed his song, his dogs joining in with him:

> 'Yo ho, yo ho, the scratching cat,
> Its tails are nine, you know,
> And when they're writ upon your back—'

What was the last line will never be known, for all of a sudden the song was stayed by a dreadful screech from the cabin. It wailed through the ship, and died away. Then was heard a crowing sound which was well understood by the boys, but to the pirates was almost more eerie than the screech.

"What was that?" cried Hook.

"Two," said Slightly solemnly.

The Italian Cecco hesitated for a moment and then swung into the cabin. He tottered out, haggard.

"What's the matter with Bill Jukes, you dog?" hissed Hook, towering over him.

"The matter wi' him is he's dead, stabbed," replied Cecco in a hollow voice.

"Bill Jukes dead!" cried the startled pirates.

"The cabin's as black as a pit," Cecco said, almost gibbering, "but there is something terrible in there: the thing you heard crowing."

The exultation of the boys, the lowering looks of the pirates, both were seen by Hook.

"Cecco," he said in his most steely voice, "go back and fetch me out that doodle-doo."

Cecco, bravest of the brave, cowered before his captain, crying, "No, no": but Hook was purring to his claw.

"Did you say you would go, Cecco?" he said musingly.

Cecco went, first flinging up his arms despairingly. There was no more singing, all listened now; and again came a death-screech and again a crow.

No one spoke except Slightly. "Three," he said.

Hook rallied his dogs with a gesture. "'Sdeath and odds fish," he thundered, "who is to bring me that doodle-doo?"

"Wait till Cecco comes out," growled Starkey, and the others took up the cry.

"I think I heard you volunteer, Starkey," said Hook, purring again.

"No, by thunder!" Starkey cried.

"My hook thinks you did," said Hook, crossing to him. "I wonder if it would not be advisable, Starkey, to honour the hook?"

"I'll swing before I go in there," replied Starkey doggedly, and again he had the support of the crew.

"Is it mutiny?" asked Hook more pleasantly than ever. "Starkey's ring-leader."

"Captain, mercy," Starkey whimpered, all of a tremble now.

"Shake hands, Starkey," said Hook, proffering his claw.

Starkey looked round for help, but all deserted him. As he backed Hook advanced, and now the red spark was in his eye. With a despairing scream the pirate leapt upon Long Tom and precipitated himself into the sea.

"Four," said Slightly.

"And now," Hook said courteously, "did any other gentleman say mutiny?" Seizing a lantern and raising his claw with a menacing gesture, "I'll bring out that doodle-doo myself," he said, and sped into the cabin.

"Five." How Slightly longed to say it. He wetted his lips to be ready, but Hook came staggering out, without his lantern.

"Something blew out the light," he said a little unsteadily.

"Something!" echoed Mullins.

"What of Cecco?" demanded Noodler.

"He's as dead as Jukes," said Hook shortly.

His reluctance to return to the cabin impressed them all unfavourably, and the mutinous sounds again broke forth.

All pirates are superstitious; and Cookson cried, "They do say the surest sign a ship's accurst is when there's one on board more than can be accounted for."

"I've heard," muttered Mullins, "he always boards the pirate craft at last. Had he a tail, captain?"

"They say," said another, looking viciously at Hook, "that when he comes it's in the likeness of the wickedest man aboard."

"Had he a hook, captain?" asked Cookson insolently; and one after another took up the cry, "The ship's doomed." At this the children could not resist raising a cheer. Hook had well nigh forgotten his prisoners, but as he swung round on them now his face lit up again.

"Lads," he cried to his crew, "here's a notion. Open the cabin door and drive them in. Let them fight the doodle-doo for their lives. If they kill him, we're so much the better; if he kills them we're none the worse."

For the last time his dogs admired Hook, and devotedly they did his bidding. The boys, pretending to struggle, were pushed into the cabin and the door was closed on them.

"Now, listen," cried Hook, and all listened. But not one dared to face the door. Yes, one, Wendy, who all this time had been bound to the mast. It was for neither a scream nor a crow that she was watching; it was for the reappearance of Peter.

She had not long to wait. In the cabin he had found the thing for which he had gone in search: the key that would free the children of their manacles; and now they all stole forth, armed with such weapons as they could find. First signing to them to hide, Peter cut Wendy's bonds, and then nothing could have been easier than for them all to fly off together; but one thing barred the way, an oath, "Hook or me this time." So when he had freed Wendy, he whispered to her to conceal herself with the others and himself took her place by the mast, her cloak around him so that he should pass for her. Then he took a great breath and crowed.

To the pirates it was a voice crying that all the boys lay slain in the cabin; and they were panic-stricken. Hook tried to hearten them; but like the dogs he had made them they showed him their fangs, and he knew that if he took his eyes off them now they would leap at him.

"Lads," he said, ready to cajole or strike as need be, but never quailing for an instant, "I've thought it out. There's a Jonah aboard."

"Aye," they snarled, "a man wi' a hook."

"No, lads, no, it's the girl. Never was luck on a pirate ship wi' a woman on board. We'll right the ship when she's gone."

Some of them remembered that this had been a saying of Flint's. "It's worth trying," they said doubtfully.

"Fling the girl overboard," cried Hook; and they made a rush at the figure in the cloak.

"There's none can save you now, missy," Mullins hissed jeeringly.

"There's one," replied the figure.

"Who's that?"

"Peter Pan the avenger!" came the terrible answer; and as he spoke Peter flung off his cloak. Then they all knew who 'twas that had been undoing them in the cabin, and twice Hook essayed to speak and twice he failed. In that frightful moment I think his fierce heart broke.

At last he cried, "Cleave him to the brisket," but without conviction.

"Down, boys, and at them," Peter's voice rang out; and in another moment the clash of arms was resounding through the ship. Had the pirates kept together it is certain that they would have won; but the onset came when they were all unstrung, and they ran hither and thither, striking wildly, each thinking himself the last survivor of the crew. Man to man they were stronger; but they fought on the defensive only, which enabled the boys to hunt in pairs and choose their quarry. Some of the miscreants leapt into the sea; others hid in dark recesses, where they were found by Slightly, who did not fight, but ran about with a lantern which he flashed in their faces, so that they were half blinded and fell an easy prey to the reeking swords of the other boys. There was little sound to be heard but the clang of weapons, an occasional screech or splash, and Slightly monotonously counting – five – six – seven – eight – nine – ten – eleven.

I think all were gone when a group of savage boys surrounded Hook, who seemed to have a charmed life, as he kept them at bay in that circle of fire. They had done for his dogs, but this man alone seemed to be a match for them all. Again and again they closed upon him, and again and again he hewed a clear space. He had lifted up one boy with his hook, and was using him as a buckler, when another, who had just passed his sword through Mullins, sprang into the fray.

"Put up your swords, boys," cried the newcomer, "this man is mine."

Then suddenly Hook found himself face to face with Peter. The others drew back and formed a ring round them.

For long the two enemies looked at one another; Hook shuddering slightly, and Peter with the strange smile upon his face.

"So, Pan," said Hook at last, "this is all your doing."

"Aye, James Hook," came the stern answer, "it is all my doing."

"Proud and insolent youth," said Hook, "prepare to meet thy doom."

"Dark and sinister man," Peter answered, "have at thee."

Without more words they fell to, and for a space there was no advantage to either blade. Peter was a superb swordsman, and parried with dazzling rapidity; ever and anon he followed up a feint with a lunge that got past his foe's defence, but his shorter reach stood him in ill stead, and he could not drive the steel home. Hook, scarcely his inferior in brilliancy, but not quite so nimble in wrist play, forced him back by the weight of his onset, hoping suddenly to end all with a favourite thrust, taught him long ago by Barbecue at Rio; but to his astonishment he found this thrust turned aside again and again. Then he sought to close and give the quietus with his iron hook, which all this time had been pawing the air; but Peter doubled under it and, lunging fiercely, pierced him in the ribs. At sight of his own blood, whose peculiar colour, you remember, was offensive to him, the sword fell from Hook's hand, and he was at Peter's mercy.

"Now!" cried all the boys; but with a magnificent gesture Peter invited his opponent to pick up his sword. Hook did so instantly, but with a tragic feeling that Peter was showing good form.

Hitherto he had thought it was some fiend fighting him, but darker suspicions assailed him now.

"Pan, who and what art thou?" he cried huskily.

"I'm youth, I'm joy," Peter answered at a venture, "I'm a little bird that has broken out of the egg."

This, of course, was nonsense; but it was proof to the unhappy Hook that Peter did not know in the least who or what he was, which is the very pinnacle of good form.

"To't again," he cried despairingly.

He fought now like a human flail, and every sweep of that terrible sword would have severed in twain any man or boy who obstructed it; but Peter fluttered round him as if the very wind it made blew him out of the danger zone. And again and again he darted in and pricked.

Hook was fighting now without hope. That passionate breast no longer asked for life; but for one boon it craved: to see Peter bad form before it was cold for ever.

Abandoning the fight he rushed into the powder magazine and fired it.

"In two minutes," he cried, "the ship will be blown to pieces."

Now, now, he thought, true form will show.

But Peter issued from the powder magazine with the shell in his hands, and calmly flung it overboard.

What sort of form was Hook himself showing? Misguided man though he was, we may be glad, without sympathizing with him, that in the end he was true to the traditions of his race. The other boys were flying around him now, flouting, scornful; and as he staggered about the deck striking up at them impotently, his mind was no longer with them; it was slouching in the playing fields of long ago, or being sent up for good, or watching the wall-game from a famous wall. And his shoes were right, and his waistcoat was right, and his tie was right, and his socks were right.

James Hook, thou not wholly unheroic figure, farewell.

For we have come to his last moment.

Seeing Peter slowly advancing upon him through the air with dagger poised, he sprang upon the bulwarks to cast himself into the sea. He did not know that the crocodile was waiting for him; for we purposely stopped the clock that this knowledge might be spared him: a little mark of respect from us at the end.

He had one last triumph, which I think we need not grudge him. As he stood on the bulwark looking over his shoulder at Peter gliding through the air, he invited him with a gesture to use his foot. It made Peter kick instead of stab.

At last Hook had got the boon for which he craved.

"Bad form," he cried jeeringly, and went content to the crocodile.

Thus perished James Hook.

"Seventeen," Slightly sang out; but he was not quite correct in his figures. Fifteen paid the penalty for their crimes that night; but two reached the shore: Starkey to be captured by the redskins, who made him nurse for all their papooses, a melancholy come-down for a pirate, and Smee, who henceforth wandered about the world in his spectacles, making a precarious living by saying he was the only man that James Hook had feared.

Wendy, of course, had stood by taking no part in the fight, though watching Peter with glistening eyes; but now that all was over she became prominent again. She praised them equally, and shuddered delightfully when Michael showed her the place where he had killed one; and then she took them into Hook's cabin and pointed to his watch which was hanging on a nail. It said, "half past one"!

The lateness of the hour was almost the biggest thing of all. She got them to bed in the pirates' bunks pretty quickly, you may be sure; all but Peter, who strutted up and down on deck, until at last he fell asleep by the side of Long Tom. He had one of his dreams that night, and cried in his sleep for a long time, and Wendy held him tight.

CHAPTER 16

THE RETURN HOME

By two bells that morning they were all stirring their stumps; for there was a big sea running; and Tootles, the bo'sun, was among them, with a rope's end in his hand and chewing tobacco. They all donned pirate clothes cut off at the knee, shaved smartly, and tumbled up, with the true nautical roll and hitching their trousers.

It need not be said who was the captain. Nibs and John were the first and second mate. There was a woman aboard. The rest were tars before the mast, and lived in the fo'c'sle. Peter had already lashed himself to the wheel; but he piped all hands and delivered a short address to them; said he hoped that they would do their duty like gallant hearties, but that he knew they were the scum of Rio and the Gold Coast, and if they snapped at him he would tear them. His bluff strident words struck the note sailors understood, and they cheered him lustily. Then a few sharp orders were given, and they turned the ship round, and nosed her for the mainland.

Captain Pan calculated, after consulting the ship's chart, that if this weather lasted they would strike the Azores about the 21st of June, after which it would save time to fly.

Some of them wanted it to be an honest ship and others were in favour of keeping it a pirate; but the captain treated them as dogs, and they dared not express their wishes to him even in a round robin. Instant obedience was the only safe thing. Slightly got a dozen for looking perplexed when told to take soundings. The general feeling was that Peter was honest just now to lull Wendy's suspicions, but that there might be a change when the new suit was ready, which, against her will, she was making for him out of some of Hook's wickedest garments. It was afterwards whispered among them that on the first night he wore this suit he sat long in the cabin with Hook's cigar-holder in his mouth and one hand clenched, all but the forefinger, which he bent and held threateningly aloft like a hook.

Instead of watching the ship, however, we must now return to that desolate home from which three of our characters had taken heartless flight so long ago. It seems a shame to have neglected No. 14 all this time; and yet we may be sure that Mrs Darling does not blame us. If we had returned sooner to look with sorrowful sympathy at her, she would probably have cried, "Don't be silly; what do I matter? Do go back and keep an eye on the children." So long as mothers are like this their children will take advantage of them; and they may lay to that.

Even now we venture into that familiar nursery only because its lawful occupants are on their way home; we are merely hurrying on in advance of them to see that their beds are properly aired and that Mr and Mrs Darling do not go out for the evening. We are no more than servants. Why on earth should their beds be properly aired, seeing that they left them in such a thankless hurry? Would it not serve them jolly well right if they came back and found that their parents were spending the weekend in the country? It would be the moral lesson they have been in need of ever since we met them; but if we contrived things in this way Mrs Darling would never forgive us.

One thing I should like to do immensely, and that is to tell her, in the way authors have, that the children are coming back, that indeed they will be here on Thursday week. This would spoil so completely the surprise to which Wendy and John and Michael are looking forward. They have been planning it out on the ship: mother's rapture, father's shout of joy, Nana's leap through the air to embrace them first, when what they ought to be preparing for is a good hiding. How delicious to spoil it all by breaking the news in advance; so that when they enter grandly Mrs Darling may not even offer Wendy her mouth, and Mr Darling may exclaim pettishly, "Dash it all, here are those boys again." However, we should get no thanks even for this. We are beginning to know Mrs Darling by this time and may be sure that she would upbraid us for depriving the children of their little pleasure.

"But, my dear madam, it is ten days till Thursday week; so that by telling you what's what, we can save you ten days of unhappiness."

"Yes, but at what a cost! By depriving the children of ten minutes of delight."

"Oh, if you look at it in that way."

"What other way is there in which to look at it?"

You see, the woman had no proper spirit. I had meant to say extraordinarily nice things about her; but I despise her, and not one of them will I say now. She does not really need to be told to have things ready, for they are ready. All the beds are aired, and she never leaves the house, and observe, the window is open. For all the use we are to her, we might go back to the ship. However, as we are here we may as well stay and look on. That is all we are, lookers-on. Nobody really wants us. So let us watch and say jaggy things, in the hope that some of them will hurt.

The only change to be seen in the night-nursery is that between nine and six the kennel is no longer there. When the children flew away, Mr Darling felt in his bones that all the blame was his for having chained Nana up, and that from first to last she had been wiser than he. Of course, as we have seen, he was quite a simple man; indeed he might have passed for a boy again if he had been able to take his baldness off; but he had also a noble sense of justice and a lion courage to do what seemed right to him; and having thought the matter out with anxious care after the flight of the children, he went down on all fours and crawled into the kennel. To all Mrs Darling's dear invitations to come out he replied sadly but firmly:

"No, my own one, this is the place for me."

In the bitterness of his remorse he swore that he would never leave the kennel until his children came back. Of course this was a pity; but whatever Mr Darling did he had to do in excess; otherwise he soon gave up doing it. And there never was a more humble man than the once proud George Darling, as he sat in the kennel of an evening talking with his wife of their children and all their pretty ways.

Very touching was his deference to Nana. He would not let her come into the kennel, but on all other matters he followed her wishes implicitly.

Every morning the kennel was carried with Mr Darling in it to a cab, which conveyed him to his office, and he returned home in the same way at six. Something of the strength of character of the man will be seen if we remember how sensitive he was to the opinion of neighbours: this man whose every movement now attracted surprised attention. Inwardly he must have suffered torture; but he preserved a calm exterior even when the young criticized his little home, and he always lifted his hat courteously to any lady who looked inside.

It may have been quixotic, but it was magnificent. Soon the inward meaning of it leaked out, and the great heart of the public was touched. Crowds followed the cab, cheering it lustily; charming girls scaled it to get his autograph; interviews appeared in the better class of papers, and society invited him to dinner and added, "Do come in the kennel."

On that eventful Thursday week Mrs Darling was in the night-nursery awaiting George's return home: a very sad-eyed woman. Now that we look at her closely and remember the gaiety of her in the old days, all gone now just because she has lost her babes, I find I won't be able to say nasty things about her after all. If she was too fond of her rubbishy children she couldn't help it. Look at her in her chair, where she has fallen asleep. The corner of her mouth, where one looks first, is almost withered up. Her head moves restlessly on her breast as if she had a pain there. Some like Peter best and some like Wendy best, but I like her best. Suppose, to make her happy, we whisper to her in her sleep that the brats are coming back.

They are really within two miles of the window now, and flying strong, but all we need whisper is that they are on the way. Let's.

It is a pity we did it, for she had started up, calling their names; and there is no one in the room but Nana.

"O Nana, I dreamt my dear ones had come back."

Nana had filmy eyes, but all she could do was to put her paw gently on her mistress's lap; and they were sitting together thus when the kennel was brought back. As Mr Darling puts his head out of it to kiss his wife, we see that his face is more worn than of yore, but has a softer expression.

He gave his hat to Liza, who took it scornfully; for she had no imagination, and was quite incapable of understanding the motives of such a man. Outside, the crowd who had accompanied the cab home were still cheering, and he was naturally not unmoved.

"Listen to them," he said; "it is very gratifying."

"Lots of little boys," sneered Liza.

"There were several adults today," he assured her with a faint flush; but when she tossed her head he had not a word of reproof for her. Social success had not spoilt him; it had made him sweeter. For some time he sat half out of the kennel, talking to Mrs Darling of this success, and pressing her hand reassuringly when she said she hoped his head would not be turned by it.

"But if I had been a weak man," he said. "Good heavens, if I had been a weak man!"

"And George," she said timidly, "you are as full of remorse as ever, aren't you?"

"Full of remorse as ever, dearest! See my punishment: living in a kennel."

"But it is punishment, isn't it, George? You are sure you are not enjoying it?"

"My love!"

You may be sure she begged his pardon; and then, feeling drowsy, he curled round in the kennel.

"Won't you play me to sleep," he asked, "on the nursery piano?" and as she was crossing to the day-nursery he added thoughtlessly, "And shut that window. I feel a draught."

"O George, never ask me to do that. The window must always be left open for them, always, always."

Now it was his turn to beg her pardon; and she went into the day-nursery and played, and soon he was asleep; and while he slept, Wendy and John and Michael flew into the room.

Oh no. We have written it so, because that was the charming arrangement planned by them before we left the ship; but something must have happened since then, for it is not they who have flown in, it is Peter and Tinker Bell.

Peter's first words tell all.

"Quick, Tink," he whispered, "close the window; bar it. That's right. Now you and I must get away by the door; and when Wendy comes she will think her mother has barred her out; and she will have to go back with me."

Now I understand what had hitherto puzzled me, why when Peter had exterminated the pirates he did not return to the island and leave Tink to escort the children to the mainland. This trick had been in his head all the time.

Instead of feeling that he was behaving badly he danced with glee; then he peeped into the day-nursery to see who was playing. He whispered to Tink, "It's Wendy's mother. She is a pretty lady, but not so pretty as my mother. Her mouth is full of thimbles, but not so full as my mother's was."

Of course he knew nothing whatever about his mother; but he sometimes bragged about her.

He did not know the tune, which was "Home, Sweet Home", but he knew it was saying, "Come back, Wendy, Wendy, Wendy"; and he cried exultantly, "You will never see Wendy again, lady, for the window is barred."

He peeped in again to see why the music had stopped; and now he saw that Mrs Darling had laid her head on the box, and that two tears were sitting on her eyes.

"She wants me to unbar the window," thought Peter, "but I won't, not I."

He peeped again, and the tears were still there, or another two had taken their place.

"She's awfully fond of Wendy," he said to himself. He was angry with her now for not seeing why she could not have Wendy.

The reason was so simple: "I'm fond of her too. We can't both have her, lady."

But the lady would not make the best of it, and he was unhappy. He ceased to look at her, but even then she would not let go of him. He skipped about and made funny faces, but when he stopped it was just as if she were inside him, knocking.

"Oh, all right," he said at last, and gulped. Then he unbarred the window. "Come on, Tink," he cried, with a frightful sneer at the laws of nature; "we don't want any silly mothers"; and he flew away.

Thus Wendy and John and Michael found the window open for them after all, which of course was more than they deserved. The alighted on the floor, quite unashamed of themselves; and the youngest one had already forgotten his home.

"John," he said, looking around him doubtfully, "I think I have been here before."

"Of course you have, you silly. There is your old bed."

"So it is," Michael said, but not with much conviction.

"I say," cried John, "the kennel!" and he dashed across to look into it.

"Perhaps Nana is inside it," Wendy said.

But John whistled. "Hallo," he said, "there's a man inside it."

"It's father!" exclaimed Wendy.

"Let me see father," Michael begged eagerly, and he took a good look. "He is not so big as the pirate I killed," he said with such frank disappointment that I am glad Mr Darling was asleep; it would have been sad if those had been the first words he heard his little Michael say.

Wendy and John had been taken aback somewhat at finding their father in the kennel.

"Surely," said John, like one who has lost faith in his memory, "he used not to sleep in the kennel?"

"John," Wendy said falteringly, "perhaps we don't remember the old life as well as we thought we did."

A chill fell upon them; and serve them right.

"It is very careless of mother," said that young scoundrel John, "not to be here when we come back."

It was then that Mrs Darling began playing again.

"It's mother!" cried Wendy, peeping.

"So it is!" said John.

"Then you are not really our mother, Wendy?" asked Michael, who was surely sleepy.

"Oh dear!" exclaimed Wendy, with her first real twinge of remorse, "it is quite time we came back."

"Let us creep in," John suggested, "and put our hands over her eyes."

But Wendy, who saw that they must break the joyous news more gently, had a better plan.

"Let us all slip into our beds, and be there when she comes in, just as if we had never been away."

And so when Mrs Darling went back to the night-nursery to see if her husband was asleep, all the beds were occupied. The children waited for her cry of joy, but it did not come. She saw them, but she did not believe they were there. You see, she saw them in their beds so often in her dreams that she thought this was just the dream hanging around her still.

She sat down in the chair by the fire, where in the old days she had nursed them.

They did not understand this, and a cold fear fell upon all the three of them.

"Mother!" Wendy cried.

"That's Wendy," she said, but still she was sure it was the dream.

"Mother!"

"That's John," she said.

"Mother!" cried Michael. He knew her now.

"That's Michael," she said, and she stretched out her arms for the three little selfish children they would never envelop again. Yes, they did, they went round Wendy and John and Michael, who had slipped out of bed and run to her.

"George, George," she cried when she could speak; and Mr Darling woke to share her bliss, and Nana came rushing in. There could not have been a lovelier sight; but there was none to see it except a strange boy who was staring in at the window. He had ecstasies innumerable that other children can never know; but he was looking through the window at the one joy from which he must be for ever barred.

Chapter 17

WHEN WENDY GREW UP

I hope you want to know what became of the other boys. They were waiting below to give Wendy time to explain about them; and when they had counted five hundred they went up. They went up by the stairs, because they thought this would make a better impression. They stood in a row in front of Mrs Darling, with their hats off, and wishing they were not wearing their pirate clothes. They said nothing, but their eyes asked her to have them. They ought to have looked at Mr Darling also, but they forgot about him.

Of course Mrs Darling said at once that she would have them; but Mr Darling was curiously depressed, and they saw that he considered six a rather large number.

"I must say," he said to Wendy, "that you don't do things by halves," a grudging remark which the twins thought was pointed at them.

The first twin was the proud one, and he asked, flushing, "Do you think we should be too much of a handful, sir? Because if so we can go away."

"Father!" Wendy cried, shocked; but still the cloud was on him. He knew he was behaving unworthily, but he could not help it.

"We could lie doubled up," said Nibs.

"I always cut their hair myself," said Wendy.

"George!" Mrs Darling exclaimed, pained to see her dear one showing himself in such an unfavourable light.

Then he burst into tears, and the truth came out. He was as glad to have them as she was, he said, but he thought they should have asked his consent as well as hers, instead of treating him as a cypher in his own house.

"I don't think he is a cypher," Tootles cried instantly. "Do you think he is a cypher, Curly?"

"No, I don't. Do you think he is a cypher, Slightly?"

"Rather not. Twin, what do you think?"

It turned out that not one of them thought him a cypher; and he was absurdly gratified, and said he would find space for them all in the drawing-room if they fitted in.

"We'll fit in, sir," they assured him.

"Then follow the leader," he cried gaily. "Mind you, I am not sure that we have a drawing-room, but we pretend we have, and it's all the same. Hoop-la!"

He went off dancing through the house, and they all cried "Hoop-la!" and danced after him, searching for the drawing-room; and I forget whether they found it, but at any rate they found corners, and they all fitted in.

As for Peter, he saw Wendy once again before he flew away. He did not exactly come to the window, but he brushed against it in passing, so that she could open it if she liked and call to him. That was what she did.

"Hallo, Wendy, good-bye," he said.

"Oh dear, are you going away?"

"Yes."

"You don't feel, Peter," she said falteringly, "that you would like to say anything to my parents about a very sweet subject?"

"No."

"About me, Peter?"

"No."

Mrs Darling came to the window, for at present she was keeping a sharp eye on Wendy. She told Peter that she had adopted all the other boys, and would like to adopt him also.

"Would you send me to school?" he inquired craftily.

"Yes."

"And then to an office?"

"I suppose so."

"Soon I should be a man?"

"Very soon."

"I don't want to go to school and learn solemn things," he told her passionately. "I don't want to be a man. O Wendy's mother, if I was to wake up and feel there was a beard!"

"Peter!" said Wendy the comforter, "I should love you in a beard"; and Mrs Darling stretched out her arms to him, and he repulsed her.

"Keep back, lady, no one is going to catch me and make me a man."

"But where are you going to live?"

"With Tink in the house we built for Wendy. The fairies are to put it high up among the tree-tops where they sleep at nights."

"How lovely," cried Wendy so longingly that Mrs Darling tightened her grip.

"I thought all the fairies were dead," Mrs Darling said.

"There are always a lot of young ones," explained Wendy, who was now quite an authority, "because you see when a new baby laughs for the first time a new fairy is born, and as there are always new babies there are always new fairies. They live in nests on the tops of trees; and the mauve ones are boys and the white ones are girls, and the blue ones are just little sillies who are not sure what they are."

"I shall have such fun," said Peter, with one eye on Wendy.

"It will be rather lonely in the evening," she said "sitting by the fire."

"I shall have Tink."

"Tink can't go a twentieth part of the way round," she reminded him a little tartly.

"Sneaky tell-tale!" Tink called out from somewhere round the corner.

"It doesn't matter," Peter said.

"O Peter, you know it matters."

"Well then, come with me to the little house."

"May I, Mummy?"

"Certainly not. I have got you home again, and I mean to keep you."

"But he does so need a mother."

"So do you, my love."

"Oh, all right," Peter said, as if he had asked her from politeness merely; but Mrs Darling saw his mouth twitch, and she made this handsome offer: to let Wendy go to him for a week every year to do his spring cleaning. Wendy would have preferred a more permanent arrangement; and it seemed to her that spring would be long in coming; but this promise sent Peter away quite gay again. He had no sense of time, and was so full of adventures that all I have told you about him is only a halfpenny-worth of them. I suppose it was because Wendy knew this that her last words to him were these rather plaintive ones:

"You won't forget me, Peter, will you, before spring-cleaning time comes?"

Of course Peter promised, and then flew away. He took Mrs Darling's kiss with him. The kiss that had been for no one else Peter took quite easily. Funny. But she seemed satisfied.

Of course all the boys went to school; and most of them got into Class III but Slightly was put first into Class IV and then into Class V. Class I is the top class. Before they had attended school a week they saw what goats they had been not to remain on the island; but it was too late now, and soon they settled down to being as ordinary as you or me or Jenkins minor. It is sad to have to say that the power to fly gradually left them. At first Nana tied their feet to the bedposts so that they should not fly away in the night; and one of their diversions by day was to pretend to fall off buses; but by and by they ceased to tug at their bonds in bed, and found that they hurt themselves when they let go of the bus. In time they could not even fly after their hats. Want of practice, they called it; but what it really meant was that they no longer believed.

Michael believed longer than the other boys, though they jeered at him; so he was with Wendy when Peter came for her at the end of the first year. She flew away with Peter in the frock she had woven from leaves and berries in the Neverland, and her one fear was that he might notice how short it had become; but he never noticed, he had so much to say about himself.

She had looked forward to thrilling talks with him about old times, but new adventures had crowded the old ones from his mind.

"Who is Captain Hook?" he asked with interest when she spoke of the arch enemy.

"Don't you remember," she asked, amazed, "how you killed him and saved our lives?"

"I forget them after I kill them," he replied carelessly.

When she expressed a doubtful hope that Tinker Bell would be glad to see her he said, "Who is Tinker Bell?"

"O Peter," she said, shocked; but even when she explained he could not remember.

"There are such a lot of them," he said. "I expect she is no more."

I expect he was right, for fairies don't live long, but they are so little that a short time seems a good while to them.

Wendy was pained to find that the past year was but as yesterday to Peter; it had seemed such a long year of waiting to her. But he was exactly as fascinating as ever, and they had a lovely spring cleaning in the little house on the tree-tops.

Next year he did not come to her. She waited in a new frock because the old one simply would not meet; but he never came.

"Perhaps he is ill," Michael said.

"You know he is never ill."

Michael came close to her and whispered, with a shiver, "Perhaps there is no such person, Wendy!" and then Wendy would have cried if Michael had not been crying.

Peter came next spring cleaning; and the strange thing was that he never knew he had missed a year.

That was the last time the girl Wendy ever saw him. For a little longer she tried for his sake not to have growing pains; and she felt she was untrue to him when she got a prize for general knowledge. But the years came and went without bringing the careless boy; and when they met again Wendy was a married woman, and Peter was no more to her than a little dust in the box in which she had kept her toys. Wendy was grown up. You need not be sorry for her. She was one of the kind that likes to grow up. In the end she grew up of her own free will a day quicker than other girls.

All the boys were grown up and done for by this time; so it is scarcely worth while saying anything more about them. You may see the twins and Nibs and Curly any day going to an office, each carrying a little bag and an umbrella. Michael is an engine-driver. Slightly married a lady of title, and so he became a lord. You see that judge in a wig coming out at the iron door? That used to be Tootles. The bearded man who doesn't know any story to tell his children was once John.

Wendy was married in white with a pink sash. It is strange to think that Peter did not alight in the church and forbid the banns.

Years rolled on again, and Wendy had a daughter. This ought not to be written in ink but in a golden splash.

She was called Jane, and always had an odd inquiring look, as if from the moment she arrived on the mainland she wanted to ask questions. When she was old enough to ask them they were mostly about Peter Pan. She loved to hear of Peter, and Wendy told her all she could remember in the very nursery from which the famous flight had taken place. It was Jane's nursery now, for her father had bought it at the three per cents from Wendy's father, who was no longer fond of stairs. Mrs Darling was now dead and forgotten.

There were only two beds in the nursery now, Jane's and her nurse's; and there was no kennel, for Nana also had passed away. She died of old age, and at the end she had been rather difficult to get on with; being very firmly convinced that no one knew how to look after children except herself.

Once a week Jane's nurse had her evening off; and then it was Wendy's part to put Jane to bed. That was the time for stories. It was Jane's invention to raise the sheet over her mother's head and her own, thus making a tent, and in the awful darkness to whisper:

"What do we see now?"

"I don't think I see anything tonight," says Wendy, with a feeling that if Nana were here she would object to further conversation.

"Yes, you do," says Jane, "you see when you were a little girl."

"That is a long time ago, sweetheart," said Wendy. "Ah me, how time flies!"

"Does it fly," asks the artful child, "the way you flew when you were a little girl?"

"The way I flew! Do you know, Jane, I sometimes wonder whether I ever did really fly."

"Yes, you did."

"The dear old days when I could fly!"

"Why can't you fly now, mother?"

"Because I am grown up, dearest. When people grow up they forget the way."

"Why do they forget the way?"

"Because they are no longer gay and innocent and heartless. It is only the gay and innocent and heartless who can fly."

"What is gay and innocent and heartless? I do wish I was gay and innocent and heartless."

Or perhaps Wendy admits that she does see something. "I do believe," she says, "that it is this nursery."

"I do believe it is," says Jane. "Go on."

They are now embarked on the great adventure of the night when Peter flew in looking for his shadow.

"The foolish fellow," says Wendy, "tried to stick it on with soap, and when he could not he cried, and that woke me, and I sewed it on for him."

"You have missed a bit," interrupts Jane, who now knows the story better than her mother. "When you saw him sitting on the floor crying, what did you say?"

"I sat up in bed and I said, 'Boy, why are you crying?'"

"Yes, that was it," says Jane, with a big breath.

"And then he flew us all away to the Neverland and the fairies and the pirates and the redskins and the mermaids' lagoon, and the home under the ground, and the little house."

"Yes! Which did you like best of all?"

"I think I liked the home under the ground best of all."

"Yes, so do I. What was the last thing Peter ever said to you?"

"The last thing he ever said to me was, 'Just always be waiting for me, and then some night you will hear me crowing.'"

"Yes."

"But, alas, he forgot all about me." Wendy said it with a smile. She was as grown up as that.

"What did his crow sound like?" Jane asked one evening.

"It was like this," Wendy said, trying to imitate Peter's crow.

"No, it wasn't," Jane said gravely, "it was like this," and she did it ever so much better than her mother.

Wendy was a little startled. "My darling, how can you know?"

"I often hear it when I am sleeping," Jane said.

"Ah yes, many girls hear it when they are sleeping, but I was the only one who heard it awake."

"Lucky you," said Jane.

And then one night came the tragedy. It was the spring of the year, and the story had been told for the night, and Jane was now asleep in her bed. Wendy was sitting on the floor, very close to the fire, so as to see to darn, for there was no other light in the nursery; and while she sat darning she heard a crow. Then the window blew open as of old, and Peter dropped on the floor.

He was exactly the same as ever, and Wendy saw at once that he still had all his first teeth.

He was a little boy, and she was grown up. She huddled by the fire not daring to move, helpless and guilty, a big woman.

"Hallo, Wendy," he said, not noticing any difference, for he was thinking chiefly of himself; and in the dim light her white dress might have been the night-gown in which he had seen her first.

"Hallo, Peter," she replied faintly, squeezing herself as small as possible. Something inside her was crying. "Woman, woman, let go of me."

"Hallo, where is John?" he asked, suddenly missing the third bed.

"John is not here now,"she gasped.

"Is Michael asleep?" he asked, with a careless glance at Jane.

"Yes," she answered; and now she felt that she was untrue to Jane as well as to Peter.

"That is not Michael," she said quickly, lest a judgement should fall on her.

Peter looked. "Hallo, is it a new one?"

"Yes."

"Boy or girl?"

"Girl."

Now surely he would understand; but not a bit of it.

"Peter," she said, falteringly, "are you expecting me to fly away with you?"

"Of course, that is why I have come." He added a little sternly. "Have you forgotten that it is spring-cleaning time?"

She knew it was useless to say that he had let many spring-cleaning times pass.

"I can't come," she said apologetically. "I have forgotten how to fly."

"I'll soon teach you again."

"O Peter, don't waste the fairy dust on me."

She had risen; and now at last fear assailed him. "What is it?" he cried, shrinking.

"I will turn up the light," she said, "and then you can see for yourself."

For almost the only time in his life that I know of, Peter was afraid. "Don't turn up the light," he cried.

She let her hands play in the hair of the tragic boy. She was not a little girl heart-broken about him; she was a grown woman smiling at it all, but they were wet smiles.

Then she turned up the light, and Peter saw. He gave a cry of pain; and when the tall beautiful creature stooped to lift him in her arms he drew back sharply.

"What is it?" he cried again.

"I am old, Peter. I am ever so much more than twenty. I grew up long ago."

"You promised not to!"

"I couldn't help it. I am a married woman, Peter."

"No, you're not."

"Yes, and the little girl in the bed is my baby."

"No, she's not."

But he supposed she was; and he took a step towards the sleeping child with his dagger upraised. Of course he did not strike. He sat down on the floor instead and sobbed; and Wendy did not know how to comfort him, though she could have done it so easily once. She was only a woman now, and she ran out of the room to try to think.

Peter continued to cry, and soon his sobs woke Jane. She sat up in bed and was interested at once.

"Boy," she said, "why are you crying?"

Peter rose and bowed to her, and she bowed to him from the bed.

"Hallo," he said.

"Hallo," said Jane.

"My name is Peter Pan," he told her.

"Yes, I know."

"I came back for my mother," he explained, "to take her to the Neverland."

"Yes, I know," Jane said. "I've been waiting for you."

When Wendy returned diffidently she found Peter sitting on the bedpost crowing gloriously, while Jane in her nighty was flying round the room in solemn ecstasy.

"She is my mother," Peter explained; and Jane descended and stood by his side, with the look on her face that he liked to see on ladies when they gazed at him.

"He does so need a mother," Jane said.

"Yes, I know," Wendy admitted rather forlornly; "no one knows it so well as I."

"Good-bye," said Peter to Wendy; and he rose in the air, and the shameless Jane rose with him; it was already her easiest way of moving about.

Wendy rushed to the window.

"No, no," she cried.

"It is just for spring-cleaning time," Jane said; "he wants me always to do his spring cleaning."

"If only I could go with you," Wendy sighed.

"You see you can't fly," said Jane.

Of course in the end Wendy let them fly away together. Our last glimpse of her shows her at the window, watching them receding into the sky until they were as small as stars.

As you look at Wendy you may see her hair becoming white, and her figure little again, for all this happened long ago. Jane is now a common grown-up with a daughter called Margaret; and every spring-cleaning time, except when he forgets, Peter comes to Margaret and takes her to the Neverland, where she tells him stories about himself, to which he listens eagerly. When Margaret grows up she will have a daughter, who is to be Peter's mother in turn; and thus it will go on, so long as children are gay and innocent and heartless.

CHILDREN'S CLASSICS

The Story of
The Treasure Seekers

E. Nesbit

The Story of The Treasure Seekers

PARRAGON

The Treasure Seekers
A Parragon Classic

This is a Siena Book
Siena is an imprint of Parragon

First published in 1899

This edition published in 1999 by
Parragon
13 Whiteladies Road
Clifton
Bristol BS8 1PB

Printed and bound in the UK

CHAPTER 1

THE COUNCIL OF WAYS AND MEANS

This is the story of the different ways we looked for treasure, and I think when you have read it you will see that we were not lazy about the looking.

There are some things I must tell before I begin to tell about the treasure-seeking, because I have read books myself, and I know how beastly it is when a story begins, "'Alas!' said Hildegarde with a deep sigh, 'we must look our last on this ancestral home'"—and then some one else says something—and you don't know for pages and pages where the home is, or who Hildegarde is, or anything about it. Our ancestral home is in the Lewisham Road. It is semi-detached and has a garden, not a large one. We are the Bastables. There are six of us besides Father. Our Mother is dead, and if you think we don't care because I don't tell you much about her you only show that you do not understand people at all. Dora is the eldest. Then Oswald—and then Dicky. Oswald won the Latin prize at his preparatory school—and Dicky is good at sums. Alice and Noël are twins: they are ten, and Horace Octavius is my youngest brother. It is one of us that tells this story—but I shall not tell you which: only at the very end perhaps I will. While the story is going on you may be trying to guess, only I bet you don't.

It was Oswald who first thought of looking for treasure. Oswald often thinks of very interesting things. And directly he thought of it he did not keep it to himself, as some boys would have done, but he told the others, and said—

"I'll tell you what, we must go and seek for treasure: it is always what you do to restore the fallen fortunes of your House."

Dora said it was all very well. She often says that. She was trying to mend a large hole in one of Noël's stockings. He tore it on a nail when we were playing shipwrecked mariners on top of the chicken-house the day H. O. fell off and cut his chin: he has the scar still. Dora is the only one of us who ever tries to mend anything. Alice tries to make things sometimes. Once she knitted a red scarf for Noël because his chest is delicate, but it was much wider at one end than the other, and he wouldn't wear it. So we used it as a pennon, and it did very well, because most of our things are black or grey since Mother died; and scarlet was a nice change. Father does not like you to ask for new things. That was one way we had of knowing that the fortunes of the ancient House of Bastable were really fallen. Another way was that there was no more pocket-money—except a penny now and then to the little ones, and people did not come to dinner any more, like they used to, with pretty dresses, driving up in cabs—and the carpets got holes in them—and when the legs came off things they were not sent to be mended, and we gave up having the gardener except for the front garden, and not that very often. And the silver in the big oak plate-chest that is lined with green baize all went away to the shop to have the dents and scratches taken out of it, and it never came back. We think Father hadn't enough money to pay the silver man for taking out the dents and scratches. The new spoons and forks were yellowy-white, and not so heavy as the old ones, and they never shone after the first day or two.

Father was very ill after Mother died; and while he was ill his business-partner went to Spain—and there was never much money afterwards. I don't know why. Then the servants left and there was only one, a General. A great deal of your comfort and happiness depends on having a good General. The last but one was nice: she used to make jolly good currant puddings for us, and let us have the dish on the floor and pretend it was a wild boar we were killing with our forks. But the General we have now nearly always makes sago puddings, and they are the watery kind, and you cannot pretend anything with them, not even islands, like you do with porridge.

Then we left off going to school, and Father said we should go to a good school as soon as he could manage it. He said a holiday would do us all good. We thought he was right, but we wished he had told us he couldn't afford it. For of course we knew.

Then a great many people used to come to the door with envelopes with no stamps on them, and sometimes they got very angry, and said they were calling for the last time before putting it in other hands. I asked Eliza what that meant, and she kindly explained to me, and I was so sorry for Father.

And once a long, blue paper came; a policeman brought it, and we were so frightened. But Father said it was all right, only when he went up to kiss the girls after they were in bed they said he had been crying, though I'm sure that's not true. Because only cowards and snivellers cry, and my Father is the bravest man in the world.

So you see it was time we looked for treasure; and Oswald said so, and Dora said it was all very well. But the others agreed with Oswald. So we held a council. Dora was in the chair—the big dining-room chair, that we let the fireworks off from, the Fifth of November when we had the measles and couldn't do it in the garden. The hole has never been mended, so now we have that chair in the nursery, and I think it was cheap at the blowing-up we boys got when the hole was burnt.

"We must do something," said Alice, "because the exchequer is empty." She rattled the money-box as she spoke, and it really did rattle because we always keep the bad sixpence in it for luck.

"Yes—but what shall we do?" said Dicky. "It's so jolly easy to say let's do *something*." Dicky always wants everything settled exactly. Father calls him the Definite Article.

"Let's read all the books again. We shall get lots of ideas out of them." It was Noël who suggested this, but we made him shut up, because we knew well enough he only wanted to get back to his old books. Noël is a poet. He sold some of his poetry once—and it was printed, but that does not come in this part of the story.

Then Dicky said, "Look here. We'll be quite quiet for ten minutes by the clock—and each think of some way to find treasure. And when we've thought we'll try all the ways one after the other, beginning with the eldest."

"I shan't be able to think in ten minutes, make it half an hour," said H. O. His real name is Horace Octavius, but we call him H. O. because of the advertisement, and it's not so very long ago he was afraid to pass the hoarding where it says "Eat H. O." in big letters. He says it was when he was a little boy, but I remember last Christmas but one, he woke in the middle of the night crying and howling, and they said it was the pudding. But he told me afterwards he had been dreaming that they really *had* come to eat H. O., and it couldn't have been the pudding, when you come to think of it, because it was so very plain.

Well, we made it half an hour—and we all sat quiet, and thought and thought. And I made up my mind before two minutes were over, and I saw the others had, all but Dora, who is always an awful time over everything. I got pins and needles in my leg from sitting still so long, and when it was seven minutes H. O. cried out—

"Oh, it must be more than half an hour!"

H. O. is eight years old, but he cannot tell the clock yet. Oswald could tell the clock when he was six.

We all stretched ourselves and began to speak at once, but Dora put up her hands to her ears and said—

"One at a time, please. We aren't playing Babel." (It is a very good game. Did you ever play it?)

So Dora made us all sit in a row on the floor, in ages, and then she pointed at us with the finger that had the brass thimble on. Her silver one got lost when the last General but two went away. We think she must have forgotten it was Dora's and put it in her box by mistake. She was a very forgetful girl. She used to forget what she had spent money on, so that the change was never quite right.

Oswald spoke first. "I think we might stop people on Blackheath—with crape masks and horse-pistols—and say 'Your money or your life! Resistance is useless, we are armed to the teeth'—like Dick Turpin and Claude Duval. It wouldn't matter about not having horses, because coaches have gone out too."

Dora screwed up her nose the way she always does when she is going to talk like the good elder sister in books, and said, "That would be very wrong: it's like pickpocketing or taking pennies out of Father's great-coat when it's hanging in the hall."

I must say I don't think she need have said that, especially before the little ones—for it was when I was only four.

But Oswald was not going to let her see he cared, so he said—

"Oh, very well. I can think of lots of other ways. We could rescue an old gentleman from deadly Highwaymen."

"There aren't any," said Dora.

"Oh, well, it's all the same—from deadly peril, then. There's plenty of that. Then he would turn out to be the Prince of Wales, and he would say, 'My noble, my cherished preserver! Here is a million pounds a year. Rise up, Sir Oswald Bastable.'"

But the others did not seem to think so, and it was Alice's turn to say.

She said, "I think we might try the divining-rod. I'm sure I could do it. I've often read about it. You hold a stick in your hands, and when you come to where there is gold underneath the stick kicks about. So you know. And you dig."

"Oh," said Dora suddenly, "I have an idea. But I'll say last. I hope the divining-rod isn't wrong. I believe it's wrong in the Bible."

"So is eating pork and ducks," said Dicky. "You can't go by that."

"Anyhow, we'll try the other ways first," said Dora. "Now, H. O."

"Let's be Bandits," said H. O. "I dare say it's wrong but it would be fun pretending."

"I'm sure it's wrong," said Dora.

And Dicky said she thought everything wrong. She said she didn't, and Dicky was very disagreeable. So Oswald had to make peace, and he said—

"Dora needn't play if she doesn't want to. Nobody asked her. And, Dicky, don't be an idiot: do dry up and let's hear what Noël's idea is."

Dora and Dicky did not look pleased, but I kicked Noël under the table to make him hurry up, and then he said he didn't think he wanted to play any more. That's the worst of it. The others are so jolly ready to quarrel. I told Noël to be a man and not a snivelling pig, and at last he said he had not made up his mind whether he would print his poetry in a book and sell it, or find a princess and marry her.

"Whichever it is," he added, "none of you shall want for anything, though Oswald did kick me, and say I was a snivelling pig."

"I didn't," said Oswald, "I told you not to be." And Alice explained to him that that was quite the opposite of what he thought. So he agreed to drop it.

Then Dicky spoke.

"You must all of you have noticed the advertisements in the papers, telling you that ladies and gentlemen can easily earn two pounds a week in their spare time, and to send two shillings for sample and instructions, carefully packed free from observation. Now that we don't go to school all our time is spare time. So I should think we could easily earn twenty pounds a week each. That would do us very well. We'll try some of the other things first, and directly we have any money we'll send for the sample and instructions. And I have another idea, but I must think about it before I say."

We all said, "Out with it—what's the other idea?"

But Dicky said, "No." That is Dicky all over. He never will show you anything he's making till it's quite finished, and the same with his inmost thoughts. But he is pleased if you seem to want to know, so Oswald said—

"Keep your silly old secret, then. Now, Dora, drive ahead. We've all said except you."

Then Dora jumped up and dropped the stocking and the thimble (it rolled away, and we did not find it for days), and said—

"Let's try my way *now*. Besides, I'm the eldest, so it's only fair. Let's dig for treasure. Not any tiresome divining-rod—but just plain digging. People who dig for treasure always find it. And then we shall be rich and we needn't try your ways at all. Some of them are rather difficult: and I'm certain some of them are wrong—and we must always remember that wrong things—"

But we told her to shut up and come on, and she did.

I couldn't help wondering as we went down to the garden, why Father had never thought of digging there for treasure instead of going to his beastly office every day.

CHAPTER 2

DIGGING FOR TREASURE

I am afraid the last chapter was rather dull. It is always dull in books when people talk and talk, and don't do anything, but I was obliged to put it in, or else you wouldn't have understood all the rest. The best part of books is when things are happening. That is the best part of real things too. This is why I shall not tell you in this story about all the days when nothing happened. You will not catch me saying, "thus the sad days passed slowly by"—or "the years rolled on their weary course" or "time went on"—because it is silly; of course time goes on—whether you say so or not. So I shall just tell you the nice, interesting parts—and in between you will understand that we had our meals and got up and went to bed, and dull things like that. It would be sickening to write all that down, though of course it happens. I said so to Albert-next-door's uncle, who writes books, and he said, "Quite right, that's what we call selection, a necessity of true art." And he is very clever indeed. So you see.

I have often thought that if the people who write books for children knew a little more it would be better. I shall not tell you anything about us except what I should like to know about if I was reading the story and you were writing it. Albert's uncle says I ought to have put this in the preface, but I never read prefaces, and it is not much good writing things just for people to skip. I wonder other authors have never thought of this.

Well, when we had agreed to dig for treasure we all went down into the cellar and lighted the gas. Oswald would have liked to dig there, but it is stone flags. We looked among the old boxes and broken chairs and fenders and empty bottles and things, and at last we found the spades we had to dig in the sand with when we went to the seaside three years ago. They are not silly, babyish, wooden spades, that split if you look at them, but good iron, with a blue mark across the top of the iron part, and yellow wooden handles. We wasted a little time getting them dusted, because the girls wouldn't dig with spades that had cobwebs on them. Girls would never do for African explorers or anything like that, they are too beastly particular.

It was no use doing the thing by halves. We marked out a sort of square in the mouldy part of the garden, about three yards across, and began to dig. But we found nothing except worms and stones—and the ground was very hard.

So we thought we'd try another part of the garden, and we found a place in the big round flower bed, where the ground was much softer. We thought we'd make a smaller hole to begin with, and it was much better. We dug and dug and dug, and it was jolly hard work! We got very hot digging, but we found nothing.

Presently Albert-next-door looked over the wall. We do not like him very much, but we let him play with us sometimes, because his father is dead, and you must not be unkind to orphans, even if their mothers are alive. Albert is always very tidy. He wears frilly collars and velvet knickerbockers. I can't think how he can bear to.

So we said, "Hallo!"

And he said, "What are you up to?"

"We're digging for treasure," said Alice; "an ancient parchment revealed to us the place of concealment. Come over and help us. When we have dug deep enough we shall find a great pot of red clay, full of gold and precious jewels."

Albert-next-door only sniggered and said, "What silly nonsense!" He cannot play properly at all. It is very strange, because he has a very nice uncle. You see, Albert-next-door doesn't care for reading, and he has not read nearly so many books as we have, so he is very foolish and ignorant, but it cannot be helped, and you just have to put up with it when you want him to do anything. Besides, it is wrong to be angry with people for not being so clever as you are yourself. It is not always their faults.

So Oswald said, "Come and dig! Then you shall share the treasure when we've found it."

But he said, "I shan't—I don't like digging—and I'm just going in to my tea."

"Come along and dig, there's a good boy," Alice said. "You can use my spade. It's much the best—"

So he came along and dug, and when once he was over the wall we kept him at it, and we worked as well, of course, and the hole got deep. Pincher worked too—he is our dog and he is very good at digging. He digs for rats in the dustbin sometimes, and gets very dirty. But we love our dog, even when his face wants washing.

"I expect we shall have to make a tunnel," Oswald said, "to reach the rich treasure." So he jumped into the hole and began to dig at one side. After that we took it in turns to dig at the tunnel, and Pincher was most useful in scraping the earth out of the tunnel—he does it with his back feet when you say "Rats!" and he digs with his front ones, and burrows with his nose as well.

At last the tunnel was nearly a yard long, and big enough to creep along to find the treasure, if only it had been a bit longer. Now it was Albert's turn to go in and dig, but he funked it.

"Take your turn like a man," said Oswald—nobody can say that Oswald doesn't take his turn like a man. But Albert wouldn't. So we had to make him, because it was only fair.

"It's quite easy," Alice said. "You just crawl in and dig with your hands. Then when you come out we can scrape out what you've done, with the spades. Come—be a man. You won't notice it being dark in the tunnel if you shut your eyes tight. We've all been in except Dora—and she doesn't like worms."

"I don't like worms neither." Albert-next-door said this; but we remembered how he had picked a fat red and black worm up in his fingers and thrown it at Dora only the day before.

So we put him in.

But he would not go in head first, the proper way, and dig with his hands as we had done, and though Oswald was angry at the time, for he hates snivellers, yet afterwards he owned that perhaps it was just as well. You should never be afraid to own that perhaps you were mistaken—but it is cowardly to do it unless you are quite sure you are in the wrong.

"Let me go in feet first," said Albert-next-door. "I'll dig with my boots—I will truly, honour bright."

So we let him get in feet first—and he did it very slowly and at last he was in, and only his head sticking out into the hole; and all the rest of him in the tunnel.

"Now dig with your boots," said Oswald; "and, Alice, do catch hold of Pincher, he'll be digging again in another minute, and perhaps it would be uncomfortable for Albert if Pincher threw the mould into his eyes."

You should always try to think of these little things. Thinking of other people's comfort makes them like you. Alice held Pincher, and we all shouted, "Kick! dig with your feet, for all you're worth!"

So Albert-next-door began to dig with his feet, and we stood on the ground over him, waiting—and all in a minute the ground gave way, and we tumbled together in a heap: and when we got up there was a little shallow hollow where we had been standing, and Albert-next-door was underneath, stuck quite fast, because the roof of the tunnel had tumbled in on him. He is a horribly unlucky boy to have anything to do with.

It was dreadful the way he cried and screamed, though he had to own it didn't hurt, only it was rather heavy and he couldn't move his legs. We would have dug him out all right enough, in time, but he screamed so we were afraid the police would come, so Dicky climbed over the wall, to tell the cook there to tell Albert-next-door's uncle he had been buried by mistake, and to come and help dig him out.

Dicky was a long time gone. We wondered what had become of him, and all the while the screaming went on and on, for we had taken the loose earth off Albert's face so that he could scream quite easily and comfortably.

Presently Dicky came back and Albert-next-door's uncle came with him. He has very long legs, and his hair is light and his face is brown. He has been to sea, but now he writes books. I like him.

He told his nephew to stow it, so Albert did, and then he asked him if he was hurt—and Albert had to say he wasn't, for though he is a coward, and very unlucky, he is not a liar like some boys are.

"This promises to be a protracted if agreeable task," said Albert-next-door's uncle, rubbing his hands and looking at the hole with Albert's head in it. "I will get another spade," so he fetched the big spade out of the next-door garden tool-shed, and began to dig his nephew out.

"Mind you keep very still," he said, "or I might chunk a bit out of you with the spade." Then after a while he said—

"I confess that I am not absolutely insensible to the dramatic interest of the situation. My curiosity is excited. I own that I should like to know how my nephew happened to be buried. But don't tell me if you'd rather not. I suppose no force was used?"

"Only moral force," said Alice. They used to talk a lot about moral force at the High School where she went, and in case you don't know what it means I'll tell you that it is making people do what they don't want to, just by slanging them, or laughing at them, or promising them things if they're good.

"Only moral force, eh?" said Albert-next-door's uncle. "Well?"

"Well," Dora said, "I'm very sorry it happened to Albert—I'd rather it had been one of us. It would have been my turn to go into the tunnel, only I don't like worms, so they let me off. You see we were digging for treasure."

"Yes," said Alice, "and I think we were just coming

to the underground passage that leads to the secret hoard, when the tunnel fell in on Albert. He is so unlucky," and she sighed.

Then Albert-next-door began to scream again, and his uncle wiped his face—his own face, not Albert's—with his silk handkerchief, and then he put it in his trousers pocket. It seems a strange place to put a handkerchief, but he had his coat and waistcoat off and I suppose he wanted the handkerchief handy. Digging is warm work.

He told Albert-next-door to drop it, or he wouldn't proceed further in the matter, so Albert stopped screaming, and presently his uncle finished digging him out. Albert did look so funny, with his hair all dusty and his velvet suit covered with mould and his face muddy with earth and crying.

We all said how sorry we were, but he wouldn't say a word back to us. He was most awfully sick to think he'd been the one buried, when it might just as well have been one of us. I felt myself that it was hard lines.

"So you were digging for treasure," said Albert-nextdoor's uncle, wiping his face again with his handkerchief. "Well, I fear that your chances of success are small. I have made a careful study of the whole subject. What I don't know about buried treasure is not worth knowing. And I never knew more than one coin buried in any one garden—and that is generally—Hullo—what's that?"

He pointed to something shining in the hole he had just dragged Albert out of. Oswald picked it up. It was a half-crown. We looked at each other, speechless with surprise and delight, like in books.

"Well, that's lucky, at all events," said Albert-next-door's uncle. "Let's see, that's fivepence each for you."

"It's fourpence—something; I can't do fractions," said Dicky; "there are seven of us, you see."

"Oh, you count Albert as one of yourselves on this occasion, eh?"

"Of course," said Alice; "and I say, he was buried after all. Why shouldn't we let him have the odd somethings, and we'll have fourpence each."

We all agreed to do this, and told Albert-next-door we would bring his share as soon as we could get the half-crown changed. He cheered up a little at that, and his uncle wiped his face again—he did look hot—and began to put on his coat and waistcoat.

When he had done it he stooped and picked up something. He held it up, and you will hardly believe it, but it is quite true—it was another half-crown!

"To think that there should be two!" he said; "in all my experience of buried treasure I never heard of such a thing!"

I wish Albert-next-door's uncle would come treasure-seeking with us regularly; he must have very sharp eyes: for Dora says she was looking just the minute before at the very place where the second half-crown was picked up from, and *she* never saw it.

Chapter 3

BEING DETECTIVES

The next thing that happened to us was very interesting. It was as real as the half-crowns—not just pretending. I shall try to write it as like a real book as I can. Of course we have read Mr Sherlock Holmes, as well as the yellow-covered books with pictures outside that are so badly printed; and you get them for fourpence-halfpenny at the bookstall when the corners of them are beginning to curl up and get dirty, with people looking to see how the story ends when they are waiting for trains. I think this is most unfair to the boy at the bookstall. The books are written by a gentleman named Gaboriau, and Albert's uncle says they are the worst translations in the world—and written in vile English. Of course they're not like Kipling, but they're jolly good stories. And we had just been reading a book by Dick Diddlington—that's not his right name, but I know all about libel actions, so I shall not say what his name is really, because his books are rot. Only they put it into our heads to do what I am going to narrate.

It was in September, and we were not to go to the seaside because it is so expensive, even if you go to Sheerness, where it is all tin cans and old boots and no sand at all. But every one else went, even the people next door—not Albert's side, but the other. Their servant told Eliza they were all going to Scarborough, and next day sure enough all the blinds were down and the shutters up, and the milk was not left any more. There is a big horse chestnut tree between their garden and ours, very useful for getting conkers out of and for making stuff to rub on your chilblains. This prevented our seeing whether the blinds were down at the back as well, but Dicky climbed to the top of the tree and looked, and they were.

It was jolly hot weather, and very stuffy indoors—we used to play a good deal in the garden. We made a tent out of the kitchen clothes-horse and some blankets off our beds, and though it was quite as hot in the tent as in the house it was a very different sort of hotness. Albert's uncle called it the Turkish Bath. It is not nice to be kept from the seaside, but we know that we have much to be thankful for. We might be poor little children living in a crowded alley where even at summer noon hardly a ray of sunlight penetrates; clothed in rags and with bare feet—though I do not mind holes in my clothes myself, and bare feet would not be at all bad in this sort of weather. Indeed we do, sometimes, when we are playing at things which require it. It was shipwrecked mariners that day, I remember, and we were all in the blanket tent. We had just finished eating the things we had saved, at the peril of our lives, from the fast-sinking vessel. They were rather nice things. Two-pennyworth of coconut candy—it was got in Greenwich, where it is four ounces a penny—three apples, some macaroni—the straight sort that is so useful to suck things through—some raw rice, and a large piece of cold suet pudding that Alice nicked from the larder when she went to get the rice and macaroni. And when we had finished some one said—

"I should like to be a detective."

I wish to be quite fair, but I cannot remember exactly

who said it. Oswald thinks he said it and Dora says it was Dicky, but Oswald is too much of a man to quarrel about a little thing like that.

"I should like to be a detective," said—perhaps it was Dicky, but I think not—"and find out strange and hidden crimes."

"You have to be much cleverer than you are," said H. O.

"Not so very," Alice said, "because when you've read the books you know what the things mean: the red-hair on the handle of the knife, or the grains of white powder on the velvet collar of the villain's overcoat. I believe we could do it."

"I shouldn't like to have anything to do with murders," said Dora; "somehow it doesn't seem safe—"

"And it always ends in the poor murderer being hanged," said Alice.

We explained to her why murderers have to be hanged, but she only said, "I don't care. I'm sure no one would ever do murdering twice. Think of the blood and things, and what you would see when you woke up in the night! I shouldn't mind being a detective to lie in wait for a gang of coiners, now, and spring upon them unawares, and secure them—single-handed, you know, or with only my faithful bloodhound."

She stroked Pincher's ears, but he had gone to sleep because he knew well enough that all the suet pudding was finished. He is a very sensible dog.

"You always get hold of the wrong end of the stick," Oswald said. "You can't choose what crimes you'll be a detective about. You just have to get a suspicious circumstance, and then you look for a clue and follow it up. Whether it turns out a murder or a missing will is just a fluke."

"That's one way," Dicky said. "Another is to get a paper and find two advertisements or bits of news that fit. Like this: 'Young Lady Missing,' and then it tells about all the clothes she had on, and the gold locket she wore, and the colour of her hair, and all that; and then in another piece of the paper you see, 'Gold locket found,' and then it all comes out."

We sent H. O. for the paper at once, but we could not make any of the things fit in. The two best were about how some burglars broke into a place in Holloway where they made preserved tongues and invalid delicacies, and carried off a lot of them. And on another page there was, "Mysterious deaths in Holloway."

Oswald thought there was something in it, and so did Albert's uncle when we asked him, but the others thought not, so Oswald agreed to drop it. Besides, Holloway is a long way off. All the time we were talking about the paper Alice seemed to be thinking about something else, and when we had done she said—

"I believe we might be detectives ourselves, but I should not like to get anybody into trouble."

"Not murderers or robbers?" Dicky asked.

"It wouldn't be murderers," she said; "but I *have* noticed something strange. Only I feel a little frightened. Let's ask Albert's uncle first."

Alice is a jolly sight too fond of asking grown-up people things. And we all said it was tommy-rot, and she was to tell us.

"Well, promise you won't do anything without me," Alice said, and we promised. Then she said—

"This is a dark secret, and any one who thinks it is better not to be involved in a career of crime-discovery had better go away ere yet it be too late."

So Dora said she had had enough of tents, and she was going to look at the shops. H. O. went with her because he had twopence to spend. They thought it was only a game of Alice's but Oswald knew by the way she spoke. He can nearly always tell. And when people are not telling the truth Oswald generally knows by the way they look with their eyes. Oswald is not proud of being able to do this. He knows it is through no merit of his own that he is much cleverer than some people.

When they had gone, the rest of us got closer together and said—

"Now then."

"Well," Alice said, "you know the house next door? The people have gone to Scarborough. And the house is shut up. But last night *I saw a light in the windows.*"

We asked her how and when, because her room is in the front, and she couldn't possibly have seen. And then she said—

"I'll tell you if you boys will promise not ever to go fishing again without me."

So we had to promise.

Then she said—

"It was last night. I had forgotton to feed my rabbits and I woke up and remembered it. And I was afraid I should find them dead in the morning, like Oswald did."

"It wasn't my fault," Oswald said; "there was something the matter with the beasts. I fed them right enough."

Alice said she didn't mean that, and she went on—

"I came down into the garden, and I saw a light in the house, and dark figures moving about. I thought perhaps it was burglars, but Father hadn't come home, and Eliza had gone to bed, so I couldn't do anything. Only I thought perhaps I would tell the rest of you."

"Why didn't you tell us this morning?" Noël asked. And Alice explained that she did not want to get any one into trouble, even burglars. "But we might watch to-night," she said, "and see if we see the light again."

"They might have been burglars," Noël said. He was sucking the last bit of his macaroni. "You know the people next door are very grand. They won't know us and they go out in a real private carriage sometimes. And they have an 'At Home' day, and people come in cabs. I daresay they have piles of plate and jewellery and rich brocades, and furs of price and things like that. Let us keep watch to-night."

"It's no use watching to-night," Dicky said; "if it's only burglars they won't come again. But there are other things besides burglars that are discovered in empty houses where lights are seen moving."

"You mean coiners," said Oswald at once. "I wonder what the reward is for setting the police on their track?"

Dicky thought it ought to be something fat, because coiners are always a desperate gang; and the machinery they make the coins with is so heavy and handy for knocking down detectives.

Then it was tea-time, and we went in; and Dora and H. O. had clubbed their money together and bought a melon; quite a big one, and only a little bit squashy at one end. It was very good, and then we washed the seeds and made things with them and with pins and cotton. And nobody said any more about watching the house next door.

Only when we went to bed Dicky took off his coat and waistcoat, but he stopped at his braces, and said—

"What about the coiners?"

Oswald had taken off his collar and tie, and he was just going to say the same, so he said, "Of course I meant to watch, only my collar's rather tight, so I thought I'd take it off first."

Dicky said he did not think the girls ought to be in it, because there might be danger, but Oswald reminded him that they had promised Alice, and that a promise is a sacred thing, even when you'd much rather not. So Oswald got Alice alone under pretence of showing her a caterpillar—Dora does not like them, and she screamed and ran away when Oswald offered to show it her. Then Oswald explained, and Alice agreed to come and watch if she could. This made us later than we ought to have been, because Alice had to wait till Dora was quiet and then creep out very slowly, for fear of the boards creaking. The girls sleep with their room door open for fear of burglars. Alice had kept on her clothes under her nightgown when Dora wasn't looking, and presently we got down, creeping past Father's study, and out at the glass door that leads on to the veranda and the iron steps into the garden. And we went down very quietly, and got into the chestnut-tree, and then I felt that we had only been playing what Albert's uncle calls our favourite instrument—I mean the Fool. For the house next door was as dark as dark. Then suddenly we heard a sound—it came from the gate at the end of the garden. All the gardens have gates; they lead into a kind of lane that runs behind them. It is a sort of back way, very convenient when you don't want to say exactly where you are going. We heard the gate at the end of the next garden click, and Dicky nudged Alice so that she would have fallen out of the tree if it had not been for Oswald's extraordinary presence of mind. Oswald squeezed Alice's arm tight, and we all looked; and the others were rather frightened because really we had not exactly expected anything to happen except perhaps a light. But now a muffled figure, shrouded in a dark cloak, came swiftly up the path of the next-door garden. And we could see that under its cloak the figure carried a mysterious burden. The figure was dressed to look like a woman in a sailor hat.

We held our breath as it passed under the tree where we were, and then it tapped very gently on the back door and was let in, and then a light appeared in the window of the downstairs back breakfast-room. But the shutters were up.

Dicky said, "My eye!" and wouldn't the others be sick to think they hadn't been in this! But Alice didn't half like it—and as she is a girl I do not blame her. Indeed, I thought myself at first that perhaps it would be better to retire for the present, and return later with a strongly armed force.

"It's not burglars," Alice whispered; "the mysterious stranger was bringing things in, not taking them out. They must be coiners—and oh, Oswald!—don't let's! The things they coin with must hurt very much. Do let's go to bed!"

But Dicky said he was going to see; if there was a reward for finding out things like this he would like to have the reward.

"They locked the back door," he whispered, "I heard it go. And I could look in quite well through the holes in the shutters and be back over the wall long before they'd got the door open, even if they started to do it at once."

There were holes at the top of the shutters the shape of hearts, and the yellow light came out through them as well as through the chinks of the shutters.

Oswald said if Dicky went he should, because he was the eldest; and Alice said, "If any one goes it ought to be me, because I thought of it."

So Oswald said, "Well, go then"; and she said, "Not for anything!" And she begged us not to, and we talked about it in the tree till we were all quite hoarse with whispering.

At last we decided on a plan of action.

Alice was to stay in the tree, and scream "Murder!" if anything happened. Dicky and I were to get down into the next garden and take it in turns to peep.

So we got down as quietly as we could, but the tree made much more noise than it does in the day, and several times we paused, fearing that all was discovered. But nothing happened.

There was a pile of red flower-pots under the window and one very large one was on the window-ledge. It seemed as if it was the hand of Destiny had placed it there, and the geranium in it was dead, and there was nothing to stop your standing on it—so Oswald did. He went first because he is the eldest, and though Dicky tried to stop him because he thought of it first it could not be, on account of not being able to say anything.

So Oswald stood on the flower-pot and tried to look through one of the holes. He did not really expect to see the coiners at their fell work, though he had pretended to when we were talking in the tree. But if he had seen them pouring the base molten metal into tin moulds the shape of half-crowns he would not have been half so astonished as he was at the spectacle now revealed.

At first he could see little, because the hole had

unfortunately been made a little too high, so that the eye of the detective could only see the Prodigal Son in a shiny frame on the opposite wall. But Oswald held on to the window-frame and stood on tiptoe and then he saw.

There was no furnace, and no base metal, no bearded men in leathern aprons with tongs and things, but just a table with a table-cloth on it for supper, and a tin of salmon and a lettuce and some bottled beer. And there on a chair was the cloak and the hat of the mysterious stranger, and the two people sitting at the table were the two youngest grown-up daughters of the lady next door, and one of them was saying—

"So I got the salmon three-halfpence cheaper, and the lettuces are only six a penny in the Broadway, just fancy! We must save as much as ever we can on our housekeeping money if we want to go away decent next year.

And the other said, "I wish we could *all* go *every* year, or else—Really, I almost wish—"

And all the time Oswald was looking Dicky was pulling at his jacket to make him get down and let Dicky have a squint. And just as she said "I almost," Dicky pulled too hard and Oswald felt himself toppling on the giddy verge of the big flower-pot. Putting forth all hig strength our hero strove to recover his equi-what's-its-name, but it was now lost beyond recall.

"You've done it this time!" he said, then he fell heavily among the flower-pots piled below. He heard them crash and rattle and crack, and then his head struck against an iron pillar used for holding up the next-door veranda. His eyes closed and he knew no more.

Now you will perhaps expect that at this moment

Alice would have cried "Murder!" If you think so you little know what girls are. Directly she was left alone in that tree she made a bolt to tell Albert's uncle all about it and bring him to our rescue in case the coiner's gang was a very desperate one. And just when I fell, Albert's uncle was getting over the wall. Alice never screamed at all when Oswald fell, but Dicky thinks he heard Albert's uncle say, "Confound those kids!" which would not have been kind or polite, so I hope he did not say it.

The people next door did not come out to see what the row was. Albert's uncle did not wait for them to come out. He picked up Oswald and carried the insensible body of the gallant young detective to the wall, laid it on the top, and then climbed over and bore his lifeless burden into our house and put it on the sofa in Father's study. Father was out, so we needn't have *crept* so when we were getting into the garden. Then Oswald was restored to consciousness, and his head tied up, and sent to bed, and next day there was a lump on his young brow as big as a turkey's egg, and very uncomfortable.

Albert's uncle came in next day and talked to each of us separately. To Oswald he said many unpleasant things about ungentlemanly to spy on ladies, and about minding your own business; and when I began to tell him what I had heard he told me to shut up, and altogether he made me more uncomfortable than the bump did.

Oswald did not say anything to any one, but next day, as the shadows of eve were falling, he crept away, and wrote on a piece of paper, "I want to speak to you," and shoved it through the hole like a heart in the top of the next-door shutters.

And the youngest young lady put an eye to the heart-shaped hole, and then opened the shutter and said "Well?" very crossly.

Then Oswald said—

"I am very sorry, and I beg your pardon. We wanted to be detectives, and we thought a gang of coiners infested your house, so we looked through your window last night. I saw the lettuce, and I heard what you said about the salmon being three-halfpence cheaper, and I know it is very dishonourable to pry into other people's secrets, especially ladies", and I never will again if you will forgive me this once."

Then the lady frowned and then she laughed, and then she said—

"So it was *you* tumbling into the flower-pots last night? We thought it was burglars. It frightened us horribly. Why, what a bump on your poor head!"

And then she talked to me a bit, and presently she said she and her sister had not wished people to know they were at home, because—And then she stopped short and grew very red, and I said, "I thought you were all at Scarborough; your servant told Eliza so. Why didn't you want people to know you were at home?

The lady got redder still, and then she laughed and said—

"Never mind the reason why. I hope your head doesn't hurt much. Thank you for your nice, manly little speech. *You've* nothing to be ashamed of, at any rate." Then she kissed me, and I did not mind. And then she said, "Run away now, dear. I'm going to—I'm going to pull up the blinds and open the shutters, and I want to do it *at once*, before it gets dark, so that every one can see we're at home, and not at Scarborough."

CHAPTER 4

GOOD HUNTING

When we had got that four shillings by digging for treasure we ought, by rights, to have tried Dicky's idea of answering the advertisement about ladies and gentlemen and spare time and two pounds a week, but there were several things we rather wanted.

Dora wanted a new pair of scissors, and she said she was going to get them with her eightpence. But Alice said—

"You ought to get her those, Oswald, because you know you broke the points off hers getting the marble out of the brass thimble."

It was quite true, though I had almost forgotten it, but then it was H. O. who jammed the marble into the thimble first of all. So I said—

"It's H. O.'s fault as much as mine, anyhow. Why shouldn't he pay?"

Oswald didn't so much mind paying for the beastly scissors, but he hates injustice of every kind.

"He's such a little kid," said Dicky, and of course H. O. said he wasn't a little kid, and it very nearly came to being a row between them. But Oswald knows when to be generous; so he said—

"Look here! I'll pay sixpence of the scissors, and H. O. shall pay the rest, to teach him to be careful."

H. O. agreed: he is not at all a mean kid, but I found out afterwards that Alice paid his share out of her own money.

Then we wanted some new paints, and Noël wanted a pencil and a halfpenny account-book to write poetry with, and it does seem hard never to have any apples. So, somehow or other nearly all the money got spent, and we agreed that we must let the advertisement run loose a little longer.

"I only hope," Alice said, "that they won't have got all the ladies and gentlemen they want before we have got the money to write for the sample and instructions."

And I was a little afraid myself, because it seemed such a splendid chance; but we looked in the paper every day, and the advertisement was always there, so we thought it was all right.

Then we had the detective try-on—and it proved no go; and then, when all the money was gone, except a halfpenny of mine and twopence of Noël's and threepence of Dicky's and a few pennies that the girls had left, we held another council.

Dora was sewing the buttons on H. O.'s Sunday things. He got himself a knife with his money, and he cut every single one of his best buttons off. You've no idea how many buttons there are on a suit. Dora counted them. There are twenty-four, counting the little ones on the sleeves that don't undo.

Alice was trying to teach Pincher to beg; but he has too much sense when he knows you've got nothing in your hands, and the rest of us were roasting potatoes under the fire. We had made a fire on purpose, though it was rather warm. They are very good if you cut away the burnt parts—but you ought to wash them first, or you are a dirty boy.

"Well, what can we do?" said Dicky. "You are so

fond of saying 'Let's do something!' and never saying what."

"We can't try the advertisement yet. Shall we try rescuing some one?" said Oswald. It was his own idea, but he didn't insist on doing it, though he is next to the eldest, for he knows it is bad manners to make people do what you want, when they would rather not.

"What was Noël's plan?" Alice asked.

"A Princess or a poetry book," said Noël sleepily. He was lying on his back on the sofa, kicking his legs. "Only I shall look for the Princess all by myself. But I'll let you see her when we're married."

"Have you got enough poetry to make a book?" Dicky asked that, and it was rather sensible of him, because when Noël came to look there were only seven of his poems that any of us could understand. There way the "Wreck of the *Malabar*", and the poem he wrote when Eliza took us to hear the Reviving Preacher, and everybody cried, and Father said it must have been the Preacher's Eloquence.

So Noël wrote:

O Eloquence and what art thou?
Ay what art thou? because we cried
And everybody cried inside
When they came out their eyes were red
And it was your doing Father said.

But Noël told Alice he got the first line and a half from a book a boy at school was going to write when he had time. Besides this there were the "Lines on a Dead Black Beetle that was poisoned":

O Beetle how I weep to see
Thee lying on thy poor back!
It is so very sad indeed.

You were so shiny and black.
I wish you were alive again
But Eliza says wishing it is nonsense and a shame.

It was very good beetle poison, and there were hundreds of them lying dead—but Noël only wrote a piece of poetry for one of them. He said he hadn't time to do them all, and the worst of it was he didn't know which one he'd written it to—so Alice couldn't bury the beetle and put the lines on its grave, though she wanted to very much.

Well; it was quite plain that there wasn't enough poetry for a book.

"We might wait a year or two," said Noël. "I shall be sure to make some more some time. I thought of a piece about a fly this morning that knew condensed milk was sticky."

"But we want the money *now*," said Dicky, "and you can go on writing just the same. It will come in some time or other."

"There's poetry in newspapers," said Alice. "Down, Pincher! you'll never be a clever dog, so it's no good trying."

"Do they pay for it?" Dicky thought of that; he often thinks of things that are really important, even if they are a little dull.

"I don't know. But I shouldn't think any one would let them print their poetry without. I wouldn't I know." That was Dora; but Noël said he wouldn't mind if he didn't get paid, so long as he saw his poetry printed and his name at the end.

"We might try, anyway," said Oswald. He is always willing to give other people's ideas a fair trial.

So we copied out "The Wreck of the *Malabar*" and the

other six poems on drawing-paper—Dora did it, she writes best—and Oswald drew a picture of the *Malabar* going down with all hands. It was a full-rigged schooner, and all the ropes and sails were correct; because my cousin is in the Navy, and he showed me.

We thought a long time whether we'd write a letter and send it by post with the poetry—and Dora thought it would be best. But Noël said he couldn't bear not to know at once if the paper would print the poetry, so we decided to take it.

I went with Noël, because I am the eldest, and he is not old enough to go to London by himself. Dicky said poetry was rot—and he was glad he hadn't got to make a fool of himself: that was because there was not enough money for him to go with us. H. O. couldn't come either, but he came to the station to see us off, and waved his cap and called out "Good hunting!" as the train started.

There was a lady in spectacles in the corner. She was writing with a pencil on the edges of long strips of paper that had print all down them.

When the train started she asked—

"What was that he said?"

So Oswald answered—

"It was 'Good hunting'—it's out of the Jungle book!"

"That's very pleasant to hear," the lady said; "I am very pleased to meet people who know their Jungle book. And where are you off to—the Zoological Gardens to look for Bagheera?"

We were pleased, too, to meet some one who knew the Jungle book.

So Oswald said—

"We are going to restore the fallen fortunes of the House of Bastable—and we have all thought of different ways—and we're going to try them all. Noël's way is poetry. I suppose great poets get paid?"

The lady laughed—she was awfully jolly—and said she was a sort of poet, too, and the long strips of paper were the proofs of her new book of stories. Because before a book is made into a real book with pages and a cover, they sometimes print it all on strips of paper, and the writer make marks on it with a pencil to show the printers what idiots they are not to understand what a writer means to have printed.

We told her all about digging for treasure, and what we meant to do. Then she asked to see Noël's poetry and he said he didn't like—so she said, "Look here—if you'll show me yours I'll show you some of mine." So he agreed.

The jolly lady read Noël's poetry, and she said she liked it very much. And she thought a great deal of the picture of the *Malabar*. And then she said, "I write serious poetry like yours myself, too, but I have a piece here that I think you will like because it's about a boy." She gave it to us—and so I can copy it down, and I will, for it shows that some grown-up ladies are not so silly as others. I like it better than Noël's poetry, though I told him I did not, because he looked as if he was going to cry. This was very wrong, for you should always speak the truth, however unhappy it makes people. And I generally do. But I did not want him crying in the railway carriage.

The lady's piece of poetry:

Oh when I wake up in my bed
And see the sun all fat and red,
I'm glad to have another day
For all my different kinds of play.

There are so many things to do—
The things that make a man of you,
If grown-ups did not get so vexed
And wonder what you will do next.

I often wonder whether they
Ever made up our kinds of play—
If they were always good as gold
And only did what they were told

They like you best to play with tops
And toys in boxes, bought in shops;
They do not even know the names
Of really interesting games.

They will not let you play with fire
Or trip your sisters up with wire,
They grudge the tea-tray for a drum,
Or booby-traps when callers come.

They don't like fishing, and it's true
You sometimes soak a suit or two:
They look on fireworks, though they're dry,
With quite a disapproving eye.

They do not understand the way
To get the most out of your day:
They do not know how hunger feels
Nor what you need between your meals.

And when you're sent to bed at night
They're happy, but they're not polite,
For through the door you hear them say:
"He's *done* his *mischief for the day!*"

She told us a lot of other pieces but I cannot remember them, and she talked to us all the way up, and when we got nearly to Cannon Street she said—

"I've got two new shillings here! Do you think they would help to smooth the path to Fame?"

Noël said, "Thank you," and was going to take the shilling. But Oswald, who always remembers what he is told, said—

"Thank you very much, but Father told us we ought never to take anything from strangers."

"That's a nasty one," said the lady—she didn't talk a bit like a real lady, but more like a jolly sort of grown-up boy in a dress and hat—"a very nasty one! But don't you think as Noël and I are both poets I might be considered a sort of relation? You've heard of brother poets, haven't you? Don't you think Noël and I are aunt and nephew poets, or some relationship of that kind?"

I didn't know what to say, and she went on—

"It's awfully straight of you to stick to what your Father tells you, but look here, you take the shillings, and here's my card. When you get home tell your Father all about it, and if he says No, you can just bring the shillings back to me."

So we took the shillings, and she shook hands with us and said, "Good-bye, and good hunting!"

We did tell Father about it, and he said it was all right, and when he looked at the card he told us we were highly honoured, for the lady wrote better poetry than any other lady alive now. We had never heard of her, and she seemed much too jolly for a poet. Good old Kipling! We owe him those two shillings, as well as the Jungle books!

Chapter 5

THE POET AND THE EDITOR

It was not bad sport—being in London entirely on our own hook. We asked the way to Fleet Street, where Father says all the newspaper offices are. They said straight on down Ludgate Hill—but it turned out to be quite another way. At least *we* didn't go straight on.

We got to St Paul's. Noël would go in, and we saw where Gordon was buried—at least the monument. It is very flat, considering what a man he was.

When we came out we walked a long way, and when we asked a policeman he said we'd better go back through Smithfield. So we did. They don't burn people any more there now, so it was rather dull, besides being a long way, and Noël got very tired. He's a peaky little chap; it comes of being a poet, I think. We had a bun or two at different shops—out of the shillings—and it was quite late in the afternoon when we got to Fleet Street. The gas was lighted and the electric lights. There is a jolly Bovril sign that comes off and on in different coloured lamps. We went to the *Daily Recorder* office, and asked to see the Editor. It is a big office, very bright, with brass and mahogany and electric lights.

They told us the Editor wasn't there, but at another office. So we went down a dirty street, to a very dull looking place. There was a man there inside, in a glass case, as if he was a museum, and he told us to write down our names and our business. So Oswald wrote—

OSWALD BASTABLE.
NOËL BASTABLE.
Business very private indeed.

Then we waited on the stone stairs; it was very draughty. And the man in the glass case looked at us as if we were the museum instead of him. We waited a long time, and then a boy came down and said—

"The Editor can't see you. Will you please write your business?" And he laughed. I wanted to punch his head.

But Noël said, "Yes, I'll write it if you'll give me a pen and ink, and a sheet of paper and an envelope."

The boy said he'd better write by post. But Noël is a bit pig-headed; it's his worst fault. So he said—

"No, I'll write it *now*." So I backed him up by saying

"Look at the price penny stamps are since the coal strike!"

So the boy grinned, and the man in the glass case gave us pen and paper, and Noël wrote. Oswald writes better than he does; but Noël would do it; and it took a very long time, and then it was inky.

DEAR MR EDITOR, I want you to print my poetry and pay for it, and I am a friend of Mrs Leslie's; she is a poet too.

Your affectionate friend,

NOËL BASTABLE.

He licked the envelope a good deal, so that that boy shouldn't read it going upstairs; and he wrote "Very private" outside, and gave the letter to the boy. I thought it wasn't any good; but in a minute the grinning boy came back, and he was quite respectful, and said—

"The Editor says, please will you step up?"

We stepped up. There were a lot of stairs and passages, and a queer sort of humming, hammering sound and a very funny smell. The boy was now very polite, and said it was the ink we smelt, and the noise was the printing machines.

After going through a lot of cold passages we came to a door; the boy opened it, and let us go in. There was a large room, with a big, soft, blue-and-red carpet, and a roaring fire, though it was only October; and a large table with drawers, and littered with papers, just like the one in Father's study. A gentleman was sitting at one side of the table; he had a light moustache and light eyes, and he looked very young to be an editor not nearly so old as Father. He looked very tired and sleepy, as if he had got up very early in the morning; but he was kind, and we liked him. Oswald thought he looked clever. Oswald is considered a judge of faces.

"Well," said he, "so you are Mrs Leslie's friends?"

"I think so," said Noël; "at least she gave us each a shilling, and she wished us 'good hunting!' "

"Good hunting, eh? Well, what about this poetry of yours? Which is the poet?"

I can't think how he could have asked! Oswald is said to be a very manly-looking boy for his age. However, I thought it would look duffing to be offended, so I said—

"This is my brother Noël. He is the poet."

Noël had turned quite pale. He is disgustingly like a girl in some ways. The Editor told us to sit down, and he took the poems from Noël, and began to read them. Noël got paler and paler; I really thought he was going to faint, like he did when I held his hand under the cold-water tap, after I had accidentally cut him with my chisel. When the Editor had read the first poem—it was the one about the beetle—he got up and stood with his back to us. It was not manners; but Noël thinks he did it "to conceal his emotion," as they do in books.

He read all the poems, and then he said—

"I like your poetry very much, young man. I'll give you—let me see; how much shall I give you for it?"

"As much as ever you can," said Noël. "You see I want a good deal of money to restore the fallen fortunes of the house of Bastable."

The gentleman put on some eye-glasses and looked hard at us. Then he sat down.

"That's a good idea," said he. "Tell me how you came to think of it. And, I say, have you had any tea? They've just sent out for mine."

He rang a tingly bell, and the boy brought in a tray with a teapot and a thick cup and saucer and things, and he had to fetch another tray for us, when he was told to; and we had tea with the Editor of the *Daily Recorder*. I suppose it was a very proud moment for Noël, though I did not think of that till afterwards. The Editor asked us a lot of questions, and we told him a good deal, though of course I did not tell a stranger all our reasons for thinking that the family fortunes wanted restoring. We stayed about half an hour, and when we were going away he said again—

"I shall print all your poems, my poet; and now what do you think they're worth?"

"I don't know," Noël said. "You see I didn't write them to sell."

"Why did you write them then?" he asked.

Noël said he didn't know; he supposed because he wanted to.

"Art for Art's sake, eh?" said the Editor, and he seemed quite delighted, as though Noël had said something clever.

"Well, would a guinea meet your views?" he asked.

I have read of people being at a loss for words, and dumb with emotion, and I've read of people being turned to stone with astonishment, or joy, or something, but I never knew how silly it looked till I saw Noël standing staring at the Editor with his mouth open. He went red and he went white, and then he got crimson, as if you were rubbing more and more crimson lake on a palette. But he didn't say a word, so Oswald had to say—

"I should jolly well think so."

So the Editor gave Noël a sovereign and a shilling, and he shook hands with us both, but he thumped Noël on the back and said—

"Buck up, old man! It's your first guinea, but it won't be your last. Now go along home, and in about ten years you can bring me some more poetry. Not before see? I'm just taking this poetry of yours because I like it very much; but we don't put poetry in this paper at all. I shall have to put it in another paper I know of."

"What do you put in your paper?" I asked, for Father always takes the *Daily Chronicle*, and I didn't know what the *Recorder* was like. We chose it because it has such a glorious office, and a clock outside lighted up.

"Oh, news," said he, "and dull articles, and things about Celebrities. If you know any Celebrities, now?"

Noël asked him what Celebrities were.

"Oh, the Queen and the Princes, and people with titles, and people who write, or sing, or act—or do something clever or wicked."

"I don't know anybody wicked," said Oswald, wishing he had known Dick Turpin, or Claude Duval, so as to be able to tell the Editor things about them. "But I know some one with a title—Lord Tottenham."

"The mad old Protectionist, eh? How did you come to know him?"

"We don't know him to speak to. But he goes over the Heath every day at three, and he strides along like a giant—with a black cloak like Lord Tennyson's flying behind him, and he talks to himself like one o'clock."

"What does he say?" The Editor had sat down again, and he was fiddling with a blue pencil.

"We only heard him once, close enough to understand, and then he said, 'The curse of the country, sir—ruin and desolation!' And then he went striding along again, hitting at the furze-bushes as if they were the heads of his enemies."

"Excellent descriptive touch," said the Editor. "Well, go on."

"That's all I know about him, except that he stops in the middle of the Heath every day, and he looks all round to see if there's any one about, and if there isn't, he takes his collar off."

The Editor interrupted—which is considered rude and said—

"You're not romancing?"

"I beg your pardon?" said Oswald.

"Drawing the long bow, I mean," said the Editor.

Oswald drew himself up, and said he wasn't a liar.

The Editor only laughed, and said romancing and lying were not at all the same; only it was important to know what you were playing at. So Oswald accepted his apology, and went on.

"We were hiding among the furze-bushes one day and we saw him do it. He took off his collar, and he put on a clean one, and he threw the other among the furze-bushes. We picked it up afterwards, and it was a beastly paper one!"

"Thank you," said the Editor, and he got up and put his hand in his pocket. "That's well worth five shillings, and there they are. Would you like to see round the printing offices before you go home?"

I pocketed my five bob, and thanked him, and I said we should like it very much. He called another gentleman and said something we couldn't hear. Then he said good-bye again; and all this time Noël hadn't said a word. But now he said, "I've made a poem about you. It is called 'Lines to a Noble Editor.' Shall I write it down?"

The Editor gave him the blue pencil, and he sat down at the Editor's table and wrote. It was this, he told me afterwards as well as he could remember—

May Life's choicest blessings be your lot
I think you ought to be very blest
For you are going to print my poems
And you may have this one as well as the rest.

"Thank you," said the Editor. "I don't think I ever had a poem addressed to me before. I shall treasure it, I assure you."

Then the other gentleman said something about Maecenas, and we went off to see the printing office with at least one pound seven in our pockets.

It *was* good hunting, and no mistake!

But he never put Noël's poetry in the *Daily Recorder*. It was quite a long time afterwards we saw a sort of story thing in a magazine, on the station bookstall, and that kind, sleepy-looking Editor had written it, I suppose. It was not at all amusing. It said a lot about Noël and me, describing us all wrong, and saying how we had tea with the Editor; and all Noël's poems were in the story thing. I think myself the Editor seemed to make game of them, but Noël was quite pleased to see them printed—so that's all right.

It wasn't my poetry anyhow, I am glad to say.

CHAPTER 6

NOËL'S PRINCESS

She happened quite accidentally. We were not looking for a Princess at all just then; but Noël had said he was going to find a Princess all by himself, and marry her—and he really did. Which was rather odd, because when people say things are going to befall, very often they don't. It was different, of course, with the prophets of old.

We did not get any treasure by it, except twelve chocolate drops; but we might have done, and it was an adventure, anyhow.

Greenwich Park is a jolly good place to play in, especially the parts that aren't near Greenwich. The parts near the Heath are first-rate. I often wish the Park was nearer our house; but I suppose a Park is a difficult thing to move.

Sometimes we get Eliza to put lunch in a basket, and we go up to the Park. She likes that—it saves cooking dinner for us; and sometimes she says of her own accord, "I've made some pasties for you, and you might as well go into the Park as not. It's a lovely day."

She always tells us to rinse out the cup at the drinking-fountain, and the girls do; but I always put my head under the tap and drink. Then you are an intrepid hunter at a mountain stream—and besides, you're sure it's clean. Dicky does the same, and so does H. O. But Noël always drinks out of the cup. He says it is a golden goblet, wrought by enchanted gnomes.

The day the Princess happened was a fine, hot day, last October, and we were quite tired with the walk up to the Park.

We always go in by the little gate at the top of Croom's Hill. It is the postern gate that things always happen at in stories. It was dusty walking, but when we got in the Park it was ripping, so we rested a bit, and lay on our backs, and looked up at the trees, and wished we could play monkeys. I have done it before now, but the Park-keeper makes a row if he catches you.

When we'd rested a little, Alice said—

"It was a long way to the enchanted wood, but it is very nice now we are there. I wonder what we shall find in it?"

"We shall find deer," said Dicky, "if we go to look but they go on the other side of the Park because of the people with buns."

Saying buns made us think of lunch, so we had it; and when we had done we scratched a hole under a tree and buried the papers, because we know it spoils pretty places to leave beastly, greasy papers lying about. I remember Mother teaching me and Dora that, when we were quite little. I wish everybody's parents would teach them this useful lesson, and the same about orange peel.

When we'd eaten everything there was, Alice whispered—

"I see the white witch bear yonder among the trees! Let's track it and slay it in its lair."

"I am the bear," said Noël; so he crept away, and we followed him among the trees. Often the witch bear was out of sight, and then you didn't know where it would jump out from; but sometimes we saw it, and just followed.

"When we catch it there'll be a great fight," said Oswald; "and I shall be Count Folko of Mont Faucon."

"I'll be Gabrielle," said Dora. She is the only one of us who likes doing girl's parts.

"I'll be Sintram," said Alice; "and H. O. can be the Little Master."

"What about Dicky?"

"Oh, I can be the Pilgrim with the bones."

"Hist!" whispered Alice. "See his white fairy fur gleaming amid yonder covert!"

And I saw a bit of white too. It was Noël's collar, and it had come undone at the back.

We hunted the bear in and out of the trees, and then we lost him altogether; and suddenly we found the wall of the Park—in a place where I'm sure there wasn't a wall before. Noël wasn't anywhere about, and there was a door in the wall. And it was open; so we went through.

"The bear has hidden himself in these mountain fastnesses," Oswald said. "I will draw my good sword and after him."

So I drew the umbrella, which Dora always will bring in case it rains, because Noël gets a cold on the chest at the least thing—and we went on.

The other side of the wall it was a stable yard, all cobble-stones. There was nobody about—but we could hear a man rubbing down a horse and hissing in the stable; so we crept very quietly past, and Alice whispered—

"'Tis the lair of the Monster Serpent; I hear his deadly hiss! Beware! Courage and despatch!"

We went over the stones on tiptoe, and we found

another wall with another door in it on the other side. We went through that too, on tiptoe. It really was an adventure. And there we were in a shrubbery, and we saw something white through the trees. Dora said it was the white bear. That is so like Dora. She always begins to take part in a play just when the rest of us are getting tired of it. I don't mean this unkindly, because I am very fond of Dora. I cannot forget how kind she was when I had bronchitis; and ingratitude is a dreadful vice. But it is quite true.

"It is not a bear," said Oswald; and we all went on, still on tiptoe, round a twisty path and on to a lawn, and there was Noël. His collar had come undone, as I said, and he had an inky mark on his face that he made just before we left the house, and he wouldn't let Dora wash it off, and one of his bootlaces was coming down. He was standing looking at a little girl; she was the funniest little girl you ever saw.

She was like a china doll—the sixpenny kind; she had a white face, and long yellow hair, done up very tight in two pigtails; her forehead was very big and lumpy, and her cheeks came high up, like little shelves under her eyes. Her eyes were small and blue. She had on a funny black frock, with curly braid on it, and button boots that went almost up to her knees. Her legs were very thin. She was sitting in a hammock chair nursing a blue kitten—not a sky-blue one, of course, but the colour of a new slate pencil. As we came up we heard her say to Noël—

"Who are you?"

Noël had forgotten about the bear, and he was taking his favourite part, so he said—

"I'm Prince Camaralzaman."

The funny little girl looked pleased.

"I thought at first you were a common boy," she said. Then she saw the rest of us and said—

"Are you all Princesses and Princes too?"

Of course we said "Yes," and she said—

"I am a Princess also." She said it very well too, exactly as if it were true. We were very glad, because it is so seldom you meet any children who can begin to play right off without having everything explained to them. And even then they will say they are going to "pretend to be" a lion, or a witch, or a king. Now this little girl just said "I *am* a Princess." Then she looked at Oswald and said, "I fancy I've seen you at Baden."

Of course Oswald said, "Very likely."

The little girl had a funny voice, and all her words were quite plain, each word by itself; she didn't talk at all like we do.

H. O. asked her what the cat's name was, and she said "Katinka." Then Dicky said—

"Let's get away from the windows; if you play near windows some one inside generally knocks at them and says 'Don't'."

The Princess put down the cat very carefully and said—

"I am forbidden to walk off the grass."

"That's a pity," said Dora.

"But I will if you like," said the Princess.

"You mustn't do things you are forbidden to do," Dora said; but Dicky showed us that there was some more grass beyond the shrubs with only a gravel path between. So I lifted the Princess over the gravel, so that she should be able to say she hadn't walked off the grass. When we got to the other grass we all sat down, and the Princess asked us if we liked "dragées' (I know that's how you spell it, for I asked Albert-next-door's uncle).

We said we thought not, but she pulled a real silver box out of her pocket and showed us; they were just flat, round chocolates. We had two each. Then we asked her her name, and she began, and when she began she went on, and on, and on, till I thought she was never going to stop. H. O. said she had fifty names, but Dicky is very good at figures, and he says there were only eighteen. The first were Pauline, Alexandra, Alice, and Mary was one, and Victoria, for we all heard that, and it ended up with Hildegarde Cunigonde something or other, Princess of something else.

When she'd done, H. O. said, "That's jolly good! Say it again!" and she did, but even then we couldn't remember it. We told her our names, but she thought they were too short, so when it was Noël's turn he said he was Prince Noël Camaralzaman Ivan Constantine Charlemagne James John Edward Biggs Maximilian Bastable Prince of Lewisham, but when she asked him to say it again of course he could only get the first two names right, because he'd made it up as he went on.

So the Princess said, "You are quite old enough to know your own name." She was very grave and serious.

She told us that she was the fifth cousin of Queen Victoria. We asked who the other cousins were, but she did not seem to understand. She went on and said she was seven times removed. She couldn't tell us what that meant either, but Oswald thinks it means that the Queen's cousins are so fond of her that they will keep coming bothering, so the Queen's servants have orders to remove them. This little girl must have been very fond of the Queen to try so often to see her, and to have been seven times removed. We could see that it is considered something to be proud of, but we thought it was hard on the Queen that her cousins wouldn't let her alone.

Presently the little girl asked us where our maids and governesses were.

We told her we hadn't any just now. And she said—

"How pleasant! And did you come here alone?"

"Yes," said Dora; "we came across the Heath."

"You are very fortunate," said the little girl. She sat very upright on the grass, with her fat little hands in ber lap. "I should like to go on the Heath. There are donkeys there, with white saddle covers. I should like to ride them, but my governess will not permit it."

"I'm glad we haven't a governess," H. O. said. "We ride the donkeys whenever we have any pennies, and once I gave the man another penny to make it gallop."

"You are indeed fortunate!" said the Princess again, and when she looked sad the shelves on her cheeks showed more than ever. You could have laid a sixpence on them quite safely if you had had one.

"Never mind," said Noël; "I've got a lot of money. Come out and have a ride now." But the little girl shook her head and said she was afraid it would not be correct.

Dora said she was quite right; then all of a sudden came one of those uncomfortable times when nobody can think of anything to say, so we sat and looked at each other. But at last Alice said we ought to be going.

"Do not go yet," the little girl said. "At what time did they order your carriage?"

"Our carriage is a fairy one, drawn by griffins, and it comes when we wish for it," said Noël.

The little girl looked at him very queerly, and said,

"That is out of a picture-book."

Then Noël said he thought it was about time he was married if we were to be home in time for tea. The little girl was rather stupid over it, but she did what we told her, and we married them with Dora's pocket-handkerchief for a veil, and the ring off the back of one of the buttons on H. O.'s blouse just went on her little finger.

Then we showed her how to play cross-touch, and puss in the corner, and tag. It was funny, she didn't know any games but battledore and shuttlecock and *les graces*. But she really began to laugh at last and not to look quite so like a doll.

She was Puss and was running after Dicky when suddenly she stopped short and looked as if she was going to cry. And we looked too, and there were two prim ladies with little mouths and tight hair. One of them said in quite an awful voice, "Pauline, who are these children?" and her voice was gruff, with very curly R's.

The little girl said we were Princes and Princesses which was silly, to a grown-up person that is not a great friend of yours.

The gruff lady gave a short, horrid laugh, like a husky bark, and said—

"Princes, indeed! They're only common children!"

Dora turned very red and began to speak, but the little girl cried out "Common children! Oh, I am so glad! When I am grown up I'll always play with common children."

And she ran at us, and began to kiss us one by one, beginning with Alice; she had got to H. O. when the horrid lady said—

"Your Highness—go indoors at once!"

The little girl answered, "I won't!" Then the prim lady said—

"Wilson, carry her Highness indoors."

And the little girl was carried away screaming, and kicking with her little thin legs and her buttoned boots, and between her screams she shrieked: "Common children! I am glad, glad, glad! Common children! Common children!"

The nasty lady then remarked—

"Go at once, or I will send for the police!"

So we went. H. O. made a face at her and so did Alice, but Oswald took off his cap and said he was sorry if she was annoyed about anything; for Oswald has always been taught to be polite to ladies, however nasty. Dicky took his off, too, when he saw me do it; he says he did it first, but that is a mistake. If I were really a common boy I should say it was a lie.

Then we all came away, and when we got outside Dora said, "So she was really a Princess. Fancy a Princess living *there*!"

"Even Princesses have to live somewhere," said Dicky.

"And I thought it was play. And it was real. I wish I'd known! I should have liked to ask her lots of things," said Alice.

H. O. said he would have liked to ask her what she had for dinner and whether she had a crown.

I felt, myself, we had lost a chance of finding out a great deal about kings and queens. I might have known such a stupid-looking little girl would never have been able to pretend, as well as that.

So we all went home across the Heath, and made dripping toast for tea.

When we were eating it Noël said, "I wish I could

give her some! It is very good."

He sighed as he said it, and his mouth was very full, so we knew he was thinking of his Princess. He says now that she was as beautiful as the day, but we remember her quite well, and she was nothing of the kind.

CHAPTER 7

BEING BANDITS

Noël was quite tiresome for ever so long after we found the Princess. He would keep on wanting to go to the Park when the rest of us didn't, and though we went several times to please him, we never found that door open again, and all of us except him knew from the first that it would be no go.

So now we thought it was time to do something to rouse him from the stupor of despair, which is always done to heroes when anything baffling has occurred. Besides, we were getting very short of money again the fortunes of your house cannot be restored (not so that they will last, that is), even by the one pound eight we got when we had the "good hunting." We spent a good deal of that on presents for Father's birthday. We got him a paper-weight, like a glass bun, with a picture of Lewisham Church at the bottom; and a blotting-pad, and a box of preserved fruits, and an ivory penholder with a view of Greenwich Park in the little hole where you look through at the top. He was most awfully pleased and surprised, and when he heard how Noël and Oswald had earned the money to buy the things he was more surprised still. Nearly all the rest of our money went to get fireworks for the Fifth of November. We got six Catherine wheels and four rockets; two hand-lights, one red and one green; a sixpenny maroon; two Roman-candles—they cost a shilling; some Italian streamers, a fairy fountain, and a tourbillon that cost eighteen-pence and was very nearly worth it.

But I think crackers and squibs are a mistake. It's true you get a lot of them for the money, and they are not bad fun for the first two or three dozen, but you get jolly sick of them before you've let off your sixpenn'-orth. And the only amusing way is not allowed: it is putting them in the fire.

It always seems a long time till the evening when you have got fireworks in the house, and I think as it was a rather foggy day we should have decided to let them off directly after breakfast, only Father had said he would help us to let them off at eight o'clock after he had had his dinner, and you ought never to disappoint your father if you can help it.

You see we had three good reasons for trying H. O.'s idea of restoring the fallen fortunes of our house by becoming bandits on the Fifth of November. We had a fourth reason as well, and that was the best reason of the lot. You remember Dora thought it would be wrong to be bandits. And the Fifth of November came while Dora was away at Stroud staying with her godmother. Stroud is in Gloucestershire. We were determined to do it while she was out of the way, because we did not think it wrong, and besides we meant to do it anyhow.

We held a Council, of course, and laid our plans very carefully. We let H. O. be Captain, because it was his idea. Oswald was Lieutenant. Oswald was quite fair, because he let H. O. call himself Captain; but Oswald is the eldest next to Dora, after all.

Our plan was this. We were all to go up on to the Heath. Our house is in the Lewisham Road, but it's quite close to the Heath if you cut up the short way opposite the confectioner's, past the nursery gardens and the cottage hospital, and turn to the left again and afterwards to the right. You come out then at the top of the hill, where the big guns are with the iron fence round them, and where the bands play on Thursday evenings in the summer.

We were to lurk in ambush there, and waylay an unwary traveller. We were to call upon him to surrender his arms, and then bring him home and put him in the deepest dungeon below the castle moat; then we were to load him with chains and send to his friends for ransom. You may think we had no chains, but you are wrong, because we used to keep two other dogs once, besides Pincher, before the fall of the fortunes of the ancient House of Bastable. And they were quite big dogs.

It was latish in the afternoon before we started. We thought we could lurk better if it was nearly dark. It was rather foggy, and we waited a good while beside the railings, but all the belated travellers were either grown up or else they were Board School children. We weren't going to get into a row with grown-up people—especially strangers—and no true bandit would ever stoop to ask a ransom from the relations of the poor and needy. So we thought it better to wait.

As I said, it was Guy Fawkes Day, and if it had not been we should never have been able to be bandits at all, for the unwary traveller we did catch had been forbidden to go out because he had a cold in his head. But he would run out to follow a guy, without even putting on a coat or a comforter, and it was a very damp, foggy afternoon and nearly dark, so you see it was his own fault entirely, and served him jolly well right.

We saw him coming over the Heath just as we were

deciding to go home to tea. He had followed that guy right across to the village (we call Blackheath the village; I don't know why), and he was coming back dragging his feet and sniffing.

"Hist, an unwary traveller approaches!" whispered Oswald.

"Muffle your horses' heads and see to the priming of your pistols," muttered Alice. She always will play boys' parts, and she makes Ellis cut her hair short on purpose. Ellis is a very obliging hairdresser.

"Steal softly upon him," said Noël; "for lo! 'tis dusk, and no human eyes can mark our deeds."

So we ran out and surrounded the unwary traveller. It turned out to be Albert-next-door, and he was very frightened indeed until he saw who we were.

"Surrender!" hissed Oswald, in a desperate-sounding voice, as he caught the arm of the Unwary. And Albert-next-door said, "All right! I'm surrendering as hard as I can. You needn't pull my arm off."

We explained to him that resistance was useless, and I think he saw that from the first. We held him tight by both arms, and we marched him home down the hill in a hollow square of five.

He wanted to tell us about the guy, but we made him see that it was not proper for prisoners to talk to the guard, especially about guys that the prisoner had been told not to go after because of his cold.

When we got to where we live he said, "All right, I don't want to tell you. You'll wish I had afterwards. You never saw such a guy."

"I can see *you*!" said H. O. It was very rude, and Oswald told him so at once, because it is his duty as an older brother. But H. O. is very young and does not know better yet, and besides it wasn't bad for H. O.

Albert-next-door said, "You haven't any manners, and I want to go in to my tea. Let go of me!"

But Alice told him, quite kindly, that he was not going in to his tea, but coming with us.

"I'm not," said Albert-next-door; "I'm going home. Leave go! I've got a bad cold. You're making it worse." Then he tried to cough, which was very silly, because we'd seen him in the morning, and he'd told us where the cold was that he wasn't to go out with. When he had tried to cough, he said, "Leave go of me! You see my cold's getting worse."

"You should have thought of that before," said Dicky; "you're coming in with us."

"Don't be a silly," said Noël; "you know we told you at the very beginning that resistance was useless. There is no disgrace in yielding. We are five to your one."

By this time Eliza had opened the door, and we thought it best to take him in without any more parleying. To parley with a prisoner is not done by bandits.

Directly we got him safe into the nursery, H. O. began to jump about and say, "Now you're a prisoner really and truly!"

And Albert-next-door began to cry. He always does. I wonder he didn't begin long before—but Alice fetched him one of the dried fruits we gave Father for his birthday. It was a green walnut. I have noticed the walnuts and the plums always get left till the last in the box; the apricots go first, and then the figs and pears; and the cherries, if there are any.

So he ate it and shut up. Then we explained his position to him, so that there should be no mistake, and he couldn't say afterwards that he had not understood.

"There will be no violence," said Oswald—he was now Captain of the Bandits, because we all know H. O. likes to be Chaplain when we play prisoners—'no violence. But you will be confined in a dark, subterranean dungeon where toads and snakes crawl, and but little of the light of day filters through the heavily mullioned windows. You will be loaded with chains. Now don't begin again, Baby, there's nothing to cry about; straw will be your pallet; beside you the gaoler will set a ewer—a ewer is only a jug, stupid; it won't eat you—a ewer with water; and a mouldering crust will be your food."

But Albert-next-door never enters into the spirit of a thing. He mumbled something about tea-time.

Now Oswald, though stern, is always just, and besides we were all rather hungry, and tea was ready. So we had it at once, Albert-next-door and all—and we gave him what was left of the four-pound jar of apricot jam we got with the money Noël got for his poetry. And we saved our crusts for the prisoner.

Albert-next-door was very tiresome. Nobody could have had a nicer prison than he had. We fenced him into a corner with the old wire nursery fender and all the chairs, instead of putting him in the coal-cellar as we had first intended. And when he said the dog-chains were cold the girls were kind enough to warm his fetters thoroughly at the fire before we put them on him.

We got the straw cases of some bottles of wine someone sent Father one Christmas—it is some years ago, but the cases are quite good. We unpicked them very carefully and pulled them to pieces and scattered the straw about. It made a lovely straw pallet, and took ever so long to make—but Albert-next-door has yet to learn what gratitude really is. We got the bread trencher for the wooden platter where the prisoner's crusts were put—they were not mouldy, but we could not wait till they got so, and for the ewer we got the toilet jug out of the spare-room where nobody ever sleeps. And even then Albert-next-door couldn't be happy like the rest of us. He howled and cried and tried to get out, and he knocked the ewer over and stamped on the mouldering crusts. Luckily there was no water in the ewer because we had forgotten it, only dust and spiders. So we tied him up with the clothes-line from the back kitchen, and we had to hurry up, which was a pity for him. We might have had him rescued by a devoted page if he hadn't been so tiresome. In fact Noël was actually dressing up for the page when Albert-next-door kicked over the prison ewer.

We got a sheet of paper out of an old exercise-book, and we made H. O. prick his own thumb, because he is our little brother and it is our duty to teach him to be brave. We none of us mind pricking ourselves; we've done it heaps of times. H. O. didn't like it, but he agreed to do it, and I helped him a little because he was so slow, and when he saw the red bead of blood getting fatter and bigger as I squeezed his thumb he was very pleased, just as I had told him he would be.

This is what we wrote with H. O.'s blood, only the blood gave out when we got to "Restored", and we had to write the rest with crimson lake, which is not the same colour, though I always use it, myself, for painting wounds.

While Oswald was writing it he heard Alice whispering to the prisoner that it would soon be over, and it was only play. The prisoner left off howling, so I pretended not to hear what she said. A Bandit Captain has to overlook things sometimes. This was the letter—

"Albert Morrison is held a prisoner by Bandits. On payment of three thousand pounds he will be restored to his sorrowing relatives, and all will be forgotten and forgiven."

I was not sure about the last part, but Dicky was certain he had seen it in the paper, so I suppose it must have been all right.

We let H. O. take the letter; it was only fair, as it was his blood it was written with, and told him to leave it next door for Mrs Morrison.

H. O. came back quite quickly, and Albert-next-door's uncle came with him.

"What is all this, Albert?" he cried. "Alas, alas, my nephew! Do I find you the prisoner of a desperate band of brigands?"

"Bandits," said H. O., "you know it says bandits."

"I beg your pardon, gentlemen," said Albert-next-door's uncle, "bandits it is, of course. This, Albert is the direct result of the pursuit of the guy on an occasion when your doting mother had expressly warned you to forgo the pleasures of the chase."

Albert said it wasn't his fault, and he hadn't wanted to play.

"So ho!" said his uncle, "impenitent too! Where's the dungeon?"

We explained the dungeon, and showed him the straw pallet and the ewer and the mouldering crusts and other things.

"Very pretty and complete," he said. "Albert, you are more highly privileged than ever I was. No one ever made me a nice dungeon when I was your age. I think I had better leave you where you are."

Albert began to cry again and said he was sorry, and he would be a good boy.

"And on this old familiar basis you expect me to ransom you, do you? Honestly, my nephew, I doubt whether you are worth it. Besides, the sum mentioned in this document strikes me as excessive; Albert really is *not* worth three thousand pounds. Also by a stranger and unfortunate chance I haven't the money about me. Couldn't you take less?"

We said perhaps we could.

"Say eightpence," suggested Albert-next-door's uncle, "which is all the small change I happen to have on my person."

"Thank you very much," said Alice as he held it out; "but are you sure you can spare it? Because really it was only play."

"Quite sure. Now, Albert, the game is over. You had better run home to your mother and tell her how much you've enjoyed yourself."

When Albert-next-door had gone his uncle sat in the Guy Fawkes armchair and took Alice on his knee, and we sat round the fire waiting till it would be time to let off our fireworks. We roasted the chestnuts he sent Dicky out for, and he told us stories till it was nearly seven. His stories are first-rate—he does all the parts in different voices. At last he said—

"Look here, young-uns. I like to see you play and enjoy yourselves, and I don't think it hurts Albert to cnjoy himself too."

"I don't think he did much," said H. O. But I knew what Albert-next-door's uncle meant because I am much older than H. O. He went on—

"But what about Albert's mother? Didn't you think how anxious she would be at his not coming home? As it happens I saw him come in with you, so we knew it was all right. But if I hadn't, eh?"

He only talks like that when he is very serious, or even angry. Other times he talks like people in books—to us, I mean.

We none of us said anything. But I was thinking. Then Alice spoke.

Girls seem not to mind saying things that we don't say. She put her arms round Albert-next-door's uncle's neck and said—

"We're very, very sorry. We didn't think about his mother. You see we try very hard not to think about other people's mothers because—"

Just then we heard Father's key in the door and Albert-next-door's uncle kissed Alice and put her down, and we all went down to meet Father. As we went I thought I heard Albert-next-door's uncle say something that sounded like "Poor little beggars!"

He couldn't have meant us, when we'd been having such a jolly time, and chestnuts, and fireworks to look forward to after dinner and everything!

CHAPTER 8

BEING EDITORS

It was Albert's uncle who thought of our trying a newspaper. He said he thought we should not find the bandit business a paying industry, as a permanency, and that journalism might be.

We had sold Noël's poetry and that piece of information about Lord Tottenham to the good editor, so we thought it would not be a bad idea to have a newspaper of our own. We saw plainly that editors must be very rich and powerful, because of the grand office and the man in the glass case, like a museum, and the soft carpets and big writing-table. Besides our having seen a whole handful of money that the editor pulled out quite carelessly from his trousers pocket when he gave me my five bob.

Dora wanted to be editor and so did Oswald, but he gave way to her because she is a girl, and afterwards he knew that it is true what it says in the copy-books about Virtue being its own Reward. Because you've no idea what a bother it is. Everybody wanted to put in everything just as they liked, no matter how much room there was on the page. It was simply awful! Dora put up with it as long as she could and then she said if she wasn't let alone she wouldn't go on being editor; they could be the paper's editors themselves, so there.

Then Oswald said, like a good brother: "I will help you if you like, Dora," and she said, "You're more trouble than all the rest of them! Come and be editor and see how you like it. I give it up to you." But she didn't, and we did it together. We let Albert-next-door be sub-editor, because he had hurt his foot with a nail in his boot that gathered.

When it was done Albert-next-door's uncle had it copied for us in typewriting, and we sent copies to all our friends, and then of course there was no one left that we could ask to buy it. We did not think of that until too late. We called the paper the *Lewisham Recorder*; Lewisham because we live there, and Recorder in memory of the good editor. I could write a better paper on my head, but an editor is not allowed to write all the paper. It is very hard, but he is not. You just have to fill up with what you can get from other writers. If I ever have time I will write a paper all by myself. It won't be patchy. We had no time to make it an illustrated paper, but I drew the ship going down with all hands for the first copy. But the typewriter can't draw ships, so it was left out in the other copies. The time the first paper took to write out no one would believe! This was the Newspaper:

The Lewisham Recorder

EDITORS: DORA AND OSWALD BASTABLE

Editorial Note

Every paper is written for some reason. Ours is because we want to sell it and get money. If what we have written brings happiness to any sad heart we shall not have laboured in vain. But we want the money too. Many papers are content with the sad heart and the happiness, but we are not like that, and it is best not to be deceitful. EDITORS.

There will be two serial stories; one by Dicky and one by all of us. In a serial story you only put in one chapter at a time.

But we shall put all our serial story at once, if Dora has time to copy it. Dicky's will come later on.

Serial Story

BY US ALL

Chapter I—*by Dora*

The sun was setting behind a romantic-looking tower when two strangers might have been observed descending the crest of the hill. The eldest, a man in the prime of life; the other a handsome youth who reminded everybody of Quentin Durward. They approached the Castle, in which the fair Lady Alicia awaited her deliverers. She leaned from the castellated window and waved her lily hand as they approached. They returned her signal, and retired to seek rest and refreshment at a neighbouring hostelry.

Chapter II—*by Alice*

The Princess was very uncomfortable in the tower, because her fairy godmother had told her all sorts of horrid things would happen if she didn't catch a mouse every day, and she had caught so many mice that now there were hardly any left to catch. So she sent her carrier pigeon to ask the noble strangers if they could send her a few mice because she would be of age in a few days and then it wouldn't matter. So the fairy godmother—(I'm very sorry, but there's no room to make the chapters any longer. ED.)

Chapter III—*by the Sub-Editor*

(I can't—I'd much rather not—I don't know how.)

Chapter IV—*by Dicky*

I must now retrace my steps and tell you something about our hero. You must know he had been to an awfully jolly school, where they had turkey and goose every day for dinner, and never any mutton, and as many helps of pudding as a fellow cared to send up his plate for—so of course they had all grown up very strong, and before he left school he challenged the Head to have it out man to man, and he gave it him, I tell you. That was the education that made him able to fight Red Indians, and to be the stranger who might have been obgerved in the first chapter.

CHAPTER V—*by Noël*

I think it's time something happened in this story. So then the dragon he came out, blowing fire out of his nose, and he said—

"Come on, you valiant man and true,
I'd like to have a set-to along of you!"

(That's bad English. ED. I don't care; it's what the dragon said. Who told you dragons didn't talk bad English? NOËL.)

So the hero, whose name was Noëloninuris, replied—

"My blade is sharp, my axe is keen,
You're not nearly as big as a good many dragons I've seen."

(Don't put in so much poetry, Noël. It's not fair, because none of the others can do it. ED.)

And then they went at it, and he beat the dragon, just as he did the Head in Dicky's part of the story, and so he married the Princess, and they lived—(No they didn't not till the last chapter. ED.)

CHAPTER VI—*by H. O.*

I think it's a very nice story—but what about the mice? I don't want to say any more. Dora can have what's left af my chapter.

CHAPTER VII—*by the Editors*

And so when the dragon was dead there were lots of mice, because he used to kill them for his tea; but now they rapidly multiplied and ravaged the country, so the fair lady Alicia, sometimes called the Princess, had to say she would not marry any one unless they could rid the country of this plague of mice. Then the Prince, whose real name didn't begin with N, but was Osrawalddo, waved his magic sword, and the dragon stood before them, bowing gracefully. They made him promise to be good, and then they forgave him; and when the wedding breakfast came, all the bones were saved for him. And so they were married and lived happy ever after.

(What became of the other stranger? NOËL. The dragon ate him because he asked too many questions. EDITORS.)

This is the end of the story.

Instructive

It only takes four hours and a quarter now to get from London to Manchester; but I should not think any one would if they could help it.

A dreadful warning. A wicked boy told me a very instructive thing about ginger. They had opened one of the large jars, and he happened to take out quite a lot, and he made it all right by dropping marbles in, till there was as much ginger as before. But he told me that on the Sunday, when it was coming near the part where there is only juice generally, I had no idea what his feelings were. I don't see what he could have said when they asked him. I should be sorry to act like it.

Scientific

Experiments should always be made out of doors. And don't use benzoline. DICKY.

(That was when he burnt his eyebrows off. ED.)

The earth is 2,400 miles round, and 800 through—at least I think so, but perhaps it's the other way. DICKY.

(You ought to have been sure before you began. ED.)

Scientific Column

In this so-called Nineteenth Century Science is but too little considered in the nurseries of the rich and proud. But we are not like that.

It is not generally known that if you put bits of camphor in luke-warm water it will move about. If you drop sweet oil in, the camphor will dart away and then stop moving. But don't drop any till you are tired of it, because the camphor won't any more afterwards. Much amusement and instruction is lost by not knowing things like this.

If you put a sixpence under a shilling in a wine-glass, and blow hard down the side of the glass, the sixpence will jump up and sit on the top of the shilling. At least I can't do it myself, but my cousin can. He is in the Navy.

Answers to Correspondents

Noël. You are very poetical, but I am sorry to say it will not do.

Alice. Nothing will ever make your hair curl, so it's no use. Some people say it's more important to tidy up as you go along. I don't mean you in particular, but every one.

H. O. We never said you were tubby, but the Editor does not know any cure.

Noël. If there is any of the paper over when this newspaper is finished, I will exchange it for your shut-up inkstand, or the knife that has the useful thing in it for taking stones out of horses' feet, but you can't have it without.

H. O. There are many ways how your steam engine might stop working. You might ask Dicky. He knows one of them. I think it is the way yours stopped.

Noël. If you think that by filling the garden with sand you can make crabs build their nests there you are not at all sensible.

You have altered your poem about the battle of Waterloo so often, that we cannot read it except where the Duke waves his sword and says some thing we can't read either. Why did you write it on blotting-paper with purple chalk? ED

(Because you know who sneaked my pencil. NOËL.)

Poetry

The Assyrian came down like a wolf on the fold,
And the way he came down was awful, I'm told;
But it's nothing to the way one of the Editors comes down on me,
If I crumble my bread-and-butter or spill my tea. NOËL.

Curious Facts

If you hold a guinea-pig up by his tail his eyes drop out.

You can't do half the things yourself that children in books do, making models or so on. I wonder why? ALICE.

If you take a date's stone out and put in an almond and eat them together, it is prime. I found this out. SUB-EDITOR.

If you put your wet hand into boiling lead it will not hurt you if you draw it out quickly enough. I have never tried this. DORA.

The Purring Class

(INSTRUCTIVE ARTICLE

If I ever keep a school everything shall be quite different. Nobody shall learn anything they don't want to. And sometimes instead of having masters and mistresses we will have cats, and we will dress up in cat skins and learn purring.

"Now, my dears," the old cat will say, "one, two, three all purr together," and we shall purr like anything.

She won't teach us to mew, but we shall know how without teaching. Children do know some things without being taught. ALICE.

Poetry

(TRANSLATED INTO FRENCH BY DORA)

Quand j'étais jeune et j'étais fou
J'achetai un violon pour dix-huit sous
Et tous les airs que je jouai
Etait over the hills and far away.

ANOTHER PIECE OF IT

Merci jolie vache qui fait
Bon lait pour mon déjeuner
Tour les matins tous les soirs
Mon pain je mange, ton lait je boire

Recreations

It is a mistake to think that cats are playful. I often try to get a cat to play with me, and she never seems to care about the game, no matter how little it hurts. H.O..

Making pots and pans with clay is fun, but do not tell the grown-ups. It is better to surprise them; and then you must say at once how easily it washes off—much easier than ink. DICKY.

Sam Redfern, or the Bushranger's Burial

BY DICKY

"Well, Annie, I have bad news for you," said Mr Ridgway, as he entered the comfortable dining-room of his cabin in the Bush. "Sam Redfern the Bushranger is about this part of the Bush just now. I hope he will not attack us with his gang."

"I hope not," responded Annie, a gentle maiden of some sixteen summers.

Just then came a knock at the door of the hut, and a gruff voice asked them to open the door.

"It is Sam Redfern the Bushranger, father," said the girl.

"The same," responded the voice, and the next moment the hall door was smashed in, and Sam Redfern sprang in, followed by his gang.

Chapter II

Annie's Father was at once overpowered, and Annie herself lay bound with cords on the drawing-room sofa. Sam Redfern set a guard round the lonely hut, and all human aid was despaired of. But you never know. Far away in the Bush a different scene was being enacted.

"Must be Injuns," said a tall man to himself as he pushed his way through the brushwood. It was Jim Carlton, the celebrated detective. "I know them," he added; "they are Apaches." Just then ten Indians in full war-paint appeared. Carlton raised his rifle and fired, and slinging their scalp on his arm he hastened towards the humble log hut where resided his affianced bride, Annie Ridgway, sometimes known as the Flower of the Bush.

Chapter III

The moon was low on the horizon, and Sam Redfern was seated at a drinking bout with some of his boon companions.

They had rifled the cellars of the hut, and the rich wines flowed like water in the golden goblets of Mr Ridgway.

But Annie had made friends with one of the gang, a noble, good-hearted man who had joined Sam Redfern by mistake, and she had told him to go and get the police as quickly as possible.

"Ha! ha!" cried Redfern, "now I am enjoying myself." He

little knew that his doom was near upon him.

Just then Annie gave a piercing scream, and Sam Redfern got up, seizing his revolver.

"Who are you?" he cried, as a man entered.

"I am Jim Carlton, the celebrated detective," said tho new arrival.

Sam Redfern's revolver dropped from his nervous fingers, but the next moment he had sprung upon the detective with the well-known activity of the mountain sheep, and Annie shrieked, for she had grown to love the rough Bushranger.

(*To be continued at the end of the paper if there is room.*)

Scholastic

A new slate is horrid till it is washed in milk. I like the green spots on them to draw patterns round. I know a good way to make a slate-pencil squeak, but I won't put it in because I don't want to make it common. SUB-EDITOR.

Peppermint is a great help with arithmetic. The boy who was second in the Oxford Local always did it. He gave me two. The examiner said to him, "Are you eating peppermints?" And he said, "No, sir." He told me afterwards it was quite true, because he was only sucking one. I'm glad I wasn't asked. I should never have thought of that, and I should have had to say "Yes." OSWALD.

The Wreck of the "Malabar"

BY NOËL

(Author of "A Dream of Ancient Ancestors.") He isn't really—but he put it in to make it seem more real.

Hark! what is that noise of rolling
Waves and thunder in the air?
'Tis the death-knell of the sailors
And officers and passengers of the good ship Malabar.

It was a fair and lovely moon
When the good ship put out of port
And peoplc said "Ah little we think
How soon she will be the elements' sport."

She was indeed a lovely sight
Upon the billows with sails spread.
But the captain folded his gloomy arms
Ah—if she had been a life-boat instead!

See the captain stern yet gloomy
Flings his son upon a rock,
Hoping that there his darling boy
May escape the wreck.

Alas in vain the loud winds roared
And nobody was saved
That was the wreck of the Malabar,
Then let us toll for the brave. NOËL.

Gardening Notes

It is useless to plant cherry-stones in the hope of eating the fruit, because they don't!

Alice won't lend her gardening tools again, because the last time Noël left them out in the rain, and I don't like it. He said he didn't.

Seeds and Bulbs

These are useful to play at shop with, until you are ready. Not at dinner-parties, for they will not grow unless uncooked. Potatoes are not grown with seed, but with chopped-up potatoes. Apple trees are grown from twigs, which is less wasteful.

Oak trees come from acorns. Every one knows that. When Noël says he could grow one from a peach stone wrapped up in oak leaves, he shows that he knows nothing about gardening but marigolds, and when I passed by his garden I thought they seemed just like weeds now the flowers have been picked.

A boy once dared me to eat a bulb.

Dogs are very industrious and fond of gardening. Pincher is always planting bones, but they never grow up. There couldn't be a bone tree. I think this is what makes him bark so unhappily at night. He has never tried planting dogbiscuit, but he is fonder of bones, and perhaps he wants to be quite sure about them first.

Sam Redfren, or the Bushranger's Burial

BY DICKY

CHAPTER IV AND LAST

This would have been a jolly good story if they had let me finish it at the beginning of the paper as I wanted to. But now I have forgotten how I meant it to end, and I have lost my book about Red Indians, and all my *Boys of England* have been sneaked. The girls say "Good riddance!" so I expect they did it. They want me just to put in which Annie married, but I shan't, so they will never know.

We have now put everything we can think of into the paper. It takes a lot of thinking about. I don't know how grown-ups manage to write all they do. It must make their heads ache, especially lesson books.

Albert-next-door only wrote one chapter of the serial story, but he could have done some more if he had wanted to. He could not write out any of the things because he cannot spell. He says he can, but it takes him such a long time he might just as well not be able. There are one or two things more. I am sick of it, but Dora says she will write them in.

Legal answer wanted. A quantity of excellent string is offered if you know whether there really is a law passed about not buying gunpowder under thirteen. DICKY.

The price of this paper is one shilling each, and sixpence extra for the picture of the *Malabar* going down with all hands. If we sell one hundred copies we will write another paper.

And so we would have done, but we never did. Albert-next-door's uncle gave us two shillings, that was all. You can't restore fallen fortunes with two shillings!

Chapter 9

The G. B.

Being editors is not the best way to wealth. We all feel this now, and highwaymen are not respected any more like they used to be.

I am sure we had tried our best to restore our fallen fortunes. We felt their fall very much, because we knew the Bastables had been rich once. Dora and Oswald can remember when Father was always bringing nice things home from London, and there used to be turkeys and geese and wine and cigars come by the carrier at Christmas-time, and boxes of candied fruit and French plums in ornamental boxes with silk and velvet and gilding on them. They were called prunes, but the prunes you buy at the grocer's are quite different. But now there is seldom anything nice brought from London, and the turkey and the prune people have forgotten Father's address.

"How *can* we restore those beastly fallen fortunes?" said Oswald. "We've tried digging and writing and princesses and being editors."

"And being bandits," said H. O.

"When did you try that?" asked Dora quickly. "You know I told you it was wrong."

"It wasn't wrong the way we did it?" said Alice, quicker still, before Oswald could say, "Who asked you to tell us anything about it?" which would have been rude, and he is glad he didn't. "We only caught Albert-next-door."

"Oh, Albert-next-door!" said Dora contemptuously, and I felt more comfortable; for even after I didn't say, "Who asked you, and cetera," I was afraid Dora was going to come the good elder sister over us. She does that a jolly sight too often.

Dicky looked up from the paper he was reading and said, "This sounds likely," and he read out—

£100 secures partnership in lucrative business for sale of useful patent. £10 weekly. No personal attendance necessary. Jobbins, 300, Old Street Road.

"I wish we could secure that partnership," said Oswald. He is twelve, and a very thoughtful boy for his age.

Alice looked up from her painting. She was trying to paint a fairy queen's frock with green bice, and it wouldn't rub. There is something funny about green bice. It never will rub off, no matter how expensive your paintbox is—and even boiling water is very little use.

She said, "Bother the bice! And, Oswald, it's no use thinking about that. Where are we to get a hundred pounds?"

"Ten pounds a week is five pounds to us," Oswald went on—he had done the sum in his head while Alice was talking—"because partnership means halves. It would be A1."

Noël sat sucking his pencil—he had been writing poetry as usual. I saw the first two lines—

I wonder why Green Bice
Is never very nice.

Suddenly he said, "I wish a fairy would come down the chimney and drop a jewel on the table—a jewel worth just a hundred pounds."

"She might as well give you the hundred pounds while she was about it," said Dora.

"Or while she was about it she might as well give us five pounds a week," said Alice.

"Or fifty," said I.

"Or five hundred," said Dicky.

I saw H. O. open his mouth, and I knew he was going to say, "Or five thousand," so I said:

"Well, she won't give us fivepence, but if you'd only do as I am always saying, and rescue a wealthy old gentleman from deadly peril he would give us a pot of money, and we could have the partnership and five pounds a week. Five pounds a week would buy a great many things."

Then Dicky said, "Why shouldn't we borrow it?"

So we said, "Who from?" and then he read this out of the paper

MONEY PRIVATELY WITHOUT FEES
THE BOND STREET BANK

Manager Z. Rosenbaum.

Advances cash from £20 to £10,000 on ladies' or gentlemen's note of hand alone, without security. No fees. No inquiries. Absolute privacy guaranteed.

"What does it all mean?" asked H. O.

"It means that there is a kind gentleman who has a lot of money, and he doesn't know enough poor people to help, so he puts it in the paper that he will help them, by lending them his money—that's it, isn't it, Dicky?"

Dora explained this and Dicky said, "Yes." And H. O. said he was a Generous Benefactor, like in Miss Edgeworth. Then Noël wanted to know what a note of hand was, and Dicky knew that, because he had read it in a book, and it was just a letter saying you will pay the money when you can, and signed with your name.

"No inquiries!" said Alice. "Oh—Dicky—do you think he would?"

"Yes, I think so," said Dicky. "I wonder Father doesn't go to this kind gentleman. I've seen his name before on a circular in Father's study."

"Perhaps he has," said Dora.

But the rest of us were sure he hadn't, because, of course, if he had, there would have been more money to buy nice things. Just then Pincher jumped up and knocked over the painting-water. He is a very careless dog. I wonder why painting water is always such an ugly colour? Dora ran for a duster to wipe it up, and H. O. dropped drops of the water on his hands and said he had got the plague. So we played at the plague for a bit, and I was an Arab physician with a bathtowel turban, and cured the plague with magic acid-drops. After that it was time for dinner, and after dinner we talked it all over and settled that we would go and see the Generous Benefactor the very next day. But we thought perhaps the G. B.—it is short for Generous Benefactor—would not like it if there were so many of us. I have often noticed that it is the worst of our being six—people think six a great many, when it's children. That sentence looks wrong somehow. I mean they don't mind six pairs of boots, or six pounds of apples, or six oranges, especially in equations, but they seem to think you ought not to have five brothers and sisters. Of course Dicky was to go, because it was his idea. Dora had to go to Blackheath to see an old lady, a friend of Father's, so she couldn't go. Alice said she ought to go, because it said, "Ladies and gentlemen," and perhaps the G. B. wouldn't let us have the money unless there were both kinds of us.

H. O. said Alice wasn't a lady; and she said *he* wasn't going, anyway. Then he called her a disagreeable cat, and she began to cry.

But Oswald always tries to make up quarrels, so he said—

"You're little sillies, both of you!"

And Dora said, "Don't cry, Alice; he only meant you weren't a grown-up lady."

Then H. O. said, "What else did you think I meant, Disagreeable?"

So Dicky said, "Don't be disagreeable yourself, H. O. Let her alone and say you're sorry, or I'll jolly well make you!"

So H. O. said he was sorry. Then Alice kissed him and said she was sorry too; and after that H. O. gave her a hug, and said, "Now I'm *really and truly* sorry," so it was all right.

Noël went the last time any of us went to London, so he was out of it, and Dora said she would take him to Blackheath if we'd take H. O. So as there'd been a little disagreeableness we thought it was better to take him, and we did. At first we thought we'd tear our oldest things a bit more, and put some patches of different colours on them, to show the G. B. how much we wanted money. But Dora said that would be a sort of cheating, pretending we were poorer than we are. And Dora is right sometimes, though she is our elder sister. Then we thought we'd better wear our best things, so that the G. B. might see we weren't so very poor that he couldn't trust us to pay his money back when we had it. But Dora said that would be wrong too. So it came to our being quite honest, as Dora said, and going just as we were, without even washing our faces and hands, but when I looked at H. O. in the train I wished we had not been quite so particularly honest.

Every one who reads this knows what it is like to go in the train, so I shall not tell about it—though it was rather fun, especially the part where the guard came for the tickets at Waterloo, and H. O. was under the seat and pretended to be a dog without a ticket. We went to Charing Cross, and we just went round to Whitehall to see the soldiers and then by St James's for the same reason—and when we'd looked in the shops a bit we got to Brook Street, Bond Street. It was a brass plate on a door next to a shop—a very grand place, where they sold bonnets and hats—all very bright and smart, and no tickets on them to tell you the price. We rang a bell and a boy opened the door and we asked for Mr Rosenbaum. The boy was not polite; he did not ask us in. So then Dicky gave him his visiting card; it was one of Father's really, but the name is the same, Mr Richard Bastable, and we others wrote our names underneath. I happened to have a piece of pink chalk in my pocket and we wrote them with that.

Then the boy shut the door in our faces and we waited on the step. But presently he came down and asked our business. So Dicky said—

"Money advanced, young shaver! and don't be all day about it!"

And then he made us wait again, till I was quite stiff in my legs, but Alice liked it because of looking at the hats and bonnets, and at last the door opened, and the boy said—

"Mr Rosenbaum will see you," so we wiped our feet on the mat, which said so, and we went up stairs with soft carpets and into a room. It was a beautiful room. I wished then we had put on our best things, or at least washed a little. But it was too late now.

The room had velvet curtains and a soft, soft carpet, and it was full of the most splendid things. Black and gold cabinets, and china, and statues, and pictures. There was a picture of a cabbage and a pheasant and a dead hare that was just like life, and I would have given worlds to have it for my own. The fur was so natural I should never have been tired of looking at it; but Alice liked the one of the girl with the broken jug best. Then besides the pictures there were clocks and candlesticks and vases, and gilt looking glasses, and boxes of cigars and scent and things littered all over the chairs and tables. It was a wonderful place, and in the middle of all the splendour was a little old gentleman with a very long black coat and a very long white beard and a hookey nose—like a falcon. And he put on a pair of gold spectacles and looked at us as if he knew exactly how much our clothes were worth. And then, while we elder ones were thinking how to begin, for we had all said "Good morning" as we came in, of course, H. O. began before we could stop him. He said:

"Are you the G. B.?"

"The what?" said the little old gentleman.

"The G. B.," said H. O., and I winked at him to shut up, but he didn't see me, and the G. B. did. He waved his hand at me to shut up, so I had to, and H. O. went on—

"It stands for Generous Benefactor."

The old gentleman frowned. Then he said, "Your Father sent you here, I suppose?"

"No he didn't," said Dicky. "Why did you think so?"

The old gentleman held out the card, and I explained

that we took that because Father's name happens to be the same as Dicky's.

"Doesn't he know you've come?"

"No," said Alice, "we shan't tell him till we've got the partnership, because his own business worries him a good deal and we don't want to bother him with ours till it's settled, and then we shall give him half our share."

The old gentleman took off his spectacles and rumpled his hair with his hands, then he said, "Then what *did* you come for?"

"We saw your advertisement," Dicky said, "and we want a hundred pounds on our note of hand, and my sister came so that there should be both kinds of us; and we want it to buy a partnership with in the lucrative business for sale of useful patent. No personal attendance necessary."

"I don't think I quite follow you," said the G. B. "But one thing I should like settled before entering more fully into the matter: why did you call me Generous Benefactor?"

"Well, you see," said Alice, smiling at him to show she wasn't frightened, though I know really she was, awfully, "we thought it was so *very* kind of you to try to find out the poor people who want money and to help them and lend them your money."

"Hum!" said the G. B. "Sit down."

He cleared the clocks and vases and candlesticks off some of the chairs, and we sat down. The chairs were velvety, with gilt legs. It was like a king's palace.

"Now," he said, "you ought to be at school, instead of thinking about money. Why aren't you?"

We told him that we should go to school again when Father could manage it, but meantime we wanted to do something to restore the fallen fortunes of the House of Bastable. And we said we thought the lucrative patent would be a very good thing. He asked a lot of questions, and we told him everything we didn't think Father would mind our telling, and at last he said—

"You wish to borrow money. When will you repay it?"

"As soon as we've got it, of course," Dicky said.

Then the G. B. said to Oswald, "You seem the eldest," but I explained to him that it was Dicky's idea, so my being eldest didn't matter. Then he said to Dicky—

"You are a minor, I presume?"

Dicky said he wasn't yet, but he had thought of being a mining engineer some day, and going to Klondike.

"Minor, not miner," said the G. B. "I mean you're not of age?"

"I shall be in ten years, though," said Dicky.

"Then you might repudiate the loan," said the G. B., and Dicky said "What?" Of course he ought to have said "I beg your pardon. I didn't quite catch what you said"—that is what Oswald would have said. It is more polite than "What."

"Repudiate the loan," the G. B. repeated. "I mean you might say you would not pay me back the money, and the law could not compel you to do so."

"Oh, well, if you think we're such sneaks," said Dicky, and he got up off his chair. But the G. B. said, "Sit down, sit down; I was only joking."

Then he talked some more, and at last he said—

"I don't advise you to enter into that partnership. It's a swindle. Many advertisements are. And I have not a hundred pounds by me to-day to lend you. But I will lend you a pound, and you can spend it as you like.

And when you are twenty-one you shall pay me back."

"I shall pay you back long before that," said Dicky. "Thanks, awfully! And what about the note of hand?"

"Oh," said the G. B., "I'll trust to your honour. Between gentlemen, you know—and ladies"—he made a beautiful bow to Alice—"a word is as good as a bond."

Then he took out a sovereign, and held it in his hand while he talked to us. He gave us a lot of good advice about not going into business too young, and about doing our lessons—just swatting a bit, on our own hook, so as not to be put in a low form when we went back to school. And all the time he was stroking the sovereign and looking at it as if he thought it very beautiful. And so it was, for it was a new one. Then at last he held it out to Dicky, and when Dicky put out his hand for it the G. B. suddenly put the sovereign back in his pocket.

"No," he said, "I won't give you the sovereign. I'll give you fifteen shillings, and this nice bottle of scent. It's worth far more than the five shillings I'm charging you for it. And, when you can, you shall pay me back the pound, and sixty per cent interest—sixty per cent, sixty per cent—"

"What's that?" said H. O.

The G. B. said he'd tell us that when we paid back the sovereign, but sixty per cent was nothing to be afraid of. He gave Dicky the money. And the boy was made to call a cab, and the G. B. put us in and shook hands with us all, and asked Alice to give him a kiss, so she did, and H. O. would do it too, though his face was dirtier than ever. The G. B. paid the cabman and told him what station to go to, and so we went home.

That evening Father had a letter by the seven o'clock

post. And when he had read it he came up into the nursery. He did not look quite so unhappy as usual, but he looked grave.

"You've been to Mr Rosenbaum's," he said.

So we told him all about it. It took a long time, and Father sat in the armchair. It was jolly. He doesn't often come and talk to us now. He has to spend all his time thinking about his business. And when we'd told him all about it he said—

"You haven't done any harm this time, children; rather good than harm, indeed. Mr Rosenbaum has written me a very kind letter."

"Is he a friend of yours, Father?" Oswald asked.

"He is an acquaintance," said my father, frowning a little, "we have done some business together. And this letter—" He stopped and then said: "No; you didn't do any harm to-day; but I want you for the future not to do anything so serious as to try to buy a partnership without consulting me, that's all. I don't want to interfere with your plays and pleasures; but you will consult me about business matters, won't you?"

Of course we said we should be delighted, but then Alice, who was sitting on his knee, said, "We didn't like to bother you."

Father said, "I haven't much time to be with you, for my business takes most of my time. It is an anxious business—but I can't bear to think of your being left all alone like this."

He looked so sad we all said we liked being alone. And then he looked sadder than ever.

Then Alice said, "We don't mean that exactly, Father. It is rather lonely sometimes, since Mother died."

Then we were all quiet a little while.

Father stayed with us till we went to bed, and when

he said good night he looked quite cheerful. So we told him so, and he said—

"Well, the fact is, that letter took a weight off my mind."

I can't think what he meant—but I am sure the G. B. would be pleased if he could know he had taken a weight off somebody's mind. He is that sort of man, I think.

We gave the scent to Dora. It is not quite such good scent as we thought it would be, but we had fifteen shillings—and they were all good, so is the G. B.

And until those fifteen shillings were spent we felt almost as jolly as though our fortunes had been properly restored. You do not notice your general fortune so much, as long as you have money in your pocket. This is why so many children with regular pocket-money have never felt it their duty to seek for treasure. So, perhaps, our not having pocket-money was a blessing in disguise. But the disguise was quite impenetrable, like the villains' in the books; and it seemed still more so when the fifteen shillings were all spent. Then at last the others agreed to let Oswald try his way of seeking for treasure, but they were not at all keen about it, and many a boy less firm than Oswald would have chucked the whole thing. But Oswald knew that a hero must rely on himself alone. So he stuck to it, and presently the others saw their duty, and backed him up.

Chapter 10

LORD TOTTENHAM

Oswald is a boy of firm and unswerving character, and he had never wavered from his first idea. He felt quite certain that the books were right, and that the best way to restore fallen fortunes was to rescue an old gentleman in distress. Then he brings you up as his own son: but if you preferred to go on being your own father's son I expect the old gentleman would make it up to you some other way. In the books the least thing does it—you put up the railway carriage window—or you pick up the purse when he drops it—or you say a hymn when he suddenly asks you to, and then your fortune is made.

The others, as I said, were very slack about it, and did not seem to care much about trying the rescue. They said there wasn't any deadly peril, and we should have to make one before we could rescue the old gentleman from it, but Oswald didn't see that that mattered. However, he thought he would try some of the easier ways first, by himself.

So he waited about the station, pulling up railway carriage windows for old gentlemen who looked likely but nothing happened, and at last the porters said he was a nuisance. So that was no go. No one ever asked him to say a hymn, though he had learned a nice short one, beginning "New every morning"—and when an old gentleman did drop a two-shilling piece just by Ellis's the hairdresser's, and Oswald picked it up, and was just thinking what he should say when he returned it, the old gentleman caught him by the collar and called him a young thief. It would have been very unpleasant for Oswald if he hadn't happened to be a very brave boy, and knew the policeman on that beat very well indeed. So the policeman backed him up, and the old gentleman said he was sorry, and offered Oswald sixpence. Oswald refused it with polite disdain, and nothing more happened at all.

When Oswald had tried by himself and it had not come off, he said to the others, "We're wasting our time, not trying to rescue the old gentleman in deadly peril. Come—buck up! Do let's do somethingl"

It was dinner-time, and Pincher was going round getting the bits off the plates. There were plenty because it was cold-mutton day. And Alice said—

"It's only fair to try Oswald's way—he has tried all the things the others thought of. Why couldn't we rescue Lord Tottenham?"

Lord Tottenham is the old gentleman who walks over the Heath every day in a paper collar at three o'clock—and when he gets halfway, if there is no one about, he changes his collar and throws the dirty one into the furze-bushes.

Dicky said, "Lord Tottenham's all right—but where's the deadly peril?"

And we couldn't think of any. There are no highwaymen on Blackheath now, I am sorry to say. And though Oswald said half of us could be highwaymen and the other half rescue party, Dora kept on saying it would be wrong to be a highwayman—and so we had to give that up.

Then Alice said, "What about Pincher?"

And we all saw at once that it could be done.

Pincher is very well bred, and he does know one or two things, though we never could teach him to beg. But if you tell him to hold on—he will do it, even if you only say "Seize him!" in a whisper.

So we arranged it all. Dora said she wouldn't play; she said she thought it was wrong, and she knew it was silly—so we left her out, and she went and sat in the dining-room with a goody-book, so as to be able to say she didn't have anything to do with it, if we got into a row over it.

Alice and H. O. were to hide in the furze-bushes just by where Lord Tottenham changes his collar, and they were to whisper, "Seize him!" to Pincher; and then when Pincher had seized Lord Tottenham we were to go and rescue him from his deadly peril. And he would say, "How can I reward you, my noble young preservers?" and it would be all right.

So we went up to the Heath. We were afraid of being late. Oswald told the others what Procrastination was—so they got to the furze-bushes a little after two o'clock, and it was rather cold. Alice and H. O. and Pincher hid, but Pincher did not like it any more than they did, and as we three walked up and down we heard him whining. And Alice kept saying, "I *am* so cold! Isn't he coming yet?" And H. O. wanted to come out and jump about to warm himself. But we told him he must learn to be a Spartan boy, and that he ought to be very thankful he hadn't got a beastly fox eating his inside all the time. H. O. is our little brother, and we are not going to let it be our fault if he grows up a milksop. Besides, it was not really cold. It was his knees—he wears socks. So they stayed where they were. And at last, when even the other three who were walking about were beginning to feel rather chilly, we saw Lord

Tottenham's big black cloak coming along, flapping in the wind like a great bird. So we said to Alice—

"Hist! he approaches. You'll know when to set Pincher on by hearing Lord Tottenham talking to himself—he always does while he is taking off his collar."

Then we three walked slowly away whistling to show we were not thinking of anything. Our lips were rather cold, but we managed to do it.

Lord Tottenham came striding along, talking to himself. People call him the mad Protectionist. I don't know what it means—but I don't think people ought to call a Lord such names.

As he passed us he said, "Ruin of the country, sir! Fatal error, fatal error!" And then we looked back and saw he was getting quite near where Pincher was, and Alice and H. O. We walked on—so that he shouldn't think we were looking—and in a minute we heard Pincher's bark, and then nothing for a bit; and then we looked round, and sure enough good old Pincher had got Lord Tottenham by the trouser leg and was holding on like billy-ho, so we started to run.

Lord Tottenham had got his collar half off—it was sticking out sideways under his ear—and he was shouting, "Help, help, murder!" exactly as if some one had explained to him beforehand what he was to do. Pincher was growling and snarling and holding on. When we got to him I stopped and said—

"Dicky, we must rescue this good old man."

Lord Tottenham roared in his fury, "Good old man be—" something or othered. "Call the dog off!"

So Oswald said. "It is a dangerous task—but who would hesitate to do an act of true bravery?"

And all the while Pincher was worrying and snarling, and Lord Tottenham shouting to us to get the dog away. He was dancing about in the road with Pincher hanging on like grim death; and his collar flapping about, where it was undone.

Then Noël said, "Haste, ere yet it be too late." So I said to Lord Tottenham—

"Stand still, aged sir, and I will endeavour to alleviate your distress."

He stood still, and I stooped down and caught hold of Pincher and whispered, "Drop it, sir; drop it!"

So then Pincher dropped it, and Lord Tottenham fastened his collar again—he never does change it if there's any one looking—and he said—

"I'm much obliged, I'm sure. Nasty vicious brute! Here's something to drink my health."

But Dicky explained that we are teetotallers, and do not drink people's healths. So Lord Tottenham said, "Well, I'm much obliged any way. And now I come to look at you—of course, you're not young ruffians, but gentlemen's sons, eh? Still, you won't be above taking a tip from an old boy—I wasn't when I was your age," and he pulled out half a sovereign.

It was very silly; but now we'd done it I felt it would be beastly mean to take the old boy's chink after putting him in such a funk. He didn't say anything about bringing us up as his own sons—so I didn't know what to do. I let Pincher go, and was just going to say he was very welcome, and we'd rather not have the money, which seemed the best way out of it, when that beastly dog spoiled the whole show. Directly I let him go he began to jump about at us and bark for joy, and try to lick our faces. He was so proud of what he'd done. Lord Tottenham opened his eyes and he just said, "The dog seems to know you."

And then Oswald saw it was all up, and he said,

"Good morning," and tried to get away. But Lord Tottenham said—

"Not so fast!" And he caught Noël by the collar. Noël gave a howl, and Alice ran out from the bushes. Noël is her favourite. I'm sure I don't know why. Lord Tottenham looked at her, and he said—

"So there are more of you!" And then H. O. came out.

"Do you complete the party?" Lord Tottenham asked him. And H. O. said there were only five of us this time.

Lord Tottenham turned sharp off and began to walk away, holding Noël by the collar. We caught up with him, and asked him where he was going, and he said, "To the Police Station." So then I said quite politely, "Well, don't take Noël; he's not strong, and he easily gets upset. Besides, it wasn't his doing. If you want to take any one take me—it was my very own idea."

Dicky behaved very well. He said, "If you take Oswald I'll go too, but don't take Noël; he's such a delicate little chap."

Lord Tottenham stopped, and he said, "You should have thought of that before." Noël was howling all the time, and his face was very white, and Alice said—

"Oh, do let Noël go, dear, good, kind Lord Tottenham; he'll faint if you don't, I know he will, he does sometimes. Oh, I wish we'd never done it! Dora said it was wrong."

"Dora displayed considerable common sense," said Lord Tottenham, and he let Noël go. And Alice put her arm round Noël and tried to cheer him up, but he was all trembly, and as white as paper.

Then Lord Tottenham said—

"Will you give me your word of honour not to try to escape?

So we said we would.

"Then follow me," he said, and led the way to a bench. We all followed, and Pincher too, with his tail between his legs—he knew something was wrong. Then Lord Tottenham sat down, and he made Oswald and Dicky and H. O. stand in front of him, but he let Alice and Noël sit down. And he said—

"You set your dog on me, and you tried to make me believe you were saving me from it. And you would have taken my half-sovereign. Such conduct is most—No—you shall tell me what it is, sir, and speak the truth."

So I had to say it was most ungentlemanly, but I said I hadn't been going to take the half-sovereign.

"Then what did you do it for?" he asked. "The truth, mind."

So I said, "I see now it was very silly, and Dora said it was wrong, but it didn't seem so till we did it. We wanted to restore the fallen fortunes of our house, and in the books if you rescue an old gentleman from deadly peril, he brings you up as his own son—or if you prefer to be your father's son, he starts you in business, so that you end in wealthy affluence; and there wasn't any deadly peril, so we made Pincher into one—and so—" I was so ashamed I couldn't go on, for it did seem an awfully mean thing. Lord Tottenham said—

"A very nice way to make your fortune—by deceit and trickery. I have a horror of dogs. If I'd been a weak man the shock might have killed me. What do you think of yourselves, eh?"

We were all crying except Oswald, and the others

say he was; and Lord Tottenham went on—

"Well, well, I see you're sorry. Let this be a lesson to you; and we'll say no more about it. I'm an old man now, but I was young once."

Then Alice slid along the bench close to him, and put her hand on his arm: her fingers were pink through the holes in her woolly gloves, and said, "I think you're very good to forgive us, and we are really very, very sorry. But we wanted to be like the children in the books—only we never have the chances they have. Everything they do turns out all right. But we *are* sorry, very, very. And I know Oswald wasn't going to take the half-sovereign. Directly you said that about a tip from an old boy I began to feel bad inside, and I whispered to H. O. that I wished we hadn't."

Then Lord Tottenham stood up, and he looked like the Death of Nelson, for he is clean shaved and it is a good face, and he said—

"Always remember never to do a dishonourable thing, for money or for anything else in the world."

And we promised we would remember. Then he took off his hat, and we took off ours, and he went away, and we went home. I never felt so cheap in all my life! Dora said, "I told you so," but we didn't mind even that so much, though it was indeed hard to bear. It was what Lord Tottenham had said about ungentlemanly. We didn't go on to the Heath for a week after that; but at last we all went, and we waited for him by the bench. When he came along Alice said, "Please, Lord Tottenham, we have not been on the Heath for a week, to be a punishment because you let us off. And we have brought you a present each if you will take them to show you are willing to make it up."

He sat down on the bench, and we gave him our

presents. Oswald gave him a sixpenny compass—he bought it with my own money on purpose to give him. Oswald always buys useful presents. The needle would not move after I'd had it a day or two, but Lord Tottenham used to be an admiral, so he will be able to make that go all right. Alice had made him a shavingcase, with a rose worked on it. And H. O. gave him his knife—the same one he once cut all the buttons off his best suit with. Dicky gave him his prize, *Naval Heroes*, because it was the best thing he had, and Noël gave him a piece of poetry he had made himself:

When sin and shame bow down the brow
When people feel just like we do now.
We are so sorry with grief and pain
We never will be so ungentlemanly again.

Lord Tottenham seemed very pleased. He thanked us, and talked to us for a bit, and when he said goodbye he said—

"All's fair weather now, mates," and shook hands.

And whenever we meet him he nods to us, and if the girls are with us he takes off his hat, so he can't really be going on thinking us ungentlemanly now.

Chapter 11

CASTILIAN AMOROSO

One day when we suddenly found that we had half a crown we decided that we really ought to try Dicky's way of restoring our fallen fortunes while yet the deed was in our power. Because it might easily have happened to us never to have half a crown again. So we decided to dally no longer with being journalists and bandits and things like them, but to send for sample and instructions how to earn two pounds a week each in our spare time. We had seen the advertisement in the paper, and we had always wanted to do it, but we had never had the money to spare before, somehow. The advertisement says: "Any lady or gentleman can easily earn two pounds a week in their spare time. Sample and instructions, two shillings. Packed free from observation." A good deal of the half-crown was Dora's. It came from her godmother; but she said she would not mind letting Dicky have it if he would pay her back before Christmas, and if we were sure it was right to try to make our fortune that way. Of course that was quite easy, because out of two pounds a week in your spare time you can easily pay all your debts, and have almost as much left as you began with; and as to the right we told her to dry up.

Dicky had always thought that this was really the best way to restore our fallen fortunes, and we were glad that now he had a chance of trying, because of course we wanted the two pounds a week each, and besides, we were rather tired of Dicky's always saying, when our ways didn't turn out well, "Why don't you try tho sample and instructions about our spare time?"

When we found out about our half-crown we got the paper. Noël was playing admirals in it, but he had made the cocked hat without tearing the paper, and we found the advertisement, and it said just the same as ever. So we got a two-shilling postal order and a stamp, and what was left of the money it was agreed we would spend in ginger-beer to drink success to trade.

We got some nice paper out of Father's study, and Dicky wrote the letter, and we put in the money and put on the stamp, and made H. O. post it. Then we drank the ginger-beer, and then we waited for the sample and instructions. It seemed a long time coming, and the postman got quite tired of us running out and stopping him in the street to ask if it had come.

But on the third morning it came. It was quite a large parcel, and it was packed, as the advertisement said it would be, "free from observation." That means it was in a box; and inside the box was some stiff browny cardboard, crinkled like the galvanized iron on the tops of chicken-houses, and inside that was a lot of paper, some of it printed and same scrappy, and in the very middle of it all a bottle, not very large, and black, and sealed on the top of the cork with yellow sealing-wax.

We looked at it as it lay on the nursery table, and while all the others grabbed at the papers to see what the printing said, Oswald went to look for the cork-screw, so as to see what was inside the bottle. He found the corkscrew in the dresser drawer—it always gets there, though it is supposed to be in the sideboard drawer in the dining-room—and when he got back the others had read most of the printed papers.

"I don't think it's much good, and I don't think it's quite nice to sell wine," Dora said; "and besides, it's not easy to suddenly begin to sell things when you aren't used to it."

"I don't know," said Alice; "I believe I could."

They all looked rather down in the mouth, though, and Oswald asked how you were to make your two pounds a week.

"Why, you've got to get people to taste that stuff in the bottle. It's sherry—Castilian Amoroso its name is—and then you get them to buy it, and then you write to the people and tell them the other people want the wine, and then for every dozen you sell you get two shillings from the wine people, so if you sell twenty dozen a week you get your two pounds. I don't think we shall sell as much as that," said Dicky.

"We might not the first week," Alice said, "but when people found out how nice it was, they would want more and more. And if we only got ten shillings a week it would be something to begin with, wouldn't it?"

Oswald said he should jolly well think it would, and then Dicky took the cork out with the corkscrew. The cork broke a good deal, and some of the bits went into the bottle. Dora got the medicine glass that has the teaspoons and tablespoons marked on it, and we agreed to have a teaspoonful each, to see what it was like.

"No one must have more than that," Dora said, "however nice it is." Dora behaved rather as if it were her bottle. I suppose it was, because she had lent the money for it.

Then she measured out the teaspoonful, and she had first go, because of being the eldest. We asked at once what it was like, but Dora could not speak just then.

Then she said, "It's like the tonic Noël had in the spring; but perhaps sherry ought to be like that."

Then it was Oswald's turn. He thought it was very burny; but he said nothing. He wanted to see first what the others would say.

Dicky said his was simply beastly, and Alice said Noël could taste next if he liked.

Noël said it was the golden wine of the gods, but he had to put his handkerchief up to his mouth all the same, and I saw the face he made.

Then H. O. had his, and he spat it out in the fire, which was very rude and nasty, and we told him so.

Then it was Alice's turn. She said, "Only half a teaspoonful for me, Dora. We mustn't use it all up." And she tasted it and said nothing.

Then Dicky said. "Look here, I chuck this. I'm not going to hawk round such beastly stuff. Any one who likes can have the bottle. *Quis?*"

And Alice got out "*Ego*" before the rest of us. Then she said, "I know what's the matter with it. It wants sugar."

And at once we all saw that that was all there was the matter with the stuff. So we got two lumps of sugar and crushed it on the floor with one of the big wooden bricks till it was powdery, and mixed it with some of the wine up to the tablespoon mark, and it was quite different, and not nearly so nasty.

"You see it's all right when you get used to it," Dicky said. I think he was sorry he had said "*Quis*" in such a hurry.

"Of course," Alice said, "it's rather dusty. We must crush the sugar carefully in clean paper before we put it in the bottle."

Dora said she was afraid it would be cheating to

make one bottle nicer than what people would get when they ordered a dozen bottles, but Alice said Dora always made a fuss about everything, and really it would be quite honest.

"You see," she said, "I shall just tell them, quite truthfully, what we have done to it, and when their dozens come they can do it for themselves."

So then we crushed eight more lumps, very cleanly and carefully between newspapers, and shook it up well in the bottle, and corked it up with a screw of paper, brown and not news, for fear of the poisonous printing ink getting wet and dripping down into the wine and killing people. We made Pincher have a taste, and he sneezed for ever so long, and after that he used to go under the sofa whenever we showed him the bottle.

Then we asked Alice who she would try and sell it to. She said: "I shall ask everybody who comes to the house. And while we are doing that, we can be thinking of outside people to take it to. We must be careful: there's not much more than half of it left, even counting the sugar."

We did not wish to tell Eliza—I don't know why. And she opened the door very quickly that day, so that the Taxes and a man who came to our house by mistake for next door got away before Alice had a chance to try them with the Castilian Amoroso. But about five Eliza slipped out for half an hour to see a friend who was making her a hat for Sunday, and while she was gone there was a knock.

Alice went, and we looked over the banisters.

When she opened the door, she said at once, "Will you walk in, please?"

The person at the door said, "I called to see your Pa, miss. Is he at home?"

Alice said again, "Will you walk in, please?"

Then the person—it sounded like a man—said, "He *is* in, then?" But Alice only kept on saying, "Will you walk in, please?" so at last the man did, rubbing his boots very loudly on the mat. Then Alice shut the front door, and we saw that it was the butcher, with an envelope in his hand. He was not dressed in blue, like when he is cutting up the sheep and things in the shop, and he wore knickerbockers. Alice says he came on a bicycle. She led the way into the dining-room, where the Castilian Amoroso bottle and the medicine glass were standing on the table all ready.

The others stayed on the stairs, but Oswald crept down and looked through the door-crack.

"Please sit down," said Alice quite calmly, though she told me afterwards I had no idea how silly she felt. And the butcher sat down. Then Alice stood quite still and said nothing, but she fiddled with the medicine glass and put the screw of brown paper straight in the Castilian bottle.

"Will you tell your Pa I'd like a word with him?" the butcher said, when he got tired of saying nothing.

"He'll be in very soon, I think," Alice said.

And then she stood still again and said nothing. It was beginning to look very idiotic of her, and H. O. laughed. I went back and cuffed him for it quite quietly, and I don't think the butcher heard. But Alice did, and it roused her from her stupor. She spoke suddenly, very fast indeed—so fast that I knew she had made up what she was going to say before. She had got most of it out of the circular.

She said, "I want to call your attention to a sample of

sherry wine I have here. It is called Castilian something or other, and at the price it is unequalled for flavour and bouquet."

The butcher said, "Well—I never!"

And Alice went on, "Would you like to taste it?"

"Thank you very much, I'm sure, miss," said the butcher.

Alice poured some out.

The butcher tasted a very little. He licked his lips, and we thought he was going to say how good it was. But he did not. He put down the medicine glass with nearly all the stuff left in it (we put it back in the bottle afterwards to save waste) and said, "Excuse me, miss, but isn't it a little sweet?—for sherry I mean?"

"The *real* isn't," said Alice. "If you order a dozen it will come quite different to that—we like it best with sugar. I wish you *would* order some."

The butcher asked why.

Alice did not speak for a minute, and then she said—

"I don't mind telling you: you are in business your self, aren't you? We are trying to get people to buy it, because we shall have two shillings for every dozen we can make any one buy. It's called a purr something."

"A percentage. Yes, I see," said the butcher, looking at the hole in the carpet.

"You see there are reasons," Alice went on, "why we want to make our fortunes as quickly as we can."

"Quite so," said the butcher, and he looked at the place where the paper is coming off the wall.

"And this seems a good way," Alice went on. "We paid two shillings for the sample and instructions, and it says you can make two pounds a week easily in your leisure time."

"I'm sure I hope you may, miss," said the butcher.

And Alice said again would he buy some?

"Sherry is my favourite wine," he said.

Alice asked him to have some more to drink.

"No, thank you, miss," he said; "it's my favourite wine, but it doesn't agree with me; not the least bit. But I've an uncle drinks it. Suppose I ordered him half a dozen for a Christmas present? Well, miss, here's the shilling commission, anyway," and he pulled out a handful of money and gave her the shilling.

"But I thought the wine people paid that," Alice said.

But the butcher said not on half-dozens they didn't. Then he said he didn't think he'd wait any longer for Father—but would Alice ask Father to write him?

Alice offered him the sherry again, but he said something about "Not for worlds!"—and then she let him out and came back to us with the shilling, and said, "How's that?" And we said "A1."

And all the evening we talked of our fortune that we had begun to make.

Nobody came next day, but the day after a lady came to ask for money to build an orphanage for the children of dead sailors. And we saw her. I went in with Alice. And when we had explained to her that we had only a shilling and we wanted it for something else, Alice suddenly said, "Would you like some wine?"

And the lady said, "Thank you very much," but she looked surprised. She was not a young lady, and she had a mantle with beads, and the beads had come off in places—leaving a browny braid showing, and she had printed papers about the dead sailors in a sealskin bag, and the seal had come off in places, leaving the skin bare.

We gave her a tablespoonful of the wine in a proper

wine-glass out of the sideboard, because she was a lady. And when she had tasted it she got up in a very great hurry, and shook out her dress and snapped her bag shut, and said, "You naughty, wicked children! What do you mean by playing a trick like this? You ought to be ashamed of yourselves! I shall write to your Mamma about it. You dreadful little girl!—you might have poisoned me. But your Mamma . . ."

Then Alice said, "I'm very sorry; the butcher liked it, only he said it was sweet. And please don't write to Mother. It makes Father so unhappy when letters come for her!"—and Alice was very near crying.

"What do you mean, you silly child?" said the lady, looking quite bright and interested. "Why doesn't your Father like your Mother to have letters—eh?"

And Alice said, "*Oh*, you . . .!" and began to cry, and bolted out of the room.

Then I said, "Our Mother is dead, and will you please go away now?"

The lady looked at me a minute, and then she looked quite different, and she said, "I'm very sorry. I didn't know. Never mind about the wine. I daresay your little sister meant it kindly." And she looked round the room just like the butcher had done. Then she said again, "I didn't know—I'm very sorry. . . ."

So I said, "Don't mention it," and shook hands with her, and let her out. Of course we couldn't have asked her to buy the wine after what she'd said. But I think she was not a bad sort of person. I do like a person to say they're sorry when they ought to be—especially a grown-up. They do it so seldom. I suppose that's why we think so much of it.

But Alice and I didn't feel jolly for ever so long afterwards. And when I went back into the dining-room I saw how different it was from when Mother was here, and we are different, and Father is different, and nothing is like it was. I am glad I am not made to think about it every day.

I went and found Alice, and told her what the lady had said, and when she had finished crying we put away the bottle and said we would not try to sell any more to people who came. And we did not tell the others—we only said the lady did not buy any—but we went up on the Heath, and some soldiers went by and there was a Punch-and-Judy show, and when we came back we were better.

The bottle got quite dusty where we had put it, and perhaps the dust of ages would have laid thick and heavy on it, only a clergyman called when we were all out. He was not our own clergyman—Mr Bristow is our own clergyman, and we all love him, and we would not try to sell sherry to people we like, and make two pounds a week out of them in our spare time. It was another clergyman, just a stray one; and he asked Eliza if the dear children would not like to come to his little Sunday school. We always spend Sunday afternoons with Father. But as he had left the name of his vicarage with Eliza, and asked her to tell us to come, we thought we would go and call on him, just to explain about Sunday afternoons, and we thought we might as well take the sherry with us.

"I won't go unless you all go too," Alice said, "and I won't do the talking."

Dora said she thought we had much better not go; but we said "Rot!" and it ended in her coming with us, and I am glad she did.

Oswald said he would do the talking if the others

liked, and he learned up what to say from the printed papers.

We went to the Vicarage early on Saturday afternoon, and rang at the bell. It is a new red house with no trees in the garden, only very yellow mould and gravel. It was all very neat and dry. Just before we rang the bell we heard some one inside call "Jane! Jane!" and we thought we would not be Jane for anything. It was the sound of the voice that called that made us sorry for her.

The door was opened by a very neat servant in black, with a white apron; we saw her tying the strings as she came along the hall, through the different coloured glass in the door. Her face was red, and I think she was Jane.

We asked if we could see Mr Mallow.

The servant said Mr Mallow was very busy with his sermon just then, but she would see.

But Oswald said, "It's all right. He asked us to come."

So she let us all in and shut the front door, and showed us into a very tidy room with a bookcase full of a lot of books covered in black cotton with white labels, and some dull pictures, and a harmonium. And Mr Mallow was writing at a desk with drawers, copying something out of a book. He was stout and short, and wore spectacles.

He covered his writing up when we went in—I didn't know why. He looked rather cross, and we heard Jane or somebody being scolded outside by the voice. I hope it wasn't for letting us in, but I have had doubts.

"Well," said the clergyman, "what is all this about?"

"You asked us to call," Dora said, "about your little Sunday school. We are the Bastables of Lewisham Road."

"Oh—ah, yes," he said; "and shall I expect you all to-morrow?" He took up his pen and fiddled with it, and he did not ask us to sit down. But some of us did.

"We always spend Sunday afternoon with Father," said Dora; "but we wished to thank you for being so kind as to ask us."

"And we wished to ask you something else!" said Oswald; and he made a sign to Alice to get the sherry ready in the glass. She did—behind Oswald's back while he was speaking.

"My time is limited," said Mr Mallow, looking at his watch; "but still—" Then he muttered something about the fold, and went on: "Tell me what is troubling you, my little man, and I will try to give you any help in my power. What is it you want?"

Then Oswald quickly took the glass from Alice, and held it out to him, and said, "I want your opinion on that."

"On *that*," he said. "What is it?"

"It is a shipment," Oswald said; "but it's quite enough for you to taste." Alice had filled the glass half-full; I suppose she was too excited to measure properly.

"A shipment?" said the clergyman, taking the glass in his hand.

"Yes," Oswald went on; "an exceptional opportunity. Full-bodied and nutty."

"It really does taste rather like one kind of Brazil nut." Alice put her oar in as usual.

The Vicar looked from Alice to Oswald, and back again, and Oswald went on with what he had learned from the printing. The clergyman held the glass at half-arm's-length, stiffly, as if he had caught cold.

"It is of a quality never before offered at the price. Old Delicate Amoro—what's its name—"

"Amorolio," said H. O.

"Amoroso," said Oswald. "H. O., you just shut up Castilian Amoroso—it's a true after-dinner wine, stimulating and yet . . ."

"*Wine?*" said Mr Mallow, holding the glass further off. "Do you *know*," he went on, making his voice very thick and strong (I expect he does it like that in church), "have you never been *taught* that it is the drinking of *wine* and *spirits*—yes, and BEER, which makes half the homes in England full of *wretched* little children, and *degraded*, MISERABLE parents?"

"Not if you put sugar in it," said Alice firmly; "eight lumps and shake the bottle. We have each had more than a teaspoonful of it, and we were not ill at all. It was something else that upset H. O. Most likely all those acorns he got out of the Park."

The clergyman seemed to be speechless with conflicting emotions, and just then the door opened and a lady came in. She had a white cap with lace, and an ugly violet flower in it, and she was tall, and looked very strong, though thin. And I do believe she had been listening at the door.

"But why," the Vicar was saying, "why did you bring this dreadful fluid, this curse of our country, to me to taste?"

"Because we thought you might buy some," said Dora, who never sees when a game is up. "In books the parson loves his bottle of old port; and new sherry is just as good—with sugar—for people who like sherry. And if you would order a dozen of the wine, then we should get two shillings."

The lady said (and it was the voice), "Good gracious! Nasty, sordid little things! Haven't they any one to teach them better?"

And Dora got up and said, "No, we are not those things you say; but we are sorry we came here to be called names. We want to make our fortune just as much as Mr Mallow does—only no one would listen to us if we preached, so it's no use our copying out sermons like him."

And I think that was smart of Dora, even if it was rather rude.

Then I said perhaps we had better go, and the lady said, "I should think so!" But when we were going to wrap up the bottle and glass the clergyman said, "No; you can leave that," and we were so upset we did, though it wasn't his after all.

We walked home very fast and not saying much, and the girls went up to their rooms. When I went to tell them tea was ready, and there was a teacake, Dora was crying like anything and Alice hugging her. I am afraid there is a great deal of crying in this chapter, but I can't help it. Girls will sometimes; I suppose it is their nature, and we ought to be sorry for their affliction.

"It's no good," Dora was saying, "you all hate me, and you think I'm a prig and a busybody, but I do try to do right—oh, I do! Oswald, go away; don't come here making fun of me!"

So I said, "I'm not making fun, Sissy don't cry, old girl."

Mother taught me to call her Sissy when we were very little and before the others came, but I don't often somehow, now we are old. I patted her on the back, and she put her head against my sleeve, holding on to Alice all the time, and she went on. She was in that laughy cryey state when people say things they wouldn't say at other times.

"Oh dear, oh dear—I do try, I do. And when Mother

died she said, 'Dora, take care of the others, and teach them to be good, and keep them out of trouble and make them happy.' She said, 'Take care of them for me, Dora dear.' And I have tried, and all of you hate me for it; and to-day I let you do this, though I knew all the time it was silly."

I hope you will not think I was a muff, but I kissed Dora for some time. Because girls like it. And I will never say again that she comes the good elder sister too much. And I have put all this in though I do hate telling about it, because I own I have been hard on Dora, but I never will be again. She is a good old sort; of course we never knew before about what Mother told her, or we wouldn't have ragged her as we did. We did not tell the little ones, but I got Alice to speak to Dicky, and we three can sit on the others if requisite.

This made us forget all about the sherry; but about eight o'clock there was a knock, and Eliza went, and we saw it was poor Jane, if her name was Jane, from the Vicarage. She handed in a brown-paper parcel and a letter. And three minutes later Father called us into his study.

On the table was the brown-paper parcel, open, with our bottle and glass on it, and Father had a letter in his hand. He pointed to the bottle and sighed, and said, "What have you been doing now?" The letter in his hand was covered with little black writing, all over the four large pages.

So Dicky spoke up, and he told Father the whole thing, as far as he knew it, for Alice and I had not told about the dead sailors' lady.

And when he had done, Alice said, "Has Mr Mallow written to you to say he will buy a dozen of the sherry after all? It is really not half bad with sugar in it."

Father said no, he didn't think clergymen could afford such expensive wine; and he said he would like to taste it. So we gave him what there was left, for we had decided coming home that we would give up trying for the two pounds a week in our spare time.

Father tasted it, and then he acted just as H. O. had done when he had his teaspoonful, but of course we did not say anything. Then he laughed till I thought he would never stop.

I think it was the sherry, because I am sure I have read somewhere about "wine that maketh glad the heart of man". He had only a very little, which shows that it was a good after-dinner wine, stimulating, and yet . . . I forget the rest.

But when he had done laughing he said, "It's all right, kids. Only don't do it again. The wine trade is overcrowded; and besides, I thought you promised to consult me before going into business?"

"Before buying one I thought you meant," said Dicky. "This was only on commission." And Father laughed again. I am glad we got the Castilian Amoroso, because it did really cheer Father up, and you cannot always do that, however hard you try, even if you make jokes, or give him a comic paper.

Chapter 12

THE NOBLENESS OF OSWALD

The part about his nobleness only comes at the end, but you would not understand it unless you knew how it began. It began, like nearly everything about that time, with treasure-seeking.

Of course as soon as we had promised to consult my Father about business matters we all gave up wanting to go into business. I don't know how it is, but having to consult about a thing with grown-up people, even the bravest and the best, seems to make the thing not worth doing afterwards.

We don't mind Albert's uncle chipping in sometimes when the thing's going on, but we are glad he never asked us to promise to consult him about anything. Yet Oswald saw that my Father was quite right; and I daresay if we had had that hundred pounds we should have spent it on the share in that lucrative business for the sale of useful patent, and then found out afterwards that we should have done better to spend the money in some other way. My Father says so, and he ought to know. We had several ideas about that time, but having so little chink always stood in the way. This was the case with H. O.'s idea of setting up a coconut-shy on this side of the Heath, where there are none generally. We had no sticks or wooden balls, and the greengrocer said he could not book so many as twelve dozen coconuts without Mr Bastable's written order. And as we did not wish to consult my Father it was decided to drop it. And when Alice dressed up Pincher in some of the dolls' clothes and we made up our minds to take him round with an organ as soon as we had taught him to dance, we were stopped at once by Dicky's remembering how he had once heard that an organ cost seven hundred pounds. Of course this was the big church kind, but even the ones on three legs can't be got for one-and-sevenpence, which was all we had when we first thought of it. So we gave that up too.

It was a wet day, I remember, and mutton hash for dinner—very tough with pale gravy with lumps in it. I think the others would have left a good deal on the sides of their plates, although they know better, only Oswald said it was a savoury stew made of the red deer that Edward shot. So then we were the Children of the New Forest, and the mutton tasted much better. No one in the New Forest minds venison being tough and the gravy pale.

Then after dinner we let the girls have a dolls' tea-party, on condition they didn't expect us boys to wash up; and it was when we were drinking the last of the liquorice water out of the little cups that Dicky said—

"This reminds me."

So we said, "What of?"

Dicky answered us at once, though his mouth was full of bread with liquorice stuck in it to look like cake. You should not speak with your mouth full, even to your own relations, and you shouldn't wipe your mouth on the back of your hand, but on your handkerchief, if you have one. Dicky did not do this. He said—

"Why, you remember when we first began about treasure-seeking, I said I had thought of something, only I could not tell you because I hadn't finished thinking about it."

We said "Yes."

"Well, this liquorice water—"

"Tea," said Alice softly.

"Well, tea then—made me think." He was going on to say what it made him think, but Noël interrupted and cried out, "I say; let's finish off this old tea-party and have a council of war."

So we got out the flags and the wooden sword and the drum, and Oswald beat it while the girls washed up, till Eliza came up to say she had the jumping toothache, and the noise went through her like a knife. So of course Oswald left off at once. When you are polite to Oswald he never refuses to grant your requests.

When we were all dressed up we sat down round the camp fire, and Dicky began again.

"Every one in the world wants money. Some people get it. The people who get it are the ones who see things. I have seen one thing."

Dicky stopped and smoked the pipe of peace. It is the pipe we did bubbles with in the summer, and somehow it has not got broken yet. We put tea-leaves in it for the pipe of peace, but the girls are not allowed to have any. It is not right to let girls smoke. They get to think too much of themselves if you let them do everything the same as men.

Oswald said, "Out with it."

"I see that glass bottles only cost a penny. H. O., if you dare to snigger I'll send you round selling old bottles, and you shan't have any sweets except out of the money you get for them. And the same with you, Noël."

"Noël wasn't sniggering," said Alice in a hurry; "it is only his taking so much interest in what you were saying makes him look like that. Be quiet, H. O., and don't you make faces, either. Do go on, Dicky dear."

So Dicky went on.

"There must be hundreds of millions of bottles of medicines sold every year. Because all the different medicines say, 'Thousands of cures daily,' and if you only take that as two thousand, which it must be, at least, it mounts up. And the people who sell them must make a great deal of money by them because they are nearly always two-and-ninepence the bottle, and three-and-six for one nearly double the size. Now the bottles, as I was saying, don't cost anything like that."

"It's the medicine costs the money," said Dora; "look how expensive jujubes are at the chemist's, and peppermints too."

"That's only because they're nice," Dicky explained; "nasty things are not so dear. Look what a lot of brimstone you get for a penny, and the same with alum. We would not put the nice kinds of chemist's things in our medicine."

Then he went on to tell us that when we had invented our medicine we would write and tell the editor about it, and he would put it in the paper, and then people would send their two-and-ninepence and three-and-six for the bottle nearly double the size, and then when the medicine had cured them they would write to the paper and their letters would be printed, saying how they had been suffering for years, and never thought to get about again, but thanks to the blessing of our ointment—

Dora interrupted and said, "Not ointment—it's so messy." And Alice thought so too. And Dicky said he did not mean it, he was quite decided to let it be in bottles. So now it was all settled, and we did not see at the time that this would be a sort of going into business, but afterwards when Albert's uncle showed us we saw it, and we were sorry. We only had to invent the medicine. You might think that was easy, because of the number of them you see every day in the paper, but it is much harder than you think. First we had to decide what sort of illness we should like to cure, and a "heated discussion ensued", like in Parliament.

Dora wanted it to be something to make the complexion of dazzling fairness, but we remembered how her face came all red and rough when she used the Rosabella soap that was advertised to make the darkest complexion fair as the lily, and she agreed that perhaps it was better not. Noël wanted to make the medicine first and then find out what it would cure, but Dicky thought not, because there are so many more medicines than there are things the matter with us, so it would be easier to choose the disease first.

Oswald would have liked wounds. I still think it was a good idea, but Dicky said, "Who has wounds, especially now there aren't any wars? We shouldn't sell a bottle a day!" So Oswald gave in because he knows what manners are, and it was Dicky's idea. H. O. wanted a cure for the uncomfortable feeling that they give you powders for, but we explained to him that grown-up people do not have this feeling, however much they eat, and he agreed. Dicky said he did not care a straw what the loathsome disease was, as long as we hurried up and settled on something. Then Alice said—

"It ought to be something very common, and only one thing. Not the pains in the back and all the hundreds of things the people have in somebody's syrup. What's the commonest thing of all?"

And at once we said, "Colds."

So that was settled.

Then we wrote a label to go on the bottle. When it was written it would not go on the vinegar bottle that we had got, but we knew it would go small when it was printed. It was like this:

BASTABLE'S
CERTAIN CURE FOR COLDS

Coughs, Asthma, Shortness of Breath, and all infections of the chest

One dose gives immediate relief
It will cure your cold in one bottle
Especially the larger size at 3*s*.6*d*.
Order at once of the Makers
To prevent disappointment

Makers:
D., O., R., A., N., & H. O. BASTABLE
150 Lewisham Road, S.E.
(*A halfpenny for all bottles returned*)

Of course the next thing was for one of us to catch a cold and try what cured it; we all wanted to be the one, but it was Dicky's idea, and he said he was not going to be done out of it, so we let him. It was only fair. He left off his undershirt that very day, and next morning he stood in a draught in his nightgown for quite a long time. And we damped his day-shirt with the nail-brush before he put it on. But all was vain. They always tell you that these things will give you cold, but we found it was not so.

So then we all went over to the Park, and Dicky went

right into the water with his boots on, and stood there as long as he could bear it, for it was rather cold, and we stood and cheered him on. He walked home in his wet clothes, which they say is a sure thing, but it was no go, though his boots were quite spoiled. And three days after Noël began to cough and sneeze.

So then Dicky said it was not fair.

"I can't help it," Noël said. "You should have caught it yourself, then it wouldn't have come to me."

And Alice said she had known all along Noël oughtn't to have stood about on the bank cheering in the cold.

Noël had to go to bed, and then we began to make the medicines; we were sorry he was out of it, but he had the fun of taking the things.

We made a great many medicines. Alice made herb tea. She got sage and thyme and savory and marjoram and boiled them all up together with salt and water, but she would put parsley in too. Oswald is sure parsley is not a herb. It is only put on the cold meat and you are not supposed to eat it. It kills parrots to eat parsley, I believe. I expect it was the parsley that disagreed so with Noël. The medicine did not seem to do the cough any good.

Oswald got a pennyworth of alum, because it is so cheap, and some turpentine which every one knows is good for colds, and a little sugar and an aniseed ball. These were mixed in a bottle with water, but Eliza threw it away and said it was nasty rubbish, and I hadn't any money to get more things with.

Dora made him some gruel, and he said it did his chest good; but of course that was no use, because you cannot put gruel in bottles and say it is medicine. It would not be honest, and besides nobody would believe you.

Dick mixed up lemon-juice and sugar and a little of the juice of the red flannel that Noël's throat was done up in. It comes out beautifully in hot water. Noël took this and he liked it. Noël's own idea was liquorice-water, and we let him have it, but it is too plain and black to sell in bottles at the proper price.

Noël liked H. O.'s medicine the best, which was silly of him, because it was only peppermints melted in hot water, and a little cobalt to make it look blue. It was all right, because H. O.'s paint-box is the French kind, with *Couleurs non Vénéneuses* on it. This means you may suck your brushes if you want to, or even your paints if you are a very little boy.

It was rather jolly while Noël had that cold. He had a fire in his bedroom which opens out of Dicky's and Oswald's, and the girls used to read aloud to Noël all day; they will not read aloud to you when you are well. Father was away at Liverpool on business, and Albert's uncle was at Hastings. We were rather glad of this, because we wished to give all the medicines a fair trial, and grown-ups are but too fond of interfering. As if we should have given him anything poisonous!

His cold went on—it was bad in his head, but it was not one of the kind when he has to have poultices and can't sit up in bed. But when it had been in his head nearly a week, Oswald happened to tumble over Alice on the stairs. When we got up she was crying.

"Don't cry silly!" said Oswald; "you know I didn't hurt you." I was very sorry if I had hurt her, but you ought not to sit on the stairs in the dark and let other people tumble over you. You ought to remember how beastly it is for them if they do hurt you.

"Oh, it's not that, Oswald," Alice said. "Don't be a pig! I am so miserable. Do be kind to me."

So Oswald thumped her on the back and told her to shut up.

"It's about Noël," she said. "I'm sure he's very ill; and playing about with medicines is all very well, but I know he's ill, and Eliza won't send for the doctor: she says it's only a cold. And I know the doctor's bills are awful. I heard Father telling Aunt Emily so in the summer. But he *is* ill, and perhaps he'll die or something."

Then she began to cry again. Oswald thumped her again, because he knows how a good brother ought to behave, and said, "Cheer up." If we had been in a book Oswald would have embraced his little sister tenderly, and mingled his tears with hers.

Then Oswald said, "Why not write to Father?" And she cried more and said, "I've lost the paper with the address. H. O. had it to draw on the back of, and I can't find it now; I've looked everywhere. I'll tell you what I'm going to do. No I won't. But I'm going out. Don't tell the others. And I say, Oswald, do pretend I'm in if Eliza asks. Promise."

"Tell me what you're going to do," I said. But she said "No"; and there was a good reason why not. So I said I wouldn't promise if it came to that. Of course I meant to all right. But it did seem mean of her not to tell me.

So Alice went out by the side door while Eliza was setting tea, and she was a long time gone, she was not in to tea. When Eliza asked Oswald where she was he said he did not know, but perhaps she was tidying her corner drawer. Girls often do this, and it takes a long time. Noël coughed a good bit after tea, and asked for

Alice. Oswald told him she was doing something and it was a secret. Oswald did not tell any lies even to save his sister. When Alice came back she was very quiet, but she whispered to Oswald that it was all right. When it was rather late Eliza said she was going out to post a letter. This always takes her an hour, because she will go to the post-office across the Heath instead of the pillar-box, because once a boy dropped fusees in our pillar-box and burnt the letters. It was not any of us; Eliza told us about it. And when there was a knock at the door a long time after we thought it was Eliza come back, and that she had forgotten the back-door key. We made H. O. go down to open the door, because it is his place to run about: his legs are younger than ours. And we heard boots on the stairs besides H. O.'s, and we listened spell-bound till the door opened, and it was Albert's uncle. He looked very tired.

"I am glad you've come," Oswald said. "Alice began to think Noël—"

Alice stopped me, and her face was very red, her nose was shiny too, with having cried so much before tea.

She said, "I only said I thought Noël ought to have the doctor. Don't you think he ought?" She got hold of Albert's uncle and held on to him.

"Let's have a look at you, young man," said Albert's uncle, and he sat down on the edge of the bed. It is a rather shaky bed, the bar that keeps it steady underneath got broken when we were playing burglars last winter. It was our crowbar. He began to feel Noël's pulse, and went on talking.

"It was revealed to the Arab physician as he made merry in his tents on the wild plains of Hastings that the Presence had a cold in its head. So he immediately seated himself on the magic carpet, and bade it bear him hither, only pausing in the flight to purchase a few sweetmeats in the bazaar."

He pulled out a jolly lot of chocolate and some butterscotch, and grapes for Noël. When we had all said thank you, he went on.

"The physician's are the words of wisdom: it's high time this kid was asleep. I have spoken. Ye have my leave to depart."

So we bunked, and Dora and Albert's uncle made Noël comfortable for the night.

Then they came to the nursery which we had gone down to, and he sat down in the Guy Fawkes chair and said, "Now then."

Alice said, "You may tell them what I did. I daresay they'll all be in a wax, but I don't care."

"I think you were very wise," said Albert's uncle, pulling her close to him to sit on his knee. "I am very glad you telegraphed."

So then Oswald understood what Alice's secret was. She had gone out and sent a telegram to Albert's uncle at Hastings. But Oswald thought she might have told him. Afterwards she told me what she had put in the telegram. It was, "Come home. We have given Noël a cold, and I think we are killing him." With the address it came to tenpence-halfpenny.

Then Albert's uncle began to ask questions, and it all came out, how Dicky had tried to catch the cold, but the cold had gone to Noël instead, and about the medicines and all. Albert's uncle looked very serious.

"Look here," he said, "you're old enough not to play the fool like this. Health is the best thing you've got; you ought to know better than to risk it. You might have killed your little brother with your precious medicines. You've had a lucky escape, certainly. But poor Noël!"

"Oh, do you think he's going to die?" Alice asked that, and she was crying again.

"No, no," said Albert's uncle; "but look here. Do you see how silly you've been? And I thought you promised your Father—" And then he gave us a long talking-to. He can make you feel most awfully small. At last he stopped, and we said we were very sorry, and he said, "You know I promised to take you all to the pantomime?"

So we said, "Yes," and knew but too well that now he wasn't going to. Then he went on—

"Well, I will take you if you like, or I will take Noël to the sea for a week to cure his cold. Which is it to be?"

Of course he knew we should say, "Take Noël" and we did; but Dicky told me afterwards he thought it was hard on H. O.

Albert's uncle stayed till Eliza came in, and then he said good night in a way that showed us that all was forgiven and forgotten.

And we went to bed. It must have been the middle of the night when Oswald woke up suddenly, and there was Alice with her teeth chattering, shaking him to wake him.

"Oh, Oswald!" she said, "I am so unhappy. Suppose I should die in the night!"

Oswald told her to go to bed and not gas. But she said, "I must tell you; I wish I'd told Albert's uncle. I'm a thief, and if I die to-night I know where thieves go to."

So Oswald saw it was no good and he sat up in bed and said—

"Go ahead."

So Alice stood shivering and said—

"I hadn't enough money for the telegram, so I took the bad sixpence out of the exchequer. And I paid for it with that and the fivepence I had. And I wouldn't tell you, because if you'd stopped me doing it I couldn't have borne it; and if you'd helped me you'd have been a thief too. Oh, what shall I do?"

Oswald thought a minute, and then he said—

"You'd better have told me. But I think it will be all right if we pay it back. Go to bed. Cross with you? No, stupid! Only another time you'd better not keep secrets." So she kissed Oswald, and he let her, and she went back to bed. The next day Albert's uncle took Noël away, before Oswald had time to persuade Alice that we ought to tell him about the sixpence. Alice was very unhappy, but not so much as in the night: you can be very miserable in the night if you have done anything wrong and you happen to be awake. I know this for a fact.

None of us had any money except Eliza, and she wouldn't give us any unless we said what for; and of course we could not do that because of the honour of the family. And Oswald was anxious to get the sixpence to give to the telegraph people because he feared that the badness of that sixpence might have been found out, and that the police might come for Alice at any moment. I don't think I ever had such an unhappy day. Of course we could have written to Albert's uncle, but it would have taken a long time, and every moment of delay added to Alice's danger. We thought and thought, but we couldn't think of any way to get that sixpence. It seems a small sum, but you see Alice's liberty depended on it. It was quite late in the afternoon when I met Mrs Leslie on the Parade. She had a brown fur coat and a lot of yellow flowers in her hands. She stopped to speak to me, and asked me how the Poet was. I told her he had a cold, and I wondered whether she would lend me sixpence if I asked her, but I could not make up my mind how to begin to say it. It is a hard thing to say—much harder than you would think. She talked to me for a bit, and then she suddenly got into a cab, and said—

"I'd no idea it was so late," and told the man where to go. And just as she started she shoved the yellow flowers through the window and said, "For the sick poet, with my love," and was driven off.

Gentle reader, I will not conceal from you what Oswald did. He knew all about not disgracing the family, and he did not like doing what I am going to say: and they were really Noël's flowers, only he could not have sent them to Hastings, and Oswald knew he would say "Yes" if Oswald asked him. Oswald sacrificed his family pride because of his little sister's danger. I do not say he was a noble boy—I just tell you what he did, and you can decide for yourself about the nobleness.

He put on his oldest clothes—they're much older than any you would think he had if you saw him when he was tidy—and he took those yellow chrysanthemums and he walked with them to Greenwich Station and waited for the trains bringing people from London. He sold those flowers in penny bunches and got tenpence. Then he went to the telegraph office at Lewisham, and said to the lady there:

A little girl gave you a bad sixpence yesterday, Here are six good pennies."

The lady said she had not noticed it, and never mind,

but Oswald knew that "Honesty is the best Policy", and he refused to take back the pennies. So at last she said she should put them in the plate on Sunday. She is a very nice lady. I like the way she does her hair.

Then Oswald went home to Alice and told her, and she hugged him, and said he was a dear, good, kind boy, and he said "Oh, it's all right."

We bought peppermint bullseyes with the fourpence I had over, and the others wanted to know where we got the money, but we would not tell.

Only afterwards when Noël came home we told him, because they were his flowers, and he said it was quite right. He made some poetry about it. I only remember one bit of it.

The noble youth of high degree
Consents to play a menial part,
All for his sister Alice's sake,
Who was so dear to his faithful heart.

But Oswald himself has never bragged about it.

We got no treasure out of this, unless you count the peppermint bullseyes.

CHAPTER 13

THE ROBBER AND THE BURGLAR

A day or two after Noël came back from Hastings there was snow; it was jolly. And we cleared it off the path. A man to do it is sixpence at least, and you should always save when you can. A penny saved is a penny earned. And then we thought it would be nice to clear it off the top of the portico, where it lies so thick, and the edges as if they had been cut with a knife. And just as we had got out of the landing window on to the portico, the Water Rates came up the path with his book that he tears the thing out of that says how much you have got to pay, and the little ink-bottle hung on to his buttonhole in case you should pay him. Father says the Water Rates is a sensible man, and knows it is always well to be prepared for whatever happens, however unlikely. Alice said afterwards that she rather liked the Water Rates, really, and Noël said he had a face like a good vizier, or the man who rewards the honest boy for restoring the purse, but we did not think about these things at the time, and as the Water Rates came up the steps, we shovelled down a great square slab of snow like an avalanche—and it fell right on his head. Two of us thought of it at the same moment, so it was quite a large avalanche. And when the Water Rates had shaken himself he rang the bell. It was Saturday, and Father was at home. We know now that it is very wrong and ungentlemanly to shovel snow off porticoes on to the Water Rates, or any other person, and we hope he did not catch a cold, and we are very sorry. We apologized to the Water Rates when Father told us to. We were all sent to bed for it.

We all deserved the punishment, because the others would have shovelled down snow just as we did if they'd thought of it—only they are not so quick at thinking of things as we are. And even quite wrong things sometimes lead to adventures; as every one knows who has ever read about pirates or highwaymen.

Eliza hates us to be sent to bed early, because it means her having to bring meals up, and it means lighting the fire in Noël's room ever so much earlier than usual. He had to have a fire because he still had a bit of a cold. But this particular day we got Eliza into a good temper by giving her a horrid brooch with pretending amethysts in it, that an aunt once gave to Alice, so Eliza brought up an extra scuttle of coals, and when the greengrocer came with the potatoes (he is always late on Saturdays) she got some chestnuts from him. So that when we heard Father go out after his dinner, there was a jolly fire in Noël's room, and we were able to go in and be Red Indians in blankets most comfortably. Eliza had gone out; she says she gets things cheaper on Saturday nights. She has a great friend, who sells fish at a shop, and he is very generous, and lets her have herrings for less than half the natural price.

So we were all alone in the house; Pincher was out with Eliza, and we talked about robbers. And Dora thought it would be a dreadful trade, but Dicky said—

"I think it would be very interesting. And you would only rob rich people, and be very generous to the poor and needy, like Claude Duval."

Dora said, "It is wrong to be a robber."

"Yes," said Alice, "you would never know a happy hour. Think of trying to sleep with the stolen jewels under your bed, and remembering all the quantities of policemen and detectives that there are in the world!"

"There are ways of being robbers that are not wrong," said Noël; "if you can rob a robber it is a right act."

"But you can't," said Dora; "he is too clever, and besides, it's wrong anyway."

"Yes you can, and it isn't; and murdering him with boiling oil is a right act, too, so there!" said Noël. "What about Ali Baba? Now then!" And we felt it was a score for Noël.

"What would you do if there was a robber?" said Alice.

H. O. said he would kill him with boiling oil; but Alice explained that she meant a real robber—now this minute—in the house.

Oswald and Dicky did not say; but Noël said he thought it would only be fair to ask the robber quite politely and quietly to go away, and then if he didn't you could deal with him.

Now what I am going to tell you is a very strange and wonderful thing, and I hope you will be able to believe it. I should not, if a boy told me, unless I knew him to be a man of honour, and perhaps not then unless he gave his sacred word. But it is true, all the same, and it only shows that the days of romance and daring deeds are not yet at an end.

Alice was just asking Noël *how* he would deal with the robber who wouldn't go if he was asked politely and quietly, when we heard a noise downstairs—quite a plain noise, not the kind of noise you fancy you hear.

It was like somebody moving a chair. We held our breath and listened—and then came another noise, like some one poking a fire. Now, you remember there was no one *to* poke a fire or move a chair downstairs, because Eliza and Father were both out. They could not have come in without our hearing them, because the front door is as hard to shut as the back one, and whichever you go in by you have to give a slam that you can hear all down the street.

H. O. and Alice and Dora caught hold of each other's blankets and looked at Dicky and Oswald, and every one was quite pale. And Noël whispered—

"It's ghosts, I know it is"—and then we listened again, but there was no more noise. Presently Dora said in a whisper—

"Whatever shall we do? Oh, whatever shall we do what *shall* we do?"

And she kept on saying it till we had to tell her to shut up.

O reader, have you ever been playing Red Indians in blankets round a bedroom fire in a house where you thought there was no one but you—and then suddenly heard a noise like a chair, and a fire being poked, downstairs? Unless you have you will not be able to imagine at all what it feels like. It was not like in books; our hair did not stand on end at all, and we never said "Hist!" once, but our feet got very cold, though we were in blankets by the fire, and the insides of Oswald's hands got warm and wet, and his nose was cold like a dog's, and his ears were burning hot.

The girls said afterwards that they shivered with terror, and their teeth chattered, but we did not see or hear this at the time.

"Shall we open the window and call police?" said

Dora; and then Oswald suddenly thought of something, and he breathed more freely and he said—

"I know it's not ghosts, and I don't believe it's robbers. I expect it's a stray cat got in when the coals came this morning, and she's been hiding in the cellar, and now she's moving about. Let's go down and see."

The girls wouldn't, of course; but I could see that they breathed more freely too. But Dicky said, "All right; I will if you will."

H. O. said, "Do you think it's *really* a cat?" So we said he had better stay with the girls. And of course after that we had to let him and Alice both come. Dora said if we took Noël down with his cold, she would scream "Fire!" and "Murder!" and she didn't mind if the whole street heard.

So Noël agreed to be getting his clothes on, and the rest of us said we would go down and look for the cat.

Now Oswald *said* that about the cat, and it made it easier to go down, but in his inside he did not feel at all sure that it might not be robbers after all. Of course, we had often talked about robbers before, but it is very different when you sit in a room and listen and listen and listen; and Oswald felt somehow that it would be easier to go down and see what it was, than to wait, and listen, and wait, and wait, and listen, and wait, and then perhaps to hear *It*, whatever it was, come creeping slowly up the stairs as softly as *It* could with *Its* boots off, and the stairs creaking, towards the room where we were with the door open in case of Eliza coming back suddenly, and all dark on the landings. And then it would have been just as bad, and it would have lasted longer, and you would have known you were a coward besides. Dicky says he felt all these same things. Many people would say we were young heroes to go down as we did; so I have tried to explain, because no young hero wishes to have more credit than he deserves.

The landing gas was turned down low—just a blue bead—and we four went out very softly, wrapped in our blankets, and we stood on the top of the stairs a good long time before we began to go down. And we listened and listened till our ears buzzed.

And Oswald whispered to Dicky, and Dicky went into our room and fetched the large toy pistol that is a foot long, and that has the trigger broken, and I took it because I am the eldest; and I don't think either of us thought it was the cat now. But Alice and H. O. did Dicky got the poker out of Noël's room, and told Dora it was to settle the cat with when we caught her.

Then Oswald whispered, "Let's play at burglars; Dicky and I are armed to the teeth, we will go first. You keep a flight behind us, and be a reinforcement if we are attacked. Or you can retreat and defend the women and children in the fortress, if you'd rather."

But they said they would be a reinforcement.

Oswald's teeth chattered a little when he spoke. It was not with anything else except cold.

So Dicky and Oswald crept down, and when we got to the bottom of the stairs, we saw Father's study door just ajar, and the crack of light. And Oswald was so pleased to see the light, knowing that burglars prefer the dark, or at any rate the dark lantern, that he felt really sure it *was* the cat after all, and then he thought it would be fun to make the others upstairs think it was really a robber. So he cocked the pistol—you can cock it, but it doesn't go off—and he said, "Come on, Dick!" and he rushed at the study door and burst into the room, crying, "Surrender! you are discovered! Surrender, or I fire! Throw up your hands!"

And, as he finished saying it, he saw before him, standing on the study hearthrug, a Real Robber. There was no mistake about it. Oswald was sure it was a robber, because it had a screwdriver in its hands, and was standing near the cupboard door that H. O. broke the lock off, and there were gimlets and screws and things on the floor. There is nothing in that cupboard but old ledgers and magazines and the tool chest, but of course, a robber could not know that beforehand.

When Oswald saw that there really was a robber, and that he was so heavily armed with the screwdriver, he did not feel comfortable. But he kept the pistol pointed at the robber, and—you will hardly believe it, but it is true—the robber threw down the screwdriver clattering on the other tools, and he *did* throw up his hands, and said—

"I surrender; don't shoot me! How many of you are there?"

So Dicky said, "You are outnumbered. Are you armed?"

And the robber said, "No, not in the least."

And Oswald said, still pointing the pistol, and feeling very strong and brave and as if he was in a book, "Turn out your pockets."

The robber did: and while he turned them out, we looked at him. He was of the middle height, and clad in a black frock-coat and grey trousers. His boots were a little gone at the sides, and his shirt-cuffs were a bit frayed, but otherwise he was of gentlemanly demeanour. He had a thin, wrinkled face, with big, light eyes that sparkled, and then looked soft very queerly, and a short beard. In his youth it must have been of a fair golden colour, but now it was tinged with grey. Oswald was sorry for him, especially when he saw that one of his pockets had a large hole in it, and that he had nothing in his pockets but letters and string and three boxes of matches, and a pipe and a handkerchief and a thin tobacco pouch and two pennies. We made him put all the things on the table, and then he said—

"Well, you've caught me; what are you going to do with me? Police?"

Alice and H. O. had come down to be reinforcements, when they heard a shout, and when Alice saw that it was a Real Robber, and that he had surrendered, she clapped her hands and said, "Bravo, boys!" and so did H. O. And now she said, "If he gives his word of honour not to escape, I shouldn't call the police: it seems a pity. Wait till Father comes home."

The robber agreed to this, and gave his word of honour, and asked if he might put on a pipe, and we said "Yes," and he sat in Father's armchair and warmed his boots, which steamed, and I sent H. O. and Alice to put on some clothes and tell the others, and bring down Dicky's and my knickerbockers, and the rest of the chestnuts.

And they all came, and we sat round the fire, and it was jolly. The robber was very friendly, and talked to us a great deal.

"I wasn't always in this low way of business," he said, when Noël said something about the things he had turned out of his pockets. "It's a great come-down to a man like me. But, if I must be caught, it's something to be caught by brave young heroes like you. My stars! How you did bolt into the room,—'Surrender, and up with your hands!' You might have been born and bred to the thief-catching."

Oswald is sorry if it was mean, but he could not own

up just then that he did not think there was any one in the study when he did that brave if rash act. He has told since.

"And what made you think there was any one in the house?" the robber asked, when he had thrown his head back, and laughed for quite half a minute. So we told him. And he applauded our valour, and Alice and H. O. explained that they would have said "Surrender," too, only they were reinforcements.

The robber ate some of the chestnuts—and we sat and wondered when Father would come home, and what he would say to us for our intrepid conduct. And the robber told us of all the things he had done before he began to break into houses. Dicky picked up the tools from the floor, and suddenly he said—

"Why, this is Father's screwdriver and his gimlets, and all! Well, I do call it jolly cheek to pick a man's locks with his own tools!"

"True, true," said the robber. "It is cheek, of the jolliest! But you see I've come down in the world. I was a highway robber once, but horses are so expensive to hire—five shillings an hour, you know—and I couldn't afford to keep them. The highwayman business isn't what it was."

"What about a bike?" said H. O.

But the robber thought cycles were low—and besides you couldn't go across country with them when occasion arose, as you could with a trusty steed. And he talked of highwaymen as if he knew just how we liked hearing it.

Then he told us how he had been a pirate captain and how he had sailed over waves mountains high, and gained rich prizes—and how he did begin to think that here he had found a profession to his mind.

"I don't say there are no ups and downs in it," he said, "especially in stormy weather. But what a trade! And a sword at your side, and the Jolly Roger flying at the peak, and a prize in sight. And all the black mouths of your guns pointed at the laden trader—and the wind in your favour, and your trusty crew ready to live and die for you! Oh—but it's a grand life!"

I did feel so sorry for him. He used such nice words, and he had a gentleman's voice.

"I'm sure you weren't brought up to be a pirate," said Dora. She had dressed even to her collar—and made Noël do it too—but the rest of us were in blankets with just a few odd things put on anyhow underneath.

The robber frowned and sighed.

"No," he said, "I was brought up to the law. I was at Balliol, bless your hearts, and that's true anyway." He sighed again, and looked hard at the fire.

"That was my Father's college," H. O. was beginning, but Dicky said—

"Why did you leave off being a pirate?"

"A pirate?" he said, as if he had not been thinking of such things. "Oh, yes; why I gave it up because because I could not get over the dreadful sea-sickness."

"Nelson was sea-sick," said Oswald.

"Ah," said the robber; "but I hadn't his luck or his pluck, or something. He stuck to it and won Trafalgar, didn't he? 'Kiss me, Hardy'?—and all that, eh? I couldn't stick to it—I had to resign. And nobody kissed *me*."

I saw by his understanding about Nelson that he was really a man who had been to a good school as well as to Balliol.

Then we asked him, "And what did you do then?"

And Alice asked if he was ever a coiner, and we told

him how we had thought we'd caught the desperate gang next door, and he was very much interested and said he was glad he had never taken to coining. "Besides, the coins are so ugly nowadays," he said, "no one could really find any pleasure in making them. And it's a hole-and-corner business at the best, isn't it?—and it must be a very thirsty one—with the hot metal and furnaces and things."

And again he looked at the fire.

Oswald forgot for a minute that the interesting stranger was a robber, and asked him if he wouldn't have a drink. Oswald has heard Father do this to his friends, so he knows it is the right thing. The robber said he didn't mind if he did. And that is right, too.

And Dora went and got a bottle of Father's ale—the Light Sparkling Family—and a glass, and we gave it to the robber. Dora said she would be responsible.

Then when he had had a drink he told us about bandits, but he said it was so bad in wet weather. Bandits' caves were hardly ever properly weathertight. And bush-ranging was the same.

"As a matter of fact," he said, "I was bush-ranging this afternoon, among the furze-bushes on the Heath, but I had no luck. I stopped the Lord Mayor in his gilt coach, with all his footmen in plush and gold lace, smart as cockatoos. But it was no go. The Lord Mayor hadn't a stiver in his pockets. One of the footmen had six new pennies: the Lord Mayor always pays his servants' wages in new pennies. I spent fourpence of that in bread and cheese, that on the table's the tuppence. Ah, it's a poor trade!" And then he filled his pipe again.

We had turned out the gas, so that Father should have a jolly good surprise when he did come home, and we sat and talked as pleasant as could be. I never liked a new man better than I liked that robber. And I felt so sorry for him. He told us he had been a war correspondent and an editor, in happier days, as well as a horse-stealer and a colonel of dragoons.

And quite suddenly, just as we were telling him about Lord Tottenham and our being highwaymen ourselves, he put up his hand and said "Shish!" and we were quiet and listened.

There was a scrape, scrape, scraping noise; it came from downstairs.

"They're filing something," whispered the robber, "here—shut up, give me that pistol, and the poker. There is a burglar now, and no mistake."

"It's only a toy one and it won't go off," I said, "but you can cock it."

Then we heard a snap.

"There goes the window bar," said the robber softly. "Jove! what an adventure! You kids stay here, I'll tackle it."

But Dicky and I said we should come. So he let us go as far as the bottom of the kitchen stairs, and we took the tongs and shovel with us. There was a light in the kitchen; a very little light. It is curious we never thought, any of us, that this might be a plan of our robber's to get away. We never thought of doubting his word of honour. And we were right.

That noble robber dashed the kitchen door open, and rushed in with the big toy pistol in one hand and the poker in the other, shouting out just like Oswald had done

"Surrender! You are discovered! Surrender, or I'll fire! Throw up your hands!" And Dicky and I rattled the tongs and shovel so that he might know there were more of us, all bristling with weapons.

And we heard a husky voice in the kitchen saying—

"All right, governor! Stow that scent sprinkler. I'll give in. Blowed if I ain't pretty well sick of the job, anyway."

Then we went in. Our robber was standing in the grandest manner with his legs very wide apart, and the pistol pointing at the cowering burglar. The burglar was a large man who did not mean to have a beard, I think, but he had got some of one, and a red comforter, and a fur cap, and his face was red and his voice was thick. How different from our own robber! The burglar had a dark lantern, and he was standing by the plate-basket. When we had lit the gas we all thought he was very like what a burglar ought to be. He did not look as if he could ever have been a pirate or a highwayman, or anything really dashing or noble, and he scowled and shuffled his feet and said: "Well, go on: why don't yer fetch the pleece?"

"Upon my word, I don't know," said our robber, rubbing his chin. "Oswald, why don't we fetch the police?"

It is not every robber that I would stand Christian names from, I can tell you; but just then I didn't think of that. I just said—

"Do you mean I'm to fetch one?"

Our robber looked at the burglar and said nothing.

Then the burglar began to speak very fast, and to look different ways with his hard, shiny little eyes.

"Lookee 'ere, governor," he said, "I was stony broke, so help me, I was. And blessed if I've nicked a haporth of your little lot. You know yourself there ain't much to tempt a bloke," he shook the plate-basket as if he was angry with it, and the yellowy spoons and forks rattled. "I was just a-looking through this 'ere Bank-ollerday show, when you come. Let me off, sir. Come now, I've got kids of my own at home, strike me if I ain't—same as yours—I've got a nipper just about 'is size, and what'll come of them if I'm lagged? I ain't been in it long, sir, and I ain't 'andy at it."

"No," said our robber; "you certainly are not."

Alice and the others had come down by now to see what was happening. Alice told me afterwards they thought it really was the cat this time.

"No, I ain't 'andy, as you say, sir, and if you let me off this once I'll chuck the whole blooming bizz; rake my civvy, I will. Don't be hard on a cove, mister; think of the missis and the kids. I've got one just the cut of little missy there; bless 'er pretty 'eart."

"Your family certainly fits your circumstances very nicely," said our robber.

Then Alice said—

"Oh, do let him go! If he's got a little girl like me, whatever will she do? Suppose it was Father!"

"I don't think he's got a little girl like you, my dear," said our robber, "and I think he'll be safer under lock and key."

"You ask yer Father to let me go, miss," said the burglar; "'e won't 'ave the 'art to refuse you."

"If I do," said Alice, "will you promise never to come back?"

"Not me, miss," the burglar said very earnestly, and he looked at the plate-basket again, as if that alone would be enough to keep him away, our robber said afterwards.

"And will you be good and not rob any more?" said Alice.

"I'll turn over a noo leaf, miss, so help me."

Then Alice said—

"Oh, do let him go! I'm sure he'll be good."

But our robber said no, it wouldn't be right; we must wait till Father came home.

Then H. O. said, very suddenly and plainly:

"I don't think it's at all fair, when you're a robber yourself."

The minute he'd said it the burglar said, "Kidded, by gum!"—and then our robber made a step towards him to catch hold of him, and before you had time to think "Hullo!" the burglar knocked the pistol up with one hand and knocked our robber down with the other, and was off out of the window like a shot, though Oswald and Dicky did try to stop him by holding on to his legs.

And that burglar had the cheek to put his head in at the window and say, "I'll give yer love to the kids and the missis"—and he was off like winking, and there were Alice and Dora trying to pick up our robber, and asking him whether he was hurt, and where. He wasn't hurt at all, except a lump at the back of his head. And he got up, and we dusted the kitchen floor off him. Eliza is a dirty girl.

Then he said, "Let's put up the shutters. It never rains but it pours. Now you've had two burglars I daresay you'll have twenty." So we put up the shutters, which Eliza has strict orders to do before she goes out, only she never does, and we went back to Father's study, and the robber said, "What a night we are having!" and put his boots back in the fender to go on steaming, and then we all talked at once. It was the most wonderful adventure we ever had, though it wasn't treasure-seeking—at least not ours. I suppose it was the burglar's treasure-seeking, but he didn't get much—and our robber said he didn't believe a word about those kids that were so like Alice and me.

And then there was the click of the gate, and we said, "Here's Father," and the robber said, "And now for the police."

Then we all jumped up. We did like him so much, and it seemed so unfair that he should be sent to prison, and the horrid, lumping big burglar not.

And Alice said, "Oh, *no*—run! Dicky will let you out at the back door. Oh, do go, go *now*."

And we all said, "Yes, *go*," and pulled him towards the door, and gave him his hat and stick and the things out of his pockets.

But Father's latchkey was in the door, and it was too late.

Father came in quickly, purring with the cold, and began to say, "It's all right, Foulkes, I've got—" And then he stopped short and stared at us. Then he said, in the voice we all hate, "Children, what is the meaning of all this?"

And for a minute nobody spoke.

Then my Father said, "Foulkes, I must really apologize for these very naughty—"

And then our robber rubbed his hands and laughed, and cried out: "You're mistaken, my dear sir, I'm not Foulkes; I'm a robber, captured by these young people in the most gallant manner. 'Hands up, surrender, or I fire,' and all the rest of it. My word, Bastable, but you've got some kids worth having! I wish my Denny had their pluck."

Then we began to understand, and it was like being knocked down, it was so sudden. And our robber told us he wasn't a robber after all. He was only an old college friend of my Father's, and he had come after dinner, when Father was just trying to mend the lock H. O. had broken, to ask Father to get him a letter to a doctor about his little boy Denny, who was ill. And Father had gone over the Heath to Vanbrugh Park to see some rich people he knows and get the letter. And he had left Mr Foulkes to wait till he came back, because it was important to know at once whether Father could get the letter, and if he couldn't Mr Foulkes would have had to try some one else directly.

We were dumb with amazement.

Our robber told my Father about the other burglar, and said he was sorry he'd let him escape, but my Father said, "Oh, it's all right: poor beggar; if he really had kids at home: you never can tell—forgive us our debts, don't you know; but tell me about the first business. It must have been moderately entertaining."

Then our robber told my Father how I had rushed into the room with a pistol, crying out . . . but you know all about that. And he laid it on so thick and fat about plucky young-uns, and chips of old blocks, and things like that, that I felt I was purple with shame, even under the blanket. So I swallowed that thing that tries to prevent you speaking when you ought to, and I said, "Look here, Father, I didn't really think there was any one in the study. We thought it was a cat at first, and then I thought there was no one there, and I was just larking. And when I said surrender and all that, it was just the game, don't you know?"

Then our robber said, "Yes, old chap; but when you found there really *was* some one there, you dropped the pistol and bunked, didn't you, eh?"

And I said, "No; I thought, 'Hullo! here's a robber! Well, it's all up, I suppose, but I may as well hold on and see what happens.'"

And I was glad I'd owned up, for Father slapped me on the back, and said I was a young brick, and our robber said I was no funk anyway, and though I got very hot under the blanket I liked it, and I explained that the others would have done the same if they had thought of it.

Then Father got up some more beer, and laughed about Dora's responsibility, and he got out a box of figs he had bought for us, only he hadn't given it to us because of the Water Rates, and Eliza came in and brought up the bread and cheese, and what there was left of the neck of mutton—cold wreck of mutton, Father called it—and we had a feast—like a picnic—all sitting anywhere, and eating with our fingers. It was prime. We sat up till past twelve o'clock, and I never felt so pleased to think I was not born a girl. It was hard on the others; they would have done just the same if they'd thought of it. But it does make you feel jolly when your pater says you're a young brick!

When Mr Foulkes was going, he said to Alice, "Good-bye, Hardy."

And Alice understood, of course, and kissed him as hard as she could.

And she said, "I wanted to, when you said no one kissed you when you left off being a pirate captain."

And he said, "I know you did, my dear."

And Dora kissed him too, and said, "I suppose none of these tales were true?"

And our robber just said, "I tried to play the part properly, my dear."

And he jolly well did play it, and no mistake. We have often seen him since, and his boy Denny, and his girl Daisy, but that comes in another story.

And if any of you kids who read this ever had two such adventures in one night you can just write and tell me. That's all.

Chapter 14

THE DIVINING-ROD

You have no idea how uncomfortable the house was on the day when we sought for gold with the divining-rod. It was like a spring-cleaning in the winter-time. All the carpets were up, because Father had told Eliza to make the place decent as there was a gentleman coming to dinner the next day. So she got in a charwoman, and they slopped water about, and left brooms and brushes on the stairs for people to tumble over. H. O. got a big bump on his head in that way, and when he said it was too bad, Eliza said he should keep in the nursery then, and not be where he'd no business. We bandaged his head with a towel, and then he stopped crying and played at being England's wounded hero dying in the cockpit, while every man was doing his duty, as the hero had told them to, and Alice was Hardy, and I was the doctor, and the others were the crew. Playing at Hardy made us think of our own dear robber, and we wished he was there, and wondered if we should ever see him any more.

We were rather astonished at Father's having anyone to dinner, because now he never seems to think of anything but business. Before Mother died people often came to dinner, and Father's business did not take up so much of his time and was not the bother it is now. And we used to see who could go furthest down in our nightgowns and get nice things to eat, without being seen, out of the dishes as they came out of the dining room. Eliza can't cook very nice things. She told Father she was a good plain cook, but he says it was a fancy portrait. We stayed in the nursery till the charwoman came in and told us to be off—she was going to make one job of it, and have our carpet up as well as all the others, now the man was here to beat them. It came up, and it was very dusty—and under it we found my threepenny-bit that I lost ages ago, which shows what Eliza is. H. O. had got tired of being the wounded hero, and Dicky was so tired of doing nothing that Dora said she knew he'd begin to tease Noël in a minute; then of course Dicky said he wasn't going to tease anybody—he was going out to the Heath. He said he'd heard that nagging women drove a man from his home, and now he found it was quite true. Oswald always tries to be a peace-maker, so he told Dicky to shut up and not make an ass of himself. And Alice said, "Well, Dora began—" And Dora tossed her chin up and said it wasn't any business of Oswald's any way, and no one asked Alice's opinion. So we all felt very uncomfortable till Noël said, "Don't let's quarrel about nothing. You know let dogs delight—and I made up another piece while you were talking

Quarrelling is an evil thing,
It fills with gall life's cup;
For when once you begin
It takes such a long time to make it up."

We all laughed then and stopped jawing at each other. Noël is very funny with his poetry. But that piece happened to come out quite true. You begin to quarrel and then you can't stop; often, long before the others are ready to cry and make it up, I see how silly it is, and I want to laugh; but it doesn't do to say so—

for it only makes the others crosser than they were before. I wonder why that is?

Alice said Noël ought to be poet laureate, and she actually went out in the cold and got some laurel leaves—the spotted kind—out of the garden, and Dora made a crown and we put it on him. He was quite pleased, but the leaves made a mess, and Eliza said, "Don't." I believe that's a word grown-ups use more than any other. Then suddenly Alice thought of that old idea of hers for finding treasure, and she said—

"Do let's try the divining-rod."

So Oswald said, "Fair priestess, we do greatly desire to find gold beneath our land, therefore we pray thee practise with the divining-rod, and tell us where we can find it."

"Do ye desire to fashion of it helms and hauberks?" said Alice.

"Yes," said Noël; "and chains and ouches."

"I bet you don't know what an 'ouch' is," said Dicky.

"Yes I do, so there!" said Noël. "It's a carcanet. I looked it out in the dicker, now then!"

We asked him what a carcanet was, but he wouldn't say.

"And we want to make fair goblets of the gold," said Oswald.

"Yes, to drink coconut milk out of," said H. O.

"And we desire to build fair palaces of it," said Dicky.

"And to buy things," said Dora; "a great many things. New Sunday frocks and hats and kid gloves and—"

She would have gone on for ever so long only we reminded her that we hadn't found the gold yet.

By this Alice had put on the nursery tablecloth, which is green, and tied the old blue and yellow antimacassar over her head, and she said—

"If your intentions are correct, fear nothing and follow me."

And she went down into the hall. We all followed chanting "Heroes." It is a gloomy thing the girls learnt at the High School, and we always use it when we want a priestly chant.

Alice stopped short by the hat-stand, and held up her hands as well as she could for the table-cloth, and said—

"Now, great altar of the golden idol, yield me the divining-rod that I may use it for the good of the suffering people.

The umbrella-stand was the altar of the golden idol, and it yielded her the old school umbrella. She carried it between her palms.

"Now," she said, "I shall sing the magic chant. You mustn't say anything, but just follow wherever I go like follow my leader, you know—and when there is gold underneath the magic rod will twist in the hand of the priestess like a live thing that seeks to be free. Then you will dig, and the golden treasure will be revealed. H. O., if you make that clatter with your boots they'll come and tell us not to. Now come on all of you."

So she went upstairs and down and into every room. We followed her on tiptoe, and Alice sang as she went. What she sang is not out of a book—Noël made it up while she was dressing up for the priestess.

Ashen rod cold
That here I hold,
Teach me where to find the gold.

When we came to where Eliza was, she said, "Get along with you"; but Dora said it was only a game, and we wouldn't touch anything, and our boots were quite clean, and Eliza might as well let us. So she did.

It was all right for the priestess, but it was a little dull for the rest of us, because she wouldn't let us sing, too; so we said we'd had enough of it, and if she couldn't find the gold we'd leave off and play something else. The priestess said, "All right, wait a minute," and went on singing. Then we all followed her back into the nursery, where the carpet was up and the boards smelt of soft soap. Then she said, "It moves, it moves! Once more the choral hymn!" So we sang "Heroes" again, and in the middle the umbrella dropped from her hands.

"The magic rod has spoken," said Alice; "dig here, and that with courage and despatch." We didn't quite see how to dig, but we all began to scratch on the floor with our hands, but the priestess said, "Don't be so silly! It's the place where they come to do the gas. The board's loose. Dig an you value your lives, for ere sundown the dragon who guards this spoil will return in his fiery fury and make you his unresisting prey."

So we dug—that is, we got the loose board up. And Alice threw up her arms and cried

"See the rich treasure—the gold in thick layers, with silver and diamonds stuck in it!"

"Like currants in cake," said H. O.

"It's a lovely treasure," said Dicky yawning. "Let's come back and carry it away another day."

But Alice was kneeling by the hole.

"Let me feast my eyes on the golden splendour," she said, "hidden these long centuries from the human eye. Behold how the magic rod has led us to treasures more Oswald, don't push so!—more bright than ever monarch—I say, there is something down there, really. I saw it shine!"

We thought she was kidding, but when she began to try to get into the hole, which was much too small, we saw she meant it, so I said, "Let's have a squint," and I looked, but I couldn't see anything, even when I lay down on my stomach. The others lay down on their stomachs too and tried to see, all but Noël, who stood and looked at us and said we were the great serpents come down to drink at the magic pool. He wanted to be the knight and slay the great serpents with his good sword—he even drew the umbrella ready—but Alice said, "All right, we will in a minute. But now I'm sure I saw it; do get a match, Noël, there's a dear."

"What did you see?" asked Noël, beginning to go for the matches very slowly.

"Something bright, away in the corner under the board against the beam."

"Perhaps it was a rat's eye,—Noël said, "or a snake's," and we did not put our heads quite so close to the hole till he came back with the matches.

Then I struck a match, and Alice cried, "There it is!"

And there it was, and it was a half-sovereign, partly dusty and partly bright. We think perhaps a mouse, disturbed by the carpets being taken up, may have brushed the dust of years from part of the half-sovereign with his tail. We can't imagine how it came there, only Dora thinks she remembers once when H. O. was very little Mother gave him some money to hold, and he dropped it, and it rolled all over the floor. So we think perhaps this was part of it. We were very glad. H. O. wanted to go out at once and buy a mask he had seen for fourpence. It had been a shilling mask, but now it was going very cheap because Guy Fawkes' Day was over, and it was a little cracked at the top. But Dora said, "I don't know that it's our money. Let's wait and ask Father."

But H. O. did not care about waiting, and I felt for him. Dora is rather like grown-ups in that way; she does not seem to understand that when you want a thing you do want it, and that you don't wish to wait, even a minute.

So we went and asked Albert-next-door's uncle. He was pegging away at one of the rotten novels he has to write to make his living, but he said we weren't interrupting him at all.

"My hero's folly has involved him in a difficulty," he said. "It is his own fault. I will leave him to meditate on the incredible fatuity—the hare-brained recklessness which have brought him to this pass. It will be a lesson to him. I, meantime, will give myself unreservedly to the pleasures of your conversation."

That's one thing I like Albert's uncle for. He always talks like a book, and yet you can always understand what he means. I think he is more like us, inside of his mind, than most grown-up people are. He can pretend beautifully. I never met any one else so good at it, except our robber, and we began it, with him. But it was Albert's uncle who first taught us how to make people talk like books when you're playing things, and he made us learn to tell a story straight from the beginning, not starting in the middle like most people do. So now Oswald remembered what he had been told, as he generally does, and began at the beginning, but when he came to where Alice said she was the priestess, Albert's uncle said—

"Let the priestess herself set forth the tale in fitting speech."

So Alice said, "O high priest of the great idol, the humblest of thy slaves took the school umbrella for a divining-rod, and sang the song of inver—what's-it's name?"

"Invocation perhaps?" said Albert's uncle.

"Yes; and then I went about and about and the others got tired, so the divining-rod fell on a certain spot, and I said, 'Dig', and we dug—it was where the loose board is for the gas men—and then there really and truly was a half-sovereign lying under the boards, and here it is."

Albert's uncle took it and looked at it.

"The great high priest will bite it to see if it's good," he said, and he did. "I congratulate you," he went on; "you are indeed among those favoured by the Immortals. First you find half-crowns in the garden, and now this. The high priest advises you to tell your Father, and ask if you may keep it. My hero has become penitent, but impatient. I must pull him out of this scrape. Ye have my leave to depart."

Of course we know from Kipling that that means, "You'd better bunk, and be sharp about it," so we came away. I do like Albert's uncle. I shall be like that when I'm a man. He gave us our Jungle books, and he is awfully clever, though he does have to write grown-up tales.

We told Father about it that night. He was very kind. He said we might certainly have the half-sovereign, and he hoped we should enjoy ourselves with our treasure-trove.

Then he said, "Your dear Mother's Indian Uncle is coming to dinner here to-morrow night. So will you not drag the furniture about overhead, please, more than you're absolutely obliged; and H. O. might wear slippers or something. I can always distinguish the note of H. O.'s boots."

We said we would be very quiet, and Father went on "This Indian Uncle is not used to children, and he is coming to talk business with me. It is really important that he should be quiet. Do you think, Dora, that perhaps bed at six for H. O. and Noël—"

But H. O. said, "Father, I really and truly won't make a noise. I'll stand on my head all the evening sooner than disturb the Indian Uncle with my boots."

And Alice said Noël never made a row anyhow.

So Father laughed and said, "All right." And he said we might do as we liked with the half-sovereign. "Only for goodness' sake don't try to go in for business with it," he said. "It's always a mistake to go into business with an insufficient capital."

We talked it over all that evening, and we decided that as we were not to go into business with our half-sovereign it was no use not spending it at once, and so we might as well have a right royal feast. The next day we went out and bought the things. We got figs, and almonds and raisins, and a real raw rabbit, and Eliza promised to cook it for us if we would wait till tomorrow, because of the Indian Uncle coming to dinner. She was very busy cooking nice things for him to eat. We got the rabbit because we are so tired of beef and mutton, and Father hasn't a bill at the poultry shop. And we got some flowers to go on the dinnerta-ble for Father's party. And we got hardbake and raspberry noyau and peppermint rock and oranges and a coconut, with other nice things. We put it all in the top long drawer. It is H. O.'s play drawer, and we made him turn his things out and put them in Father's old portmanteau. H. O. is getting old enough now to learn to be unselfish, and besides, his drawer wanted tidying very badly. Then we all vowed by the honour of the ancient House of Bastable that we would not touch any of the feast till Dora gave the word next day. And we gave H. O. some of the hardbake, to make it easier for him to keep his vow. The next day was the most rememorable day in all our lives, but we didn't know that then. But that is another story. I think that is such a useful way to know when you can't think how to end up a chapter. I learnt it from another writer named Kipling. I've mentioned him before, I believe, but he deserves it!

Chapter 15

"LO, THE POOR INDIAN!"

It was all very well for Father to ask us not to make a row because the Indian Uncle was coming to talk business, but my young brother's boots are not the only things that make a noise. We took his boots away and made him wear Dora's bath slippers, which are soft and woolly, and hardly any soles to them; and of course we wanted to see the Uncle, so we looked over the banisters when he came, and we were as quiet as mice—but when Eliza had let him in she went straight down to the kitchen and made the most awful row you ever heard, it sounded like the Day of Judgement, or all the saucepans and crockery in the house being kicked about the floor, but she told me afterwards it was only the teatray and one or two cups and saucers, that she had knocked over in her flurry. We heard the Uncle say, "God bless my soul!" and then he went into Father's study and the door was shut—we didn't see him properly at all that time.

I don't believe the dinner was very nice. Something got burned I'm sure—for we smelt it. It was an extra smell, besides the mutton. I know *that* got burned. Eliza wouldn't have any of us in the kitchen except Dora—till dinner was over. Then we got what was left of the dessert, and had it on the stairs—just round the corner where they can't see you from the hall, unless the first landing gas is lighted. Suddenly the study door opened and the Uncle came out and went and felt in his greatcoat pocket. It was his cigar-case he wanted. We saw that afterwards. We got a much better view of him then. He didn't look like an Indian but just like a kind of brown, big Englishman, and of course he didn't see us, but we heard him mutter to himself—

"Shocking bad dinner! Eh!—what?" When he went back to the study he didn't shut the door properly. That door has always been a little tiresome since the day we took the lock off to get out the pencil sharpener H. O. had shoved into the keyhole. We didn't listen really and truly—but the Indian Uncle has a very big voice, and Father was not going to be beaten by a poor Indian in talking or anything else—so he spoke up too, like a man, and I heard him say it was a very good business, and only wanted a little capital—and he said it as if it was an imposition he had learned, and he hated having to say it. The Uncle said, "Pooh, pooh!" to that, and then he said he was afraid that what that same business wanted was not capital but management. Then I heard my Father say, "It is not a pleasant subject: I am sorry I introduced it. Suppose we change it, sir. Let me fill your glass." Then the poor Indian said something about vintage—and that a poor, broken-down man like he was couldn't be too careful. And then Father said, "Well, whisky then," and afterwards they talked about Native Races and Imperial something or other and it got very dull.

So then Oswald remembered that you must not hear what people do not intend you to hear—even if you are not listening; and he said, "We ought not to stay here any longer. Perhaps they would not like us to hear—"

Alice said, "Oh, do you think it could possibly matter?" and went and shut the study door softly but quite tight. So it was no use staying there any longer, and we went to the nursery.

Then Noël said, "Now I understand. Of course my Father is making a banquet for the Indian, because he is a poor, broken-down man. We might have known that from 'Lo, the poor Indian!' you know."

We all agreed with him, and we were glad to have the thing explained, because we had not understood before what Father wanted to have people to dinner for—and not let us come in.

"Poor people are very proud," said Alice, "and I expect Father thought the Indian would be ashamed, if all of us children knew how poor he was."

Then Dora said, "Poverty is no disgrace. We should honour honest Poverty."

And we all agreed that that was so.

"I wish his dinner had not been so nasty," Dora said, while Oswald put lumps of coal on the fire with his fingers, so as not to make a noise. He is a very thoughtful boy, and he did not wipe his fingers on his trouser leg as perhaps Noël or H. O. would have done, but he just rubbed them on Dora's handkerchief while she was talking. "I am afraid the dinner was horrid." Dora went on, "The table looked very nice with the flowers we got. I set it myself, and Eliza made me borrow the silver spoons and forks from Albert-next-door's Mother."

"I hope the poor Indian is honest," said Dicky gloomily, "when you are a poor, broken-down man silver spoons must be a great temptation."

Oswald told him not to talk such tommy-rot because the Indian was a relation, so of course he couldn't do anything dishonourable. And Dora said it was all right any way, because she had washed up the spoons and forks herself and counted them, and they were all there, and she had put them into their wash-leather bag, and taken them back to Albert-next-door's Mother.

"And the brussels sprouts were all wet and swimmy," she went on, "and the potatoes looked grey—and there were bits of black in the gravy—and the mutton was bluey-red and soft in the middle. I saw it when it came out. The apple-pie looked very nice—but it wasn't quite done in the apply part. The other thing that was burnt—you must have smelt it, was the soup."

"It is a pity," said Oswald; "I don't suppose he gets a good dinner every day."

"No more do we," said H. O., "but we shall tomorrow."

I thought of all the things we had bought with our half-sovereign—the rabbit and the sweets and the almonds and raisins and figs and the coconut: and I thought of the nasty mutton and things, and while I was thinking about it all Alice said—

"Let's ask the poor Indian to come to dinner with us to-morrow." I should have said it myself if she had given me time.

We got the little ones to go to bed by promising to put a note on their dressing-table saying what had happened, so that they might know the first thing in the morning, or in the middle of the night if they happened to wake up, and then we elders arranged everything.

I waited by the back door, and when the Uncle was beginning to go Dicky was to drop a marble down between the banisters for a signal, so that I could run round and meet the Uncle as he came out.

This seems like deceit, but if you are a thoughtful

and considerate boy you will understand that we could not go down and say to the Uncle in the hall under Father's eye, "Father has given you a beastly, nasty dinner, but if you will come to dinner with us tomorrow, we will show you our idea of good things to eat." You will see, if you think it over, that this would not have been at all polite to Father.

So when the Uncle left, Father saw him to the door and let him out, and then went back to the study, looking very sad, Dora says.

As the poor Indian came down our steps he saw me there at the gate. I did not mind his being poor, and I said, "Good evening, Uncle," just as politely as though he had been about to ascend into one of the gilded chariots of the rich and affluent, instead of having to walk to the station a quarter of a mile in the mud, unless he had the money for a tram fare.

"Good evening, Uncle." I said it again, for he stood staring at me. I don't suppose he was used to politeness from boys—some boys are anything but—especially to the Aged Poor.

So I said, "Good evening, Uncle," yet once again. Then he said—

"Time you were in bed, young man. Eh!—what?"

Then I saw I must speak plainly with him, man to man. So I did. I said—

"You've been dining with my Father, and we couldn't help hearing you say the dinner was shocking. So we thought as you're an Indian, perhaps you're very poor"—I didn't like to tell him we had heard the dreadful truth from his own lips, so I went on, "because of 'Lo, the poor Indian'—you know—and you can't get a good dinner every day. And we are very sorry if you're poor; and won't you come and have dinner with us to-morrow—with us children, I mean? It's a very, very good dinner—rabbit, and hardbake, and coconut—and you needn't mind us knowing you're poor, because we know honourable poverty is no disgrace, and—" I could have gone on much longer, but he interrupted me to say—

"Upon my word! And what's *your* name, eh?"

"Oswald Bastable," I said; and I do hope you people who are reading this story have not guessed before that I was Oswald all the time.

"Oswald Bastable, eh? Bless my soul!" said the poor Indian. "Yes, I'll dine with you, Mr Oswald Bastable, with all the pleasure in life. Very kind and cordial invitation, I'm sure. Good night, sir. At one o'clock, I presume?"

"Yes, at one," I said. "Good night, sir."

Then I went in and told the others, and we wrote a paper and put it on the boy's dressing-table, and it said—

"The poor Indian is coming at one. He seemed very grateful to me for my kindness."

We did not tell Father that the Uncle was coming to dinner with us, for the polite reason that I have explained before. But we had to tell Eliza; so we said a friend was coming to dinner and we wanted everything very nice. I think she thought it was Albert-next-door, but she was in a good temper that day, and she agreed to cook the rabbit and to make a pudding with currants in it. And when one o'clock came the Indian Uncle came too. I let him in and helped him off with his greatcoat, which was all furry inside, and took him straight to the nursery. We were to have dinner there as usual, for we had decided from the first that he would enjoy himself more if he was not made a stranger of. We agreed to treat him as one of ourselves, because if we were too polite, he might think it was our pride because he was poor.

He shook hands with us all and asked our ages, and what schools we went to, and shook his head when we said we were having a holiday just now. I felt rather uncomfortable—I always do when they talk about schools—and I couldn't think of anything to say to show him we meant to treat him as one of ourselves. I did ask if he played cricket. He said he had not played lately. And then no one said anything till dinner came in. We had all washed our faces and hands and brushed our hair before he came in, and we all looked very nice, especially Oswald, who had had his hair cut that very morning. When Eliza had brought in the rabbit and gone out again, we looked at each other in silent despair, like in books. It seemed as if it were going to be just a dull dinner like the one the poor Indian had had the night before; only, of course, the things to eat would be nicer. Dicky kicked Oswald under the table to make him say something—and he had his new boots on, too!—but Oswald did not kick back; then the Uncle asked

"Do you carve, sir, or shall I?"

Suddenly Alice said—

"Would you like grown-up dinner, Uncle, or play-dinner?"

He did not hesitate a moment, but said, "Play-dinner, by all means. Eh!—what?" and then we knew it was all right.

So we at once showed the Uncle how to be a dauntless hunter. The rabbit was the deer we had slain in the green forest with our trusty yew bows, and we toasted the joints of it, when the Uncle had carved it, on bits of firewood sharpened to a point. The Uncle's piece got a little burnt, but he said it was delicious, and he said game was always nicer when you had killed it yourself. When Eliza had taken away the rabbit bones and brought in the pudding, we waited till she had gone out and shut the door, and then we put the dish down on the floor and slew the pudding in the dish in the good old-fashioned way. It was a wild boar at bay, and very hard indeed to kill, even with forks. The Uncle was very fierce indeed with the pudding, and jumped and howled when he speared it, but when it came to his turn to be helped, he said, "No, thank you; think of my liver. Eh!—what?"

But he had some almonds and raisins—when we had climbed to the top of the chest of drawers to pluck them from the boughs of the great trees; and he had a fig from the cargo that the rich merchants brought in their ship—the long drawer was the ship—and the rest of us had the sweets and the coconut. It was a very glorious and beautiful feast, and when it was over we said we hoped it was better than the dinner last night. And he said:

"I never enjoyed a dinner more." He was too polite to say what he really thought about Father's dinner. And we saw that though he might be poor, he was a true gentleman.

He smoked a cigar while we finished up what there was left to eat, and told us about tiger shooting and about elephants. We asked him about wigwams, and wampum, and mocassins, and beavers, but he did not seem to know, or else he was shy about talking of the wonders of his native land.

We liked him very much indeed, and when he was going at last, Alice nudged me, and I said—

"There's one and threepence farthing left out of our half-sovereign. Will you take it, please, because we do like you very much indeed, and we don't want it, really; and we would rather you had it." And I put the money into his hand.

"I'll take the threepenny-bit," he said, turning the money over and looking at it, "but I couldn't rob you of the rest. By the way, where did you get the money for this most royal spread—half a sovereign you said—eh, what?"

We told him all about the different ways we had looked for treasure, and when we had been telling some time he sat down, to listen better; and at last we told him how Alice had played at divining-rod, and how it really had found a half-sovereign. Then he said he would like to see her do it again. But we explained that the rod would only show gold and silver, and that we were quite sure there was no more gold in the house, because we happened to have looked very carefully.

"Well, silver, then," said he; "let's hide the plate-basket, and little Alice shall make the divining-rod find it. Eh!—what?"

"There isn't any silver in the plate-basket now," Dora said. "Eliza asked me to borrow the silver spoons and forks for your dinner last night from Albert-next-door's Mother. Father never notices, but she thought it would be nicer for you. Our own silver went to have the dents taken out; and I don't think Father could afford to pay the man for doing it, for the silver hasn't come back."

"Bless my soul!" said the Uncle again, looking at the hole in the big chair that we burnt when we had Guy Fawkes' Day indoors. "And how much pocket-money do you get? Eh!—what?"

"We don't have any now," said Alice; "but indeed we don't want the other shilling. We'd much rather you had it, wouldn't we?"

And the rest of us said, "Yes." The Uncle wouldn't take it, but he asked a lot of questions, and at last he went away. And when he went he said—

"Well, youngsters, I've enjoyed myself very much. I shan't forget your kind hospitality. Perhaps the poor Indian may be in a position to ask you all to dinner some day.

Oswald said if he ever could we should like to come very much, but he was not to trouble to get such a nice dinner as ours, because we could do very well with cold mutton and rice pudding. We do not like these things, but Oswald knows how to behave. Then the poor Indian went away.

We had not got any treasure by this party, but we had had a very good time, and I am sure the Uncle enjoyed himself.

We were so sorry he was gone that we could none of us eat much tea; but we did not mind, because we had pleased the poor Indian and enjoyed ourselves too. Besides, as Dora said, "A contented mind is a continual feast," so it did not matter about not wanting tea.

Only H. O. did not seem to think a continual feast was a contented mind, and Eliza gave him a powder in what was left of the red-currant jelly Father had for the nasty dinner.

But the rest of us were quite well, and I think it must have been the coconut with H. O. We hoped nothing had disagreed with the Uncle, but we never knew.

Chapter 16

THE END OF THE TREASURE-SEEKING

Now it is coming near the end of our treasure-seeking, and the end was so wonderful that now nothing is like it used to be. It is like as if our fortunes had been in an earthquake, and after those, you know, everything comes out wrong-way up.

The day after the Uncle speared the pudding with us opened in gloom and sadness. But you never know. It was destined to be a day when things happened. Yet no sign of this appeared in the early morning. Then all was misery and upsetness. None of us felt quite well; I don't know why: and Father had one of his awful colds, so Dora persuaded him not to go to London, but to stay cosy and warm in the study, and she made him some gruel. She makes it better than Eliza does; Eliza's gruel is all little lumps, and when you suck them it is dry oatmeal inside.

We kept as quiet as we could, and I made H. O. do some lessons, like the G. B. had advised us to. But it was very dull. There are some days when you seem to have got to the end of all the things that could ever possibly happen to you, and you feel you will spend all the rest of your life doing dull things just the same way. Days like this are generally wet days. But, as I said, you never know.

Then Dicky said if things went on like this he should run away to sea, and Alice said she thought it would be rather nice to go into a convent. H. O. was a little disagreeable because of the powder Eliza had given him, so he tried to read two books at once, one with each eye, just because Noël wanted one of the books, which was very selfish of him, so it only made his headache worse. H. O. is getting old enough to learn by experience that it is wrong to be selfish, and when he complained about his head Oswald told him whose fault it was, because I am older than he is, and it is my duty to show him where he is wrong. But he began to cry, and then Oswald had to cheer him up because of Father wanting to be quiet. So Oswald said—

"They'll eat H. O. if you don't look out!"

And Dora said Oswald was too bad.

Of course Oswald was not going to interfere again, so he went to look out of the window and see the trams go by, and by and by H. O. came and looked out too, and Oswald, who knows when to be generous and forgiving, gave him a piece of blue pencil and two nibs, as good as new, to keep.

As they were looking out at the rain splashing on the stones in the street they saw a four-wheeled cab come lumbering up from the way the station is. Oswald called out

"Here comes the coach of the Fairy Godmother. It'll stop here, you see if it doesn't!"

So they all came to the window to look. Oswald had only said that about stopping and he was stricken with wonder and amaze when the cab really did stop. It had boxes on the top and knobby parcels sticking out of the window, and it was something like going away to the seaside and something like the gentleman who takes things about in a carriage with the wooden shutters up, to sell to the drapers' shops. The cabman got down, and some one inside handed out ever so many parcels of different shapes and sizes, and the cabman stood holding them in his arms and grinning over them.

Dora said, "It is a pity some one doesn't tell him this isn't the house." And then from inside the cab some one put out a foot feeling for the step, like a tortoise's foot coming out from under his shell when you are holding him off the ground, and then a leg came and more parcels, and then Noël cried—

"It's the poor Indian!"

And it was.

Eliza opened the door, and we were all leaning over the banisters. Father heard the noise of parcels and boxes in the hall, and he came out without remembering how bad his cold was. If you do that yourself when you have a cold they call you careless and naughty. Then we heard the poor Indian say to Father

"I say, Dick, I dined with your kids yesterday—as I daresay they've told you. Jolliest little cubs I ever saw! Why didn't you let me see them the other night? The eldest is the image of poor Janey—and as to young Oswald, he's a man! If he's not a man, I'm a nigger! Eh!—what? And Dick, I say, I shouldn't wonder if I could find a friend to put a bit into that business of yours—eh?"

Then he and Father went into the study and the door was shut—and we went down and looked at the parcels. Some were done up in old, dirty newspapers, and tied with bits of rag, and some were in brown paper and string from the shops, and there were boxes. We wondered if the Uncle had come to stay and this was his luggage, or whether it was to sell. Some of it smelt of spices, like merchandise—and one bundle Alice felt certain was a bale. We heard a hand on the knob of the study door after a bit, and Alice said—

"Fly!" and we all got away but H. O., and the Uncle caught him by the leg as he was trying to get upstairs after us.

"Peeping at the baggage, eh?" said the Uncle, and the rest of us came down because it would have been dishonourable to leave H. O. alone in a scrape, and we wanted to see what was in the parcels.

"I didn't touch," said H. O. "Are you coming to stay? I hope you are."

"No harm done if you did touch," said the good, kind, Indian man to all of us. "For all these parcels are *for you.*"

I have several times told you about our being dumb with amazement and terror and joy, and things like that, but I never remember us being dumber than we were when he said this.

The Indian Uncle went on: "I told an old friend of mine what a pleasant dinner I had with you, and about the threepenny-bit, and the divining-rod, and all that, and he sent all these odds and ends as presents for you. Some of the things came from India."

"Have you come from India, Uncle?" Noël asked; and when he said "Yes" we were all very much surprised, for we never thought of his being that sort of Indian. We thought he was the Red kind, and of course his not being accounted for his ignorance of beavers and things.

He got Eliza to help, and we took all the parcels into the nursery and he undid them and undid them and undid them, till the papers lay thick on the floor. Father came too and sat in the Guy Fawkes chair. I cannot begin to tell you all the things that kind friend of

Uncle's had sent us. He must be a very agreeable person.

There were toys for the kids and model engines for Dick and me, and a lot of books, and Japanese china tea-sets for the girls, red and white and gold—there were sweets by the pound and by the box—and long yards and yards of soft silk from India, to make frocks for the girls—and a real Indian sword for Oswald and a book of Japanese pictures for Noël, and some ivory chessmen for Dicky: the castles of the chessmen are elephant-and-castles. There is a railway station called that; I never knew what it meant before. The brown paper and string parcels had boxes of games in them—and big cases of preserved fruits and things. And the shabby old newspaper parcels and the boxes had the Indian things in. I never saw so many beautiful things before. There were carved fans and silver bangles and strings of amber beads, and necklaces of uncut gems turquoises and garnets, the Uncle said they were—and shawls and scarves of silk, and cabinets of brown and gold, and ivory boxes and silver trays, and brass things. The Uncle kept saying, "This is for you, young man," or "Little Alice will like this fan," or "Miss Dora would look well in this green silk, I think. Eh!—what?"

And Father looked on as if it was a dream, till the Uncle suddenly gave him an ivory paper-knife and a box of cigars, and said, "My old friend sent you these, Dick; he's an old friend of yours too, he says." And he winked at my Father, for H. O. and I saw him. And my Father winked back, though he has always told us not to.

That was a wonderful day. It was a treasure, and no mistake! I never saw such heaps and heaps of presents, like things out of a fairy-tale—and even Eliza had a shawl. Perhaps she deserved it, for she did cook the rabbit and the pudding; and Oswald says it is not her fault if her nose turns up and she does not brush her hair. I do not think Eliza likes brushing things. It is the same with the carpets. But Oswald tries to make allowances even for people who do not wash their ears.

The Indian Uncle came to see us often after that, and his friend always sent us something. Once he tipped us a sovereign each—the Uncle brought it; and once he sent us money to go to the Crystal Palace, and the Uncle took us; and another time to a circus; and when Christmas was near the Uncle said—

"You remember when I dined with you, some time ago, you promised to dine with me some day, if I could ever afford to give a dinner-party. Well, I'm going to have one—a Christmas party. Not on Christmas Day, because every one goes home then—but on the day after. Cold mutton and rice pudding. You'll come? Eh!—what?"

We said we should be delighted, if Father had no objection, because that is the proper thing to say, and the poor Indian, I mean the Uncle, said, "No, your Father won't object—he's coming too, bless your soul!"

We all got Christmas presents for the Uncle. The girls made him a handkerchief case and a comb bag, out of some of the pieces of silk he had given them. I got him a knife with three blades; H. O. got a siren whistle, a very strong one, and Dicky joined with me in the knife, and Noël would give the Indian ivory box that Uncle's friend had sent on the wonderful Fairy Cab day. He said it was the very nicest thing he had, and he was sure Uncle wouldn't mind his not having bought it with his own money.

I think Father's business must have got better perhaps Uncle's friend put money in it and that did it good, like feeding the starving. Anyway we all had new suits, and the girls had the green silk from India made into frocks, and on Boxing Day we went in two cabs—Father and the girls in one, and us boys in the other.

We wondered very much where the Indian Uncle lived, because we had not been told. And we thought when the cab began to go up the hill towards the Heath that perhaps the Uncle lived in one of the poky little houses up at the top of Greenwich. But the cab went right over the Heath and in at some big gates, and through a shrubbery all white with frost like a fairy forest, because it was Christmas time. And at last we stopped before one of those jolly, big, ugly red houses with a lot of windows, that are so comfortable inside, and on the steps was the Indian Uncle, looking very big and grand, in a blue cloth coat and yellow sealskin waistcoat, with a bunch of seals hanging from it.

"I wonder whether he has taken a place as butler here?" said Dicky. "A poor, broken-down man—"

Noël thought it was very likely, because he knew that in these big houses there were always thousands of stately butlers.

The Uncle came down the steps and opened the cab door himself, which I don't think butlers would expect to have to do. And he took us in. It was a lovely hall, with bear and tiger skins on the floor, and a big clock with the faces of the sun and moon dodging out when it was day or night, and Father Time with a scythe coming out at the hours, and the name on it was "Flint. Ashford. 1776"; and there was a fox eating a stuffed duck in a glass case, and horns of stags and other animals over the doors.

"We'll just come into my study first," said the Uncle, "and wish each other a Merry Christmas." So then we knew he wasn't the butler, but it must be his own house, for only the master of the house has a study.

His study was not much like Father's. It had hardly any books, but swords and guns and newspapers and a great many boots, and boxes half unpacked, with more Indian things bulging out of them.

We gave him our presents and he was awfully pleased. Then he gave us his Christmas presents. You must be tired of hearing about presents, but I must remark that all the Uncle's presents were watches; there was a watch for each of us, with our names engraved inside, all silver except H. O.'s, and that was a Waterbury, "To match his boots," the Uncle said. I don't know what he meant.

Then the Uncle looked at Father, and Father said, "You tell them, sir."

So the Uncle coughed and stood up and made a speech. He said—

"Ladies and gentlemen, we are met together to discuss an important subject which has for some weeks engrossed the attention of the honourable member opposite and myself."

I said, "Hear, hear," and Alice whispered, "What happened to the guinea-pig?" Of course you know the answer to that.

The Uncle went on—

"I am going to live in this house, and as it's rather big for me, your Father has agreed that he and you shall come and live with me. And so, if you're agreeable, we're all going to live here together, and, please God, it'll be a happy home for us all. Eh!—what?"

He blew his nose and kissed us all round. As it was

Christmas I did not mind, though I am much too old for it on other dates. Then he said, "Thank you all very much for your presents; but I've got a present here I value more than anything else I have."

I thought it was not quite polite of him to say so, till I saw that what he valued so much was a threepenny-bit on his watch-chain, and, of course, I saw it must be the one we had given him.

He said, "You children gave me that when you thought I was the poor Indian, and I'll keep it as long as I live. And I've asked some friends to help us to be jolly, for this is our house-warming. Eh! what?"

Then he shook Father by the hand, and they blew their noses; and then Father said, "Your Uncle has been most kind—most—"

But Uncle interrupted by saying, "Now, Dick, no nonsense!"

Then H. O. said, "Then you're not poor at all?" as if he were very disappointed.

The Uncle replied, "I have enough for my simple wants, thank you, H. O.; and your Father's business will provide him with enough for yours. Eh!—what?"

Then we all went down and looked at the fox thoroughly, and made the Uncle take the glass off so that we could see it all round; and then the Uncle took us all over the house, which is the most comfortable one I have ever been in. There is a beautiful portrait of Mother in Father's sitting-room. The Uncle must be very rich indeed. This ending is like what happens in Dickens's books; but I think it was much jollier to happen like a book, and it shows what a nice man the Uncle is, the way he did it all.

Think how flat it would have been if the Uncle had said, when we first offered him the one and threepence farthing, "Oh, I don't want your dirty one and three-pence! I'm very rich indeed." Instead of which he saved up the news of his wealth till Christmas, and then told us all in one glorious burst. Besides, I can't help it if it is like Dickens, because it happens this way. Real life is often something like books.

Presently, when we had seen the house, we were taken into the drawing-room, and there was Mrs Leslie, who gave us the shillings and wished us good hunting, and Lord Tottenham, and Albert-next-door's Uncle—and Albert-next-door, and his Mother (I'm not very fond of her), and best of all our own Robber and his two kids, and our Robber had a new suit on. The Uncle told us he had asked the people who had been kind to us, and Noël said, "Where is my noble editor that I wrote the poetry to?"

The Uncle said he had not had the courage to ask a strange editor to dinner; but Lord Tottenham was an old friend of Uncle's, and he had introduced Uncle to Mrs Leslie, and that was how he had the pride and pleasure of welcoming her to our house-warming. And he made her a bow like you see on a Christmas card.

Then Alice asked, "What about Mr Rosenbaum? He was kind; it would have been a pleasant surprise for him."

But everybody laughed, and Uncle said—

"Your father has paid him the sovereign he lent you. I don't think he could have borne another pleasant surprise."

And I said there was the butcher, and he was really kind; but they only laughed, and Father said you could not ask all your business friends to a private dinner.

Then it was dinner-time, and we thought of Uncle's talk about cold mutton and rice. But it was a beautiful dinner, and I never saw such a dessert! We had ours on plates to take away into another sitting-room, which was much jollier than sitting round the table with the grown-ups. But the Robber's kids stayed with their Father. They were very shy and frightened, and said hardly anything, but looked all about with very bright eyes. H. O. thought they were like white mice; but afterwards we got to know them very well, and in the end they were not so mousy. And there is a good deal of interesting stuff to tell about them; but I shall put all that in another book, for there is no room for it in this one. We played desert islands all the afternoon and drank Uncle's health in ginger wine. It was H. O. that upset his over Alice's green silk dress, and she never even rowed him. Brothers ought not to have favourites, and Oswald would never be so mean as to have a favourite sister, or, if he had, wild horses should not make him tell who it was.

And now we are to go on living in the big house on the Heath, and it is very jolly.

Mrs Leslie often comes to see us, and our own Robber and Albert-next-door's uncle. The Indian Uncle likes him because he has been in India too and is brown; but our Uncle does not like Albert-next-door. He says he is a muff. And I am to go to Rugby, and so are Noël and H. O., and perhaps to Balliol afterwards. Balliol is my Father's college. It has two separate coats of arms, which many other colleges are not allowed. Noël is going to be a poet and Dicky wants to go into Father's business.

The Uncle is a real good old sort; and just think, we should never have found him if we hadn't made up our minds to be Treasure Seekers!

Noël made a poem about it

Lo! the poor Indian from lands afar,
Comes where the treasure seekers are;
We looked for treasure, but we find
The best treasure of all is the Uncle good and kind.

I thought it was rather rot, but Alice would show it to the Uncle, and he liked it very much. He kissed Alice and he smacked Noël on the back, and he said, "I don't think *I've* done so badly either, if you come to that, though I was never a regular professional treasure seeker. Eh!—what?"